Spear-Shaker

Francis Bacon's Legacy

Spear-Shaker

Francis Bacon's Legacy

Kenric McKenzie

SpearShaker Book Publications

Copyright © 2010 by Kenric McKenzie

First Edition published in the United States of America
in 2010 by Lightning Source, a subsidiary
of Ingram Industries Inc.

First Edition published in Great Britain in 2010
by Lightning Source, a subsidiary
of Ingram Industries Inc.

ISBN 978-0-9564185-0-0

A SpearShaker Book Publication

http://www.SpearShaker.com

*"Truth is so hard to tell,
it sometimes needs fiction to make it plausible"*

Fr. Bacon

Dedication

For Isabella

FACTS

1. 1561, Dictionary of National Biography XVI, page 114, "*It is herein recorded that on Jan. 21 1560/1 Queen Elizabeth was secretly married to Robert Dudley in the House of Lord Pembroke before a number of witnesses.*"
2. Jan 22, 1561 - The Queen was in residence at York Place and had no public engagements or interviews – Francis Bacon was born this day.
3. Francis Bacon was referred by his contemporaries as a supreme poet & leader of all other poets. One who wrote poetry secretly and philosophy publicly.
4. Francis Bacon was still alive when the Shakespeare First Folio (complete works) was published in 1623, seven years after the death of the attributed author from Stratford-Upon-Avon. The First Folio also contained 14 other known plays and six unknown plays.
5. The letter 'B' (for *Bote-swaine*), the first word of the first play *The Tempest* published in the Folio of 1623 featured curly adornments. These adornments were found to contain the words "Francis" and "Bacon" contained within its design. This discovery was first published in 1931 in the Cincinnati Times-Star newspaper & the Literary Digest that same year.
6. After 250 years of scholarly research, nothing has been discovered which unequivocally links William Shakspere of Stratford-upon-Avon with literature. No manuscripts or other documents of a literary nature by him have emerged.
7. The famous Martin Droeshout Engraving of Shakespeare in the First Folio (1623) has been pattern matched to two existing portraits of Francis Bacon.
8. Francis Bacon had dark brown/hazel eyes, like those of his secret brother, Robert Devereux, as well as Queen Elizabeth I, her mother, Anne Boleyn, and also Robert Dudley. Francis bore no resemblance to Sir Nicholas Bacon, his supposed father (Bacon family traits were predominantly grey-blue eye

colouring), but he did look like Robert Dudley, as shown in the Hilliard miniatures.

9. Anthony Bacon, brother to Francis, had his passport signed by four French noblemen while he toured Navarre in 1583, their names, Biron, Dumaine, Longville, and Boyesse, were all characters in the Shakespeare play *Love's Labour's Lost*. This passport still exists, and is on display at the British Museum, England.

10. Francis Bacon kept a private memorandum book which he called 'The Promus of Formularies and Elegancies' which contained thousands of unique phrases, expressions, and more. Hundreds of these entries are reproduced in the Shakespeare plays. His *Promus* is held at the British Museum, England.

11. In 1909, a collection of books was discovered in Francis Bacon's old Gorhambury home, and along with them were eight Shakespeare quartos published between 1599-1615, among them *Titus Andronicus, Richard II & III, King Lear, King John, Romeo and Juliet, Hamlet*, and *Henry the IV*.

12. While Francis held the prominent position of co-treasurer at the Law courts of Gray's Inn, he oversaw the play *The Comedy of Error's* as it undertook its first performance there as part of a Christmas revel.

13. A handwritten document dating back to the 1590s describing a scene very similar to one from the play *Henry IV* was validated by a handwriting expert to belong to Francis Bacon. An article validating the findings was published in the *London Evening Standard* newspaper on July 30, 1992.

14. In the play *Henry VIII*, in being relieved of the *Great Seal*, the four lords who relieved Wolsey are the same four in title that also relieved Francis Bacon when he was disgraced. Historically though, Wolsey was relieved by only two.

15. Between 1597-1598 two poets, Joseph Hall & John Marston referred to the author of the Shakespeare poems *Venus and Adonis* & *The Rape of Lucrece* in a series of published satires, referring to the author by the name of 'Labeo' and accusing the author of hiding behind a mask. They made associations of the motto 'Mediocria firma' and that the author was a jurist. This motto is part of the Bacon family crest, and between Francis and his brother Anthony, only Francis was a jurist.

16. Manuscripts later labelled as 'The Northumberland Manuscripts', discovered in 1867 among some documents at Northumberland House, England, contained documents in Francis Bacon's own handwriting (confirmed) with the signature 'Mr Francis William Shakespeare' written on one of the pages. The documents are now kept at Alnwick Castle, in the possession of the Duke of Northumberland.

The Past

PROLOGUE

𝔉rom the serenity of a seemingly empty Royal palace, the agonising scream of a woman shakes its very foundation, forcing a number of birds that had nestled on an external window ledge of the palace to take flight for their safety.

The scream is traced back to a large majestic room in the northern part of the Palace, which had been lit with an excessive amount of candles.

The room with its gold panelled designs on the doors and walls was sectioned in part, by a high white curtain, now stained on one side with splatters of blood, and alive with eerie shadows.

Behind the curtain, there is a hive of activity as a number of women shuttle pass each other busily.

Their focus is a large Queen sized bed, or more to the point, the woman who lay atop it stretched out on her back, her swollen pregnant belly the real focus of everyone's attention.

The woman, in her ceaseless misery had thrown off her cover, uncaring that her swollen naked body was exposed. She was beyond thinking, almost beyond the searing pain that receded quickly, only to explode again with greater ferocity within her belly, tearing hoarse screams from her parched throat.

"Anne" the woman cried through her painful ordeal, calling for her friend, Anne Bacon.

"I am right here!" Anne quickly responded in a reassuring tone, rushing to her side.

"Water" the pregnant woman gasped in a weakened tone.

"Yes, of course!" Anne flustered an answer, embarrassed that her friend had to ask in her weakened state.

Anne immediately picked up a glass of water from a nearby table, and with her free hand, placed it behind the pregnant woman's head, lifting it from her sweat soiled pillow, and as she did, the woman's thick sweat sodden red hair fell down in clumps.

Almost immediately, another woman removed the damp pillow that had revealed itself and quickly replaced it with a fresh one.

Anne pressed the glass of water to her dear friend's mouth, allowing her to take her fill as she quenched her thirst, and after a few moments she raised two fingers to indicate she had had enough, causing Anne to withdraw the glass and lay her friend's head to rest back down onto the fresh new pillow.

As Anne was about to attend some other duties, the Doctor approached them both.

"Doctor?" Anne greeted him, waiting to receive new orders.

"It is time!" the Doctor replied sharply.

The pregnant woman gave a weakened nod in response while Anne ordered some of the other women to ready themselves for the impending delivery of a newborn child.

As all the women made ready, the Doctor leaned in close to the pregnant woman.

"When I tell you, you will need to bear down with all your strength as we had discussed. Are you in agreement?" the Doctor explained humbly in a low tone.

The woman swayed her head from left to right as she fought the pain within her wanting so desperately to detach herself from her gross child-filled body, but again nodded weakly in agreement, hoping her ordeal would soon be over.

The Doctor smiled and then made his way to a table where he hoped to grab a clean towel to clean his hands, but the table was empty.

"Where are those damned towels?" the Doctor bellowed in frustration to the group of women around him.

"They should be here any moment now, Doctor!" one of the women apologised in a sheepish tone.

The Doctor shook his head in dismay and stepped out from behind the curtain.

The physician, a grey-haired large-bellied man, with sweat dripping from his forehead, emerged from behind the curtain, shaking his head as he surveyed his bloodstained hands and apron.

This will not do. She is losing too much blood! The Doctor considered worriedly to himself.

His bloodshot eyes betrayed his exhaustion as the thirty-six arduous hours tending to the impending delivery were beginning to wear him down.

To combat his tiredness, he retrieved a small vial containing smelling salts from his pocket, wafting it under his nostrils, which caused an almost violent reaction as the smelling salts snapped his senses back sharply to the task at hand.

Suddenly, in a far corner of the room, two tall and wide gold encrusted double doors sprung open, exposing a tiny maid, who rushed into the room clutching an armful of clean towels.

Her face was reddened and sweaty due to her rushed roundtrip from the palace laundry room which was a great distance on the other side of the palace.

Behind her in the large grand hallway were two anxious looking men, one young, slim and handsome named Robert Dudley, Earl of Leicester, while the other larger man some 20 years older is Nicholas Bacon, husband to Anne.

The men took advantage of the open doors to peer in, but it only lasted mere seconds before the heavy doors swung back to their original closed positions, once again shutting them out.

The maid rushed towards the Doctor extending the towels in hand to him.

"The towels, Doctor!" the maid flustered as she approached him, her cheeks flushed from her ordeal of racing across the large breadth of the palace to where the laundry room was located.

"It's about time!" the Doctor responded impatiently, grabbing a handful of the towels before making haste back behind the curtains to attend to the pregnant woman.

The maid huffed quietly at the Doctor's rudeness, stacking the remainder of the towels next to a collection of basins next to a table laid out with an array of tools arranged like implements of torture, some of which were already used and bloodied.

In a heap near the curtain, the main eyed a bundle of bloodied used towels, and taking the initiative, collected them up and rushed back out of the room, grateful to escape the madness of the room.

As she made her exit, the two men eager for news arched their heads inside stealing another quick look into the room, before the doors closed again in their faces.

Back behind the curtain as the Doctor anxiously examined the swollen stomach of his patient, he flinched nervously as his patient let out a horrible shriek as the vicious contractions tore through her body.

The Doctor quickly eased his hand inside her for another examination. His facial expression turned from worry to a look of dread.

"Push!" the Doctor ordered the pregnant woman with urgency in his tone as he felt the baby's head crowning.

The Doctor hesitated only for the briefest of moments, before smoothly placing his hands across her belly, methodically pressing on her stomach to help the baby down turn from its precarious position.

After some tense minutes of the Doctor directing the mother to help the baby on its journey into the world by pushing with all her might, she finally let out an exhausted gasp of relief as the baby's first cry signified an end to her ordeal, much to the relief of her Doctor.

As the Doctor attended to the new mother, repairing her ravaged body, the baby was carefully washed and swaddled in a beautiful green and white shawl by her friend, Anne.

With a free moment, one of the women attending rushed from behind the curtain back to the large doors, opening one of them just enough to talk personally with the two waiting anxious men.

"What news?" the younger man asked eagerly as he stepped forward to the door.

"It is a healthy baby boy sire!" the maid shrieked with a huge smile, revealing her yellowing teeth.

Robert was ecstatic, but his happiness quickly subsided as he remembered some deep dark secret.

"Both mother and baby are in good health!" she added, still smiling broadly before letting the heavy door's close again as she returned to her duties.

"That is wonderful news!" Robert commented proudly, letting out a small sigh of relief.

"Congratulations Robert!" the older man offered gleefully, grabbing Robert's hand, shaking it.

As they shook hands however, Robert's eyes welled up with tears, and thinking them as tears of joy, Nicholas patted Robert on the shoulder, in a commending fashion.

Back behind the curtain, the newborn is finally placed into his mother's arms, and tears of joy fell uncontrollably from her cheeks as she held him close.

✝

A short time later, with the curtain now removed, the new mother, a young tired looking red haired woman, sat upright in a newly made up bed holding the baby, Robert Dudley, the father, stood next to the bed, stroking the baby's head, while Anne and her husband Nicholas Bacon, looked on.

The Doctor sat at a discrete distance allowing them some privacy.

The mother held the baby close to her bosom, as the baby gripped tightly onto one of Robert's fingers.

"God bless him!" Robert commented tearfully, as they shared a warm moment as a family of three.

As the mother noticed how sweetly the baby wrapped his tiny hand around his father's finger, she smiled sadly before whispering a prayer.

Becoming unsettled by the new mother's actions, Anne opened her mouth to ask a question, but was interrupted by the Doctor.

"It is time I am afraid!" the Doctor informed the new mother in a solemn tone, causing her to burst into floods of tears.

She offered up her child to the Doctor, looking away with sorrow filled eyes.

"What is going on?" Anne now asked, becoming distressed by the mother and Doctor's strange actions.

"Doctor, will you please tell me what is going on?" she pressed, turning to the Doctor, whose face was now full of dread as he held the new born child.

"The baby cannot live. His destiny was already decided before his birth!" he stated, unable to make eye contact with Anne.

"What?" Anne screamed in disbelief as she stared at the innocent baby now in the Doctor's arms, turning immediately to the new mother.

"The child is to be murdered? Tell me this is not true!" Anne bawled, shaking her head erratically in disbelief, unable to take in the gravity of what she had just been told.

"It must be done for the good of the country!" the mother cried in her defence, as she dropped her head in her hands, sobbing.

"No! I beg of you, do not do this!" Anne cried out as she fell to her knees in front of the new mother, clasping both hands together, begging for the child's life.

Heartfelt cries of woe echoed through the great halls of the palace.

1. THE FUNERAL

13th April 1626, St Albans, England

Amidst blankets of snow, a line of men and women all dressed solemnly in black, trudged through an icy April morning, making their way down a path towards a small church named St. Michael's, for the funeral of the enigmatic statesman, Sir Francis Bacon.

Waiting outside the church entrance is a young widow, Mrs Alice Bacon, also dressed in black and looking ghostly pale. Next to her is a priest, trying to offer her some level of comfort for her pain.

The widow smiled uncomfortably as some of the mourners acknowledged her as they made their way pass her and into the church.

As she waited outside the church entrance, it was unclear as to whether it was the icy April winds that had made her facial expression cold, or the knowledge that she had lived estranged from her now dead husband for so long.

Nonetheless, she waited, not so patiently, for the dead body of her husband to arrive.

"Where is that damned hearse?" she muttered through her chattering teeth to the frowns of the priest standing next to her.

"I am sure it is not too far now!" the priest replied, putting his arm around her shoulder as he tried to safeguard her from the cold winds.

It was the clattering of hoof beats that first caught their attention, and as they peered down the path obscured by a blanket of snow, the head's of two stallions majestically broke through, dragging a hearse behind them.

"Ah, here it is!" the priest commented with a soft smile, bowing his head as if to offer up a prayer.

As the horse-drawn hearse neared them, they then caught sight of a solemn entourage of coffin bearers following behind it.

With the hearse now at the church entrance before them, as they locked eyes on the coffin through a long rectangular glass pane of the wooden hearse, they both seemed to become lost in their own thoughts as they reflected on different memories they had of Francis Bacon, both feeling a sudden rush of renewed sadness.

Oblivious to the widow and the priest, the coffin bearers grouped together and after a brief discussion on what they had to do, they separated into two lines of four men behind the hearse and helped to hold the coffin as it was slid out into their waiting arms.

With a regimental precision, the coffin bearers lifted the coffin up onto their shoulders, before making a slow entry into the church.

The widow lowered her head and her eyes filled uncontrollably with tears as the coffin bearer's passed them with the coffin held high.

"We have been separated for some time now," she commented in a sorrowful tone as she turned to the priest.

"Yes, I am aware of that," the priest nodded uneasily as he considered the reason for her separation from her husband, which Francis had explained to him some years before.

"It was good of you to come, and I am sure Francis would have appreciated it," the priest continued, placing his hand gently on her shoulder to comfort her.

"I had not seen him for quite a while," she continued, remembering back to better times they had shared before they separated.

"Will I get a chance to see him before he is buried?" she asked, staring back at the priest, her eyes welling up with tears of regret.

"Sadly, I am afraid not. His will make's explicit instructions for a closed casket," the priest advised her, shaking his head, to which she slumped her shoulders, letting out a heavy sigh.

Though her expression had been cold up to that point, she fought the tears that involuntary rolled down her cheeks for her dead husband, taking her seemingly by surprise.

She quickly retrieved a handkerchief from her purse, pressing it madly against the tears on her cheeks, as if to blot out the true loss she felt.

Dropping her head in sadness, she eyed her wedding ring finger, now naked from the ring she had once worn.

Pulling back some strength she walked with the priest as he directed her into the church with the final mourners, making her way down the aisle to the front pew with the priest, where he then left her.

The priest then disappeared up a spiral staircase which led up to a small pulpit with afforded a commanding view above the church pews.

As she stood alone, she briefly turned back behind her, scanning the final mourners entering the church, seemingly searching the crowd, not really sure who she was looking for, but eventually giving up and taking her seat at the front pew, next to a plainly dressed young man named John Underhill.

As she sat, he held her hand to comfort her, and maybe also to offer a little affection of his own.

Meanwhile, at the front of the church, the coffin bearers set down the coffin on a pedestal in front of the altar, arranging flowers around it, before finding some of the seats to the side of the church.

Out of nowhere, a huge big bellied man the widow recognised as the poet and actor, Ben Jonson, makes his way solemnly to the coffin, picking out a single long stemmed rose from a beautiful rose bouquet and laying it on top of the coffin before making his way to one of the vacant seats a few rows behind her.

Back at the pulpit, the priest checked the contents of some pages of writing that were to form the sermon for the funeral, and he readied himself to begin.

As the winds began to gather strength blowing snow into the open church doors, the priest, from his pulpit, caught the attention of one of his ushers and pointed to the church doors, indicating that they should now be closed.

The usher nodded to the priest and made his way to close the doors, pausing to allow any final mourners an opportunity to enter and take their seats.

Seeing the last of the mourners make their way into the church, the usher began to close the doors, but was hampered by the late arrival of a final mourner who inserted a cane between the doors, blocking the usher's efforts.

The usher frowned as he reopened the doors to get an icy fold gush of wind in his face.

The late mourner, an elderly man wearing a long dark coat and matching hat, ambled into the church leaning on his walking stick, nodding briefly at the usher as he entered, who merely frowned in return.

The user did a quick final check outside the church to see if there were any more late arrivals, and seeing none, quickly closed the doors and shuffled away.

As the elderly man took his seat in one of the rear pews in a darkened section of the church, he pushed down on his hat to ensure he was not recognised. Like an owl, the elderly man watched the other mourners take their seats among the long aisles, greeting friends they recognise with handshakes and hugs, and nodding at those they don't recognise.

The elderly man smiled as he admired the polite nature of English etiquette, thinking about its origins.

It is such an interest to watch how people greet each other, how formality dictates that names are exchanged as a means of being remembered. We all strive to some degree to make a name for ourselves in the short time we have on this earth, but stripped of our birth name, how would we answer the philosophical question, Who am I?

"We are here to celebrate the life of Sir Francis Bacon, 1st Viscount of St. Albans, born 22nd January 1561, and dying sadly on 9th April 1626. Born in York House or York Place, Strand, London, entering Trinity College, Cambridge at the age of twelve, studying law and becoming a barrister in 1582, then taking a seat in the House of Commons two years later." the Priest declared as he began his oration, interrupting the elderly man's thoughts.

The elderly man pauses upon hearing the priest's comment about *York Place*, one of the favoured palaces of Queen Elizabeth when she was alive, smiling briefly to himself, before returning to his thoughts.

The man whose memory is being honoured here today will be remembered in history as a politician, philosopher, and historian - a man who did all in his means to serve his country, but there is more to this man than the history books will ever be able to tell.

*A man that pondered such philosophical questions as **who am I? Why am I here? How can I best serve my country?***

*To truly know the man behind the name Sir Francis Bacon, I must tell you a story - **his** story,* the elderly man considered further, staring at the closed coffin at the front of the church.

2. INNOCENCE

Hampton Court, England, 1576

Manoeuvring effortlessly through the many corridors revealing themselves before him, young Francis Bacon seemed to know the whole palace by heart.

The young Francis was dressed in an exquisite new blue doublet with matching trousers, a level of attire some levels above his normal level of dress wear, and as he walked, he felt as fine as any noble man in the palace.

The Latin phrase *persona grata*, meaning '*welcome person*' would be the best way to describe him as he went about his business in the Royal court.

The Queen's guards, in their typical Royal regalia, wearing steel helmets and breastplates blocked the entrances of numerous doors with crossed pikes, signifying that access required permission from the Queen or the powerful Privy Council. However, as soon as they caught sight of Francis, the guards immediately retracted their pikes and stepped aside to allow him to pass without intervention.

He seemed to know everyone, and everyone seemed to know him.

Francis had been a visitor to the royal courts for as long as he could remember and had grown to believe it was because his father, Sir Nicholas Bacon, held a prominent position as the *Keeper of the Seal* in Queen Elizabeth's England, giving his family certain privileges.

This day, however, Francis would uncover the *real* reason for such freedom of access since his birth, which would change his life *forever*.

As he navigated the many corridors, he came upon his younger cousin, Robert Cecil, a diminutive figure, physically incapable of standing upright with his head erect due to a slightly disfiguring hunched-back from birth.

Robert was the son of William Cecil, Lord Burghley, one of the highest ranked men in England. Lord Burghley held a prominent position as a key advisor to Queen Elizabeth, and was a leading voice on the Privy Council, a select group of people who advised the Queen on important matters of state.

Francis and Robert shared a unique friendship, as Lady Anne Bacon was Lord Burghley's sister-in-law, and as such, the cousins often played together when they were younger.

Robert's disfigurement had never bothered Francis, but others would mock Robert often, so much so that Robert had become bitter against many of the palace patrons, always thinking they mocked him in their whispered conversations as he passed them.

As Robert grew older though, his retribution against those that mocked him would leave a gruesome trail.

"Francis! Are you en-route for another tutoring session?" queried Robert.

Robert had become accustomed to seeing him around this particular time of the day on a Tuesday morning, knowing that Francis had a recurring tutoring session with Dr John Dee, Queen Elizabeth's court astrologer, who was also a very learned scholar. Today, Francis was late for his weekly session.

"Yes!" Francis huffed with a smile as he rushed past Robert.

"Sorry, I cannot stop! Maybe I will see you later?" Francis continued quickly.

"Okay!" Robert returned as Francis flashed past him.

Francis carried on for a few minutes, walking briskly through the labyrinth of hallways, and as he turned into a new hallway, he eyed a pretty girl of similar age to himself whom he had not seen before, coming from the other end.

From her apron and overalls, Francis deduced she must be working in the nearby palace kitchens. As he neared her, the girl did not seem to notice him, staring glumly down at the ground, seemingly lost in her own thoughts.

Francis thought that she looked unhappy.

As she heard his footsteps, she realised she was no longer alone in the hallway, and looked up straight into his dark brown eyes.

As Francis let out a confident smile, the girl's demeanour changed from sadness to a scowl, and she quickly turned her face away, rushing past him.

Francis was stunned. He was not prepared for such outright rudeness.

As she made her way pass him, Francis was certain he heard her muffled cries and he paused briefly to consider whether he should find out why she was so upset, but by the time he had turned to chase after her, she was gone.

What did I do? Did I offend her in some way? Francis thought critically of himself.

Francis thought he was normally quite good at courting the palace ladies, and could not stop thinking about why the girl's demeanour had so quickly turned sour as soon as she saw him.

She must have taken one of the side corridors, Francis thought as he tried to retrace the girl's steps, frustrated that he had lost sight of her so quickly.

Francis made haste down a nearby side corridor in pursuit, but the hallway was empty apart from a plump old woman, also wearing a stained apron making her way towards him.

"Excuse me, but did you see a young girl come through here?" he asked as he came within earshot of the old woman.

"Ay, I did see a little 'un pass me master, but I don't know which way she went to sir!" the servant responded in a crude northern accent.

Although Francis was fluent in a number of languages, he found it difficult to understand the crude and almost barbaric accent of the old woman, but this was typical of the level of English being spoken across the land at that time by the common people.

As he tried to make sense of her response, his nose crinkled as he caught the scent of a rank odour, and realising the smell was coming from the withered old woman, he smiled at her politely, holding his breath, trying not to inhale the pungent smell any longer than he had to, continuing quickly past her, reaching the end of the long corridor before gasping for air as he began to breathe properly again.

As he panted at the end of this corridor he realised he had to make a decision, because the corridor forked off in three routes, straight ahead, left or right.

The girl was nowhere to be seen, and Francis was at a loss as to which way he should turn, and as he tried to decide, he shook his head at the madness of his actions, realising the time of day and the appointment he was now very late for.

Francis decided to abandon his pursuit, turning and hurrying back towards his original destination, eventually arriving at the Long Gallery, and as he walked down the empty hallway still thinking about the girl, he heard a faint scream, causing the hairs on the back of his neck to prick up.

Realising his location, Francis remembered a story he was told about Queen Catherine, one of King Henry VIII's many wives, and how, when she was arrested in Hampton Court in 1542, she was dragged down the very same hallway, screaming for Henry to save her. Soon afterwards she was executed.

Francis was told that many people had since reported hearing a ghastly scream in the same area of the palace, but this was a first time for him. He composed himself, and quietly tiptoed across the hallway, before quickening his walk once again, finally arriving at his appointment and banged his knuckles on the door, but there was no reply.

After waiting for a few moments, Francis banged on the door again, but still, there was no reply. On checking the door knob, and finding the door unlocked, he made his way into the room.

The room itself was set up like a small classroom, with a few chairs facing a large blackboard, showing a partially rubbed out set of math formulae's on it.

Francis had been here before, and he settled on one of the desks towards the back of the room near a small window, and began unpacking some books from his satchel onto it.

"Francis!" a familiar Welsh voice whispered, startling him.

As Francis turned back at the doorway, he found his mentor Dr. John Dee standing before him with his own small stack of books under his arm, smiling.

He was a tall and slender man, his face a clear sanguine complexion, sporting a long beard as white as milk, and greying hair on top, mostly hidden by a close fitting coif styled cap. Although he was in his 50s, Dr. Dee had the sharp alert eyes of a much younger man.

"Master Dee!" Francis asked with a wry smile.

"Must you always surprise me so?" Francis complained.

"Oh, let an old man have his vices!" his tutor replied with a teasing smile.

Francis relaxed a little, shaking his head with a little chuckle as he finished unpacking the last of the items in his satchel.

Dr. Dee, still smiling, put down his own stack of books from under his arm and placed them onto the table at the front of the classroom, picking up a cloth from the table, wiping the stray chalk markings on the blackboard with it.

As Dr. Dee waited for Francis to ready himself for the day's lessons, he admired the snug fitting blue doublet Francis was wearing.

"So, how are you today? You are looking very smart!" he commented, causing Francis to beam proudly.

"Thank you Master. I have just come from a sitting! My parents felt I was overdue a painting to record my sixteenth year!" Francis replied as he stood up briefly showed off the doublet to his mentor.

"Wonderful! Are you ready to begin?" he asked warmly.

"Yes!" Francis responded still smiling as he sat back down.

Dr. Dee then turned to the blackboard and began scribbling a number of mathematical problems for Francis to solve, and over the next two hours, he tutored Francis in advanced maths and other sciences.

Francis had shown a great acumen for numbers from an early age, where at the age of 3, he could multiply four digit numbers in his head, and by the age of 6, was translating Latin works into English.

His early tutoring revealed a great intellect in his young mind.

As Dr. Dee stood with his back to Francis, scribbling yet another maths problem for Francis to solve, Francis looked down at one of the margins on his page and began sketching an image of a rose, adding to other sketches he had already made.

Outside, a small bird flapped its wings against one of the nearby windows attracting his attention, landing on the window ledge. As Francis studied the bird, he decided to sketch a still portrait of it, realising he would have to be quick before the bird flew away.

When Dr. Dee had finished marking up the maths formulae on the blackboard, he turned back to Francis and saw that he was distracted by writing something in his notes about the bird.

Dr. Dee had decided to sneak up on Francis, and looking over his shoulder, made an evaluation of the drawing.

"Hmm, very good!" Dr. Dee nodded stroking his beard, startling Francis.

"My apologies, master Dee. Forgive me!" Francis pleaded as he turned to face Dr. Dee looking over his shoulder.

As Francis tries to cover up his sketch, Dr. Dee just waves his hand, discounting his apology.

"No apologies necessary Francis, I know your love of nature. It is a love that we both share!" Dr. Dee replied as the bird spread its wings, flying away from the ledge.

Dr. Dee went to the window to observe the path of the bird, and as he looked outside he smiled in appreciation at the grand palace gardens before him.

"What bliss! The greatest joy of nature is the absence of man!" Dr. Dee continued, before turning back to Francis.

"If you are lucky Francis, one day maths will unravel the mysteries of all that you see and believe!" Dr. Dee added, with a smile. Intrigued, Francis arched his brow.

"How Master Dee?" Francis asked, now intrigued.

"You are young, but time will reveal it to you if you have the determination to find it!" Dr. Dee responded with a glint of knowing in his eyes.

This confused Francis, but before he could think of a follow-on question, Dr. Dee interrupted.

"Okay Francis, one last problem for the day, and then I will leave you to the great outdoors!" Dr. Dee announced, as he made his way back to the blackboard.

"There you go!" Dr. Dee explained as he pointed to the maths problem on the blackboard.

Francis looked back to the heavily complex formulae on the blackboard, and after a few seconds of deep analytical thought, he rose from his seat and made his way to the blackboard and solved the problem set for him - it took him less than 30 seconds, impressing his mentor.

"Francis, you have solved a problem in seconds that would take a math professor at least an hour to accomplish. You have a natural gift for numbers my boy!" he grinned proudly at his protégé.

Francis simply smiled as he made his way back to his seat.

"As promised, we will finish a little earlier today!" he replied, winking at Francis before putting away his books, finally tying them up with some string.

Great! Francis thought as he jumped out of his seat and began backing away his own books.

"Thank you again for your tutoring sir!" Francis replied as he continued packing away his books.

"See you next week!" Dr. Dee replied in a jovial tone as he left the room.

Pausing from packing away his books, Francis stepped over to the window and looked out, trying to contemplate the meaning of Dr. Dee's earlier cryptic statement.

As Dr. Dee made his way down a hallway of the royal court to leave, he crossed paths with Queen Elizabeth of England, and her entourage of ladies-in-waiting, all en-route to her presence chamber.

Here, the red-haired Queen's face is the same face, although now older, as the woman who had delivered unto the world a newborn boy in the empty palace, 16 years before.

As she eyed her trusted advisor on astrological and scientific matters, the Queen's face lit up. Dressed in a regal crimson velvet gown, trimmed with ermine, she waved to her ladies-in-waiting to wait as she walked on ahead to talk to Dr. Dee privately.

"Your Majesty!" Dr. Dee exclaimed, bowing humbly before his Queen as she approached him.

"Master Dee!" she replied in a jovial tone, bidding him to rise, noticing the stack of books under his arm.

"Have you just finished a tutoring session with young Francis?" she queried in a happy tone.

"Yes, I have your Majesty!" he replied, nodding enthusiastically.

"Good! How is his learning?" she queried.

"He is a child prodigy ma'am. He has the making of a very learned individual." He continued.

"Well, he is being tutored by one of the best minds in the country!" she commended.

"You are very kind, your Majesty!" Dr. Dee replied with a grin, tilting his head in appreciation.

"Good day, Dr. Dee!" Queen Elizabeth finished before waving her hand behind her, ushering for her ladies-in-waiting to follow as she continued down the hallway.

Dr. Dee gave a courteous nod as the entourage of the Queen's ladies made their way past him, before he continued on his way out of the palace.

The Past

3. HIDDEN TRUTH

As Francis left the classroom, he decided to go in search of his cousin, Robert, and as he navigated back through the many hallways of the palace he thought the most logical thing to do would be to head towards the office of his uncle, Lord Burghley, father to Robert.

En-route to his uncle's office however, he recognised the young girl with whom he had shared the strange encounter earlier, finding her sitting on a bench crying.

I knew she was upset! Francis confirmed to himself as he headed towards her.

"Hello, are you alright? Do you need some help?" he asked sympathetically.

As the young girl looked up and realised it was Francis, her cries grew louder causing Francis to consider that he should have left her well alone, backing away a couple of steps.

What is it with this girl? Francis wondered to himself as her cries grew louder.

"YOU!" she shouted with a fierce look in her deep brown eyes, prodding Francis in the chest.

Immediately, the girl plunged one of her hands into her thick brown hair, which was styled in a tight bob, pulling out a long hairpin, causing her hair to fall down around her face, revealing curly locks.

With the hairpin retrieved, measuring some four inches with a sharpened end, she launched herself madly at Francis, forcing him against a nearby wall.

Before he could respond, the girl had positioned the sharpened end of the hairpin against the thin skin of his throat, just below his adam's apple, and as her nostrils flared with anger, Francis knew he was in trouble.

"What are you doing? Stop this!" Francis pleaded, shocked and fearful at the dire turnaround of events.

The girl maintained the pressure of the hairpin against his throat as she continued to sob.

"Please! How have I wronged you to act in such a way?" he continued as the sharpened end of the hairpin dug into his neck.

"It is because of you that my sister is dead!" she cried out.

"Because of me?" Francis returned with a confused stare.

Francis was taken aback by this awful accusation.

"I don't even know who you are! How is it that you have come to believe I was involved in the death of your sister? Who was she?" Francis continued, straining to keep the hairpin from perforating his neck.

"Is your name not Francis Bacon?" the young girl screamed – her eyes now wild with anger, releasing the tension of the hairpin a little from his neck.

"Yes. It is!" he stuttered back, giving her a confused stare at her knowledge of knowing who he was.

"Then I have the right person!" she responded as she pressed the hairpin back against his neck again.

"If I kill you, I will finally have retribution for my sister's death!" she continued seemingly determined in carrying out her assault on him.

"Please, I beg mercy!" Francis cried as he tried to reason with her.

The girl wiped the tears from her face using her free arm.

"Please tell me how am I to blame for your sister's death?" Francis pleaded.

As the girl became more distraught thinking about her sister, the tension in her arm holding the hairpin slackened a little, giving Francis hope that she could be calmed.

"She was a lady-in-waiting to our Queen, until she was executed along with many others!" the girl replied, trying to catch her breath in between her sobbing.

"Executed by whose order?" Francis asked, staring at her distraught teary face.

"By the Queen, who else!" the girl cried.

"The Queen?" Francis repeated with a puzzled stare.

"If it was the Queen's doing, then why do you blame me?" Francis continued, wondering if the Queen was capable of such grim actions.

"All I know is that they whispered gossip about YOU, and for that, they were all executed!" she replied, crying some more, pressing the hairpin back against his neck with renewed ferocity against the person she believed responsible for her sister's execution.

"Gossip?" repeated Francis as his eyes widened.

"What gossip?" he continued, intrigued by her story.

"You tell me! I want to know how our Queen can be judge, jury, and executioner to someone who never harmed anyone in her life."

Being completely distraught now and sobbing uncontrollably, she let the hairpin fall to the ground, and then collapsed to the floor herself, holding her head in her hands as she cried, causing Francis to let out a deep sigh of relief.

His immediate thought was to summon a guard to arrest the girl, but something inside him felt there must be some truth to her madness, and he wanted to know what that truth was.

Francis composed himself, wiping away the accumulated sweat from his forehead and then dropped to his knees to talk to the girl.

"Please, tell me about your sister!" Francis asked as he lifted her chin up from her hands so he could see her grief stricken face.

The girl was surprised by his kindness, especially after her attack on him, and instead tried to bury her face back into her tear-soaked hands, but Francis held firm, and as she saw the compassion in his eyes, she began to explain herself.

"I was told the matter could not be discussed, because it involved state secrets!" she explained.

State secrets? Francis thought critically, thinking that if such an atrocity had occurred it would make sense for all those involved to remain quiet for fear of retribution from the Privy Council.

Over the years as Francis enjoyed the numerous visits from Queen Elizabeth in his youth, the freedom of the many Royal palaces, and the many privileges bestowed on him by Queen Elizabeth herself, but recently began wondering if there was a deeper reasoning to it all.

Francis had started to notice occasional unexplained strange looks from some of the senior members of the Privy Council and wondered if there was a possible state secret that would explain why no one spoke to him about it.

He removed a handkerchief from his pocket and handed it to the girl.

"I swear to you that I will find out what happened to your sister and clear my name in having anything to do with her fate!" he told her adamantly.

She looked up at him apologetically as she considered the ordeal she had just put him through.

"You are not going to have me arrested?" she asked, almost resolved to now be thrown in jail.

Francis seriously considered it as he felt a bruise on his neck where she had pressed the hairpin against.

"I should, but I think your cause is just. You want answers, and now so do I!" he responded with a determined look.

The girl wiped the remaining tears from her face.

"What was your sister's name?" Francis asked.

"Scales, her name was Jane Scales," she replied, fighting back some more tears.

Francis nodded as he considered what to do next.

"I will get to the bottom of this, I swear!" Francis told her, picking up the hairpin now lying on the floor.

"Maybe I should hold onto this for now?" he advised the girl.

As she eyed the hairpin, she bowed her head in shame at her actions.

"I am so sorry. My emotions got the better of me. I hope you can forgive me somehow," she asked, feeling desperately sorry for her violent actions.

Francis did not satisfy her with a response and simply rose to his feet, making his way down one of the corridors away from her in search of his own answers.

4. STATE SECRETS

$\mathfrak{F}$illed with a set of burning questions, Francis manoeuvred through the maze of hallways, strangely still en-route to Lord Burghley's office.

Instead of innocence on his face however, there was now anxiousness to find out the truth, and after a few minutes, he arrived at his uncle's office.

As Secretary of State, and close advisor to Queen Elizabeth, Lord Burghley would know if there had been such an execution's as the girl had stated.

Francis knocked urgently on the door, but with no reply, and finding the door unlocked, opened it and made his way in.

Lord Burghley's office was of a simple design, with little furniture and ornaments, reflecting his own humble beginnings and as Francis surveyed the room, he eyed a great oak desk at the back of it, littered with letters and vellum parchments in piles.

Behind the desk was a single elevated grand chair where Lord Burghley usually sat, which had a side view out of the only window in the room, while on the other side of the desk in front of Francis were two shorter simpler chairs for receiving guests.

On one wall there was a wide cabinet full of books, the bottom three shelves containing some 40 or so books of varying sizes and colours on each row, while the top row contained books of matching size and colour. Although the cabinet had many doors, they were all controlled by a central lock.

Francis had been in this office many times before, meeting Robert and his uncle, and remembered being told the books on the top row were *day books* that spanned the decades that his uncle had been employed in the Queen's service.

The journals went back before Francis was even born.

These day books detailed journal styled entries that Lord Burghley filled in on a day-to-day basis and contained key events and actions that he had been present to or had a part to play, such as meetings with foreign dignitaries and events or actions from Queen Elizabeth or other members of the Privy Council.

For Francis, the journals were the fountain of all knowledge that belonged to Lord Burghley. If such an execution had indeed been carried out as the girl has said, Francis thought they would surely have been noted in one of these books.

Realising he was alone in the room Francis considered the unthinkable, which was to sneak a read of the journals in the cabinet, knowing that if caught it could mean dire consequences for himself and possibly his father, Sir Nicholas Bacon.

If I am quick, no one will know, Francis thought.

He made his way to the central cabinet doors and pulled on one of the handles, but found it locked.

"Dammit!" Francis whispered under his breath.

Thinking back some months when he was last in this office with his uncle, he remembered that his uncle usually kept the key to the cabinet in his desk drawer, but as Francis made his way around the desk he found that the drawer was also locked.

Not having much success, Francis decided he would return later to talk to his uncle instead, but just as he was about to leave the office, he remembered the young girl's hairpin still in his pocket and retrieved it.

As he looked at the hairpin, he recalled an occasion a few weeks earlier, at his Gorhambury home, where he had success opening the lock of a jewellery drawer for his mother Lady Anne, by using a similar hairpin, and with this in mind he decided to try his skills on the locked drawer.

Francis inserted the hairpin into the keyhole of the drawer, jiggling it against the internal lock mechanism until disaster struck.

"No!" Francis lamented as he withdrew the hairpin, finding that it had snapped in two, leaving one half of it still embedded in the lock.

Try as he might, he could not retrieve the other half of the hairpin.

Francis was worried now, thinking that his uncle could discover the broken piece of the hairpin the next time he unlocked his drawer, then realising that someone had been in his office and had tampered with the lock.

He placed the broken half of the hairpin in his pocket and decided to leave the room quickly before he was caught, and as he made his getaway, in anger at his failure, he slammed the top of the desk with his fist, and as a consequence, he heard a faint *click*.

"Huh?" Francis murmured, stopping dead in his tracks.

He quickly returned to the drawer and tried to open it again, and realised that the bang of his fist on the desk had somehow managed to open the lock.

As he reviewed the contents of the drawer, he found the other half of the hairpin and quickly retrieved it, putting it in his pocket, but as he scanned the rest of the contents, he could not find the elusive key to the cabinet.

It must be here! Francis thought defiantly, hoping that his efforts had not been in vain.

He quickly rummaged through the numerous items in the drawer finding spare quills, ink, and some blank parchments, but no key.

It must be here! Francis thought in frustration.

Standing up and looking at the untidy desk full of papers, he wonders if the key could be possibly be under the mess and starts sifting under the many piles of papers there, and to his surprise, he finds it.

Francis stared in disbelief at the key, realising it was on the desk the whole time. He picked it up and immediately went over to the cabinet, inserting it into the lock. It clicked open.

"It works!" Francis whispered to himself, letting out a little smile of relief.

As he scanned the binders of each of the day books on the top row, he found they were all dated, so he reviewed the complete list of books and extracted a number of random journals not knowing which dates were actually going to be relevant. Upon seeing a day book corresponding with the year of his birth, he selected this one as well.

He laid the pile of journals on the desk, sat down, and opened the first book, noting all the entries were written in Latin, and being well versed, he easily translated the text back into English.

Finding nothing of importance, he put the book aside and began flipping through the pages of some of the other journals, not finding anything of interest. He decides to review the day book that overlapped the year of his birth.

First Francis scanned dates in the journal some months before his birth and discovered a list of entries of names and dates where dignitaries had commented on how Queen Elizabeth *looked* pregnant.

This immediately spikes his interest, since he knew that Queen Elizabeth had no children, and assumed the dignitaries were being critical of her weight.

Francis then found an interesting entry from his uncle, Lord Burghley stating that a Bishop De Quadra, a representative of the King of Spain and the mouthpiece of the Continental nations, who was visiting the English Court at the time, had also commented at her weight.

The Bishop was noted as stating he thought Queen Elizabeth *looked pregnant and should be careful not to be foolish enough to marry her protestant childhood sweetheart Robert Dudley, and bring the English back into a protestant religious order.*

Francis knew full well that Queen Elizabeth, as the head of a young Protestant nation, had to play a very wary game against this man and other Catholic Ambassadors to prevent England being plunged into a possibly bloody religious war, even now sixteen years later, not much had changed in the threat from the Spanish.

As he read further, he found an underlined entry, stating that a secret despatch was intercepted from Bishop De Quadra to King Philip of Spain, indicating that the Queen was expecting a child by her childhood sweetheart, Robert Dudley, Earl of Leicester.

This cannot be true! Francis thought, shaking his head in disbelief.

As he checked the entries for the month of his birth, he found an entry dated the day before his birth, 21st January, 1561, stating that Queen Elizabeth and Robert Dudley were married in the private home of a Lord Pembroke, and then listed the witnesses, noting his father, Sir Nicholas, as being one of them.

Francis raised his head from the journal perplexed.

Recognising the hand writing to be that of his uncle, Francis could only conclude that the entries were accurate and true.

Francis had heard that on more than one occasion, a member of the Queen's ladies-in-waiting had become pregnant and hid it from everyone, including the Queen, and carried out her day to day duties until it was time for delivery.

Why not our Queen? Francis thought critically as he considered the details of the Queen's supposed pregnancy. He was now spurred on to read more.

As he read the next entry dated the 22nd January, corresponding with the date of his own birth, he realised that the Queen was carrying a child at the same time as his mother, Lady Anne.

As he turned the page of the journal, Francis discovered an entry that would change his life forever.

The entry stated that Queen Elizabeth gave birth to a healthy baby boy and also listed the people who were witnesses to the birth, and he could not believe that his own mother, Anne Bacon, was present.

Now Francis became anxious and confused.

This must be wrong! Francis considered, jerking his head up from the journal.

How could my mother be in attendance to Queen Elizabeth on the same day she gave birth to me?

Confused, he rechecked the dates and the journal entry was indeed the date of his birth.

Francis continued reading, and almost immediately the next few sentences brought tears to his eyes.

He read that Queen Elizabeth and the Earl of Leicester, named the child Francis, and fearing retribution from England's Catholic enemies, the Queen handed the child over to her trusted friends, Anne and Nicholas Bacon to be secretly brought up as one of their own.

Spain and France, pushing for a Catholic reformation had warned they would invade England and bring about a religious war if they believed Queen Elizabeth was forging a Protestant union with Robert Dudley, Earl of Leicester.

Unbeknown to Francis, the initial intention was that as a babe, he was not meant to live, murdered at birth, but due to the fact that Lady Anne had begged for his life to be spared, possibly due to her own recent miscarriage, Queen Elizabeth and Robert Dudley reluctantly agreed.

Francis shook his head in disbelief, devastated by what he had just read.

"No, no, it can't be true!" Francis whispered as he slumped back into his uncle's chair. Unable to sit any longer, he got up and began to pace the floor.

An overwhelming feeling of betrayal took hold of him, and with an angry outburst, he picked up the nearest thing to him on the desk, an ink pot.

"No!" Francis exploded, throwing the ink pot against the row of cabinets.

As the ink pot hit one of the cabinet doors, it shattered one of its inset glass panels, which seemed to jolt Francis back to his senses.

He inhaled deeply as if to calm his nerves and then went back to sit at the desk. As he sat there, all he could do was stare at the day book as he tried to make sense of it all.

It must be wrong, it must! Francis kept on telling himself as he tried to disprove what he had read, but his logical mind tried to understand it.

Could such a secret of immense consequence really be kept from the palace patrons and courtiers who surrounded her every day, and worse still, the people of England? Francis tried to reconcile with himself.

As tears rolled down his face onto the aged writings of his uncle, Francis had a realisation. He choked at the thought that his mother, Lady Anne, was NOT his mother after all.

The noise of activity outside the room brought Francis back to the reality of his situation as he considered the possibility that his angry outburst may have attracted undue attention.

Realising his time may now be running out before he is discovered, Francis quickly scanned some of the later entries and found an entry that detailed how, some weeks afterward, his father Sir Nicholas Bacon, was given a prestigious position in Government and also the London home of York House in the Strand next door to the London palace of Queen Elizabeth.

He reads a few more pages but then came to the end of the journal.

Francis sighed as he put the journal aside and quickly picked up a later volume, and began earnestly flipping through its pages as well, which seemed to have skipped a few years.

In this journal, he found a number of entries relating to imprisonments and executions, all in the name of ensuring the state secret that Queen Elizabeth had borne a child remained private. Here, Francis eventually finding the name of Jane Scales listed among those that were beheaded to maintain the secret.

Francis again slouched back in his uncle's chair bewildered.

On the desk in front of him was undeniable proof that his kinsmen had been imprisoned or killed to ensure that no one knew about his secret birth, written in his uncle's own handwriting!

He rubbed his eyes still not believing what was written before him, knowledge that a secret about him had caused the death and imprisonment of his kinsmen simply telling the truth.

It was little consolation to read Lord Burghley's reasoning for keeping it a secret even though at the time of his birth, the royal court seemed to be buzzing with gossip of such an event.

Although Francis was supposedly born within wedlock, he was conceived during the time that Robert Dudley's wife was alive, and her mysterious accidental death, falling down some stairs would forever taint their affair.

With Francis born five months after her death, it was impossible, in view of the Roman Catholic opposition, that Queen Elizabeth could admit the marriage, let alone the pregnancy.

For any subject of Queen Elizabeth to have repeated such an accusation openly and unproven would have been high treason, and for that reason, Lady Scales and her associates were executed.

As the young Francis pondered the sum of his falsified life, his uncle, Lord Burghley entered the room with his son, Robert, at his side.

"What the" Lord Burghley started, but was lost for words as he surveyed the state of his office, taking stock of his cabinet doors being open and damaged, and realising to his horror that Francis had no doubt been reading some of the secrets contained within them.

Knowing full well that he had committed many offences of state by his actions, Francis sat uncaring and dejected, simply staring at the open journal in front of him, lost in thought.

Francis expected his uncle to be angry, but he was not, instead, Lord Burghley's face went as white as a sheet. Lord Burghley was frightened.

"Francis, what have you done?" Lord Burghley shouted with a hint of fear in his voice as he rushed to review the day books that Francis had been looking at, pulling Francis out of his chair.

When Lord Burghley took stock of the many day books on his desk, the gravity of the situation filled him with dread, and he realised that he had no option, but to report the whole thing to Queen Elizabeth at once.

"Come with me!" he shouted finally, grabbing Francis by the arm and leading him out of the office.

As Lord Burghley led Francis out passing his son Robert, he remembered the journals open on his desk, and the damage Francis had caused.

"Robert, put the journals back into the cabinet and clean this mess up!" he explained firmly as he examined the damage to his cabinet one more time, realising he would have to get that fixed as well.

"Call a carpenter to come and repair the cabinets, but do not leave him in the room alone! Do I make myself clear?" his father demanded in an aggravated tone.

Robert nodded quickly in agreement, without saying a word as his father reached inside one of his pockets and took out a key.

"Use this key to lock my office when you are done!" he continued, handing Robert the key.

"Yes father!" Robert quickly answered, looking into his father's fearful face.

Lord Burghley huffed as he left the room with Francis.

Now alone, Robert was eager to find out what had caused Francis to lose his temper in such a way and his father to be fearful, and sat down in his father's chair to review the open journals. This day, his cousin Robert would also discover the secrets that would change his relationship with Francis forever.

5. TRUTHS REALISED

Red-faced and seemingly lost in his own thoughts, Lord Burghley dragged Francis through a myriad of halls like a spoiled brat.

As they made their way down one hall that Francis had walked many times before, Francis caught sight of one of the hanging portrait's that had perplexed him from the very first time he had laid eyes on it.

It was a portrait of a mysterious young pregnant lady, painted by one of the Queen's artists, Marcus Gheeraerts.

The portrait depicted a young lady wearing a dress beautifully made of fine muslin covering a long silk gown with Tudor roses and bird designs. Her left hand was resting on her hip, while her right hand rested on the head of a stag, and around her neck hung a ring from a thin purple ribbon, not unlike a wedding ring.

He always thought that the portrait had all the elements of stateliness, riches, and royalty, but no matter who he had asked, no one could tell him who it was.

Was that a picture of Queen Elizabeth all along? Francis considered as the portrait disappeared from view as he was dragged down the hall.

More thoughts began to flood his mind.

As part of his legal studies, he remembered reading that when the Queen came to the throne, the Act of Succession 1563 stated that the Crown after her death would go to the issue of her body "lawfully to be begotten", but five years ago this phrase was changed, to read "the natural issue of her body", with the words *lawfully to be begotten* omitted.

This change in Law made it a penal offence to speak of any other successor to the crown of England other than the *natural* issue of the Queen.

He had thought it was a curious statute change when he first read of it, and contended that the term *natural* distinctly meant a birth out of wedlock, and that *lawful* was the only proper term to have been used.

Was the term added to allow me to one day become King of England? Francis considered. His mind was awash with this and many more questions, but no answers.

As the tranquillity of the near empty hallways was replaced with a buzz of activity, Francis snapped back to his current predicament, realising his uncle had dragged him into a grand room, filled with many royal patrons involved in numerous conversations.

As he scanned the huge room, he immediately saw Queen Elizabeth, elevated up some steps sitting in a grand golden throne, talking to one of her courtiers, who was kneeling several steps below her, while her ladies-in-waiting sat behind her talking among themselves.

They were in the Queen's presence chamber.

As Francis glanced at the ladies-in-waiting his thoughts went to the girl who started it all earlier that day, when she attempted to take his life with her hairpin. Realising he didn't even know her name, he reached for the broken hairpin deep inside his pocket, and for a moment, he wished she had finished the job.

Lord Burghley continued to drag Francis through some of the court patrons towards a set of steps that led up to where Queen Elizabeth was seated, and for the first time, Francis became anxious, realising that Lord Burghley was probably going to inform her about what happened in his office.

As Queen Elizabeth noticed them, she smiled and jumped up.

"Lord Burghley!" she announced aloud in a happy tone above the buzz of the room.

Lord Burghley smiled uncomfortably in return, putting her on edge, and seeing a look of fear in Lord Burghley's face, she realised something dire must have happened. She sat uncomfortably back down into her throne.

Can it be true? Francis wondered, fighting back tears as he stared up at his Queen, looking into her face and considering how he had always thought it *coincidental* that he and Queen Elizabeth shared the same dark brown eyes with unique flecks of hazel, different from the grey-blue Bacon family trait.

His head dropped as more thoughts ran through his mind wondering what other traits they may also share.

As Lord Burghley and Francis reached the steps leading to her seat, Francis froze and refused to go any further.

As Lord Burghley pulled at him to continue up the stairs, Francis was determined to stay put, and as Lord Burghley scanned the busy room, he decided it was probably better not to cause a scene.

"Wait here then!" he ordered Francis in an aggravated tone, continuing up the stairs on his own.

Getting within earshot of Queen Elizabeth, Lord Burghley bent over and whispered in her ear as to what had happened in his office, explaining that Francis had read certain day books containing particulars about his birth, and possibly other matters.

The Queen's eyes betrayed her shock and anger at the news and immediately rose to her feet, clapping her hands together several times to get the urgent attention of the assembled court patrons in the hall.

The many conversations in the great room stopped instantly and the court patrons froze as if they were statues.

"Attention! I want this room cleared NOW!" she shrieked.

Amidst some puzzled looks, everyone scurried out of the room, fearing her Tudor wrath if they did not comply. Francis wished he could leave as well, knowing that the Queen's anger could be very deadly when provoked.

Lord Burghley watched the patrons leave and also wished he could join them, feeling uncomfortable at the prospect of a private audience with Queen Elizabeth, knowing full well that he would be severely punished for allowing his state-secret journals to be read.

Lord Burghley had been warned many years ago by Queen Elizabeth herself that under no circumstances should anyone reveal the truth to Francis except for her, when she was ready, but now her hand had been forced.

After the last of the patrons had left the room, the guards made their exit, closing the doors behind them, leaving Lord Burghley, Francis and Queen Elizabeth alone.

In the silence of the room, Queen Elizabeth appeared noticeably agitated, and as she considered her next move, she locked eyes with Francis.

"I understand you have been behaving very badly Francis!" she asked delicately as a small frown formed on her forehead.

Francis tried hard to respond, but nothing came out, and simply nodded his head sheepishly instead.

Queen Elizabeth nodded a little herself, recognising his response.

"I understand you have also caused some damage to Lord Burghley's office, and read some of his private diaries?" she continued, still frowning.

"Yes, your Majesty," Francis replied, finally getting his words out.

Queen Elizabeth smiled uncomfortably as she considered her next words.

"Francis, we have been friends for a long time, have we not?" she asked, trying to be tactful in her questioning.

"Yes ma'am. I have known you all my life," Francis responded hesitantly.

"Ma'am I am confused by what I have read in my uncle's journals," Francis continued, changing the subject.

"I am sure you are. There is a lot to consider," Queen Elizabeth returned, nodding her head as she wondered what must be running through his mind.

As she looked toward Lord Burghley she gave him an angry stare as she tried to find the right words to say next.

"Do you remember that my primary role is that of Queen of this land, above all else?" she asked uncomfortably, returning her focus back to Francis.

"Yes ma'am," Francis nodded.

"Above all else?" she stressed, before becoming a little tearful.

"Yes ma'am," Francis replied, nodding again and feeling a little awkward as tears fell down her cheeks.

"Before family?" she stressed again.

"Yes ma'am?" Francis replied again giving Queen Elizabeth a confused stare, unsure what she was trying to say.

Queen Elizabeth hesitated, unsure of what to say next, deciding the truth was the best option.

"It may take some time for you to understand Francis, but it IS true. I am your mother. You are my son," she confessed finally, believing it better to tell the truth than to drag the whole thing out.

Francis began to shake uncontrollably.

"What?" Francis asked, not wanting to believe his ears.

"I am your mother, Francis, you are my own flesh and blood!" she continued with more conviction.

"I don't understand. I have a mother, Lady Anne, and a father, Sir Nicholas. You know of them. Why are you lying to me?" Francis replied, becoming hysterical.

"Francis! I am your mother I tell you!" Queen Elizabeth piped back.

Francis looked at his uncle who was staring back at him, nodding, as if to confirm Queen Elizabeth's confession.

Oh God, it's true? Francis thought to himself, not really able to believe it.

He looked back to Queen Elizabeth, eyeing her squarely.

"No, you lie!" Francis shouted, shaking his head in disbelief.

Lord Burghley felt very uncomfortable at being placed in the middle of this private conversation, but he knew he could not leave.

"Lady Anne Bacon is my dearest friend, and she adopted you at my request!" Queen Elizabeth tried to argue.

"No! My father is Sir Nicholas!" responded Francis, interrupting her.

"No he is not. Your Father is Lord of Leicester, Robert Dudley," Queen Elizabeth returned with a cold tone.

"You are my son, but you, though truly royal, of fresh and masterly spirit shall" Queen Elizabeth continued, trying to be sincere.

"No! No! No!" Francis interrupted, shaking his head furiously, causing Queen Elizabeth to become even angry at being interrupted again.

She stood up and stamped her foot on the ground as her own anger now flared.

"You will have respect for your Queen!" she shouted stamping her foot, causing Francis to flinch a little, remembering that he was talking to the Queen of England, irrespective of whether she was his mother or not.

"I am sorry for shouting Francis," Queen Elizabeth responded softly, realising her anger had gotten the better of her, but Francis wasn't listening, now lost in his own thoughts of his supposed Bacon family.

"I have a family, a brother" Francis finally responded with pain in his voice.

"My brother Anthony, is he not my brother?" Francis queried, looking back to his Queen, trying to make sense of it all.

Queen Elizabeth sat back down on her throne chair, thinking briefly before answering.

"Yes, he is your brother, but NOT my son," she replied, trying to give Francis some solace.

Francis slumped to the ground dejected, grasping his chest in pain.

Queen Elizabeth rose to her feet and started to make her way down the stairs towards Francis, her maternal instincts pushing her to go to his aid.

"Get away from me!" Francis shouted as Queen Elizabeth neared him, causing her to flinch at his outburst.

"My life is a lie! The love of my parents, another lie! Your love, the ultimate lie of all! My whole life is a lie, and it is of your inception!" Francis told her angrily.

Lord Burghley became even more embarrassed at his attendance to what he considered a family argument between mother and son, dropping his head in embarrassment.

"My heart feels as though a dagger has pierced it, one from my mother, one from my father, and one from you. All those that I trusted have made my whole life a lie!" he cried.

Lord Burghley tried to catch Queen Elizabeth's attention.

"Maybe I" Lord Burghley started in a sheepish tone.

"Maybe you should not!" Queen Elizabeth interrupted, eyeing him squarely, causing Lord Burghley to humbly bow his head down low again.

Queen Elizabeth turned back to Francis and took a deep breath as she tried to calm herself.

"Francis, I am your mother, and I have always loved you, even from afar," she strained, holding back her tears.

From the floor as he held his chest, Francis once again did not hear her words of comfort, and instead looked up and around the great room, remembering a time when he was twelve years old and starred in a little play held here for her benefit, called *The Philosopher King*.

Francis recalled that drama was a moving and eloquent story of philosophy and morality, and remembered his part well, and likened his current predicament to that of actors playing parts in the fictitious life he was having.

"You do not know love! To you all the world's a stage, and the men and women merely players!" he shouted back at his Queen.

The strain of the conversation now showed on the Queen's face, and she eyed Lord Burghley with furious contempt for some seconds, trying to consider her next actions.

"Take him home until I decide what to do," she huffed, now deflated at how the discussions had gone awry.

"Yes, your majesty!" Lord Burghley nodded quietly.

As Lord Burghley made his way back down the steps, he led a dejected Francis out of the great room.

Francis knew he should have been afraid of what was to become of him, but he didn't care. As far as he was concerned, his young life was in ruins.

Meanwhile back inside, Queen Elizabeth sat alone in the great hall saddened by the way the discussions with Francis had played out and also on being reminded of his secret birth she became unsettled as she thought back to poor Amy Robsart, Robert Dudley's wife, in whose murder, enemies would say Queen Elizabeth was implicated in.

6. GORHAMBURY

Against the backdrop of beautiful rolling hills was the Bacon family home of Gorhambury Manor on the outskirts of St. Albans. The Bacon home was a fine house in an open country setting with extensive acreage of both gardens and farmland.

A maid, but one of the 70 or so staff that worked around the clock to maintain the manor grounds and its family, was lost in the mundane task of sweeping up stray leaves that littered the main entrance.

Finishing her task, she started to make her way back into the house, but paused as she felt a slight rumbling on the ground beneath her.

Looking towards the main gate in the distance she saw a horse-drawn carriage bearing down on the house which caused her to hasten her way back inside.

As she rushed back inside, she immediately bumped into the stout stomach of the master of the manor, Sir Nicholas Bacon, a broad shouldered rosy-cheeked man who towered over her.

As his inquisitive greyish-blue eyes stared down at the maid, he frowned as tried very hard to recall her name, but with so many servants at any given time tending to the needs of his family, her name evades him.

"You there, why the rush?" he asks finally, sidestepping her name.

"Sorry sire, but there is a carriage approaching!" she responded apologetically, curtsying.

"What? I was not aware of any visitors due today!" Sir Nicholas replied, perplexed, passing the maid and stepping outside the house to see for himself.

As he looked anxiously towards the main gate of the manor, he saw the carriage for himself and quickly returned into the house where the maid was still waiting.

"Quickly! Prepare the house to receive our guests!" he ordered the maid, ushering her away.

"Yes sire!" the maid responded before quickly dashing off.

Some seconds later, a bell rang, causing a number of frantic maids to appear from various rooms, criss-crossing past Sir Nicholas, hurriedly preparing the house for the unexpected guests.

With all the maids buzzing around him getting him agitated, Sir Nicholas stepped back outside the main doors to the calm outdoors, and waited patiently for the carriage to reach the main entrance of the manor.

When the carriage finally pulled up the main door, Francis impatiently jumped out, and went straight into the house, storming past Sir Nicholas.

"Francis!" his father shouted as Francis rushed past him, striding up the grand stairs.

"What the hell is going on here?" Sir Nicholas asked himself, having never seen Francis in such a foul mood.

As Francis leapt up the steps to the first floor, his gaze paused on his left hand as it gripped the banister rail, staring critically at his long slender fingers, many times commented as *Musician's fingers*.

His memory drifted back to an event where he was in the presence of Queen Elizabeth, and she raised her hand against his, commenting that their hands were similarly shaped, with Francis making the same assessment.

He felt like such a fool.

As Francis then thought back to Queen Elizabeth's mother, the famed Anne Boleyn and her infamous extra finger, Francis felt a chill run down his spine, curling up his fist fearfully.

Looking to his right at all the pictures lined up against the stair wall, Francis then faced a framed portrait of Sir Nicholas dressed in his Cambridge colours, and now understood why, instead of being sent to Sir Nicholas' college in Cambridge, *Corpus Christi* like the rest of the Bacon boys, he was instead sent to Trinity College, founded by Henry VIII, Queen Elizabeth's father.

Facing the thought that his grandfather was therefore Henry VIII, he almost lost his footing.

He let out a huge sigh to calm himself before continuing up the stairs.

Back outside the manor, Lord Burghley then exited the carriage, eyeing a confused Sir Nicholas at the main entrance.

As Sir Nicholas watched Lord Burghley coming out of the carriage, he realised something had happened.

"What's going on?" Sir Nicholas asked, approaching Lord Burghley.

"He has discovered the truth about his true royal lineage," Lord Burghley whispered back in hushed tone.

"Oh!" Sir Nicholas replied, saddened at the news.

"How did he find out?" Sir Nicholas continued, now understanding Francis' anger, escorting Lord Burghley into the house. As they entered the house, Lord Burghley explained how he found Francis reading the day books in his office.

Anthony Bacon, older brother to Francis by two years, was standing nearby in the shadows of the hallway when he overheard his father's conversation with Lord Burghley and discovered for himself that Francis was not his real brother, but a prince, a secret prince to the throne of England no less.

As brothers go, Francis and Anthony were very close, and the news saddened him as well, wondering how this revelation would now change their relationship.

It certainly explains why Francis bears no resemblance to our mother or father, and indeed possesses no Bacon family traits whatsoever Anthony considered as he made his way around the side of the house towards the nearby forest to get away from the bad atmosphere in the house.

Moments later upstairs, Francis knocked on a bedroom door.

"Who is it?" the faint female voice of Lady Anne Bacon responded.

"It is me, Francis. May I please come in?" Francis queried in a distressed tone.

"Of course!" the faint voice responded.

As Francis entered the room, he found Lady Anne, second wife to Sir Nicholas, resting in bed, her face pale and gaunt as she recovered from an unknown sickness. She managed a weak smile for Francis as he entered, but noticing the redness of his eyes, she knew that something was wrong.

"Francis, whatever is the matter?" she asked in a concerned tone.

Francis sat at the edge of her bed and sobbed.

"Is is true? Is the Queen my mother?" Francis cried.

Lady Anne's face dropped, realising that this inevitable day had finally arrived.

She nodded regrettably, holding him close to her as he broke down in her arms, sobbing.

7. LEAVING HOME

Thick leather suitcases are loaded onto the back of a number of horse-drawn carriages parked outside the Bacon Gorhambury home, supervised by Sir Nicholas Bacon himself.

Francis is going on a trip to Europe.

Looking on with Sir Nicholas is Sir Amias Paulet, a grey haired man in his early fifties. The original plan was for Francis to be escorted by his brother Edward on this trip, but it was later decided that it would be too dangerous without a dignitary escort, so Sir Amias was selected instead.

Sir Amias had been the French tutor to Francis for a number of years, and had recently been knighted and given the title of *Ambassador to France* taking over the post left vacant by Sir Francis Walsingham.

"Keep him safe Master Paulet!" Sir Nicholas requested with seriousness in his tone.

"The Queen has entrusted the boy to me, and I will guard him with my life sir!" Sir Amias returned, receiving an agreeable nod back from Sir Nicholas.

Just then, Anthony, brother to Francis came out to check on the progress of the loading.

"How are things progressing father?" he asked sadly, as he is bumped out of the way as another suitcase is brought out to the carriages.

"The last of his luggage is now being loaded. Can you fetch Francis?" his Father responded in a dejected tone.

Anthony slowly nodded and went back inside the house, making his way through numerous doors, which finally led to a side door leading out to the vast acreage of land surrounding the rear of the manor.

Anthony headed towards a familiar wooded area of the grounds in search of his brother.

Meanwhile, deep within the wooded area, Francis walked aimlessly, lost in his thoughts, all dressed for his trip and finding it difficult to walk on the damp fallen leaves with his new shoes. He was sad to be leaving his childhood home.

He breathed in the autumnal smells of the forest, and let out a deep sigh.

Days after young Francis had unearthed the truth about his royal lineage, the Queen, his mother, had made the decision to send him on a *fact finding* mission to Europe.

Francis had his own suspicions that he was being sent abroad to calm his now wild emotions, no doubt fearing that his anger might get the better of him, and end up exposing his true lineage, much to *her* detriment. Whatever the reason, he was going on the trip and he had no choice in the matter.

One simply cannot say no, Francis realised as he kicked a branch in frustration, laying in his way.

Having spent much of his childhood in the wooded area enjoying and tending to the varied plant life around him, he wondered who would tend to them while he was away, not sure when he would return.

He carried on walking until he came to a big old Oak tree and reminisced at the countless cycles of seasons where he had gone for long solitary walks ending up at this tree, sitting amidst the pure beauty of nature.

Francis could not help but be reminded of the words of wisdom quoted from the great ancient Greek philosopher Pythagoras, *Learn to be silent, let your quiet mind listen and absorb.*

As he reviewed a portion of the tree bark, he felt the outline carving of a pig (part of the Bacon family logo) which had the initials 'F.B.' and 'Anthony' etched below it. Francis smiled to himself as he remembered happier times, when he and Anthony had made their mark on the tree many years before.

Suddenly, his tranquillity is interrupted as a strong wind blew across his face distracting him.

When he managed to look back at the forest, everything around him seemed to slow down to a halt, seemingly frozen in time.

As he scanned his surroundings, he noticed a rabbit bobbing through the forest earlier had been frozen as it paused to chew some grass, while a bird just flying above his head was now stuck too, frozen in mid-flight, and as he looked to his feet, the leaves that were blown up into the air from the ground in front of him were also similarly frozen in mid-air.

Although these things would have alarmed a normal person, Francis remained calm. This had happened to him before, many times before in fact.

Time is out of joint again he thought to himself as he surveyed the stillness of the forest.

It was always the same, first everything around him would slow to a halt, as if frozen in-place, and then he would find himself in another time, the Roman era as far as he could gather based on the toga styled clothing he would find himself wearing.

Feeling a slight weight on top of his head, he felt a wreath woven from leaves, and looking down to his clothing, he could see that he was holding a bow in one hand, with a rope across his now manly chest connected to a small circular satchel resting on his back, housing many arrows.

Reviewing his surroundings, he looked through a gap in a nearby bush, exposing a Roman city in the distance, bustling with activity, in contrast to his Gorhambury home that should have blocked such a view. All this was strange to Francis, yet wonderful, but he wished he knew what it all meant.

Suddenly, the sound of his name "Francis" echoed from somewhere behind him, jerking him back to his own reality and time.

As he re-examined the forest once again, everything seemed to spring back to life, and he smiled as he watched the rabbit chewing on its piece of grass, and as he arched his head upwards, he just managed to catch sight of the bird that was frozen in mid air, now soaring up high, disappearing out of sight.

He was back in his world, his time, his home in Gorhambury.

Behind him, he could hear footsteps, and as he swung around, Anthony appeared through the forest.

"Ah, there you are!" Anthony called out as he neared Francis, a little irritated.

"Oh, it's you. What's up?" Francis returned.

"I have come to get you. It's time for you leave!" Anthony responded shortly, upset that it was time for Francis to leave home.

"Already?" Francis asked, now saddened as he looked up at the sky to get an idea of the time, realising he must have been in the forest for some hours.

"Oh, I didn't realise I was out here so long!" Francis continued as he let out a sigh.

Seeing the sadness in Anthony's face, Francis put his arm on Anthony's shoulder.

"You know when I am settled, you will have to come and visit!" Francis commented, which caused Anthony's spirit's to rise.

"We'll see!" Anthony responded.

The boys then talked a bit about the trip as they walked back to the house.

As the boys approached the rear of their home and stepped inside, the 70 or so servants and maids employed by the Bacon's, lined the path to the main entrance of the house wishing Francis a good journey, causing his eyes to well up with tears.

The boys eventually arrived back at the main entrance, where Sir Nicholas, Sir Amias and Lady Anne Bacon were both waiting.

Anthony hugged Francis briefly before retreating back into the house. They had already said their goodbyes earlier and Anthony did not want Francis to see the sadness in his eyes. He would miss his brother dearly.

Lady Anne stood before Francis, her cheeks red from the tears she had shed a short while earlier for the boy she had brought up as her own.

As Francis tried to think of something to say, he could not help but feel bitter at her for keeping something so important from him.

"Francis, I hope that one day you will understand that it was for the best," she explained in a sorrowful tone.

"It was for your own safety that our Queen acted as she did," she continued, fighting to hold back her tears.

"I think the Queen did it for her own safety and her status as Queen of England!" Francis responded bitterly.

"You know, there were so many times when I wanted to tell you the truth, but I was sworn to secrecy by the crown," she returned, hearing the bitterness in his voice.

Unable to hold back any longer, she allowed the tears to flow freely down her cheeks.

Francis felt responsible now, knowing full well that she, like everyone else, was simply following orders. He hugged her tightly, forgiving her as much as he could. He kissed her, and then made his way to the carriage where Sir Nicholas and Sir Amias were waiting.

As he closed in on them, Sir Amias shook hands with Sir Nicholas and boarded the carriage, leaving Francis and Sir Nicholas alone.

"Francis, I hope that Anne and I have instilled enough compassion in you to understand and forgive the actions of our Queen and ourselves," Sir Nicholas told him, placing a reassuring hand on his shoulder.

"I know you may think that your mother abandoned you as a babe Francis and maybe you think we were merely doing our duty to our Queen, bringing you up as our own, but know this, I am your father, and Lady Anne is your mother, and you will always be our son," he added, squeezing Francis' shoulder.

"The love we have for you, goes beyond flesh and bone my son, it is a love deep within our hearts," he added tearfully.

"Father" Francis began, wanting to apologise for his bad attitude for the last few days.

"I am proud of the Bacon man who stands before me!" Sir Nicholas interrupted, using his big hands to pull Francis towards him, hugging him tightly.

As they finished their embrace, Francis boarded the carriage where Sir Amias waited, waving his goodbyes to everyone as the carriage left his family home.

8. Virgin Voyage

Errie sounds permeated the top deck of the great galleon *dreadnought* due in part to the strong winds permeating the deck, and also because of the strong winds billowing through its sails as it made a hazardous journey across the fierce seas to France.

The Dreadnought, an 80 foot, 41-gun galleon of the English Navy Royal, was a large, multi-decked sail-powered ship. It was a solid galleon, but due to the dips and tilts forced on it by the harsh weather, many passengers could not help emptying their stomachs, and although Francis was not seasick, as the ship left the shores of England, he began to feel *homesick*.

Oblivious to the harsh sea winds blowing hard on his face, he reminisced at the typical days that were now lost to him, which started out with family prayers and ended with stories of classical adventures, morality tales and the ancient myths.

Lady Anne had made her home a shrine for her children, shielding them from the hypocrisy, corruption and vulgar debauchery that went on in London, but the innocence that Francis had about him disappeared forever when he found out about his royal lineage.

As he looked up to the distant stars partially hidden by dark clouds he let out a deep sigh.

As he tried to comprehend how miniscule he was in the world and what a facade his life had been, he wondered what his *telos* was destined to be.

Telos, taken from the term *teleology*, was a word used by philosophers such as Aristotle, which referred to the idea that *everything* had an inner goal or purpose.

In his early years, Francis was home schooled by his able mother and other learned individuals such as Dr. Dee across a broad range of subjects, which included languages, the arts, religion, fencing, sciences, and philosophy.

What's my telos? Francis pondered for many seconds as he stared up at the distant Northern star Polaris, failing to find an answer.

As the ship advanced across the seas, Francis decided to exercise one of the many skills learned from his favourite mentor, after his mother, Dr. John Dee, which was the art of *Navigation*.

Dr. Dee had repeatedly advocated a policy of political and economic strengthening of England and imperial expansion into the New World and pushed a claim that a welsh prince named *Madog ab Owain Gwynedd* had discovered the New World in 1170 with Dee intending to prove that England's claim to the New World was stronger than that of Spain through their famed navigator, Christopher Columbus and his Spanish sponsored travels.

Ship Navigation required a multitude of skills working in harmony, such as tracking the movement of the sun during the days, and the stars at night, a faithful map, a compass, a log, a lead line, a quadrant or astrolabe, and last but not least, dead reckoning.

Francis pushed his hand into a satchel which lay at his feet, and pulled out a small wooden object shaped like a crucifix. This object was commonly known as a *Cross Staff*, a relatively new tool used by navigator's to aid in determining their location as they embarked on a trip across the seas.

The object consisted of a staff some 33 inches in length with a shorter moveable cross piece and Francis held the staff to his cheekbone and lined it up with the horizon sliding the smaller cross-piece down the staff until the end of it was lined up with the North Star Polaris.

Francis then made a number of notes relating to the altitude he had read from the angled measurements on the main staff and after a short time spent checking his notes, he returned the wooden object back into his satchel.

Across the deck, a pale faced Sir Amias had been looking on, recovering from a recent bout of sea sickness. He decides to make his way over to Francis to find out what Francis was up to. As Sir Amias reached Francis they both nodded to acknowledge each other.

Francis looked out to sea.

"What were you doing with that instrument?" Sir Amias asked, spitting overboard as he tried to remove a sickly taste still in his mouth.

"I am pinpointing our current location," responded Francis, bemused that he was being watched. As he glanced at traces of sickness on Sir Amias' now stained doublet, he sniggered a little before returning back to view the wild waves.

"Why are you doing that?" Sir Amias continued with a perplexed stare as he inhaled some of the cold sea air.

"I am tracking our journey. By my estimations, we are slowly veering off course due to the high winds!" Francis replied confidently as he stared at the sail's billowing above him.

"I am sure the Captain and his crew have that in hand. You should not concern yourself with such matters Francis!" Sir Amias added, shaking his head.

As the galleon jerked up over the rough seas, Sir Amias felt his stomach lurch, and turned to face the deck, holding his tender stomach.

As the ship lurched over another huge wave, Sir Amias grasped his stomach as he contemplated whether he was going to throw up again.

Francis smiled a little as he watched his old French tutor in such a state, but as the smell of bile on Sir Amias reached his nostrils he decided to make his excuses.

"By my estimates, this ship is slightly off track, so I think it is my duty to share my findings with the Captain!" Francis informed his old tutor, picking up his satchel to leave.

"What? I do not think it is a good idea to question a Captain's navigational abilities, especially on his own ship!" Sir Amias argued, but before he could finish, Francis was gone.

9. Staying the Course

Rough winds continued to rock the dreadnought as Francis risked his life to fight his way across the top deck, eventually arriving at the navigation room of the ship.

The Captain, a large burly character, with a rounded face, and short greying beard was busy trying to control the wheel of his ship against the strong winds and didn't even notice Francis approach.

"Captain!" Francis shouted above the noise of the strong winds hammering the sails.

The Captain glanced over at the young Francis, eyeing him from top to bottom, before returning his focus to the important task before him – he tightened his grip on the steering wheel and a frown formed on his forehead at the interruption.

"This is no place for a boy! Get off this deck immediately!" he bellowed.

"I fear I cannot sire, and I am not a boy! I am nearly seventeen!" Francis replied defensively, pouting a little from the Captain calling him a boy.

The Captain glanced over at Francis once again.

"BOY I do not have time for this foolishness! Go now, or I will have you forcibly returned to your quarters!" he returned angrily as an out of breath Sir Amias finally caught up with Francis' exchange with the Captain.

"Francis, do as the Captain says! Let's go!" Sir Amias wheezed.

The Captain briefly eyed Sir Amias and recoiled as soon as he got a whiff of stale vomit, shaking his head in disgust and returning his attention to the wheel.

Stubbornly, Francis continued.

"Captain, by my reckoning, we are slowly drifting off course!" Francis continued.

"What?" the Captain murmured. "Are you still here boy?" he shouted again as he scrutinized Francis still standing before him.

The Captain began to chuckle a little at Francis' insolence.

"You are persistent boy, I will give you that!" he added, shaking his head.

"Explain yourself, and tell me how you have come to this assessment?" he continued, now looking straight at the young innocent boy before him, questioning his authority and knowledge.

"Captain forgive him, he is young!" Sir Amias interjected, apologising on behalf of Francis.

The Captain continued to ignore Sir Amias.

"Well? Come on boy I don't have all day!" the Captain bellowed impatiently.

Francis almost jumped out of his skin when the Captain shouted at him, but took a deep breath and explained himself.

"I have been noting down the ship's position at regular intervals since we left port, and"

The captain interrupted.

"You have been tracking our position have you?" the Captain asked cynically, causing him and his men chuckle at the very idea.

Francis was not impressed at being the butt of their joke and almost decided to leave.

"So you feel we are off course do you?" asked the Captain, sniggering a little.

"I do not *feel* Captain, I know! I have been tracking our path, through the use of my Cross Staff, and I" Francis responded in an angry tone.

"What? You have a Cross Staff?" interrupted the Captain again, now intrigued.

"Yes!" Francis responded tersely.

"Show it to me!" the Captain demanded, wanting to see proof.

Francis hesitantly removed the Cross Staff from his satchel and held it out in his hands.

"Take the wheel!" the Captain instructed one of his men, swapping the wheel and accepting the Cross Staff from Francis, inspecting its craftsmanship closely, noting a number of carvings beyond the notches on the main piece, which was used to measure the sun's altitude. The Captain was impressed.

"This is a good design. Where did you get it?" The Captain asked inquisitively.

"I made it myself!" responded Francis proudly.

The Captain was impressed and stroked his beard, eyeing Francis now with fascination.

"Who taught you how to make it?"

"Dr John Dee. He has been my mentor in many doctrines," Francis responded.

"Dee?" asked the Captain, even more impressed at the mention of Dr. Dee.

"Yes. Do you know him?" Francis asked, noting a strange change in the Captain's tone.

The Captain began to laugh heartily.

"He is one of the most learned men I have ever had the honour of meeting!" the Captain beamed.

"He has helped me expand my knowledge of the sea's more than I could measure. I am indebted to him!" the Captain continued, handing the Cross Staff back to Francis.

"I humbly apologise to you young sire, for if you have indeed been mentored by Master Dee and are as proficient in the use of the Cross Staff as you portray yourself to be, I owe it to Master Dee to at least listen to what you have to say!" the Captain apologised.

"Thank you sire!" responded Francis, smiling a little at the Captains change of attitude.

"Come with me lad. Let's have a look at your measurements," the Captain replied, escorting Francis back to his quarters to review navigational maps of their journey.

As Sir Amias watched Francis and the Captain leave, he was puzzled by the change in the Captain, but also angered by the stubborn attitude of Francis.

After a few minutes, Francis and the Captain emerged with some minor adjustments to the course originally set by the Captain and his men.

These adjustments were based on new formulae's Francis had explained to the Captain aimed at counteracting the strong winds that had slightly put the ship off their course.

Towards the evening, as the seas finally calmed, Francis took some time out to look up at the stars in the night sky, wishing he could see the star's more closely.

Not seeing the star's clearly reminded him of the design of a handheld device called a *telescope*, an anticipated invention by an English philosopher and

Franciscan friar named Roger Bacon, born some 300 years prior, whom Francis had partially modelled himself after.

Roger Bacon was an advocate of a more modern scientific method inspired by the works of Plato and Aristotle via early Islamic scientists and Jewish scholars such as Vicenna, Averroes, and Maimonides.

Francis remembered reading one of Roger Bacon's published works, which detailed treatments of maths and optics, alchemy and a controversial section where the friar anticipated inventions such as the microscope, spectacles, flying machines, hydraulics, steam ships, and *telescopes* - all written as though the friar had actually seen them.

The friar was also known as the first westerner to write down exact instructions for the making of gunpowder.

As the evening drew on, Francis eventually grew tired and decided to get some rest, making his way below deck towards his cabin.

On the 25th September 1576, the ship arrived in Calais, France, and as the passengers disembarked, the Captain personally thanked Francis for his help and wished him well on his European tour.

After their luggage had been unloaded from the ship into a number of waiting carriages, Francis and Sir Amias left the docks of Calais and set out for the Royal court of Navarre.

10. THE WITCH BURNING

𝕹ight turned to day as the carriage containing Francis and Sir Amias made its way across the French countryside, causing Francis to become mesmerised by the beauty of the French landscape as it rolled past his window, that was, until one of the carriage wheels dipped into a pot hole, causing Francis and Sir Amias to bounce off their seats hitting the roof of the carriage.

"Gods nails!" Francis yelped.

"Driver, watch those damned holes!" Sir Amias shouted through the carriage above their heads, to a French voiced apology from the driver above.

"How far is it now sir?" Francis moaned as he rubbed the bruise on his head caused by the unexpected jolt.

"Not far!" Sir Amias snapped, still angry at the French driving. He returned his focus back to a book he was reading.

Francis shook his head, quietly complaining about the rough journey to himself before peering back out the window and followed the route of the carriage as it passed through a number of towns, getting an improved understanding of the life of a typical French villager, as they went about their usual meanderings, selling their wares, be it meats, clothing, vegetables, cheese, or otherwise.

As the carriage passed through one village however, Francis immediately noticed how deserted it was. There were no villagers wandering the streets, and the market stall sellers had gone, strangely leaving their wares on their stalls as well.

Francis wondered what had happened to everyone.

As the carriage continued through the village, he began to hear raised voices in the distance, which seemed to be getting progressively louder, with the carriage seemingly heading straight towards the source of the commotion.

As the carriage turned a corner into the main town square, Francis finally saw the source of the noise, eyeing a crowd of villagers surrounding a large mound of bushels of hay and wood. In the centre of the mound, Francis could see a wooden stake some nine feet high, with a woman, battered and bloodied, shackled to it.

"Gods blood, it's a witch burning!" shouted Francis, causing Sir Amias to look up from his book, joining Francis as they peered out of the carriage window to get a better view.

As the carriage neared the crowd, Francis could see some of the villagers throwing stones and rotten food at the woman, whilst others were simply shouting abuse in French.

As the carriage moved closer still, Francis got a clearer view of the accused witch, as she sluggishly moved her arms and legs trying desperately to free herself from her restraints.

"She is still alive!" Francis shouted excitedly, feeling there was still hope for her survival.

The supposed witch wore a white dress, causing her long flowing black hair to stand out and also hide much of her bloodied face and body. She had been beaten badly from head to toe.

Francis guessed she was taller than him and perhaps in her thirties.

The dress she wore was like none he had ever seen. The weave of the fabric was fine and smooth, and bore none of the lace or frills he was used to seeing in England, no prints or colours to distract from the way it caressed her form. The dress was elegant in its simplicity.

"Look away Francis, look away!" beckoned Sir Amias.

"Look away? We must do something to help her!" Francis argued.

"It is not our concern Francis. We cannot meddle in the laws of this land!" Sir Amias explained to him as he returned to his seat in the carriage.

"She is one of God's creatures sire, and I will not stand idly by!" Francis returned in disbelief that Sir Amias would do nothing to change the woman's fate.

"You are not standing idly by – you are in a moving carriage, and it is not our concern!" Sir Amias snapped.

As Francis looked into the eyes of his old French tutor, he could see no compassion for the poor woman, only fear for himself as to what the villagers might do to him for interfering.

"Stop the carriage sir!" Francis demanded from Sir Amias.

"No Francis! We will not stop! It is not our concern!" Sir Amias repeated defiantly, staring back at Francis.

Realising that Sir Amias was not going to do anything to help the woman, Francis decided it was down to him alone, but if he was to help the woman, he was going to have to get out of the carriage.

He watched the carriage as it passed through the crowd trying to judge its speed and decided it should be safe enough to jump out as long as the path ahead had no obstructions.

As he glanced to Sir Amias sitting in his seat looking inquisitively back at Francis, he knew he would have to act quickly else Sir Amias may try to stop him.

Looking again at the path beside the speeding carriage he spotted a mound of stray bushels of hay and decided he would jump out of the carriage with the aim of softening his fall by landing on the hay.

As he locked eyes with Sir Amias one last time, his tutor realised Francis was up to something. Just as Sir Amias was going to warn Francis to not do anything rash Francis had opened the carriage door and jumped out, rolling as he landed, and barely managing to land on the bushels of hay.

"Good God!" shouted Sir Amias as he watched Francis jump out the carriage fearing the worst. As he strained his head to look behind, he saw Francis getting back on his feet, breathing a sigh of relief.

As he recovered from the shock of seeing Francis jump from the moving carriage, Sir Amias banged on the roof of the carriage.

"Stop the carriage!" he screamed.

Instantly, the coachman reigned in his horses, bringing the carriage to an abrupt halt, causing Sir Amias to lose his footing in the carriage again.

This abrupt stop caused a chain reaction in the rest of the carriages behind that were carrying their suitcases, and they all barely stopped in time, with some of the carriages bumping into each other.

Behind the trail of carriages, Francis was still checking himself, relieved to see that he had escaped the fall unscathed.

He began dusting off some loose strands of hay from his fine doublet, and upon hearing the voices of the angry villagers ahead of him, he hastened his way to the crowd of villagers.

Some of the villagers, having seen him jump from the moving carriage separated to let him pass, thinking Francis to be quite a madman.

Back in the carriage with Sir Amias, after managing to get back on his feet, he opened the carriage door and jumped out, briefly turning to look up at the coachman, giving him an angry stare before then making his way after Francis on foot.

11. CONNECTIONS

In the thick of the jostling crowd of villagers, Francis pushed his way towards the accused witch, receiving angry elbows for his pains.

As he got closer to the woman he was amazed to see she had a wild tattoo on her right leg, exposed through a tear on her dress. The tattoo was of a snake entwined around her leg from her ankle upwards.

As he got closer still, he could hear a village spokesman, who stood between her fate and the crowd, reading from an official declaration.

"By a vote of 5 out of 5 by the village council, you have been found guilty of performing witchcraft, and are hereby sentenced to death!" the village spokesman shouted to the rapturous applause of the villagers.

As the villagers got excited at the opportunity to watch a witch burning, many of them cheered, whilst some continued to throw rocks and rotten food at her as she looked down at them with pity.

Just as Francis reached the front of the crowd, one of the villagers handed the village spokesman a lit torch. The village spokesman rested the torch against a portion of the dry bushels of hay and almost immediately, they lit up in flames and spread to the rest of the bushels positioned around the shackled woman in its centre, forcing the villagers and Francis back.

As the flames erupted, Francis was appalled as the villagers laughed, jumped up and down, clapping their hands, shouting and stomping their feet in such a high spirited fashion.

As Francis stared on at the villagers, if he could not feel the searing heat of the bushels burning and the accused witch screaming, one could have been forgiven for thinking they were at a village barn dance.

As Francis frantically tried to find a way through the flames, the fire erupted higher around the woman, and she screamed even louder as the flames closed in around her.

Fearing all was lost in trying to save the woman himself, Francis turned to the crowd.

"Stop this injustice!" he begged the villagers, shouting at the top of his voice, but the villagers ignored his pleas and continued cheering at the spectacle before them.

As Francis turned back to the accused witch, he managed to exchange eye contact with her briefly before some of the crowd began to turn on Francis, pushing and shoving him.

"Who are you?", "What are doing here?", "Are you one of her servants?" the villagers shouted at him accusingly.

Luckily, as one of the lit flames came in contact with the accused witch' rope-based constraints tying her wrists to the stake behind her, it burned away at them, allowing the woman to free her hands, before proceeding to release the restraints on her legs.

The crowd, seeing her break free, stopped their cheering and stared at her in disbelief and fear.

As she fought her way through the fire, working her way to the edge of the lit hay bushels, she jumped off, her hair still alight with the flames, she landed in the middle of the crowd, and they all backed away from her, almost afraid.

Francis managed a sigh of relief.

"She's free!" he whispered jubilantly to himself as she stood among the villagers, staring at some of them that she had once called friends.

The villagers seemed unsure of what to do next.

The woman attempted to push her way through the crowd past Francis, but as she did, some of the villagers began to regain their confidence and started pushing her back towards the fire.

Francis realised he needed to help her.

He fought his way across the crowd towards her, reaching out his hand to help pull her free from the villager's hold.

"Take my hand! Take my hand!" Francis begged her.

The woman looked around her, taking in the enormity of the crowd she would need to triumph over and then back at Francis, and realising he was the only one that offered to help she decided it was worth a try.

She lunged with all her might towards him, stretching out one of her arms through the crowd, exposing a strange tattoo on her palm, which depicted a triangle with an inset eye which some aged scholar's would have recognised as the *all-seeing eye*.

After straining through the crowd from opposing sides, Francis and the accused witch managed to connect their hands, locking in an embrace, but as soon as this happened, memories of the accused witch flooded Francis' own consciousness.

Through a series of visions, Francis relived some past events.

In the first vision, he saw the accused witch, free of her now battered face and body, in a darkened room, lit only by an open fire and some candles.

He watched as she mixed potions and read out strange incantations up to the heavens from what looked like a very old brown book adorned with the carving of a tree on its earthly cover, seemingly made from the bark of a tree itself.

The vision then changed to images of two naked people, one man, one woman, two pure souls, in a heavenly place, and as they stood before a low hanging aged apple tree, the woman picked an apple and ate it, with Francis now associating the image as a depiction of Adam and Eve in the Garden of Eden.

After the woman bit into the apple, the tree withered away, and the two naked people somehow became lost and dehydrated in a barren desert.

As they wandered the desert, they found the same old brown book the accused witch was reading. As the man and woman read the book, they used the knowledge within it to find a lake where they were able to find drink and food.

The vision then changed again, to a man building a huge ark for all the animals of the earth. The man read from the same old brown book, which gave him the knowledge to build the ark.

Another vision then appeared, showing a man being guided by the old brown book to build whole cities from an initial barren land in the middle of a desert.

The images changed yet again, focusing on recent days, as the accused witch wore her white dress, although in the vision, the dress was in a pristine state, clean and brilliant white and not the dirty, blood stained, ripped version it was now.

Foreign memories then showed the supposed witch sitting in the same darkened room again, reading aloud from the old brown book.

Suddenly, her actions were disturbed by the shouting of angry men outside the door of her home trying to gain access.

The woman jumped up, immediately taking the book, holding it close to her as if it had some immense importance, kneeling on the floor in the middle of the room and pulling at a secret fitting that allowed part of the floorboard beneath her to open up, revealing a secret compartment. The woman kissed the book before placing it into the compartment, quickly closing it.

Having to think quickly, she rushed over to a shelf containing a number of unimportant books and grabbed one at random, a simple grey covered book.

She then raced over to the open fire and stoked it up, making the flames more aggressive, and then whispered a strange incantation that transformed the simple grey book to resemble the one she had just hidden under the floorboards.

She kept her position next to the open fire holding the book, as the men banged fiercely at her front door trying to gain entry.

Eventually, the banging on the door became progressively louder until an axe ripped a hole through it, and after three more decisive hacks at the door, there was a gaping hole, allowing a burly hand to reach in through the hole and open the door by undoing its internal latch.

A burly unshaven man then made his way into the room, immediately locking eyes with the woman.

As he neared her, she screamed at him to leave, and hung the brown book over the flames of the open fire taunting him to stay back.

The next man who entered the room was a young man in his mid 20s. His long hair, black as night, nestled on his shoulders, and taut, angry cords stood out in his neck as he eyed the brown book in her hands.

"Give me the book witch!" he shouted, showing off his strong white teeth in a grimace.

"I feel you are evil, and will certainly abuse its powers! By my life, you will never have it!" she shouted back defiantly, finally throwing the book into the back of the open fire.

"No!" shouted the younger man, as the pages of the book quickly ignited in the high flames.

"Get her!" the young man ordered his burly associate.

As his burly associate rushed towards the woman and wrapped his big arms around her restraining her, the younger man raced to the fire and knelt in front of it as he tried to retrieve the burning book.

"Argh!" he screamed, as the searing flames burned the flesh on his hand.

The book, being deep within the open fire, forced him to surrender his whole hand into the flames to try and retrieve it, but with the book being fully alight and the flames being wild and intense, it was too late.

The book was all but reduced to ashes.

The burly henchman grimaced as he smelled the burning flesh of his master's hand.

As the young man got up from the open fire, there was no mistaking the raw fury in his dark grey eyes. He raced over to the woman, and slapped her several times with the one good hand he had left.

"By your life, you say?" the young man told her, before slapping her again.

"If that is your wish, then so be it!" the young man shouted angrily.

He took one last look at the ashes of the book he had sought before continuing his assault against the woman.

After beating the woman black and blue, the two men left, with the burly man dragging the limp lifeless body of the woman out of the house and away into the night.

The last vision Francis saw, was a makeshift town trial of the woman.

She was tried by the town's people for practicing witchcraft, and condemned to death by burning. The same young man who had abused her in her home watched the proceedings, nursing a bandage for the burn on his hand.

Suddenly, the accused witch's hand released her grip on Francis, and he awakened from a dream-like state back to the screaming mob of reality.

Although it seemed like it had taken several minutes to re-live the memories, Francis could tell that only seconds had actually passed.

As Francis again focused on the woman and the crazed villagers, he was overpowered by some of them and pulled away from her as another group dragged her back to the edge of the burning hay.

To his confusion, as the woman was forced back into the fire, instead of fear on her face, she now had a contented look of *knowing* as she stared back at Francis.

This time, the woman did not fight the villagers, and seemingly accepted her fate, and smiled continually at Francis as the villagers threw her into the centre of the flames, at which point their eye contact was broken.

The flames engulfed her and for a few seconds all he could hear were her painful screams as she lost her fight to live, with Francis helpless to save her.

As the crowd watched the finale of the witch burning, their hold on Francis weakened, and Sir Amias was finally able to push his way through the crowd to get to Francis, pulling him away.

"You must come quickly Francis. The villagers will rip you apart for your interference!" Sir Amias told him in a low fearful tone.

"Let me go! Let me go!" Francis argued through his tears for the woman.

"I cannot! I am sworn by Queen Elizabeth to ensure your safety. My life will be forfeit if you are harmed! You MUST stop!" Sir Amias begged.

As Francis looked back to where the woman had been thrown, he realised that her life was lost and there was nothing more he could do. He quietly whispered a prayer for her before going limp all over, allowing Sir Amias to drag him back to the waiting carriage.

Francis felt numb.

12. NAVARRE

Through reddened teary eyes, Francis sat dejected in the carriage with Sir Amias.

It wasn't long before the carriages turned into the grand palace of Navarre, and it was the hive of activity of nobles coming and going from the majestic court that finally brought Francis out of his sadness.

As Francis looked on at the daily meandering of the French court, he was amazed at the differing colours and fashions of the French aristocracy, and as the carriages finally slowed to a halt, Francis and Sir Amias got out.

Francis wiped the remaining tears from his cheeks as he tried to compose himself in front of the French noble men and women that immediately began to stare at his foreign attire.

"Are we to be met?" Francis queried as he began to feel unsettled by the strange stares they were receiving.

"Yes, a dear friend of mine, Lord Beaumont is to meet us here," responded Sir Amias, searching the faces of the many people passing them.

After a few minutes, Sir Amias smiled as he recognises a particularly well dressed French aristocrat with greying black hair and light green eyes walking towards them grinning, showing off his strong white teeth.

It was Lord Beaumont.

"It is good to see you again!" greeted Lord Beaumont, shaking hands with Sir Amias.

"I hear congratulations are in order on your knighthood!" he continued.

Sir Amias let out a wry smile.

"News does travel fast in France!" Sir Amias joked.

Lord Beaumont himself also began looking around for someone.

"Is there a problem?" queried Sir Amias.

"No, not at all! My nephew is around here somewhere, and as usual, he has gone missing!" Lord Beaumont replied, scanning various groups of people around them.

After a few seconds, Lord Beaumont eyed his nephew talking to a group of well dressed ladies and beckoned him over.

As the nephew approached, Francis was stunned to recognise the nephew as one of the men in the visions he had when he touched the accused witch earlier that day.

"You remember my nephew?" Lord Beaumont queried Sir Amias.

Sir Amias looked eyed Damien from head to toe.

"Yes of course! You have indeed grown into a fine man. How are you Damien?"

"I am well sire!" Damien replied, showing his strong white teeth as he smiled.

"May I introduce you to Francis Bacon," Sir Amias declared to Lord Beaumont and his nephew.

Francis exchanged handshakes with Lord Beaumont, but was speechless as he noticed Damien's bandaged hand.

As Francis recalled the woman's memories he had somehow tapped into earlier that day, he remembered that the younger man had also burned his hand whilst attempting to retrieve a brown book from a roaring fire.

Francis felt he must be going mad and became lost in his own thoughts as he stared at Damien's bandaged hand.

"Are you alright?" Damien queried, wondering why Francis was staring at the bandage.

Francis snapped out of his thoughts.

"Forgive me, I am just a little tired," Francis replied, feeling a bit wary of Damien.

"I foolishly tried a spot of cooking. I should leave such tasks to the women eh?" Damien explained as he offered up an impromptu explanation for the burn on his hand, laughing, but Francis was stone-faced.

"Are you sure you are okay my dear boy? You don't look at all well!" Sir Amias asked as he noticed Francis' pale face.

"I'll be OK!" replied Francis as he managed a forced smile for Lord Beaumont and his nephew.

"Come, they are expecting us in the palace!" Lord Beaumont informed Sir Amias.

"Oh, yes! We cannot be late!" Sir Amias exclaimed.

With that, they all continued into the palace, but Francis was still wary of Damien and wondered if there was any truth to the vision he had experienced.

13. QUEEN MARGUERITE

As Francis followed Sir Amias, Lord Beaumont, and his nephew into the grand palace of Navarre, he considered that royal life in Navarre did not seem much different to the ways of English aristocracy, except for the richer colours being exercised on their fashions.

After a short walk down one of the corridors of the palace they all stopped at the entrance to a grand hall buzzing with activity and Lord Beaumont whispered some details to a crier who waited at its entrance.

"Sir Amias Paulet, English Ambassador to France!" the crier bellowed in a deafening voice. As the crier's voice echoed through the grand hall, the many conversations in the hall slowed to a whisper as they all turned to see the new Ambassador from England.

"François Bacon from England!" the crier continued after a short pause, introducing Francis.

When the crier shouted his name, it served as a sore reminder to Francis that his name did not reflect the hidden royalty in him, instead only serving as a painful reminder of the facade of his Bacon life.

As all the court patrons stared at him and Sir Amias, Francis felt alone and began to miss his family and friends, but his thoughts were interrupted when out of nowhere, the silence of the great hall was broken by the tapping of foot steps on the marble floor.

As Francis looked towards the source of the tapping sound, his face softened as he stared at the majestic sight of a beautiful young woman. Her snowy white complexion and hair as black as night, blew him away.

Each gesture, each turn of her head and hands, gracefully gliding towards him as women dropped into curtsies and men fell to their knees on every side of her path.

She must be a member of the royal family Francis thought, mesmerised by her astonishing beauty.

Sir Amias quickly pinched Francis in his side, jerking him back to his senses.

"Ouch!" Francis yelped, turning to Sir Amias.

"Kneel!" Sir Amias whispered apprehensively, directing Francis to bow in the presence of royalty.

Realising his serious error in judgement, Francis immediately dropped to his knee before her, bowing his head.

With Queen Marguerite now standing before him, Francis felt embarrassed for gawping, a serious lapse in royal etiquette.

"Welcome! You must be Francis Bacon! I was told of your arrival!" she beamed, her eyes twinkling as she looked into his.

"I am Queen Marguerite!" she continued in a joyful tone.

Marguerite was born into the last generation of the Valois family, which had ruled France for over 200 years, and was now Queen of France and Navarre via an arranged marriage.

Head still bowed, Francis was immediately set at ease.

"Your Majesty!" Francis responded in a flustered tone.

Queen Marguerite extended her hand, inviting Francis to acknowledge her and immediately took her hand and performed the customary action of kissing it.

Behind Sir Amias and Lord Beaumont, Damien looked on, jealous of the attention Francis was receiving by his Queen. He finally did an about turn and left the court in disgust, and although Queen Marguerite saw his action, she pretended not to notice.

"Rise young prince!" she whispered to Francis.

Francis was initially shocked that she knew of his secret, but as he remembered the writing's in his uncle's day books, it seemed that news of his birth had been whispered across the seas and must have been known to many in high positions of power, and particularly royal families.

Francis returned to his feet to face the French Queen.

Sir Amias, not to be upstaged by Francis any longer, made a few steps forward putting him in line with Francis, introducing himself to Queen Marguerite.

"Your Majesty, I am Sir Amias Paulet, English Ambassador for France!" Sir Amias explained as he introduced himself.

"Welcome Sir Amias!" she responded with a smile, extending her hand for him to kiss as well.

As she beckoned Sir Amias to rise, a servant entered the hall with a tray, catching Queen Marguerite's attention.

"Ah, here are some refreshments I ordered for you in anticipation of your arrival!" she explained as the servant offered Francis and Sir Amias drinks.

With the formalities now relaxed, Sir Amias, Lord Beaumont, and Francis bowed in appreciation and gratefully accepted some of the refreshments as they conversed with Queen Marguerite.

As they passed the time in the royal court, Queen Marguerite introduced Francis and Sir Amias to some of the other distinguished patrons there, which included Queen Marguerite's brother, the Duke of Anjou, an attractive man just past his twentieth year, whose face was unfortunately scarred by smallpox as a child.

It was to be a strange series of events that, a few years later, the Duke of Anjou would be offered as a potential French suitor to Queen Elizabeth of England, he being some 20 years younger than her.

As Francis passed some of the younger female ladies in the hall, many of them eyed his every move, while others smiled seductively at him, making him blush.

Breaking through the crowd heading towards Francis and Sir Amias, was a lone nobleman also styled in English clothing.

His name was Edward De Vere and as he neared them, he bowed to Queen Marguerite.

"Your Majesty!" he responded with an accent that Francis recognised as a noble Englishman.

"Master De Vere!" Queen Marguerite replied, recognising him.

"I hope you will forgive my rudeness to re-introduce myself to the young Francis and the Ambassador?" he asked.

Re-introduce? Francis thought, trying desperately to recognise the name.

"Of course not, please continue!" Queen Marguerite replied, beckoning him forward.

Edward De Vere smiled in appreciation, and then turned to Francis.

"Master Bacon!" Edward De Vere exclaimed bowing lowly.

"Do I know you sir?" asked Francis, feeling his name was indeed familiar.

"I would hope so! I am Edward De Vere!" he explained.

As Francis took stock of the full name, his eyes widened as he suddenly recalled where he recognised the name.

"I do know you! Are we not related?" asked Francis, inquisitively.

"Yes we are! I have recently married Anne, daughter of Lord Burghley, your uncle!" Edward De Vere responded.

"Of course!" Francis responded in a joyful tone as his memory finally returned about the joining of the De Vere & Cecil family's.

Francis and Edward De Vere shook hands eagerly.

"My tour of Europe is coming to an end, whilst yours is just beginning!" Edward De Vere added joyfully.

As they shook hands, Francis thought back to when he was back in England, remembering the news of Lord Burghley's daughter's engagement to Edward, also remembering some gossip that the marriage was forced upon Edward De Vere as he was of a ward of Lord Burghley's, with family wealth.

He now wondered if that was why Edward had taken up a solo tour of Europe so soon after the marriage, a trip, which would have separated him from his wife for many months.

"You must join us then, as your time here is short!" added Queen Marguerite.

"As you wish, your Majesty!" accepted Edward De Vere nodding graciously.

Francis and Sir Amias spent the rest of the day talking to Edward and Queen Marguerite about life in France and also other parts of Europe that Francis would be visiting during his travels.

As Francis practiced his French, he managed to take the lead in many of the conversations covering religion, literature, languages, art and music and although Francis was some seven years younger than Queen Marguerite, she was impressed by the breadth of his knowledge and his enthusiasm to know as much of France as possible.

Through these conversations, Francis realised that her infinite variety of knowledge enthralled him as well.

The Past

14. A RENAISSANCE

Through countless one-to-one engagements with Queen Marguerite, it took Francis quite some time to realise that she was hardly ever joined by her husband the King. In fact, Francis became aware that he had been spending more time with her than with anyone else.

He enjoyed her company, and believed the feeling was mutual, but deep within him, he knew it was somehow wrong.

One fine day, when Francis had been given an invite by Queen Marguerite to meet some special friends of hers, he asked Lord Beaumont if he would escort him to his appointment, deciding to broach the subject of the King and Queen's marriage with Lord Beaumont.

"I have a sensitive question to ask?" Francis fumbled.

"Yes of course! What do you need to know?" Lord Beaumont responded.

"It is a question about your King and Queen?" Francis asked delicately.

"You wish to know why they do not share the same bedchambers?" Lord Beaumont clarified bluntly.

"No, no, not at all sire! I merely wondered why they do not spend time together!" Francis piped back in defence, his face now red with embarrassment.

Lord Beaumont gave Francis a mischievous smile.

"It is no secret that they live separate lives. They were forced into marriage to join their two royal families and have been living apart ever since, occupying separate apartments within the palace," Lord Beaumont responded casually as they walked in the sunshine.

"They must have loved each other once, surely?" Francis asked.

"Not as far as I am aware," Lord Beaumont replied, shaking his head.

"The King stayed outside the church on the day of their wedding until the last possible moment, whilst Queen Marguerite was forced to accept him as her husband under duress standing at the altar!" continued Lord Beaumont, laughing out loud.

Francis was shocked at the level of intimidation Queen Marguerite and her husband had been faced to endure for the good of France and the demands of their respective families.

"Never have I met two more different people!" Lord Beaumont added shaking his head sadly.

"If you were to enter the King's apartments, you would find it always crowded with politicians, schemers, and wasters, being a hotbed of intrigue where dangerous plots were constantly being hatched. By comparison, when you enter Queen Marguerite's apartments you will see it is frequented by people of a very different calibre," Lord Beaumont continued.

"That is where we are going?" Francis queried.

Lord Beaumont nodded.

"On any given day, you will meet philosophers, scientists, poets, inventors, and the like, attracted by the sheer genius of her own intellectual personality," Lord Beaumont explained.

As Francis considered asking another question about why the Queen's apartments were littered with scholars, they arrived at their destination.

"This is where we part company Francis!" Lord Beaumont informed him.

"Hey you!" Lord Beaumont shouted to a passing courtier, causing the courtier to turn and nod at Francis and Lord Beaumont, forcing a smile.

"Escort this young gent to Queen Marguerite will you?"

The courtier begrudgingly nodded.

"I will see you later perhaps?" Lord Beaumont queried Francis.

Francis nodded appreciatively before following the courtier inside the private quarters, passing many groups of scholars deep in conversation, reminding him of his studies at Trinity College, back in England.

In the thick of the many groups, the courtier spotted Queen Marguerite talking with two men from the royal printers relating to some impending literary publications.

"Francis!" Queen Marguerite giggled with joy as she saw him nearing her, ushering her printers away as Francis made his way to her.

"Welcome! Come, let me show you around!" she offered, and they both took a stroll around the many groups engrossed in varying discussions.

"Who are all these scholars and thinkers?" he asked inquisitively.

She eyed all the men and women conversing in numerous groups, "This is my invisible college!" she giggled mischievously.

"I must confess, it does remind me of my schooling in England!" Francis laughed.

She smiled in return, before becoming a little serious.

"Look around you," she offered as she swept her hand out.

"Where you stand right now is the nexus of the French Renaissance!" she boldly declared.

Francis became somewhat confused, but remained quiet, hoping she would clarify the matter and seeing the confusion in his face, Queen Marguerite realised she would have to explain some more.

"The French Renaissance that is seeping through France, enriching the very fabric of our society, and more importantly, French literature is being sharpened and stimulated from within these great walls," she continued.

"Do you mean to say that the French Renaissance is merely an artificially inspired programme stimulated by these earnest scholars?" Francis asked, trying to make sense of what he was being told.

Believing Francis had ridiculed her programme, Queen Marguerite became defensive.

"Merely? Mark my words, in years to come, the French language will be rich in its vocabulary, smooth in its delivery, and will be the language of choice across the world!" she responded defiantly.

Francis bowed his head apologetically.

"My apologies, my Queen, I did not mean to speak out of turn!" Francis replied, realising he had offended her in some way.

Seeing Francis flustered, Queen Marguerite realised that perhaps she was being overprotective of her programme, laughing at herself.

"No it is I who should apologise, maybe I am too defensive of my programme!" she added with a warm smile back at Francis.

"Please arise dear Francis, you have done nothing wrong!" she commanded.

Francis, moved by her humility, stood upright at her command.

"Please allow me to explain," she asked, giving him a warm smile.

"Thank you!" Francis encouraged, wanting to understand what she was trying to get at.

"Let us walk this way," directed Queen Marguerite, and as they walked down a corridor lined with many stone busts of historical people, they initially passed a bust of Julius Caesar, and as Francis eyed the toga design on the bust, everything and everyone around him seemed to slow to a stop, apart from him.

As he looked down to what he was wearing, he found himself dressed in a large woollen cloth in the style of a toga, with sandals on his now bare feet.

Suddenly, Queen Marguerite began talking, which snapped Francis out of what must have been the briefest of day dreams.

"As you know, the French language was born from a vulgar version of Latin, which was brought to Northern Beaumont with the Roman conquest in the 1st BC."

Francis looked down and was relieved to see that the stylish blue doublet, trousers, and shoes he chose to wear that morning had now returned. He began rubbing his forehead thinking he would need to get a grip on these day dreams before it was too late.

"Francis?" prompted Queen Marguerite seeing Francis lost in his own thoughts.

"Oh, please carry on!" Francis replied, realising he was not paying attention, forcing a smile.

A small crease covered Queen Marguerite's forehead, as she wondered why Francis was so distracted, but she nonetheless continued her explanation.

"Later in the 5th to 8th centuries, this vulgar version Latin had grown in its own right to make it distinct from the mainstream Latin spoken in other regions of the Roman Empire."

"Is that the language being used in the *Reichenau Glosses* literature of that time?" Francis queried, thinking back to something Lady Anne had taught him about the origins of various languages.

"It is!" she answered, smiling at his ceaseless knowledge, causing Francis to blush a little.

"Don't be embarrassed Francis, it is a very admirable quality to be so learned!" She added as she noticed Francis getting a little embarrassed.

"I am impressed that you have taken the time to familiarise yourself with history beyond that of England." she explained.

"Anyway, between the 9th and 13th centuries, the dialect of the Northern Beaumont flourished into a separate language with a grammar of its own that we now call the French language. In the past couple of centuries, the French language has undergone many changes to elevate it to the level of the structured Latin language as a medium for our own literary expression," she continued.

Queen Marguerite paused as she considered how the programme was funded.

"The recent royal decree proclaiming 'French' as the official language of the public administration has meant the government are now actively involved in developing and standardising it. Because of this, I, as Queen of Navarre, have a vested interest in ensuring that the people of Navarre will be proud of their country's language," she added finally.

This piece of detail offered by Queen Marguerite only served to remind Francis of how unrefined the English language was, remembering that back in England, he found it difficult to understand the common man on a daily basis.

15. PALLAS ATHENA

In resuming their walk, it was not long before they came upon a full sized cast of what looked to be a female warrior, based on the breast plated armour and helmet she wore, and the spear she wielded in her hand.

"Do you know who this bust represents Francis? You actually have some things in common with her!" she asked, smiling mischievously.

As Francis eyed the statue, he immediately recognised her, but was intrigued by Queen Marguerite's comments.

"Do I?" Francis asked with interest.

Queen Marguerite nodded, giving Francis a knowing grin.

Francis was sure he recognised the statue to be Pallas Athena, the Greek Goddess of War as he had always had an interest in the Greek history, being much in awe of the ancient period that gave so many gifts to the world such as the invention of Mathematics, Science and Philosophy.

As he stared at the facial cast of the statue though, he could not help but notice that it bore a strong resemblance to the accused witch that he failed to save. He shook his head as her face now seemed to haunt him.

"She looks like Pallas Athena, the Greek Goddess of War?" Francis suggested.

"Almost!" Queen Marguerite responded.

"She is Pallas Athena, Goddess of WISDOM, and although she was always depicted as a warrior, she is known more as a judge, diplomat, and mediator to her people. More than any other of the Greek goddesses, Athena remains to this day a symbol of civilisation, useful knowledge, noble reasoning, logic and wisdom!" Queen Marguerite added.

Although Francis was already fully versed in the history of Pallas Athena, he simply smiled with interest as he took in all of Queen Marguerite's French eloquence.

"You said we had something in common?" Francis asked, looking for her to expand on her teasing.

"Oh yes!" she remembered.

"The German origins of *François,* derives from the name *Spear,* which to me is a very special connection," she answered with a playful smile as she touched the long spear the statue held in her hand.

Francis turned his focus back to the long spear the statue held.

"She also has some connection with your English Queen," she teased again.

Although Francis did not want to be reminded of Queen Elizabeth, he was again intrigued.

"How so?" he asked, feeling uncomfortable talking about his English Queen.

"In her time, she had no consorts or lovers, and was called 'Athena Parthenos', which means 'Virgin Athena', much like your English Queen," she explained.

Francis felt saddened by the reminder of his birth and Queen Marguerite realised she had somehow struck a nerve.

Francis turned away, and after a few tense seconds of silence, he realised he had dampened the mood of the conversation. To hide his sadness, he took out a small notebook, quill, and ink, and began scribbling this new found piece of information into it. Queen Marguerite was now intrigued.

"What do you have there? A diary?" she asked trying to catch a glimpse of the writing on the pages.

"No, not at all, this is my storehouse! As I learn new words, phrases, proverbs, and the like, I write them down. It helps me to remember. I am just writing notes concerning the Greek goddess Athena that you explained," Francis responded.

This 'storehouse' Francis would later call the *Promus of Formularies and Elegancies*, and by his death, would contain over 1,600 proverbs, metaphors, aphorisms, and salutations from many sources such as Seneca, Horace, and Virgil.

"You are sure it is not a diary?" she asked, glaring nosily at the book.

"No I am afraid not! You are welcome to look though!" Francis added, breathing a sigh of relief as he managed to bring the conversation back to a more jovial level.

"May I?" Queen Marguerite asked, her eyes lighting up with excitement as Francis handed her the diary.

Queen Marguerite excitedly flicked through the many notations within the pages of the diary as Francis continued reviewing the bust of Pallas Athena.

"You have noted some beautiful quotes in here Francis!" Queen Marguerite replied, handing the book back to him, and as she did, their hands touched causing them to share a tender exchange.

Love sought is good, but given unsought, is better Francis considered as he looked into her eyes. Becoming a little embarrassed, he accepted the book and turned his eyes away.

"You seem to respect her greatly," Francis queried as attempted to resume a less intimate conversation which managed to snap Queen Marguerite back to the conversation as well.

"Yes!" she replied, now giggling at his embarrassment again.

"I believe the goddess Athena reminds us that we can successfully use our intellect and creativity in the pursuit of any goal we choose," she added now back on her train of thought.

Still staring at the bust, Francis looked back down at the snake figure at Pallas Athena's feet, causing Queen Marguerite to explain the snake.

"To understand the significance of the snake, you must first understand the spear," she added mysteriously.

"Oh, why is that?" he asked curiously.

"Pallas Athena was commonly known in her day as a spear-shaker, due to the spear of knowledge she carried in her right hand, which represented a ray of wisdom."

"She would often shake her spear at the dragon of ignorance, represented here as a snake," Queen Marguerite explained, thrusting out her hand, pretending she had a spear of her own, causing Francis to smile some more.

"You seem to model yourself after her?" Francis queried with interest.

"As much as a mere mortal can do, I try to act as a guiding spirit to the scholars I have around me to keep them focused, and I look to Pallas Athena to guide me," she responded as she looked around at the many scholar's that surrounded them.

Francis gave Queen Marguerite a look of being impressed at her thinking, before considering the consequences of her programme.

"From my understanding of the history of a language, for centuries, it has been a natural evolution for a language to develop over time to the reach of the people," Francis explains thoughtfully, and then realises that she may take his comment as a criticism, but luckily, Queen Marguerite is impressed by his honesty.

"That is true, but I feel that my countrymen should be able to articulate themselves to the highest of their abilities, and currently the French language restricts them in that area," she answered critically.

"How are you to achieve such an enormous task?" Francis asked, now thinking about how useful it would be if something similar was done for his own countrymen in England.

"By educating my people in the structured reading and writing of an enriched French language, inspired by the literature of the ancient philosophers of old, the French language will be the envy of the world!" she continued in a wishful tone.

"Our programme adds more and more translations of the Latin vocabulary to the French language every day, which we then introduce into the language our countrymen use every day," Queen Marguerite added.

"I must admit, on many occasions I find myself thinking in Latin, as it allows me to express my thoughts more clearly, and then verbalising it back into English," responded Francis talking almost to himself.

She smiled, believing that Francis now appreciated the reasoning behind their government induced *Renaissance*.

"I believe the English language may also benefit from such a programme, as I fear it suffers too?" she asked.

"It does suffer, but I think to educate the masses is a monumental task in itself," responded Francis, nodding in agreement.

"Our strategy is to convert translations of historical literature into smaller more comprehensible subject areas of educational and moral interest that our countrymen can understand and appreciate and publishing it as newsworthy stories, poetry, and also in interesting re-enactments for the stage as plays to broaden its appeal," she explained.

Francis now came to understand how the enrichment of the masses was being orchestrated by her programme.

"I wondered for some time why there was little notable English literature to date, and I think I understand why," she continued.

"Oh? How so?" Francis asked.

"I think it is because the language is too brittle," she continued.

"I beg to differ, your Majesty, there is indeed some fine English literature! Sir Thomas Eliot wrote one called *The Governor*, another author wrote one called *The Schoolmaster*, and Thomas Wright authored one called *Arts of Rhetoric*," Francis piped back defending England's weak literary heritage.

"Yes, and you are good to know them all as valid English texts, but they are of the few that exist!" she responded critically.

"I think there were some recent translations of Chaucer," added Francis grasping at his knowledge of more English literary publications.

A tiny frown puckered on his forehead. He knew that she was right. There was very little quality English literature available, and he had exhausted his literary knowledge to defend his England.

Seeing Francis lost for words, Queen Marguerite realised now that she had dampened his spirits.

"I apologise if it seems I am criticising the English language Francis, that was not my intention!" she apologised.

"Many countries around the world, including ours have an evolving language, but I and my countrymen are trying to do something about it NOW to ensure its onward survival," she added.

"It is a magnificent programme, and I grow envious that my England will continue to stagnate," Francis replied, dejected at the state of England's literary weaknesses.

"You have every right to love your country Francis, for no doubt its strengths far outweigh the lack of literary knowledge!" she added with a smile.

"You have undertaken a great task. Do you believe you will be able to complete it in your own lifetime?" Francis queried, wondering what timescales she was working towards.

"I fear not, but I hope this entire programme will continue well after my bones have turned to dust!" she smiled.

"There are many here up to the challenge, and I have faith in them. Come, let me introduce you to some of these fine scholars that are working hard to enrich the French language," she added.

As Francis looked again at the buzz of activity around him, his understanding of what was going on now was becoming clearer to him.

Francis now understood that all the scholars around him were all strategising their next move to progress the programme.

16. THE PLEIADES

Scanning the various groups of scholars, Queen Marguerite paused for a moment to decide which ones to introduce to Francis, making an instant decision as she eyed a particular group of grey haired scholars huddled around a game of chess.

As Francis and Queen Marguerite approached, the group parted a little to expose the faces of the two chess opponents, one being Jean-Antoine de Bauf and the other being Pierre De Ronsard, two more grey bearded scholars.

As the group gave way some more, Francis was taken aback to find another bystander watching the game, Damien.

Although Pierre and Jean-Antoine were deep in thought over their game of chess, they immediately stood up as their Queen approached. They all bowed as their Queen approached.

"Francis, I think you already know Damien, but may I introduce you to Pierre De Ronsard, Jean-Antoine de Bauf and Joachim du Bellay."

Francis could see a part of Damien's disfigured hand protruding from his bandage, reminding him of the strange visions he had when he connected with the supposed witch.

He nodded courteously at Damien, and then at the other men.

The men all nodded in return.

"My Queen tells me you are well versed in the arts," Jean-Antoine queried immediately, strangely interested in the young man before him.

"I was fortunate enough to have been home tutored by a very capable teacher, my mother," Francis responded with a hint of pride in his voice.

"Your mother?" asked Damien, sniggering a little.

"She failed to send you to school?" Damien added smugly.

Queen Marguerite frowned at Damien's attitude towards Francis.

Lady Anne Bacon was a perfect housewife with a strong character, and her accomplishments were many and varied. Her father's high teaching skills were used to tutor members of the English royal family of his time, so she was fortunate to have had a high level of teaching from him.

Lady Anne Bacon had been the tutor to the young King Edward, being a specialist in languages. In her private letters, she quoted Latin freely and in her early twenties she translated and published *Ochines Sermons* from an Italian edition.

"My mother is educated to a higher level than most teachers I have ever known, and was called, like her father before her to tutor one of the Kings of England!" Francis responded defensively.

As Francis defended his mother however, a lump raised in his throat as he realised the privileged royal tutoring he had received, without even knowing its full implications.

"I do not know the level of teachings in France, but I will tell you that it would take much to compete with her level of knowledge!" Francis continued defensively, which caused Queen Marguerite to smile at Francis' appreciation of women being learned in the fine arts like she was.

"Where did you study?" asked Jean-Antoine.

"I was enrolled at Trinity College, Cambridge, aged 12, but did not enjoy it as I disagreed with many of their teachings," Francis responded frankly.

Jean-Antoine was very intrigued with Francis.

"At age 12 you disagreed with the learned scholars?" Jean-Antoine asked with interest.

"I disagreed with the manner by which they taught philosophy among other things," Francis responded flatly.

With that, Jean-Antoine's right eyebrow rose up a good inch, while Joachim's eyes widened. Pierre however, seemed indifferent, whilst Damien just huffed in disbelief.

The home schooling of scientific training Francis had received showed him the rare defects in existing academic debate, and Francis became opposed to the teachings at Trinity College.

Francis disagreed with their teaching's, which argued that facts be collected before deducing scientific truths, and that physical science was not carried out by observations from the natural world, but by arguments based solely on tradition and prescribed authorities.

"Do you think you were in a position to know more than the learned fellows at Trinity College?" Joachim asked in disbelief.

"For its value and utility, it must be plainly avowed that wisdom, which we have derived principally from the Greeks is but like the boyhood of knowledge and has the characteristic property of boys: it can talk but it cannot generate: for it is fruitful of controversies but barren of works.

In laymen terms, my professors could debate year on year how many teeth a donkey had, but no one would ever consider to go and physically count for themselves to prove it!"

Queen Marguerite, Jean-Antoine, Joachim, and Pierre all laughed, while Damien was not impressed that Francis seemed to be winning the others over.

"As Sophocles once said, *one must learn by doing the thing, for though you think you know it, you have no certainty until you try,*" Francis added.

Francis impressed Jean-Antoine with his knowledge of the ancient Greek tragedians.

"In my mind, that is a fruitless endeavour, I believe actions speak louder than words. One must prove their ideas else their ideas are merely hearsay. One needs a physical analysis to prove, or disprove of a theory, it is the only way to evolve our stagnant understandings!" Francis continued further with strong conviction.

Joachim smiled at his panache.

"You have much vitality Francis, where do you get your inspiration?"

Francis had an interest in ancient Greek history and literature for as long as he could remember, ever since he had started having flashbacks where he visualised himself as some sort of Roman soldier.

Looking at the group, Francis realised there was no way he was going to tell them that it was because he dreamed of life as a Roman.

"I don't know," Francis replied, dropping his head, lost for words.

"No matter!" responded Joachim, thinking Francis had become a bit embarrassed.

"Yes! To take such a stance against that of the recognised professors of philosophy, indeed against the whole authority of the university takes great courage!" added Jean-Antoine.

Francis let out a little smile.

"I fear it is stubbornness more than anything else to reject the teachings of learned professors!" criticised Damien.

Pierre nodded slightly, agreeing with Damien.

"I assure you sir, all they had to teach me I already knew, and all relevant teachings meant for me, was duly received. I acquired much of my knowledge of Latin and Greek languages through my home schooling and am the better for it!" Francis replied defiantly.

"A fan of languages eh?" asked Jean-Antoine.

"Yes, but those languages were in addition to my learning's in French, Italian, and Spanish, and some Hebrew. I have been told that I have a natural aptitude for languages, and I hope this appreciation will aid me as I further my skills in Law," Francis added.

"A noble profession!" added Jean-Antoine in agreement.

Francis had managed to impress them all, except Damien, who just shrugged his shoulders.

He was angry at having to entertain Francis and had had enough.

"Linguistics is for people with a precision for maths, but not the intelligence!" Damien responded sarcastically.

Queen Marguerite, who had remained quiet for most of the discussion, had finally had enough of Damien's rude comments.

"Damien!" scolded Queen Marguerite in an angry tone.

Damien nodded apologetically, "My apologies, Majesty!"

"I have urgent matters elsewhere, so please forgive me," he added eyeing Francis jealously before hastily withdrawing from the group.

Queen Marguerite, now feeling embarrassed, turned to Francis.

"My apologies for Damien, Francis, I do not know what has gotten into him!"

Francis nodded in appreciation, but was happy that Damien had left.

"Ignorance of all things is an evil neither terrible nor excessive, nor yet the greatest of all, but great cleverness and much learning, if they be accompanied by a bad training, are a much greater misfortune." Francis added, reciting another quote.

"Ah, quotes from the ancient Plato too! You are indeed learned Francis!" added Jean-Antoine.

"I have a great interest in literature of all ages, sire," Francis added meekly.

As they continued their discussions, Pierre looked back down to the incomplete game of chess, moving one of the pieces.

"Check!" announced Pierre, now with a grin on his face, nudging Jean-Antoine.

"What? Again? I thought this was going to be the day that I beat you!" responded Jean-Antoine, looking back to the game.

"Today is not that day, plus I am always two moves ahead of you!" Pierre responded smugly.

As Jean-Antoine sat back down to review his options, Francis reviewed the placement of pieces on the chess board and used his mathematical analysis to play out all the possible permutations of potential moves, taking mere seconds to decide a strategy for winning the game.

"May I advise you on your next move?" Francis asked Jean-Antoine.

"If you can see a way out this mess, then by all means, please go ahead!" Jean-Antoine responded in a playful tone.

With this, Francis made his move against Pierre and almost immediately, Pierre countered with another one.

Francis advised Jean-Antoine on the next few more moves, placing him in a winning position.

"That's check-mate!" declared a confident Francis after Jean-Antoine moved his Queen.

"What?" Pierre replied, stunned that he had lost.

"I like to play three moves ahead!" Francis added, smiling to the agreeable laughter of the group.

As Francis commended himself for helping Jean-Antoine to beat Pierre, he could hear a haunting female voice whispering behind him.

"Francis"

The ghostly voice frightened him for a moment, but as he turned behind him to where he heard the voice, he could see there was no one there.

He truly wondered if he was going out of his mind.

"I understand that in England, writers face retribution if their written words go against the state's views, no?" asked Jean-Antoine, which snapped Francis out of his thoughts. Francis blinked a few times as he focused on the question.

"Yes! My father fell foul of such bias," Francis replied, nodding as he thought back to his uncle's day books, remembering the people executed for merely stating his very existence as a child of Queen Elizabeth.

The consequences of being outspoken against those of power could be very dire indeed.

"So there are no restrictions as to what can be published in France then?" Francis asked wide eyed.

"You do have to be careful, but in France it is held to be discreditable for a gentleman NOT to be amorous of the learned arts. In fact, you are honoured for it!" commented Joachim in a jovial response.

"Saying or writing the wrong thing has sent many to prison, or even worse to be executed," Francis responded solemnly.

"I know of a number of English gents that write under a pseudonym to avoid being linked to their writing," responded Pierre, nodding in agreement.

"You have friends in England?" Francis asked with a surprised look.

"Yes, many years ago, I spent time in England as a page to James V [of Scotland]," Pierre responded casually.

"Don't be fooled Francis, Pierre is known the world over for his writing! Queen Elizabeth herself sent him a diamond in appreciation of his written prose!" Joachim added.

Francis was impressed.

"With all these skilled patrons of the arts, I am sure you will achieve great things!" Francis told Queen Marguerite.

"We already have Francis, and my dream is that some day after I am dead, the world will honour the French language as the sweetest, most charismatic language of them all!" she beamed.

"With your dedication, I cannot see how it could possibly fail!" Francis commented as he looked longingly into her eyes.

"That is what I and my countrymen strive for. I am their muse, and will stay their path to the enrichment of France!" she responded joyfully, to the shared agreement of Joachim, Pierre, and Jean-Antoine.

As the group engaged in many other discussions talking well into the evening, Francis continued to make a great impression on the trio, particularly on Queen Marguerite, and completely forgot about the ghostly whisper's he had heard.

As his time in France progressed, Francis learned that these men formed part of a secret fellowship named the *Pleiades*. This group, led by Pierre, took their knowledge from the original Alexandrian Pleiades, which were a famous ancient group of philosophers, who took their name after the open star cluster in the Taurus constellation.

Their key task, as part of the *artificial* French Renaissance, was to break with earlier traditions of French poetry, to attempt to ennoble the French language by injecting it with poetry of these great Ancient Greek and Latin philosophers.

At the centre of this progressive literary circle Queen, Marguerite funded and guided their every turn.

The Past

17. THE APPARITION

One warm summer's evening some months later, Francis had just dressed for a dinner reception, but feeling tired and drained from the high temperatures of the day, he decides to have a quick nap before joining the party.

He laid himself out on his bed and closed his eyes, drifting quickly off to sleep, thinking fond thoughts of Queen Marguerite, but suddenly, out of nowhere the tranquillity of his peaceful thoughts was disturbed as a voice whispered, seemingly into his thoughts.

"Francis"

He immediately opened his eyes and jumped off his bed, scanning the empty room, finding he was alone, but instead of being afraid this time, he became angry.

"I don't know where you are, but this will stop NOW! Show yourself!" Francis shouted defiantly.

After a few seconds of eerie silence, a strong wind blew open the double windows of his room giving him a fright. He immediately went to close the windows, but as he did, he felt a strange feeling that someone or something had floated in through the window past him.

As he turned around, he froze on the spot as he saw a ghostly female apparition, her bodily form seemingly transparent as he could see straight through her.

As he studied her face, there was no mistaking the resemblance she bore to the accused witch he had failed to save when he first journeyed to Navarre.

The accused witch haunts me everywhere! Francis thought fearfully.

Eyeing her from top to bottom however, he noticed she had no bruises, and the white dress she had worn whilst tied to the stake had been replaced by a Roman styled toga robe and typical roman styled slippers on her feet.

"Francis." the ghostly apparition whispered again.

"You? But you're dead, are you not?" Francis finally asked her.

"I cannot die Francis, I am immortal." the apparition explained in a smooth and calming voice.

As he looked down at her naked right leg extruding from a slit in her dress, it exposed the same tattoo of a snake curled around her leg that he had seen before whilst she was tied to the stake.

It must be the same woman Francis thought.

"Have you come to haunt me for failing to save you?" he asked worriedly.

The apparition simply smiled, shaking her head.

Francis found it difficult to comprehend exactly who or what she was, and as he tried to touch her ghostly form, he discovered that his hand passed through her.

He didn't know what to think and started to wonder if she was indeed haunting him.

"There is no need to fear me Francis. I am not here to haunt you, but instead to HELP you!" the ghostly aura confided in him.

"To help me? But why?" Francis asked, still confused.

"Your destiny has been foretold even before your birth Francis. You have been chosen." she continued.

"Chosen?" questioned Francis, now confused.

"You have been chosen to wield a great power, but with that power you will have great responsibility." she responded.

A Great Power? Francis thought.

"But why me?" Francis stuttered back in confusion.

Without moving her lips, the words *E pluribus unum* [Latin for 'Out of many, one'] echoed through his thoughts somehow from the ghostly apparition, which gave Francis a chill down his spine.

"For many, many reasons Francis. It is sufficient to say that in your lifetime, you will make choices that will ultimately have an influential affect on the world you know." she continued.

"Me?" Francis asked, staggering back in disbelief.

"I think you have the wrong person?" Francis told her, shaking his head.

"When I was in my physical form and we touched, I saw you past and your future Francis. You are the one." she responded confidently.

She has seen my whole life? Francis thought critically.

"I am the one to do what?" he asked urgently.

That, I cannot say, but know that it will be your life's work." she added.

Francis could not believe what he was hearing.

"But how will I know if I am doing what it is I am supposed to be doing?" he continued, becoming more and more frustrated.

"You will simply *know*." she responded with the same air of confidence in her voice.

Everything Francis had asked the ghostly aura only seemed to confuse him more and more, and noticing the Roman garb she was now dressed in, he wondered if he was having another one of his day dreams.

"No Francis, you are not daydreaming again" she told him as if she was reading his mind.

"What?" Francis replied, wondering how she knew his thoughts.

"I know what you are thinking Francis, and no, this is NOT one of your dreams." she added.

Francis started to rub his forehead, not knowing what to think.

"You know about my day dreams?" he asked, thinking logically now.

The apparition nodded.

Giving up on making sense of it all, Francis decides to go along with it a little.

"If you know about my day dreams, maybe you can explain them?" he asked.

"The dreams that you have, are fragment thoughts of a previous life that you have once lived." she responded knowingly.

Francis was dumbstruck as he considered her response and considered the possibility that he had been reliving memories of a previous life. He had never thought of reincarnation.

"A previous life?" he asked, now a little shaken.

She nodded again.

"Do you know who I was?" Francis asked, trying to think logically about the dreams he had experienced, remembering himself as some sort of soldier in Roman times based on the type of clothing he had always found himself dressed in, and armed with a bow and arrow.

"In one of your previous lives, you were Apollo, son of Zeus." she responded in her calming voice again.

Francis was not prepared for this. It was one thing to consider that he was having memories of a past life, but for the life to be that of a mythical Greek god, that was something else.

"Apollo?" he gulped.

"The Greek God?" he continued.

His legs weakened with this information, and he decided to sit down on the edge of his bed.

She nodded again.

"How can that be? The Greek gods are a myth!" Francis argued.

"I speak only the truth Francis." she continued.

He dropped his face in his hands.

"This must all be a dream, it has to be!" he tried to tell himself as he became flustered.

"This is not a dream Francis." the ghostly aura responded flatly, changing from her previous calming voice.

"Just as Apollo had many names in his day, so will you. You will be a King to your countrymen Francis, and the world will know your name, although it will be known by another." she continued.

When the ghostly aura stated he would be a King, Francis' ears pricked up.

I will be King? Francis thought for a few seconds, before trying to understand the rest of what the ghostly aura had told him.

"My name will be known by another?" he now asked, confusion covering his face.

"Yes. I cannot say any more than that, for it is something you will find out for yourself in due course." she added.

Suddenly, her ghostly aura shimmered, disappearing briefly.

"What happened?" Francis asked, thinking something was wrong with her.

"My time is running out. I must go." she replied, eyeing the closed windows by which she had entered the room, and raised her hand gently towards the windows forcing the doors to blow open again, causing a strong wind to billow into the room.

"What? But I have so many questions to ask!" Francis asked her anxiously as she floated towards the open window.

"Wait, about your death, I think I saw some men torturing you when we held hands! I wish I could have saved you from them!" Francis shouted after her.

"It is of no consequence now, my task has been completed." she told him, smiling the same way as he remembered when the crazed villagers threw her back into the fire after her brief escape.

"When I saw your past, why did those men hurt you?" Francis queried, thinking about the pain she had to endure at the hands of Damien and his henchman.

"Power!" she responded solemnly.

"Power? Power to do what?" Francis asked.

"Since the beginning of time, there has been a war between good and evil Francis. Make no mistake, those men are on the side of evil and left unchecked, they could do great harm to the world you love."

"I met one of them, Damien. He must be bought to justice for what he did to you!" responded Francis, saddened that he had not done anything to avenge her death.

"There is nothing you can do Francis." she responded sternly, knowing his thoughts.

"I can at least try!" he answered defiantly.

"Heed my advice and stay away from him. He is very dangerous." she warned in a defiant tone, one of her few displays of emotion.

"You and he are not so dissimilar. He was educated to a high standard just as you were, with strong morals, but Damien lost his way." she explained.

Francis was confused by her sudden display of compassion for a man that led her to her death, her physical one at least.

"What do you mean?" Francis asked.

"In his never-ending quest for knowledge, he followed the path of the dark arts and black magic, which turned his thirst for knowledge into that of power." she responded as her ghostly aura shimmered again.

"Magic? There is no truth in such a thing. It is just the excuse of men and women to dabble in the beliefs of the devil is it not? If he has taken up such a trade then his soul must already be lost." Francis declared, shaking his head in disgust.

"To dabble in magic is to forsake all that is good and dear!" Francis added defiantly, totally against the practice.

The apparition gave Francis a knowing smile.

"In the days of Jesus, the Jews frequently described him as a magician - would you mark him as well?"

"No, I suppose not," Francis responded as his face turned to a confused expression.

"Magic is not only true and real, but lawful when applied by those pure in heart, but there are two distinct types of magic; *permitted* (white) and *forbidden* (*black*) magic - it is not the knowledge that is good or bad, but the <u>way</u> it is used." she explained.

The way it is used? Francis considered to himself.

"Damien was ultimately turned to the temptation of black magic in his quest for ultimate power." she continued.

"So he has given into his temptations?" Francis queried.

"Unfortunately, yes." she responded.

"To wield such power, one needs to be strong of faith." she continued.

"Was that his downfall?" Francis asked, trying to understand.

"It was simply his emotions that led to him being consumed by the darkness." she tried to explain.

"His mother was killed trying to help the sick due to claims she was a witch, and because of this, Damien was forever consumed by hate for institutions that held power. This hate drives him to tirelessly build on his arcane knowledge to make him omnipotent," she finished.

Francis became saddened at the story.

"You will achieve great things Francis. I believe in you." she explained, focusing back to Francis.

"You do?" Francis replied, unsure as to whether he would be able to live up to her expectations.

She nodded again, smiling.

"Since you have already seen my life, have you also seen my death?" he asked, now thinking back to something she had said earlier.

The apparition smiled again.

"Francis you should not fear death, for you will bring great joy and knowledge to this earth long before then," she confided in him.

"When our hands touched in my physical self, I felt the pain of betrayal in your heart," she continued, causing Francis to look away, hiding the bitterness he still felt about his life.

"I know you feel as though your whole life is a lie and that your identity is in crisis Francis, but who you are does not come from your father or mother, or from your status or family crest. Who you are will come from within you and the choices you make in life," she declared.

Francis looked away as he considered the ghostly aura's words.

"The pain you feel now will be your strongest attribute. Your efforts on this earth will bring about a worldwide change," she continued.

He turned back towards her, his eyes now widened with interest.

"A worldwide change?" Francis asked incredulously.

"Yes, a worldwide change that will bring about a new world power that will pay homage to your efforts. Your legacy will shine across this earth, and knowledge is the key that shall set you free!" she added.

"Knowledge?" he asked.

"*Knowledge is power* Francis, but remember, *power corrupts*," she responded as her ghostly form began to fade away some more.

"Know this about your death, you will die twice, but live forever," she told him as she edged towards the window some more.

"I will die twice? What do you mean?" he shouted after her with more questions above the loud winds now swirling around the room.

"Remember, *one lives best by the hidden life!*" she whispered as her ghostly aura floated towards the open windows, finally raising her arm and opening her clenched fist, exposing the *Eye of Providence* tattoo she had on her palm that Francis had seen before.

As he looked into the eye, a bright light shone out from it, temporarily blinding him.

18. FUTURE INSIGHTS

Slowly, blinding spots faded away and Francis regained his vision, realising he was now looking out of a window at a bright sun, and as he looked away from the sun downwards back to mother earth, he noticed a wide road containing a number of shops with strange unfamiliar names in English.

One of the stores, selling beers and malts, had a placard entitled 'Philadelphia Liquor Store' above its entrance.

Where am I? Francis thought, not recognising the style of buildings or the name 'Philadelphia'.

Is Philadelphia the name of this place? Francis thought as he looked again at the shops lining the road.

As he observed some of the locals making their way down the road on horseback, he was immediately drawn to dark Negro styled tans of these otherwise white men, clothed in strange riding trousers made of leather and wide brimmed hats, doing that they could to stave off the hot sun.

As he also noticed the holsters around their waists, he realised they were wearing guns as well, and looking down to their feet past their leather styled trousers, he saw spurs on the heels of their leather boots.

He shook his head at the fashions they were wearing, having never seen anything like it on any of his European travels.

As one of the men spat out a blackened mound of something he had been chewing on the ground, Francis grimaced.

What manner of place is this? He wondered uncomfortably.

As he caught sight of himself in the reflection of a dusty window, he realised his face was aged some 50 years, and had greyed hair mostly hidden under a wide rimmed tall hat.

Looking at his clothing, he found himself wearing an unfamiliar tan leather overcoat that matched his hat.

Spinning around, he now surveyed his immediate surroundings, realising that he was inside an unfamiliar building, standing in a long hallway.

Looking down one end of the hallway, he could see a stream of 50 or so men dressed in fine clothing making their way towards him. The clothes they wore were also nothing like Francis had ever seen before.

As the men made their way down the hallway past Francis in an orderly line, each nodded and smiled at him as they passed.

They all seem to know me, but I am sure I have never met any one of them before Francis considered, confused by their actions of acknowledging him. He nodded uncomfortably back.

One of the men that passed him seemed to be holding an important document in front of him, and as he passed, Francis managed to glimpse some partial words on the document title page, 'Declara' and 'Independ'.

The men eventually disappeared into a room at the other end of the hallway, and Francis decided to follow them, stopping just inside an open doorway, nodding courteously at two men who were also watching the events from the doorway.

The room itself was bustling with distinguished men, most of which were seated in rows along two sides of the room, and at the far end of the room, in its centre sat one lone important looking man, behind an oak desk.

The man seated behind the desk seemed to be in the middle of reviewing the same document that Francis had seen earlier in the hands of one of the men that had passed him in the hallway.

That same man and a few others crowded around the other side of the desk.

Trying to figure out his location, he looked around him and noticed a display of flags on the walls just above him, of four flags layered over each other, enhanced with horns and a drum.

As he stared up at the flags, he recognised one of them being the St George's Cross, a red cross on a white background, the flag of England, but was confused when he saw the other three flags. Of these flags, he only partly recognised them as they seemed to be a mesh of the St. George's flag and the flag of Scotland, a white cross over a blue field.

Does the mesh of the English and Scottish flags mean that there is one ruler of England and Scotland? Francis shuddered as he considered such a ghastly idea.

As he scanned the many distinguished men in the room talking among themselves, Francis tried again to find someone he recognised, but as he checked every face in the room, he recognised no one, and finally settled into just understanding what was going on.

After a few minutes of people talking among themselves, the important looking man behind the desk put down the document he had been reviewing and stood up from the desk to address the gathered audience.

"I, John Hancock, bring this meeting to order. On this 2nd day of July, in the year 1776 of Philadelphia, we are here to vote that these united colonies, are, and of right ought to be free and independent states, and as such, they have, and of right ought to have full power to make war, conclude peace, establish commerce, and do all the other acts and things, which other states may rightfully do."

"1776?" Francis gasped to himself, realising that he was seemingly watching something nearly 200 years in the future.

At the end of the speech all the men in the room broke out in a loud applause with some clapping their hands, while others stamped their heels repeatedly onto the wooden floor in a jovial sign of their agreement.

For Francis though, the deafening noise brought on a headache, and as he closed his eyes and covered his ears to mute out the noise, he somehow still managed to hear someone calling his name.

"Francis..."

19. Dreaming

Again, Francis heard his name being called out, but louder.

"Francis!" the muffled male voice shouted again, followed by more banging.

Francis opened his eyes and found himself laid out on his bed, seemingly waking from a dream.

He wearily rose from his bed and answered the door, finding Sir Amias waiting impatiently, just about to rap his knuckles on the door again.

"Francis! I was starting to worry, when you didn't answer!" Sir Amias exclaimed impatiently.

"Sorry! I must have dozed off!" replied Francis, rubbing his eyes.

"Are you alright?" Sir Amias continued.

"Yes, I am fine!" Francis responded still a little distracted by the contents of his latest dream.

"Are you still alright for the dinner tonight?" Sir Amias continued, seeing Francis was actually dressed for dinner.

"Yes, I should be OK, but I think I will go for a walk to wake up a little. Can I meet you there?" Francis queried, his eyelids barely open.

Sir Amias shook his head, but agreed.

"OK, I will see you there!' Sir Amias snapped before leaving.

Francis rubbed his eyes some more as he contemplated his latest dream and then donned a cloak, leaving his room.

20. THE BALCONY

In the cool night, as dusk gave way to nightfall, Francis made his way across the palace grounds clearing his thoughts, noticing that many of the palace windows above ground level had been left open to allow the rooms within to ventilate.

As he walked aimlessly around the palace grounds for some time trying to make sense of the dream he had, his thoughts were interrupted by two women talking above him, with one voice sounding familiar to him.

As he looked to the source of the voices, he realised that a conversation was taking place on a balcony above him with one of the voices he identified as Queen Marguerite. Looking around, he realised that he had unconsciously made his way to the grounds below her private apartments.

Framed like the painting of a master artist, Queen Marguerite leaned on her balcony in a clinging white silk nightdress, looking up at the stars, oblivious to Francis staring up at her.

Heart pounding and fearful of being caught, Francis quickly hid behind some nearby bushes beneath the balcony, realising he had made a bad hiding choice as he sat within a bushel filled with wild nettles, stinging him all over.

Wanting to shout out, he gritted his teeth holding it in, eventually laughing quietly at his misfortune on picking such a painful location.

Is love a tender thing? It is too rough, too rude, and too boisterous; and it pricks like thorns? Francis thought of his predicament as he looked up and realised he nonetheless had a good view of the activities in the Queen's private apartments, but as he tried to listen in on their conversations, he realised he was now too far away to hear anything useful, but watched her longingly as she gazed up at the stars anyway.

"Oh, Francis, wherefore art thou?" Queen Marguerite whispered to herself dreamily as her lady-in-waiting stood behind her brushing her hair, smiling at her Queen's happiness.

"Are you ready to be dressed?" her lady-in-waiting asked.

"Just a few minutes more?" Queen Marguerite queried, as she continued looking up at the stars.

"Are you thinking of Francis?" her lady-in-waiting asked, seeing the sparkle in her Queen's eyes.

"Is it that obvious?" Queen Marguerite returned, looking back to her lady-in-waiting, who nodded several times.

"His eyes make me feel safe. He makes my heart smile. It has been so long since I felt this way," Queen Marguerite explained, letting out a sigh.

"He is very charming. Many of the ladies of court find him very appealing!" giggled her lady-in-waiting.

Queen Marguerite smiled a little at how much attention Francis was receiving from the ladies at court, wondering if he had eyes for any of them.

"Come, let us get you ready, or you will be late!" her lady-in-waiting advised.

Queen Marguerite finally agreeing, stepped inside, but due to the inner doors and curtains not being drawn, Francis had a clear view of Queen Marguerite getting dressed.

Inside the room, Queen Marguerite stood surrounded by her ladies-in-waiting as they pulled off the shoulder straps of her nightdress, letting it drop to the floor. Before Francis could avert his gaze, he eyed her naked torso due to his angle of view from below. He was truly transfixed by her beauty.

When he finally turned away, the image of her naked torso had burned itself in his mind, and he had to shake his head several times before he could get the image out of his thoughts.

Seconds later, Queen Marguerite's ladies-in-waiting fitted her with a corset, tying its many strings, before dressing her in a beautiful red evening gown, as one of the ladies-in-waiting combed her long black hair.

As a strong wind blew into the room interrupting the efforts of her hairdresser, one of her ladies-in-waiting closed the balcony doors, also drawing the curtains, finally ending Francis' prying eyes.

Francis took a deep breath as he revelled in what he had witnessed, before becoming anxious that he was now late for the reception, and quietly edged out of the dangerous bushes, pulling out some thorns that had lodged in his buttocks through his trousers before making his way back around the palace grounds, joining the other already assembled guests without anyone noticing.

Later that night, Francis and other guests enjoyed a flamboyant ball with their hosts, Queen Marguerite and the King of Navarre.

As the guests drank wine and ate canapés before the main dinner, some of the young female guests begged Francis to entertain them with stories of his encounters with Queen Elizabeth, describing some of the hundreds of dresses she owned, styled from the finest cloth from all around Europe.

Although Francis loathed talking about Queen Elizabeth, the crowd of young ladies around him badgered him to continue.

As the guests made their way to the grand banqueting table for the elaborate dinner, Francis was mesmerized and could not take his eyes off Queen Marguerite, feeling embarrassed as he visualised her naked torso of earlier that night. When Queen Marguerite felt no one was watching, she would steal her own discreet looks at Francis. She was completely smitten by this secret prince.

When Francis returned to his room that night, he was charged with a burning desire to preserve the image of Queen Marguerite's naked torso, immediately opening up one of his suitcases and retrieving a blank canvas and some chalk.

On the canvas, he began feverishly sketching an outline of Queen Marguerite's naked torso as he remembered it.

"The best part of beauty is that which no picture can express, but one can at least try," he whispered to himself as he sketched feverishly well into the early hours of the morning.

21. PROLIFERATION

Over many weeks, Francis observed the efforts of the various writing groups of the Renaissance programme as they influenced French culture, through the publication of poems, plays and stories.

One day, as Francis enjoyed a theatrical rendition of a play written by one of the writing groups, he watched as the enriched French grammar of the play was relayed to the audience, and as he left the playhouse after the show, he was amazed at how his fellow theatre goers were enamoured by the new phrases and words that captured their imagination.

They had no idea that they had been touched by the work of the Queen Marguerite's programme.

Francis was now a believer, realising that Queen Marguerite's programme for the enrichment of the French language *could* be accomplished.

22. THE SECRET AUTHOR

During his time abroad, Francis was to keep up his end of the bargain he had made with Sir Francis Walsingham to tour Europe and meet with certain men and women who had sworn allegiance to the English crown, and as much of his time was spent travelling between these contacts, Francis dedicated his long hours in the carriage to good use, by writing.

Before he knew it, Francis had accumulated a manuscript that detailed the first part of a history of the activities of members of the various writing groups under Queen Marguerite's charge.

Arriving in the town of Blois, he arranged to have it published under a pseudonym with the title *Académie Francoise par Pierre de la Primaudaye Esceuyer, Seignor dudict lieu et de la Barrée, Gentilhomme ordinaire de la chambre du Roy.*

Some nine years later, back in England, Francis would eventually translate the French manuscript into English through publisher's he was acquainted with, a George Bishop and Ralph Newbery.

23. THE INVITATION

Some weeks later after a tour of other parts of Europe, Francis found himself back in Navarre. Sitting on a wooden bench in the grounds of the Navarre palace, he reviewed some recent publications by members of the various writing groups when he was startled by a gentle hand being placed on his shoulder from behind.

"Master Paulet!" Francis exclaimed, as he turned his head to see who it was, recognising it as his old French tutor.

"Apologies, Master Bacon!" Sir Amias responded in a low voice, scanning their surroundings to ensure their conversation could not be overheard.

"Do you have a moment?" Sir Amias queried in a low tone.

Francis nodded and slid across the bench to give Sir Amias more space to sit.

Sir Amais nodded in appreciation and sat down.

"I have an invitation for you," Sir Amias responded proudly.

Francis now intrigued, put down the papers he was reviewing.

"An invitation?" Francis queried suspiciously.

Sir Amias made subtle checks of their immediate vicinity again to ensure no one was within earshot before he continued, which unnerved Francis a little.

"Over the centuries, there are many unseen powers that strive to shape the world we know. One such power is a group of men who seek to make connections with similar minded individuals around the world," Sir Amias explained as he looked out across the well maintained lawns of the palace still validating their privacy.

"This group would like to offer you an opportunity to join them," he continued eyeing Francis squarely.

"A secret organisation?" Francis asked with a hint of scepticism in his voice.

"A private group if you will." Sir Amias corrected.

"Many people in prominent positions and with great influence have been, or are still a member of such private groups," Sir Amias explained some more.

"What would you have me do?" Francis asked flatly, frowning a little.

"You have been given the option to attend an initial secret meeting to make your assessment of them, and of course them of you," Sir Amias responded ominously.

"Why would they want me to join them? I have no power or position that would be of use to them," Francis asked, now eyeing Sir Amias squarely.

"You may not have any power now Francis, but one day you may become King of England," Sir Amias replied, clarifying the reason, which Francis knew all too well.

With this information, Francis could now understand that the secret group sought to sign up the possible King of England to their membership list.

Francis nodded thoughtfully. They were not fools, but then neither was he.

"Tonight a carriage will come for you at the main gate at 9pm, but it will not wait long," Sir Amias explained.

"Should I go?" Francis asked, looking to Sir Amias to advise him.

"Only you can decide that Francis," Sir Amias responded ominously, before rising from the bench, leaving Francis to ponder the invitation.

24. THE SPY NETWORK

Country Home of Dr John Dee, Mortlake, England

In England a year earlier, Francis and one of his half-brothers, Edward, some 11 years older than Francis, had been invited to Dr. Dee's home in Mortlake to attend a meeting with Dr. Dee and Sir Francis Walsingham, a lawyer, politician, diplomat, and more recently, a secret spymaster for England.

The boys were to be prepped on a possible visit to Europe, and waited in Dr. Dee's library. The library, reputed to be the largest in England, and one of the biggest in Europe, stored thousands of books, stacked methodically on shelves that lined every wall of the huge library.

As they waited for their early morning meeting to begin, Francis and Edward walked the many shelves, scanning the titles of some of the books.

As Francis reviewed one section of the library away from his half-brother Edward, he eyes a series of books on some higher shelves with titles such as Agrippa's *De occulta philosophia* and Giorgi's *De harmonia mundi* Latin translations. These and other books on the shelf covered subject areas such as cabalism, demonology, alchemy, Gnosticism, and other heresies.

Francis was certain that these books were banned literature editions, knowing that at the very least just owning one of more of them would have meant imprisonment.

He looked away fearfully, pretending not to notice them, and moved swiftly on to another section of the library.

"I heard Master Dee presented a visionary plan for the preservation of old books, manuscripts, and records in the founding of a national library some 20 years ago, but the proposal was not taken up," Edward commented as he leaned against a nearby bookshelf, browsing through one of the books that had caught his interest.

"Yes, Dr. Dee said something about that to me too. He told me after Queen Mary's refusal to create a national library, he took it upon himself to create this library, at great personal cost to himself," Francis answered, remembering a conversation that had taken place with his mentor some years before.

As Francis stopped and picked out an old book from a shelf entitled *The Travels of Marco Polo*, he could not stop thinking about the set of occult books he had seen earlier and had to laugh to himself at how he used the fashionable word *Occult* to slander others of different religious beliefs and backgrounds, which could ultimately give someone's belief or practices a sinister reputation.

Francis knew too well that the word 'Occult', coming from the Latin word *Occultus*, mealy meant 'the hidden' or 'the unseen', and knew the word was generally used to describe spiritual knowledge that was difficult to explain, but the word was now being used to taint things as being sinister.

He shook his head as he considered how the recent revelations stating that the Earth was NOT the centre of the universe was initially thought to be an Occultist idea.

Looking back at the published date of the book he was now holding, Francis was shocked to see that the book was over 150 years old, causing him to return the fragile book back to its shelf for fear of damaging it.

"I understand there is an observatory here as well. Do you think he will let us view it?" Edward asked, interrupting Francis' thoughts.

In the daytime? Francis thought sarcastically, shaking his head as his brother's stupidity.

"I don't know!" Francis responded defensively, still thinking about the occult books he had seen.

"What is wrong with you?" Edward queried, sensing the mood change in Francis, but Francis just shrugged his shoulders and tried to put some more distance between them.

Edward stopped reading and returned his book to its rightful shelf before making his way towards Francis.

Dammit! Francis thought as his half-brother approached him.

"I have heard whispers that Dr. Dee dabbles in magic, and talks to angels through the use of some sort of crystal gazer," whispered Edward as he neared Francis, hoping Francis could confirm the gossip.

Francis shrugged his shoulders in response as he eyed the nearby shelf of occult books that would have easily validated Edward's questions and started to sweat a little, worrying that Edward may also notice the banned books and get his old mentor into trouble.

Edward continued talking regardless.

"I was told Dr. Dee was imprisoned once for dabbling in magic! Did he ever talk to you about that in one of your tutoring lessons?" Edward continued, still pressing Francis.

Francis had also heard similar gossip about his mentor dabbling in alchemy and other arcane lore that teetered on the brink of the forbidden and had often been associated with witchcraft, but so far his many clients in the nobility had always stood by him, and most of the slanders had not been taken seriously.

Edward's incessant questions about his mentor, Dr. Dee was beginning to aggravate Francis, and he was doing all he could to remain calm.

"No, and I will not talk about Dr. Dee like that. He is one of the greatest minds of England, and is held in great regard all over Europe, even by our own Queen Elizabeth!" Francis answered defensively.

Just then, Sir Francis Walsingham and Dr. Dee entered the library interrupting their discussion.

"Come, let us sit at the table!" instructed Dr. Dee as he pointed to a large table in the middle of the library with some books on it.

Francis was thankful to get away from Edward as he moved towards the large table.

Dr. Dee and Sir Francis Walsingham eyed each other as they noticed the friction between Francis and Edward.

"Maybe it is a bad idea to pair them up on the journey?" Dr. Dee whispered to Sir Francis Walsingham.

Sir Francis Walsingham shrugged his shoulders as he gave Dr. Dee an undecided look in return.

They all took their seats on the large desk with Sir Francis Walsingham and Dr. Dee sitting on one side of the desk while Francis and Edward sat on the other side.

As Francis surveyed the items on the table, he stared at pile of books trying to read their titles, and as he looked up, he realised Dr. Dee was staring at him, smiling. Francis smiled back and then they all got down to business.

Sir Francis Walsingham and Dr. Dee took the boys through the itinerary of their European tour.

After a long session, they stopped for a short break, at which point Francis twisted his head as he attempted to read the titles of the books, thus catching Dr. Dee's eye.

"What do you think of my library then?" Dr. Dee queried as he arched back in his chair.

"You have a truly magnificent and extensive collection, Master Dee. I hope you will allow me the honour to come back and read some of these wonderful books one day!" Francis responded gleefully.

"My door is always open to you!" Dr. Dee replied, smiling back at his once student.

As the meeting reconvened, Sir Francis Walsingham placed a document with a list of names, dates and locations in front of the boys.

"This list contains sensitive information about your travels, so guard it well," Sir Francis Walsingham commented in a serious tone.

"As you know, you are both to act as good-will ambassadors for England as you travel across Europe," Dr. Dee added, reminding the boys of their roles abroad.

"Who are the people on this list?" Francis queried as he scrutinised the document.

"Those people are loyal to England, and will aid you in understanding the customs of the locations you visit. Guard their names well as their lives may depend on it!" Sir Francis Walsingham warned them.

"But why the secrecy of their names?" asked Edward.

"We have many enemies across the seas, and these loyal patrons of the crown keep us informed. Exposing their names could endanger their lives!" Sir Francis Walsingham informed Edward before turning to Francis, frowning at the naivety of Edward's question.

Edward and Francis eyed each other suspiciously believing there was more to the list than they were being told.

Sir Francis Walsingham, who had once acted as a secret spy whilst holding the post of secretary to an English Ambassador for France before Sir Amias Paulet, had over time, managed to build up his own network of undercover agents across France, Spain, and Italy, effectively setting up what amounted to the first organised foreign espionage service to operate from England.

The Bacon boys now realised they were to become part of this growing spy network.

As they all continued their discussion, it was not difficult for Francis and Edward to see that their *innocent* visit to Europe was not so innocent after all, as it now seemed that one of their tasks would be to link up with informants loyal to the Crown.

Later in their discussions, Francis and Edward were also educated on the different secret societies that they may encounter on their travels. Their orders were that if they received an invitation to join such organisations, they were instructed to accept, and gain as much information about the secret society members as possible.

As Dr. Dee, Sir Francis Walsingham and Edward became engrossed in an argument concerning how much spending money the boys were to receive as part of the tour, Francis turned his attention back to the pile of books near him, being particularly interested in one of the books entitled *Utopia* by Thomas More.

With the others distracted in their argument, Francis attempted to slide the book out from the middle of the stack in order to review it, but in doing so, the whole pile of books toppled off the edge of the table.

As the books fell, he noticed a folded letter fall from one of the book pages.

"Sorry!" Francis apologised profusely to all as the books continued to fall, crashing to the floor. He immediately jumped from his chair onto his hands and knees, collecting up the books from under the table, and in doing so he spotted a folded letter on the floor, which had fallen from pages of one of the books.

Still under the table, he paused from collecting up the books and picked up the letter and opened it.

As he scanned the letter, he noticed that it was addressed to Queen Elizabeth, and in thick writing at the bottom of the letter he saw a peculiar symbol resembling two zero's and the number seven written backwards above them.

There was no actual signature at the bottom of the letter, only this symbol.

"I will take that Francis!" announced Dr. Dee suddenly from out of nowhere, his head now peering under the table, pulling the letter from out of Francis' hand before he had an opportunity to read the contents.

Dr. Dee folded the letter and placed into one of his pockets.

Embarrassed, Francis quickly gathered up the pile of books and emerged from under the table, placing them back on the table as he received a stern glare from Dr. Dee.

Francis returned his focus to the discussions, although he was secretly still trying to make sense of what he had just seen.

It would be some years later that Dr. Dee would confide in Francis the significance of the '007' signature, explaining that when he was away on business for Queen Elizabeth, he would sign all correspondence to her with two circles symbolising he was her secret eyes whilst abroad.

The two circles would be guarded by what may be considered a square root sign or an elongated seven, a sacred cabbalistic and lucky number for Dr. Dee.

The Past

25. SECRET SOCIETIES

As the carriage made its journey to the outskirts of Navarre that evening, with Francis its only passenger, he pulled a cloak he was wearing tightly around him to keep him warm as the temperature had dropped significantly to a cold chill.

Just as Francis' patience was wearing thin, the carriage came to a stop at the edge of a forest with the coachman stamping his heel on the ceiling of the carriage, signifying they had finally reached their destination.

As Francis looked out the carriage window, seeing only a dark road with a line of thickly forested trees on one side and open grassland on the other he became apprehensive.

"This is your stop sire!" the coachman reminded him as he bellowed down from his seat atop the carriage.

"Are you sure?" queried Francis as he scanned their isolated location.

"Yes sire! My orders are to drop you off here!" the coachman continued impatiently.

"But there is nothing here!" Francis responded back in a wary tone.

"You are to be met sire," the coachman continued, as he jumped down and opened the carriage door to coax Francis out.

Francis peered out of the carriage, but still saw no one. However, being prompted by the coachman he got out of the carriage to show the coachman that he was not afraid, even though he was terrified.

As he exited the carriage, Francis wrapped his cloak around him as a cold chill crept up his back, and as he stood in the middle of the empty road, he began to feel very vulnerable, deeply regretting his decision to come.

Quietly, the coachman closed the carriage door and jumped back on top to his seat, and as Francis considered what to do next, the coachman jerked his reins, forcing his horses into action, bolting off into the darkness, leaving him all alone.

"Wait!" Francis shouted, but the carriage and the sound of hooves and wheels disappeared among the trees, leaving Francis to face his fate.

"Dammit!" Francis exclaimed angrily, but before he had time to consider his next step, Damien appeared out of nowhere, startling him.

"Come with me!" he ordered grumpily before turning back into the forest.

Francis was speechless, but ran over to the spot where Damien had disappeared, and found a not so obvious man made pathway through the woods. Trying to decide whether he should stay or go, Francis decided it is better to follow Damien than to remain on the deserted road.

"Where are we going?" Francis demanded as he rushed to keep up with Damien, but Damien remained silent, continuing his brisk walk deep into the forest.

As Francis found himself getting progressively deeper within the forest, he became more and more concerned for his own safety.

Just as he considered making a stand against Damien, they both came upon a large wooden lodge in the middle of a man made clearing. The lodge itself seemed to be internally lit, and they neared it, Francis could see shadows moving around inside it.

Now what? Francis thought fearfully.

As the door of the lodge opened, Sir Amias and Lord Beaumont emerged giving Francis cause to let out a sigh of relief.

"Welcome Francis!" Lord Beaumont exclaimed.

"Come on inside so we can talk," he continued, beckoning Francis to come into the lodge.

Francis had been terrified walking into the dark woods alone with Damien, fearing he was about to be initiated into some demonic sect led by men in hooded gowns but thankfully that was not to be, at least not this night.

Francis followed Lord Beaumont into the wooden lodge, passing a smiling Sir Amias, and Damien, still in a grumpy mood.

26. LAID BARE

Late that same evening, Queen Marguerite looking as radiant as ever, was the centre of the attention at yet another of her lavish dinners and although she smiled, laughed and was attentive to her guests, her eyes betrayed her sadness as she glanced at the empty chair beside her reserved for Francis.

Even though she had received his message saying that he would not be able to attend the dinner, she kept his seat free, just in case he turned up.

Engaging herself in many fruitful conversations to distract her thoughts had not worked, and she glanced often at the empty seat, missing him desperately.

At the end of the dinner, she thanked her many guests and retired to her private quarters earlier than usual, telling her guests that she felt unwell; a small untruth.

Back in her private quarters, her ladies-in-waiting attended to her, changing her out of her evening wear and into her nightwear, and as soon as they were finished, she relieved them of their duties, dismissing them for the night, not feeling up to her usual gossip about the evening's highs and lows.

After the last of her ladies-in-waiting had left, she went to bed, but being restless and unable to sleep, thinking constantly about her English prince, she finally decides to get up again.

Sitting on the end of her majestic bed, yearning to see Francis, she decided she would make a secret and unlawful visit to his private quarters on the other side of the palace.

Opening one of her drawer's, she picked out a red scarf and wrapped it around her face to disguise it and then donned a gilt-bordered hooded cloak made of velvet, bearing her royal crest, normally worn by her ladies-in-waiting.

She went to her dressing table, opening a small drawer revealing a key, which was a copy of the master key of the palace, used by the maids and guards as they went about their daily duties. She took the key and dropped it into a hidden pocket of the cloak.

Placing the hood over her head, she hurried out of her quarters, navigating the many palace hallways, eventually stopping at the doorway outside the personal quarters assigned to Francis.

After a few pensive seconds, she knocked on the door, but was relieved that there was no answer.

Feeling that she had made a mistake coming, she decided to leave, but just as she turned, she saw a group of dignitaries approaching from one end of the hallway.

As she watched the group making their way down the hallway towards her, her heartbeat began to race, and tried the door finding it locked, but remembering the master key in her pocket, she quickly retrieved it, and used it to open the door, rushing into the room and closing it behind her.

Listening with her ear against the door, she heard the group of people making their way past the door and continuing down the hallway and out of earshot.

With the immediate danger behind her, she removed her hood and scarf disguise, finally breathing a sigh of relief.

Now alone in the room, she smiled earnestly as she stared at the foreign items belonging to Francis.

She gathered up her courage and made her way around the room, running her fingers over his personal effects such as family pictures, a small baby portrait of him, his Promus on a side desk, and other items.

It was not long before she noticed a canvas frame covered with a large purple velvet cloth, poised on an easel in a corner of the room.

With great curiosity, she approached it to see if anything had been painted.

As she pulled away the velvet cloth, revealing a torso painting of a dark haired young woman, she immediately saw that it had a striking resemblance to her, which moved her to tears as she admired its beauty and depth.

Hearing more activity outside the room she realised that Francis could return at any moment and knew that she should leave before she was discovered.

She quickly replaced the velvet cloth over the portrait and then donned her scarf, being very careful to wrap it around her face as she did before, before hurrying from the room.

Making her way back through the many corridors to her own royal quarters, her eyes now sparked with happiness at her mischievous actions.

27. THE INITIATION

ack at the lodge, Francis, Lord Beaumont, Sir Amias, and a handful of other men who represented the council of the secret order that had an interest in Francis, sat around a large rectangular oak table.

Being a high ranking member of the council, Lord Beaumont led the explanations of the virtues of the order to Francis, with Damien sitting in a far corner of the room watching the proceedings, unimpressed.

Due to his distrust of Damien, Francis had serious misgivings about the intentions of the secret order, and probed every facet of their manifesto.

From the discussions, Francis learned that the secret order boasted many thousands of members across Europe, including royalty, politicians, and prominent clergymen, as well as having an ambitious expansion programme.

The secret order had a compelling story, but Francis was no fool, as through a prep talk with Dr. Dee and Sir Francis Walsingham before he left England, he knew that joining a fraternity enabled one to tap into a network of influential people when it was needed. Having a possible future King of England would give any secret order considerable influence in their ongoing recruitment.

Damien was unimpressed by how the secret order pandered to Francis, believing it an erroneous decision to offer membership to their enemy, the English.

Slowly but surely, the council members made their impressions on the young Francis Bacon and he eventually accepted their offer of membership, and due to key council member's being in attendance, they made an impromptu agreement to accept.

Lord Beaumont, not wanting to miss out on an opportunity to add Francis to their secret group, decided to perform his initiation *that* night.

As a few of the council members prepared their initiation process, Lord Beaumont beckoned Damien to retrieve a pile of white robes from a store, handing them out to everyone.

With everyone now dressed in robes, the senior council members led the way into an adjoining room.

As Francis followed the men into the room, he saw that it was mostly empty except for a large stone altar and was swiftly led to stand facing the altar with flanked by some of the other council members, except Lord Beaumont, who being the highest ranking member there, took his position behind the altar itself directing the proceedings.

Looking around the room he noticed a strange logo painted on one of the walls beside him, thinking it reminded him of an Egyptian design.

Francis would later discover this to be true since it symbolised the *Eye of Osaris*, one of the symbols the order used to identify itself by.

As he turned back to the great altar before him, he could see a number of items laid on it, which included a large thick aged book duly opened facing Lord Beaumont, and a smaller closed rectangular book closer to Francis.

Other items on the altar were a gold chalice, a gold jug filled with what looked like red wine, a fresh new quill and a filled inkpot and wondered apprehensively, exactly what the secret order had in store for him.

The initiation began with Lord Beaumont reading phrases out loud from the aged book, and everyone, including Francis, repeated it.

After the reading, Lord Beaumont beckoned Damien forward who stood out of the way at the back of the proceedings. Damien approached the altar, filling the chalice with wine before backing away again.

Lord Beaumont then picked up the liquid filled chalice and offered it to Francis, who duly accepted it, taking a small sip.

The proceedings were then followed by some more reading by Lord Beaumont, where finally, new members were required to swear an oath of compliancy to the new order and their rules.

"All that is now needed to complete this initiation is that you sign the book of allegiance to the order of the *Alumbrados* in front of the assembled witnesses!" Lord Beaumont declared loudly, eyeing Francis with intent.

Lord Beaumont opened the smaller book to a preset bookmark, and asked Francis to come forward, offering him the quill.

Francis stepped to the altar, and accepted the quill, and as he viewed the opened page of the small book, he could see a list of signatures and dates that filled half of the page.

Noting the book was actually a registration book for new initiates, Francis quickly scanned the annotations on the page, recognising a few names of French noblemen.

Feeling that many eyes were on him, he quickly dipped his quill into the inkpot and then signed his name on the next available line, assigning a date to it as well before handing the quill back to Lord Beaumont.

The assembled members all started to clap their hands in celebration of their new member, but Francis was unsure as to whether they were celebrating his joining or their possible coupe of signing him. Either way, Francis smiled in appreciation at the men assembled in the lodge, relieved the initiation proved to be a simple process and not something eerie as he had earlier thought.

At the back of the assembled group, Damien's face turned to disgust, and he stormed out of the room.

At the end of the initiation, all the assembled people congratulated Francis as they left the lodge with Francis eventually putting his cloak back on again to warm him in the cold night. Lord Beaumont and Sir Amias led him out of the lodge.

They all walked a little way through the forest path arriving at the main road where Francis had been dropped off earlier. The same horse-drawn carriage was now waiting to return him back to the palace.

"Here you go Francis!" offered Sir Amias, opening the carriage door.

"Tonight was a turning point for our order, young Francis!" declared a jubilant Lord Beaumont, no doubt ecstatic about signing him up.

"I thank you for granting me membership sir," responded Francis courteously.

"Honour the order my son, and we will achieve great things!" Lord Beaumont beamed.

"I will do my best!" replied Francis agreeably. He nodded a farewell and then boarded the waiting carriage.

"Take him back to the palace!" Sir Amias beckoned to the waiting coachman.

The coachman nodded and whipped his horses into action, causing both the carriage to jerk off down the road back to the palace.

Lord Beaumont looked around for someone.

"What is it Lord Beaumont?" asked Sir Amias.

"That nephew of mine has disappeared again!" he scowled.

"I am sure he is not up to any mischief. Shall we go back inside for some refreshments?" Sir Amias queried, eyeing the surrounding area as well, not seeing anyone.

Lord Beaumont nodded in agreement as they both turned back through the wooded area towards the lodge.

28. FAMILIAR ROAD

As the carriage rattled on the uneven roads back to the palace, it passed through a number of villages, and one of them seemed familiar to Francis, even more so as the carriage turned into the village centre.

As he tried to take stock of his surroundings, he realised that it was the same village where the accused witch was sentenced and burned alive in front of his very eyes when he first journeyed to Navarre.

As they drew closer to the location where the accused witch had been burned alive, a painful headache took hold of him.

"Argh!" Francis moaned as the pain got stronger.

As he closed his eyes and tried to suppress the pain, he suddenly started having flashbacks of the memories that belonged to the accused witch that had been burned to death.

In his flashbacks, he saw her being frightened for her life as the door of her home was being beaten down by an axe wielding brute as Francis had seen before.

Francis banged on the side of his carriage to alert his driver.

"Stop the carriage!" Francis shouted urgently, causing the coachman to jerk on the reins of his horses, bringing the carriage to an abrupt halt, skidding on the rocky road surface.

As Francis struggled with the painful headache, he had another flashback, seeing new memories of her being beaten and then dragged out of her home and down a narrow cobbled street, past a cake shop.

"Are you alright sire?" The coachman shouted down in a concerned tone.

As Francis opened his eyes and stared out of the carriage window, he was shocked to see that same cake shop in the distance down one of the side roads.

"Yes...I am fine, just a headache," Francis managed through the pain.

Wearily, he got out of the carriage.

"Wait here, I will just be a minute!" Francis shouted up to the coachman, as he walked towards the cake shop.

"Are you sure sire? You don't look very well," the coachman queried, eyeing Francis' pale complexion.

"I'm fine, I just need to get some air," Francis informed him, as he staggered down a cobbled street.

The coachman shook his head, but leaned back in his seat, grateful for the rest.

Bracing himself, Francis continued down the narrow street passing the cake shop, remembering the same cobbled stone road from his flashback.

He quickly arrived at a dwelling matching the one he had seen in his flashback that matched her home.

As he eyed what was left of the door, in pieces on the floor of the dwelling, Francis believed he had found her house, and as he ambled over the remains of the door, split in half by the axe wielding madman, he surveyed the smashed remains of her home, eyeing room after room full of rubble and broken woodwork.

As he walked back into the main room that he remembered, Francis experienced an excruciating painful flashback that caused him to drop to his knees.

In this flashback, Francis saw a repeat of a previous vision where the accused witch knelt in the same room, hiding a very old book in a secret hollow floorboard, before grabbing a different book from her bookshelf and then goading her attackers into her home as he had seen before.

In the flashback, Francis again saw her throwing this non-important book into the roaring fire before his painful headache finally subsided, letting out a long sigh of relief, collapsing to the floor.

As he knelt down, staring at the old wooden floorboards, it finally dawned on him that he was kneeling at the location of the secret location in the floorboard.

She hid the real book they were after! Francis remembered, banging his fist on the floorboard for not understanding the signs earlier.

As Francis felt the floorboard with his hands, he found the same secret panel he remembered the woman had opened, and pulled the secret latch.

The hollow floorboard loosened with a *click*.

Francis impatiently opened the secret panel revealing the ancient brown book he had seen in his visions.

He was eager to open the book there and then but a noise elsewhere in the house startled him, and he decided to wait until he was back in the safety of his quarters at the palace instead.

He placed the book under his cloak and left the remains of the house, making his way back to his waiting carriage.

"Continue to the palace as quickly as you can!" Francis shouted up to the coachman as he jumped into the carriage. The coachman, waking up from a nap, wearily nodded, whipping the calmed horses back into action again.

As the carriage jerked away from the fateful village once more, Francis retrieved the book from under his cloak, and studied its cover, fearful of the forces that had directed him to retrieve it, and wondering why the accused witch died to keep the book safe from Damien.

29. THE BROWN BOOK

When Francis finally arrived back at his private quarters, he removed the book from under his cloak, placing it in a prominent position on his desk and then took a seat. He stared at the book cover for many pensive seconds admiring the curious carving of a tree on its wooden cover.

As he opened the book, turning to the first few pages, his faced turned to confusion as he stared at a mixed array of strange symbols. He had no idea what the symbols meant and just dropped his shoulders in frustration.

Looking at the page full of symbols, Francis thought back to his mother's lessons on the history of the written word, where she explained that writing was an invention by the Egyptians as far back as 4000 BC, starting off as symbols, and then over thousands of years, evolving to the conventionalised alphabet he was now used to today.

They must represent some sort of age old coding system Francis considered with a renewed interest.

Flipping through some more pages, he found much of the same, pages filled full of symbols, although in a later page, he came upon an illustration which he recognised as the *Tree of Life*, which some ancient philosophy's viewed as a diagrammatic representation of the process by which the Universe came into being.

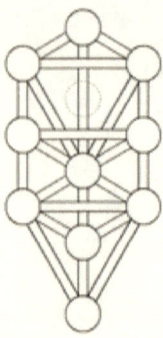

As his eyelids began to droop, he realised he was completely knackered, and looking out his window he saw it was early morning. He had to get some sleep.

He decided to close the book, hiding it under some clothes in one of his chest drawers.

Tomorrow is a better day to deal with such complexities Francis considered, knowing it could take days, weeks or even months to understand the symbols in the book he had found.

As he donned his nightwear, he extinguished his night lamp and jumped into bed.

As he snuggled up to a soft pillow however, he thought that he must have missed turning off a lamp, as part of the room was still lit.

As he dragged himself out of bed to investigate the light source, he found it was actually coming from the drawer concealing the brown book he had found.

Hesitantly, he reached out to the chest and opened the brightly lit drawer, removing a layer of clothing to expose the book. The book itself was glowing.

There is definitely magic at work here, but that is impossible. There is no such thing! Francis thought as he tried to reassure himself.

Newly intrigued by the glowing aspect, he picked up the aged book and brought it back to his desk and sat in his chair again, staring at its cover again, before opening its pages.

As he stared at the obscure symbols that adorned each of the pages, he exhaled deeply before starting the arduous task of deciphering the hidden secrets of the book.

30. A Queen's Indignity

Since Queen Marguerite and her husband reigned over France and Navarre, they would travel between these states many times in a given year, and on one of these occasions, Francis followed them as well as their huge entourage to Paris.

On their arrival in Paris, a huge flamboyant ball was organised in the palace to celebrate the arrival of their King and Queen, and at the initial reception in a grand hall, Francis enjoyed a conversation with Sir Amias, but kept on braking away to scan the room.

"Are you even talking to me?" Sir Amias asked, as Francis scanned the many dignitaries in the ball.

"I am sorry Master Paulet," Francis apologised.

Some weeks before Francis had received news that his brother Anthony Bacon had also been given a position that required him to travel across Europe, and had arranged to meet Francis at the ball that evening in Paris.

Making his way through a crowd, Francis finally glimpsed his brother Anthony with some friends trailing behind him and again broke off the conversation with Sir Amias to rush across the Grand hall to greet him.

"It is so good to see you brother!" Francis beamed with happiness as he embraced his brother.

"You are looking well!" Anthony commented as he admired the French styled clothing Francis was now wearing.

As they talked, Anthony's associates finally caught up with them.

"Francis, may I introduce Lords Dumaine, Longaville, Berowne and Boyesse!" Anthony informed him, as he proudly introduced his new found friends.

Francis nodded in acknowledgement, and they all engaged in a number of topical conversations throughout the evening's festivities.

As Francis talked with his brother and his friends over dinner, he could not help but steal secret looks at Queen Marguerite across the huge dining table where all the guests were seated.

He could not keep his eyes off of her.

With the dinner now finished, and the assembled guests enjoying after dinner drinks, the ball had so far been a great success.

As Queen Marguerite enjoyed a quiet moment away from her guests, she discreetly glanced around the hall until she saw Francis. Her eyes betrayed the deep affection she felt for him, and unbeknown to her, Damien had managed to sneak up on her from behind, observing her longing stare at Francis.

"Good evening my Queen!" he whispered into her ear, startling her.

"Damien!" she responded with a disapproving tone as she turned to face him.

He smiles mischievously.

"Is he the reason you do not respond to my messages? My bed grows cold," Damien teased as he gestured to Francis with his eyes.

"That is of no concern to you!" she responded back in an angry tone.

"Be careful with that tongue of yours, remember I am your Queen!" she added giving him an angry stare before storming off.

Damien was jealous of her affection for Francis, and decided to head towards him and his group to question him on his relations with her.

"Francis! Nice to see you again!" Damien greeted as he closed in on Francis and his friends.

As Francis turned to face Damien, he began feeling very uncomfortable.

"Mr Beaumont" he replied, aiming a cool glance back with a superficial smile.

"How is your burn?" Francis continued as he struggled to think of a conversation piece.

"Oh, it's much better!" advised Damien, lifting his hand to show Francis, the bandages now gone, leaving a small scab.

"How did it happen again?" Francis quizzed, in no mood to talk to him.

Damien paused to think.

"Didn't you say you burned it, whilst trying to take something out of a fire?" Francis continued, which unnerved Damien a little.

"If you will excuse me, I have something important to do!" Francis announced quickly, distancing himself before Damien could respond.

As Francis made his way away from Damien, he inadvertently bumped into Queen Marguerite.

They both stopped and exchanged a tender look, before being distracted by the sound of glass smashing on the marble floor.

As all eyes turned towards the source of the noise, they realised it was a glass goblet that had fallen out of the hand of the King of Navarre.

He was completely drunk.

In his drunkenness, he grabbed a nearby respectable attractive young woman who stood with her parents, and whispered lewd suggestions in her ear, squeezing her buttocks at the same time, to the horrified stares of the attended guests.

The woman shrieked in embarrassment at the assault before running out of the ball in tears.

With that embarrassing turn of events, all eyes then turned to Queen Marguerite standing with Francis, to watch her response.

Immediately, her face turned to shame in light of her husband's actions, and she also burst into tears, with her ladies-in-waiting quickly crowding around her protecting her from the unwelcome stares of their guests.

Francis was stunned, and as the ladies-in-waiting encircled Queen Marguerite, he made his way back to his group.

"How can he disrespect her so?" Francis queried angrily as he arrived back at his group, which included his brother Anthony, his associates, and Sir Amias.

"Queen Marguerite and her King were married for reasons of State. It is whispered that they despise each other," commented Lord Longaville.

"I believe he has many mistresses, the main one being the Baroness de Sauvé, who virtually lives with him," added Lord Dumaine, with Lords Longaville, Berowne and Boyesse all nodding in agreement that they had also heard the same gossip.

"It is said, that the King and Queen live separate lives," continued Lord Dumaine.

"That much I already know!" replied Francis angrily.

"Does that mean he can treat her so?" Francis scowled, angry at everyone's seemingly non-caring attitude towards their Queen.

"They are the King and Queen. They dictate their own destinies here!" Sir Amias declared to Francis.

Francis looked on in disbelief.

As a tearful Queen Marguerite made her exit from the ball with her ladies-in-waiting, she and Francis exchanged a last glance, and he could see the utter shame she felt for her husband's actions.

The King, oblivious to the Queen's embarrassment, attempted to grab another glass of wine from a servant, but missed, falling over a table onto the floor in a drunken state.

A crowd of servants immediately went to his aid, as some of the aristocrats in the ball looked on in embarrassment. Francis shook his head in contempt.

As Francis attempted to chase after Queen Marguerite, Sir Amias grabbed hold of his arm.

"No Francis!" Sir Amias told him in a lowered tone.

"She is in need!" Francis returned, feeling her pain.

"Perhaps, but not by you! She is married to the King and you would do well not to interfere!" Sir Amias told him sternly, still in a hushed tone.

Francis stared angrily at Sir Amias' grip on his arm.

"Unhand me sir!" Francis demanded.

Embarrassed, Sir Amias released his grip on Francis, not sure what to say.

Francis gave Sir Amias an angry stare before making his way out of the ball, careful to leave in the opposite direction of Queen Marguerite and her ladies-in-waiting.

31. LABOUR OF LOVE

Inside her private chambers, a tearful Queen Marguerite lay on her bed sobbing whilst her ladies-in-waiting hovered around her, trying to console her.

Becoming irritated by them crowding her, she rose to her feet, and as she stood among them, raised her arms in the air, bidding them take the initiative and undress her, undoing her stays which let her gown fall to the floor revealing a red satin under bodice. Her ladies quickly removed the under bodice and replaced it with a silk cream nightdress.

"Leave me!" she finally ordered them after she had been changed into her nightwear, causing her ladies-in-waiting to stop what their duties and leave her alone in her quarters.

Finally finding some peace, she curled up on her bed crying some more, but her cries were interrupted by someone calling out.

"My Queen!" a voice called out in a whispered tone.

As she stopped her crying, unsure if she heard correctly, she heard it again.

"My Queen!" the voice repeated.

Intrigued, she jumped up, wiping away some of the tears on her cheeks before donning a dressing gown over her nightwear and following the sound of the voice, which drew her to her balcony.

As she opened the doors to her balcony, she was amazed to find a sheepish looking Francis looking up at her.

"What are you doing here? It is dangerous for you if you are seen!" she whispered down to him.

"I am sorry," Francis whispered back in an embarrassed tone, but as he contemplates leaving, she beckons him forward.

"Come, over here!" she urgently directs him, point to some green foliage against the wall that covered the walls from the ground up to her balcony.

Not knowing what to do, Francis obeys his Queen and approaches the green foliage, finding some wooden decking behind the foliage that seemed strong enough to support his weight.

He looked up at his Queen unsure what she would bid him to do, but she continued to urge him up the green foliage, using the wooden beams as support.

"Come on then!" she urged him, giggling at his indecision.

Francis grimaced a little at the steep climb, but took a deep breath and then lumbered up the side of the wall and into her balcony. As he landed inside her balcony, they both laughed heartily to themselves at their spontaneous actions.

Out of view nearby in the grounds of the palace, Sir Amias secretly watched the events as they occurred, and a look of worry covered his face as he saw Francis climbing into Queen Marguerite's private chambers via her balcony. He made his way back to his own quarters, shaking his head worriedly.

As Queen Marguerite helped Francis up, they made their way into the privacy of her chambers.

Within her quarters now, Francis and Queen Marguerite stood in front of each other, eyeing each other tenderly.

After an uncomfortable silence of a few seconds, Queen Marguerite burst out laughing, tears mixing in with her laughter, allowing Francis to relax a little himself, smiling back at her.

"Where are all your ladies?" Francis queried, realising they were both alone.

"I sent them away," responded Queen Marguerite, smiling through her tears.

"Maybe I should go as well?" offered Francis, feeling awkward now.

A small frown appeared on her otherwise smooth forehead.

"Do you want to go?" she asked, biting her tongue.

"No," Francis responded softly shaking his head, eyeing the floor.

"I am glad you are here Francis," she told him tenderly.

Queen Marguerite sat down in a nearby chair, wiping some tears from her eyes.

"You must think me a fool!" she lamented.

Francis shook his head.

"On the contrary my Queen, I think you have great courage and determination," he responded in a serious tone.

Queen Marguerite found comfort in his words and managed a little smile.

"You always have a calming effect on me Francis," she explained as her face started to show signs of happiness.

Francis smiled again, and thought about telling her how much he loved her, but he was frustrated as the words just wouldn't come out.

"Why are you here Francis?" Queen Marguerite asked as she looked up to him from her chair, eyeing him softly.

Once again, Francis searched for the words to express just how deep his love was for her, but alas his extensive vocabulary failed him.

"I had to speak to you!" he responded softly.

"I just wanted to say that when I came to Navarre, I was in so much pain," he began, as he thought back to his initial journey across the seas to France from his home in England.

"I have carried the pain that my supposed mother, Queen Elizabeth, abandoned me as a baby so that she could keep her English crown. A hard pain to bear," he continued, as he knelt before her.

"Your kindness and generosity helped me to believe in myself again, and to focus on how I can best serve my country, just as you do for yours," Francis added.

Francis hesitated before his next words, but believed he must say what was on his mind.

"Forgive me if I speak out of turn your Majesty, but I learned recently that you and the King were only married to join two royal families. The regal life it seems is full of compromise," Francis added.

With that comment, Queen Marguerite found it difficult to stop her tears from falling down her cheeks.

Francis held her hand and whispered "just as you have been my helping hand, I shall be yours," he finished as he looked into her tear soaked eyes.

With a deep desire to feel his hand on her face, Queen Marguerite took his hand and used it to stroke her wet cheeks.

Realising that Queen Marguerite had now indicated a reciprocal feeling towards him, Francis slowly pulled her up from her chair and close to him, and in that moment, they both came to understand the love they had for each other and began kissing.

As their passion grew, Queen Marguerite pulled away from him, and as he stared at her feeling embarrassed thinking she had refused him, she began to giggle as she opened her dressing gown, letting it fall to the ground, before she then began to unfasten the buttons on her nightdress.

There was no hesitation in her, no fear, only her beautiful face flushed with excitement and anticipation.

And when her nightdress fell to the floor revealing her nakedness, he took the initiative and pulled her close. With a welcoming soft moan, she cried out and he took her cries into his mouth, and gave himself to her completely.

After their romantic encounter in her private chamber, Francis and Queen Marguerite began to spend more and more time together as they explored their feelings for each other, and as their love affair blossomed, it became common knowledge to everyone in the royal courts that Queen Marguerite had taken Francis as her lover.

Under normal circumstances, this would have been viewed as a royal scandal, but Francis was not her first lover, and behind the facade of a marriage, Queen Marguerite and her King had been quietly seeking a divorce.

The love that blossomed between Francis and Queen Marguerite was to reach the point where they wished to marry, assuming Marguerite's divorce from her husband, the King, but for this to happen, Francis had to gain permission from Queen Elizabeth, to marry his French mistress, but the marriage was quickly rejected.

There was to be no new uniting of English and French royalty under Queen Elizabeth's rule, and although they were both devastated, this did not stop their love for each other.

By this time, Sir Amias Paulet was called back to England by a now angry Queen Elizabeth. He would be chastised for allowing such a relationship to manifest.

32. MYSTICAL LEARNING

Over some weeks, Francis would retrieve the Book of Raziel as he settled down for the evening on the days when he was not with Queen Marguerite, and would work feverishly hard into the early hours of the following morning, studying its many pages of symbolism.

He knew, like many others before him that had studied cryptology, the key was literally to find a *key* that would decipher the possibly hidden knowledge it held. The key however, was not always so easy to figure out.

As he began making advances in his efforts, he discovered that the symbols were more a compendium of ancient prayers that, when repeated in a favourable environment, could supposedly draw on the long forgotten powers.

The prayers it seemed were a way to tap into long-forgotten psychic abilities that humanity had somehow lost, allowing an intimate conversation with the powers of nature, the heavens, and the animal kingdom.

33. Numbers

One fine sunny day, Francis and Queen Marguerite was enjoying a picnic in the grounds of the royal palace, and as they lazed back on plump silk cushions and feasted on strawberries, cake, and sweet wines, Francis retrieved a folded note from inside his fine French-styled doublet.

"I have written you a sonnet!" Francis declared proudly.

"Really?" she asked, her eyes now wide eyed.

"Read it!" she carried on, insistently.

Smiling, Francis unfolded the letter containing the sonnet, but no sooner had he opened the letter, a sudden gust of wind blew it from his hands up into the sky, and although Francis jumped up and chased after it as it flittered just out of reach, try as he might, the letter blew high up in the air and out of sight.

Queen Marguerite rolled on the grass, laughing out loud at his misfortune, but Francis was disappointed as he lost the poem he had written.

"Never mind Francis, I am sure there is much we can still discuss! I would rather you told me something more of yourself! I know so little about you!" Queen Marguerite replied, trying to lift his spirits as she tried to contain her laughter.

"What do you wish to know?" he asked as he took his seat beside her again, seeing the humour at his misfortune as well.

"I know you have a love for literature and languages, but what else do you like besides that, such as a favourite colour, or number, or a place?" she giggled.

As Francis leaned back on a cushion, he smiled and thought for a few seconds about his answer as he remembered back to his tutoring by Dr. Dee.

"I do have a love of numbers and science! I suppose I do have a 'lucky' number I suppose. It is the numbers *thirty-three*," he responded in a proud tone.

"33? A curious number! Why?" Queen Marguerite queried with interest.

Francis took a few seconds to consider how best to answer her.

"My math's tutor once told me that through science and numbers, all that nature had to offer would be revealed," he replied, taking a second to survey the wonderful gardens around them.

"He told me that with careful diligence, science and maths would unlock the wonders that this world," Francis explained.

"What does that mean?" she queried in wonder.

"I don't know! He is a little eccentric!" Francis responded with a perplexed look, causing Queen Marguerite to laugh as well.

"But I do not understand how the number 33 fits into all of this?" she added, giving Francis a confused stare in return. He smiled.

"Let me explain. The number 33 relates to the use of secret ciphers in cryptology. A long time ago, in the day of the ancient ruler Julius Caesar, worried that he had enemies all around him, he invented a technique which allowed him to write messages within messages when he corresponded with people he trusted."

"Messages within messages?" she asked, now even more intrigued.

"Essentially, Caesar would write a letter to someone and then afterwards, modify the letter in such a way as to provide an alternative message, like, for example, he would purposefully mark certain letters in the letter incorrectly as a capital letter, which would spell out his real message. Those he trusted would know to look out for such irregular notations in his writing," Francis clarified.

"But in plain view? Would these irregular letters eventually not cause suspicion to Caesar?" asked Queen Marguerite, now confused.

"Yes they would, but in many cases, he would have a numerical equivalent to all the letters of the alphabet to further confuse those that were spying on him, in effect, another layer of encoding," Francis clarified.

"Ahh!" Queen Marguerite replied, understanding a little more.

"Taking the numerical equivalent for the letters of my surname 'Bacon' and adding them up would give a *signature* of **33**," he added finally.

SIMPLE CIPHER

A	B	C	D	E	F	G	H	I	K
1	2	3	4	5	6	7	8	9	10

L	M	N	O	P	Q	R	S	T	V
11	12	13	14	15	16	17	18	19	20
W	X	Y	Z						
21	22	23	24						

B	2
A	1
C	3
O	14
N	13
	33

"A very boring scientific 'lucky' number I am afraid," Francis explained.

"Nothing about you is ever boring Francis!" she added, smiling as she picked up a strawberry and inserted it into his mouth playfully.

Queen Marguerite may not have been so forgiving if she had known that Francis actively used such techniques when he corresponded with his uncle back in England on the affairs of France, in his guise as an English spy.

It was to be this simple cipher key that Francis would later use to secretly *sign* his correspondence with the world, just as his mentor Dr. Dee signed his name with the '007' signature.

Over his lifetime, Francis was to use, extend and invent many different methods of encoding messages such as the *Kay, Reverse Key, and bilateral* ciphers, but generally keeping to the simple cipher keys as a base means of signing his main written correspondence.

Notable cipher signature keys were as follows:

Signature	Simple	Kay	Reverse
Francis	**67**	171	108
Bacon	**33**	111	92
Francis Bacon	**100**	282	200

Cryptography was to be one of the many gifts Francis left for the world.

34. Secret Messages

Some days later, the young Francis sat quietly at a desk in the palace library.

He had spent much of the day in the library reviewing a number of recently published poems that had been written by various members of Queen Marguerite's writing groups.

As he sifted through the pile of publications, deciding which one to read next, a pattern of character misprints on one particular poem caught his attention.

Looking at the author's name, he cringed when he realised it was a poem written by Damien.

Francis had been told that Damien was very learned in literature and writing poetry, which enabled his membership in Queen Marguerite's writing programme, but Francis had no desire to read anything that Damien had penned, however he was sure there was something odd on the first page of this long poem.

As he examined the poem more closely and fixated on further misprints on the first page, sensing that the character misprints seemed to be spelling out recognisable words.

Francis used his analytical mind to make sense of the seemingly random misprints, collating the letters together in his mind, and then making mental substitutions until he came up with a meaningful word.

The first word that seemed to make sense was the French word 'reunion'.

reunion = meeting

"Meeting?" Francis whispered curiously to himself, as he translated the French word into English.

Thinking the text to be accidental, he continued reading the text to the end of the page, turning the sheet to read the next page.

He again scanned for character misprints, making substitutions as he did on the previous page, and again noticed some peculiarities, and after a few seconds, he deciphered some more French words, converting them into English, 'Church', 'of', 'Santa', and then 'Maria'.

More words? The odds are too great for it to be a coincidence! Francis thought as he stared at the text in confusion.

As he continued to decipher, the hidden code detailed the day of the meeting being that very same day at 10pm.

Francis could not believe what he had discovered and tried to think what sort of meeting would require such an elaborate cipher to broadcast its occurrence to the French reading public.

Out of nowhere, his brother Anthony appeared, startling Francis.

"Anthony! What are you doing here?" Francis asked in a happy tone.

"I was told you were here! I just wanted to check that you will be joining my associates and me for the dinner party tonight?"

As Francis dwelled on the encoded message detailing the secret meeting that very night, Francis made a decision that he would instead investigate the meeting at the church.

"No, I am afraid I will not be able to make the dinner tonight, as I have a prior engagement," Francis explained.

Do I? Francis thought critically to himself, unsure of what he was getting involved in.

"Oh, don't worry!" replied Anthony without a second thought.

"How about having lunch tomorrow then?" Anthony asked.

"That will be wonderful!" Francis nodded with a smile.

"Okay, I will see you tomorrow then!" Anthony responded as he turned to leave.

"Wait!" shouted Francis, as he suddenly remembered a note he needed to write.

"What's wrong?" asked Anthony as he turned back to Francis.

Francis quickly scribbled down a message, folding it up and handing it to Anthony.

"Can you please give this to Queen Marguerite? It's just to say that I won't be able to make the dinner party tonight," Francis requested, pushing the note into Anthony's hand.

"Yes of course! What are you reading anyway?" Anthony asked, eyeing the pile of papers in front of Francis.

"Just some recent publications," Francis answered, not wishing to involve his brother in anything that could endanger him.

"How are they?" asked Anthony.

"There is much depth to the words," Francis responded ominously.

"Well, I will disturb you no longer! I bid you farewell!" Anthony replied as he rushed off to meet his friends.

Francis waved as his brother made his way out of the library.

As Anthony left, Francis dwelled on the encoded message he found in Damien's poem, wondering what mischief Damien was up to.

35. YEARNINGS

In her private quarters, Queen Marguerite joked playfully with her ladies-in-waiting as she prepared for her dinner party that evening, when their fun was interrupted by a knock on the door.

As one of her ladies-in-waiting answered the door, a messenger handed her a note, which she quickly delivered to Queen Marguerite.

As Queen Marguerite recognised the handwriting as belonging to Francis she became excited, but her joy quickly turned to sadness as the note advised her that Francis would not be attending the dinner party that night.

Her mood became sombre as she considered the evening ahead, already missing his company.

36. DEVILISH GATHERINGS

A carriage with Francis as its only passenger arrived outside a large old church bearing the name 'Church of Santa Maria' above its double doors.

As Francis looked out of the carriage window and saw the darkened interior of the church, confusion covered his face.

"Are you sure this is the church?" Francis shouted up to the coachman.

"It is the only one I know of sire," the coachman responded back.

Francis jumped out of the carriage, paying the coachman for his services.

As the carriage left, he surveyed the exterior of the church again, and not seeing any light or activity inside it, he wondered if his whole interpretation of the supposed cipher in Damien's poem was a figment of his imagination.

As he stood outside the church, he heard the rumbling of another carriage heading towards him, and he immediately hid out of sight, watching from the shadows of a corner of the church.

The carriage stopped outside the church, and a young French nobleman hopped out, ushering the carriage away.

The man knocked on the church door, in a melodic series of taps, and a few seconds later, a thin secret shutter opened with enough space to allow two eyes to peer out.

After a brief exchange of words, the young man was allowed entry into the church.

"This is the place!" Francis whispered to himself excitedly.

Francis waited a few seconds to compose himself before making his way to the church door, copying the melodic tap that he had heard the previous gentleman had made, and after a few tense seconds, the thin shutter opened again, with just enough space for a pair of dark blue piercing eyes to peer out.

"Name?" a gruff voice asked impatiently.

Francis was speechless for a second as he realised he could not reveal his real name for fear of retribution.

"Shakespeare," he blurted out, as he remembered back to the discussion he had some weeks before with Queen Marguerite as they talked about the Greek goddess, Pallas Athena.

Before Francis could think of a first name, the shutter immediately closed, and he heard the sound of a heavy lock being released before one of the huge doors of the church opened.

"Come in, you are late!" the voice scolded, not showing his face from behind the door, beckoning Francis inside.

As Francis entered the church and eyed the doorman behind the door, he saw that the doorman was wearing a white robe, and just caught the doorman rolling a hood back down over his face, noting a scar on the side of his face.

Francis deduced the doorman had to lift up his hood to see through the door shutter.

Although Francis had never met this man before, he was sure he recognised the scar on his face.

"In there!" the doorman pointed impatiently, directing Francis to a small side room.

As Francis entered the room, he could see a table piled high with robes similar to the one worn by the doorman.

"You better hurry up, it's already started!" shouted the doorman in a grumpy tone.

What's already started? Francis wondered ominously, as he pulled one of the robes over his clothes before hurrying back out of the room.

"Follow me!" the doorman grunted as he led the way through another door, exposing a set of steps leading downwards.

As they made their way down the many steps, Francis spotted an old sign indicting they were on route to basement crypts in the lower levels of the church. As they went deep below the church Francis began to hear eerie chanting sounds, which started to spook him.

They eventually arrived at a floor which had a number of tunnels that led off in different directions.

As the doorman led Francis through one of the tunnels, passing some crumbling coffins, the chanting seemed to get progressively louder.

No wonder there are no lights on in the church, the meeting is being held underground! Francis realised to himself.

They eventually arrived at a small door which they entered, which finally led them to a huge clearing lit by numerous torches on the surrounding walls.

The noise was now deafening.

Francis found himself at the back of a crowd of 40-50 people dressed in similar garb to himself.

Thankfully, no one seemed to notice his arrival.

Francis assumed the people chanting around him to be followers of some sort, knowing the ways of secret fraternities.

The doorman nodded at him before disappearing back through the small door.

With the noise now extreme, Francis searched his pocket to find something, anything he could use to dampen the loud sounds, luckily finding a piece of parchment where he had written the address of the church.

He immediately threw the parchment into his mouth, softening it before ripping it in half and jamming the pieces into each ear, finally dulling the loud chanting noise. He exhaled at the relief of the dampened noise.

As he observed the followers chanting in front of him, he wondered why they were not being deafened as well.

Looking into the eyes of one of the men to his left, he shuddered as he noticed that the man's eyes were wide open and fixed in a cold stare.

Francis tapped the man's gently, but got no reaction. He then tried waving his hand in front of the man's eyes but again got no reaction whatsoever - the man's eyes did not even blink.

Looking to his right, Francis gently prodded another man, and again got no reaction, trying further still, but again no reaction.

It is as if they are all under some sort of spell Francis thought to himself.

They were indeed under a spell, but unbeknown to Francis, the Book of Raziel was protecting him from the effects.

As Francis looked in the general direction of where the followers were staring, he realised they were all focused on some sort of activity at one end of the room, but he could not see what, as his view was blocked.

As he pushed partly through the crowd, he could finally see the back of a man wearing a black and red robe seemingly leading the chanting. The man seemed distracted, looking for something in a box behind him.

As the mysterious man turned around to face the assembled followers, he raised his hands in the air, with one hand holding a long sharp dagger that glinted against the backdrop of the torches.

As the man stood facing the assembled group, Francis could finally see his face, stopping dead in his tracks, recognising the man immediately as Damien.

Instinctively, Francis ducked his head down to hide his face under the hood he was wearing, positioning himself a little behind a nearby pillar to watch the rest of the proceedings.

As Francis looked down in front of Damien, his face turned to dread as he eyed a woman dressed in a long flowing white dress. She was laying on a makeshift altar, her hands and feet bound by chains and as she jerked to life, trying to free herself, Francis went pale as he considered what Damien was about to do.

As the woman struggled with her restraints, she seemed too weak to break free, not that it would do her any good, since her huge chains looked strong enough to hold even a bull at bay.

As Francis looked further downwards to the floor, he noticed a white chalk design etched onto the stone ground between Damien and his assembled followers.

The design was of a pentagram, with strange symbols around its edge not unlike the ones Francis had seen in the Book of Raziel, but this one had the face of a goat in its centre.

As Francis watched the proceedings seemingly building up to some climactic event, his heart began to beat so fast he thought it was going to explode.

He swallowed hard as he stared back up at Damien, who had his hands still in a raised position, seemingly deep in some sort of prayer, repeating a particular phrase repeatedly, as if calling forth someone, or something.

Suddenly, the room began to shake from its very foundation.

As the room shook, Francis had to consider who or *what* was responding.

As the room shook, a pair of windows blew open causing some strong winds to power around the room blowing hard at the many lit torches, causing them to cast many eerie shadowy images off the dark empty walls.

What the hell is going on? Francis wondered as he watched Damien's body convulse seemingly in ecstasy.

Damien moaned ecstatically as some invisible power surged within him, causing Francis to think hard about leaving.

What is he doing? Francis thought worriedly as he again looked to a nearby exit, considering whether he should leave before he gets caught, but he decides to stay to try and help the poor woman being held captive.

Damien made his way to the makeshift altar where the woman lay, and after some more whispered incantations, he suddenly thrust the dagger into her chest, resulting in the woman jerking violently, screaming out loud in a painful shrill as her life left her body.

"No!" Francis gasped in shock as his eyes filled with tears.

37. CALLING DEMONS

For a moment Francis just stood there, scarcely able to comprehend what he had been a party to.

This can't be happening! Francis tried to tell himself, but he knew there was no denying what he had just witnessed.

As Francis stared up at Damien's merciless face and then back down to the poor woman, he knew it was too late to help her as her blood gushed out dripping off the altar.

You are indeed the devil incarnate! Francis thought fearfully as he looked at Damien.

Now afraid for his own life and having no reason to stay, Francis studied the small door near him with earnest, turning back to Damien's activities to consider when best to make his escape without being seen.

Damien gave an evil laugh that sent a chill down Francis' spine, and then without feeling or compassion for the life he had just taken, he jerked his dagger free from her limp body. Damien stepped from behind the altar and stood before the pentagram markings he had made earlier on the stone floor.

Damien held the bloodied dagger above the pentagram and allowed a few drops of blood to fall from the blade into the centre of the pentagram.

His mother named him right! Francis whispered in anger as he wiped away the tears from his face and stared at the sight of the now dead woman.

Here Francis was referring to the origin of the name *Damien*; a French form of Latin *Damianus*, meaning "to tame, to subdue" and euphemistically "to kill".

As Damien extended the blood drenched dagger in the air, some dark mysterious creatures began to form, manifesting around the dagger, echoing howling noises across the room, which caused Francis to become rooted to the spot.

Slowly, the dark forms changed position and converged just above the pentagram merging into a single form that then began to grow in size, before stabilizing into that of a bare-chested goat-like beast with wings on its back and cloven hooves with three horns on its goat-like head, the middle of which shot out a torch of fire as hot as Hades itself.

The expression on its face was a twisted battle between pain and rage as it turned its focus to Damien, struggling to recover from the journey it had just involuntarily taken.

Francis looked on in fearful disbelief at the demon that had just appeared before his very eyes, trying to comprehend what he was seeing.

"Who calls me from to this world!" the demon hissed as its eyes were still adjusting to the lit room.

"I do! I am Allocen" Damien responded confidently, stating his demonic alternate name known in the hellish world where the demon was summoned from.

The beast's centre horn blasted out a red-hot shot of flames as it focused its thoughts.

"You have a question about the ancient book of Raziel?" the demonic beast hissed.

"Yes, and I have a sacrifice in payment for your assistance," Damien explained.

"The book was burned to dust before my eyes, but I am confused, as I have since learned that the book is indestructible!" Damien continued, sounding frustrated.

"It is indestructible," the beast hissed gleefully as it stroked its goatee.

Anger covered Damien's face.

"Dammit! Where is it? Can you locate it?" he asked impatiently.

The beast considered Damien's request.

"The alchemic teachings in that book would be a very powerful addition to your own powers," taunted the beast as another blast shot from its centre horn.

The beast eyed the woman shackled to the table and attempted to grab her, but Damien quickly whispered a spell to push the beast out of her reach.

"Not until you answer me!" ordered Damien.

The beast's face twisted in anger at being denied the sacrifice and reluctantly returned its focus back to Damien, shrugging its shoulders.

"Let me see," it hissed.

The beast concentrated for a few moments, trying to sense the book's location, but could not.

"Hmm…the book's location seems to be hidden from me. I cannot find it," the beast hissed with confusion in its black eyes.

"Dammit!" Damien shouted to himself, as his frustration now turned to anger.

Feeling its usefulness had expired, the beast attempted to grab at the human sacrifice again, but it was too far away from her lifeless body.

"If you cannot locate the book, then you are of no use to me!" Damien shouted angrily to the beast, and whispered an incantation to vanquish it.

The beast's form immediately began to fade away into black smoke, but as it thirsted for the sacrificial bounty just inches away, it began thinking of how it could still be of use to Damien.

"Wait, there is still a way!" it hissed, shooting more fire from its centre horn.

Intrigued, Damien whispered an incantation delaying the beast's expulsion.

"Speak!" Damien ordered it, his eyes now wide with interest.

"If you truly seek the book, I can tell you that the guardian of the book wore a magical ring, which could pinpoint its location should it ever become lost," the beast hissed knowingly.

A ring? Damien thought, rubbing his chin.

Meanwhile, behind the pillar, Francis was slouched on the floor holding his head in his hands, suffering from an excruciating headache brought on when the beast had tried to locate the Book of Raziel.

Francis had felt a probing feeling in his thoughts, which seemed to be getting worse by the minute.

"Do you know the whereabouts of the ring?" Damien asked the beast.

The beast nodded.

"The ring was retrieved by an English pirate who found it among a stolen Spanish bounty which was once part of King Solomon's treasures. The English pirate wears the ring on his finger unaware of its hidden power," the beast hissed playfully.

Knowing that any beast summoned to this earthly plane was bound by age old arcane laws forcing them to tell the truth, Damien had to believe what the demon was saying.

There is still a chance to have it! Damien thought defiantly, salivating at the thought of possessing the Book.

Damien whispered a spell that ushered the beast within earshot of him.

"Tell me about this pirate," Damien whispered.

"The pirate rides with the English buccaneer, Francis Drake," the beast whispered back.

At the same time, the headaches afflicting Francis had become much more severe, causing him to have visions once again.

Images raced through his thoughts of an army of demons waging war with English galleons. More images then showed English galleons being overcome and the crew slaughtered before final images, which showed Spanish armies parading through London streets, past the dead bodies of fallen English soldiers and local men and women who had battled in vain for their lives.

As the visions finally subsided, Francis was left with the last image of Damien leading a triumphant army of demons through the streets of London.

Suddenly, the beast jerked towards the crowd of followers, its nostrils flaring and smoke bellowing from the fiery torch on its head.

It could sense the power of the Book of Raziel within the room protecting Francis.

"I sense the book!" the beast hissed as it scanned Damien's followers.

"What? Who?" asked Damien urgently, scrutinizing the crowd in front of him.

Hearing the exchange between Damien and the beast, Francis flattened his body against the pillar to hide himself, fearing he would be caught.

The beast, somehow sensing Francis, looked straight in his direction, but could not see him due to the pillar obstructing its view.

The beast turned back to Damien.

"One of your follower's has the book!" the beast whined playfully.

"Hmm, there is great power growing within him!" the beast added as it tried to learn more.

Power? What power? Francis considered as he listened to the beast's comments, above his racing heartbeat.

"Who is it?" Damien asked again, still eyeing his followers all masked and dressed in the same white gowns.

"He will be an obstacle to your aspirations!" the beast laughed.

Damien looked into the crowd of followers trying to see if anyone stood out, but he realised they all looked the same in their hooded robes.

"Which one is it?" Damien demanded again from the beast.

"He is out there," the beast replied, pointing in the direction of the pillar with one of its bony human-like fingers.

"I have completed my part of the bargain and now it is time for you to do your part!" the beast demanded in return.

As Damien looked down at the human sacrifice on the table, he realised the beast had to be paid for its information, and reluctantly whispered an incantation allowing the beast to collect its due.

Upon its release, the beast immediately leapt onto the woman's still warm body, shackled to the table, and began devouring her.

"Everyone, take off your hoods!" Damien ordered finally as he returned his attention back to his crowd of followers.

Like drones, all the assembled followers removed their hoods, and one by one Damien checked their faces to see if there was someone he did not recognise, but as they each slowly removed their hoods, Damien's impatience got the better of him and jumped into the crowd, pulling off some of the hoods himself.

As the beast finished its feast revealing its blood soaked face, it let out an unearthly groan before disappearing back to the dark hell it had been summoned from.

At the same time, back behind the pillar, Francis decided he would have to make a run for the door, eyeing it desperately if he was to have any chance of escaping. As he peered behind the pillar, he saw Damien closing in on him, as he continued to unmask his followers.

It's now or never! Francis thought as he bolted for the door.

"You there, come back at once! I want that intruder! Get him!" Damien shouted as he spotted the mysterious cloaked intruder escaping via the nearby side door.

All of his followers chased sluggishly after Francis, blocking Damien's own chase, causing him to get angry.

"Get out of the damn way!" Damien shouted in frustration as he fought his way through the crowd in pursuit of the mysterious intruder himself.

As Francis bolted through the small door, he ran aimlessly through a myriad of tunnels, fearing he was getting completely lost. As he realised the tunnel he was in seemed like a dead end, he became fearful as he checked behind him and saw Damien and his followers closing in on him.

Luckily, when he got to the end of the tunnel, he found it led to a spiral staircase curving upwards as far as the eye could see.

He immediately made his way up the stairs, gasping as he lifted each leg up what must have been a hundred or so wooden steps.

Please god, let there be a way out soon! Francis hoped as his energy started to dwindle as clambered up the seemingly never ending steps.

As he reached to the top of the spiral staircase, he was completely winded, but saw hope of escape as he came upon another door, but it was locked.

"Dammit!" Francis gasped, feeling his heart pounding wildly.

As he glanced back and saw that Damien and his followers were hot on his heels, making their way up the spiral staircase after him, he knew he had to get through the door. He braced himself and made a run for the door, putting all his might into his shoulder to break the lock, and after a couple of tries, he managed to break the flimsy lock.

Finally stumbling through the door, Francis found himself back at ground level, outside the confines of the church.

In the deadness of his location, the only sounds he could hear was the thudding of his heart and his harsh efforts to recapture his breath.

As Francis inhaled deeply, his senses filled with an almighty pungent smell, and looking around, he saw a nearby stable with a huge pile of horse manure at its entrance.

A horse, a horse, I would give anything for a horse! Francis thought anxiously as he panted.

He rushed to the stables, covering his nose as he passed the foul smelling manure, looking around wildly, eventually eyeing a lone stallion already saddled, with its reins tied to a post.

Thank god! Francis thought, relieved at seeing a horse at the ready.

He headed straight for the stallion, jumping onto its already saddled back and quickly released the reins, spurring the horse out of the stable, holding on for dear life, directing it into a nearby forest pass a fox, which instinctively jumped for cover out of the way.

As Damien and his followers made their way out of the broken door, they just managed to catch a glimpse of their mysterious intruder on horseback, escaping into the forest.

Dammit, I must know who that was! Damien thought angrily, as the mysterious intruder disappeared from view.

As Damien helplessly watched the intruder escaping, he noticed the fox that had just saved itself from being trampled by the stolen stallion.

The fox stared coldly at Damien, seemingly sensing the evil within him.

As Damien and the fox exchanged glares, Damien had an idea.

He whispered a powerful incantation directed at the fox, causing it to become caught up in some form of mutation incantation, transforming the small fox into a large unearthly beast.

"Get him!" Damien whispered, ordering the beast into action, his whisper's seemingly entering the beast's very thoughts.

The beast grunted for a few seconds, its breath dissipating into the cold night air, seemingly confused, before sniffing out the lingering smell of its prey, Francis and the stolen horse.

Finding a scent, the beast's long tail flailed around wildly before charging into the forest after Francis.

38. A Beast

A relieved Francis made an exhaustive escape through the forest on the stolen horse. His whole body was in agony from running up a seemingly never ending spiral staircase, and he now ached from the hard and fast gallop back to the palace.

As his horse sped through the forest, his robe continually tore as it caught on tree branches and bushels that his steed had ridden too close against.

Several times, he was almost pulled from the horse, but he was too worried that he was being chased although saw no evidence that anyone was following him through the forest.

Feeling confident he had evaded Damien and his followers, Francis decided it was safe enough to stop for a minute to catch his breath and discard his troublesome robe.

As he approached a clearing, he pulled on the reins, and the horse slowed to a halt, but as he tried to dismount, a tear from his robe caught on the hilt of a sheathed sword hooked onto the saddle, causing him to fall off the horse to the ground haphazardly.

"Dammit!" he shouted to himself, as he fell flat on his back.

Now that wasn't at all graceful! Francis thought, and he couldn't help but laugh at himself.

The horse seemingly taken by Francis started pulling at his clothes with its teeth, trying to help him up to his feet. He laughed a little at his situation, before remembering the butchery he had seen in the depths of the church at the hands of Damien, which brought him abruptly back to the seriousness of his predicament.

He pulled himself up, ripping the robe purposefully to release the cloth from the sheathed sword, and now back on his feet he checked his horse, stroking its back.

"You served me well," he whispered to the horse in gratitude.

As he stood there, he arched his back, trying to work out a pain in the base of his spine from the hard ride from the church.

As his thoughts began to calm after his rushed escape, he took pause to listen to the whistling of the winds flowing between the trees and the placid rippling of water in a nearby stream, which helped to soothe his heart, which was still beating wildly.

Hearing the sound of running water though gave Francis an immediate desire to urinate, and he quickly made his way to some nearby bushels, pulling down his trousers and letting out a sigh of relief.

Part way through, Francis heard a growling noise nearing him on the other side of the clearing, causing him to abruptly stop, peeing on himself in the process. He pulled his trousers back up and ducked down behind the bushels, realising he was crouched in his own urine, wincing a little at its fresh pungent smell.

As he looked some thirty or so feet through the clearing in front of him, the fading evening light reflected in a set of glowing green eyes belonging to a large bear-like animal on all fours, paused as it tried to pick up on Francis' scent, sensing he was close.

Unbeknown to Francis, the beast was searching for him.

Thick brown fur covered the great body of the beast everywhere except its chest and stomach, which were covered with a smooth, glossy, pinkish skin that was rippled with corded muscles.

Throwing back its head, the beast opened its mouth, showing its huge sharp teeth. As it hissed up into the cold night air, Francis gulped as he watched its hot breath turn to vapour.

As Francis attempted to steady himself, he accidentally stepped on a twig which made an audible *crack* as it broke. With that, the beast raised its head to the side and pricked its short, rounded ears, listening.

Francis froze on the spot, and eyeing his horse, grazing some feet away from him, he prayed it would not make a noise to spark the beast's attention.

As the beast moved closer, Francis began to realise that the beast could possibly smell him, or his urine. As he considered he may have to fight it, he looked at his only weapon, a sword hooked onto the saddle of the horse.

Not wanting to bring attention to himself, he dared not move unless absolutely necessary, but the horse, sensing danger, started to snort and whine, catching the beast's attention.

The beast pricked its short rounded ears again and this time it spotted the horse, letting out an almighty growl as it immediately charged towards the stallion.

"No!" Francis shouted, fearing the worst for the poor defenceless horse.

He jumped up and raced towards the horse as well, his eyes now firmly locked on the sheathed sword hooked on the saddle.

As the beast saw Francis however, it let out an unearthly roar and changed its direction towards him, sliding menacingly in the soil of the forest as it did so.

"God's blood!" Francis shouted as he realised that the beast was now heading towards him, and as he raced towards the sword, he knew timing was going to be all important.

As the beast neared him, it used its back legs to propel itself into an air assault on Francis.

As if in slow motion, Francis managed to get to the horse, closing his fingers around the hilt of the sword, pulling the sword free, and in one smooth manoeuvre, ducked as he swung the sword high above him, meeting the underbelly of the beast, its claws just inches from ripping him to shreds.

The beast gave a load pained roar as the blade pierced its skin, causing it to land erratically some feet away from Francis. The beast took several seconds as it surveyed its wound before turning back to eye Francis.

Struggling to control his rising panic, Francis knew he had to control his fear of the beast. There was strength in control.

Closing his eyes for just a moment, he searched within himself for calming thoughts, blocking out his fears and confusion, quickly coming to a peaceful state. He then re-opened his eyes.

He was now calm, and focused, breathing slowly as he faced the beast, with a bloodied sword still in his hand.

If it bleeds, then it can die! Francis thought defiantly to himself with a renewed confidence, gripping the sword with both hands tightly as the beast growled and blinked, flexing its great muscles.

As Francis hunched down with his feet slightly apart, old sword playing rules of engagement popped into his head from his fencing teacher, William Joyner.

As Francis remembered the training he received in the use of a sword by Master Joyner back at a small fencing hall in Blackfriars, England, he smiled as he recalled the family and friends he had left behind in England.

Think! Francis thought, forcefully trying to clear his mind of distractions, remembering the lessons his fencing teacher had taught him.

Francis tried to recall the *fifteen* rules he was taught to win a sword fighting contest.

What were they? Francis asked himself impatiently.

One by one, the rules started to come back to him.

The first one, he had already done, which was *Draw your sword.*

The second was to *Relax* but Francis was still shaking like the stray leaves floating around him.

The third, *Keep your body balanced*, made him steady himself some more in the soft wet soil of the forest.

The fourth rule, *Assess the situation* was important.

With the beast now hurt and ready to pounce, Francis had to take stock of his surrounding area quickly, in case he needed to make a hasty escape.

Behind him, he noticed a low hanging thick branch with a sharpened spear-like end, and realised he would need to be careful not to back into it as it could run him through.

Francis considered the fifth rule to be easy enough, *Engage with care.*

He had no intention of going anywhere near the beast.

The sixth rule, *Have a strong defence*, caused Francis to visualise how he may need to defend himself from the beast should it attack again, believing the best defence would be to repeat the cut on its underbelly, extending the existing wound.

The seventh rule, *Keep your weapon ready* was easy enough, there was no way Francis was going to drop his guard and tightened his grip on the sword some more.

As Francis thought hard to remember the eighth rule, the beast raised its head high, eyeing Francis squarely with a glint of vengeance in its fiery green eyes, as it started to charge at him.

"God's blood!" Francis whispered to himself, thinking quickly about his next move, wondering whether he should run. He braced himself, realising he could not outrun it forever.

He looked behind him at the sharpened low hanging branch and edged back towards it a little, stopping just inches away from it.

As the beast closed in, it made a similar air launch at Francis, again pushing itself off the ground with its hind legs, which Francis had hoped it would do.

Francis stood his ground, waiting for the right moment.

Wait, wait, wait Francis thought calmly as he held back on his attack as the beast blocked out the moon behind it as gravity brought the beast down on top of him again.

With the beast just about to dig its claws into him from above, Francis swung his blade wide aiming it at the gaping gash of the beast's underbelly, ducking at the same time. The beast was so close, its claws combed through Francis' long locks, barely missing his scalp.

Again Francis managed to make another decisive cut on the underbelly of the beast, ripping an even bigger hole than before, causing some of the beast's innards to fall out.

Furthermore, as Francis had hoped, the momentum of the beast forced its perforated underbelly to land on the spear-like branch which Francis had cleverly revealed when he ducked.

Francis had jumped to the tenth rule, *Measure twice, cut once*, remembering that this rule was all important, because historically, in the vast majority of cases, a real sword fight was decided and ended with the first blow struck, and often took less than 30 seconds.

As he breathed a sigh of relief, he remembered what his fencing teacher had always reminded him about the tenth rule.

Be sure of your attack, for it is likely that if you miss with your first strike, your opponent will take advantage, and end the fight himself with a fatal blow.

Master Joyner would have been proud of him that night.

As he approached the dying beast, he could see its exposed heartbeat slowing finally to a stop, and was amazed because, on its last beat, the beast transformed into the fox it once was.

"A fox?" Francis whispered to himself perplexed.

This abomination was a result of Magic? Francis realised, with fear in his face.

When he was finally able to snap out of the shock of the transformation, he considered the possibility that there may be more of these beasts on route to kill him and quickly cleaned himself up and remounted his horse, and riding hard all the way back to the palace without stopping.

As he approached the palace boundary, he dismounted, and let the horse go free, making his way into the palace on foot, eventually entering his quarters.

Tired, he slumped to the floor of his room, aching all over, weakened and exhausted.

As he sat on the floor, his blurred eyes focused on the glowing light in the drawer where he had hidden the book, and he began to wonder exactly what secrets and power it wielded.

Deciding to clean himself up, he set a bath, throwing off his clothes, and slipping into the tin bath, soaking his weary body.

After some bath-time spent contemplating his situation, his eyes were again drawn back to the glowing light from the nearby chest, deeply worried about the books dark side.

Finally, fear gets the better of him, and he gets out of the bath and dons a robe before making his way to the chest, pausing at the handle of the drawer, as he considered his actions.

I have witnessed Damien using magic to his own depraved ends, I must destroy it! Francis finally decides, fearing the power the book must hold.

He opened the drawer and removed a layer of clothing, exposing the Book of Raziel.

But what if the ghost was right about white and black magic? Am I destined to also dabble in this arcane art to balance out the evil doing I have seen tonight? Francis thought fearfully.

He shook his head, undecided about that to do, taking the book from the drawer and carefully placing it on his desk, staring at it for some time.

Just as Francis considered whether to open its pages one last time, the book then flipped opened of its own accord, causing him to back away from it some steps. One by one, the pages turned as if some invisible hand was flicking through its many pages full of symbols.

This frightened him.

Finally, with a resolve, Francis quickly closed the book and returned it to the drawer, hiding it back under some clothes, and closing the drawer itself, dragging his weary bones to bed, and passing out almost immediately.

The next morning he had hoped he would wake up and believe it all to be a bad dream, but at the end of his bed lay the pile of bloodied clothes he had worn and also the stolen sword he had used to slay the beast.

It wasn't a dream Francis realised with dread in his heart.

After a few days, Francis finally mustered up the courage to retrieve the book from the drawer again, continuing the process of unravelling its ancient symbolism, slowly deciphering segments of the book into that of phrases, which he would later understand to be mystical incantations that could unlock ancient power and knowledge.

39. SCOTTISH SPIES

A messenger makes his way down the hallway of a large palace adorned with Scottish artefacts, making his way into a majestic room with a letter in his hand. As he entered the room, the door is accidentally left ajar.

"What news?" an unidentified voice with a deep Scottish accent asked.

"It is from one of our spies in London sire," the messenger responded.

"What information do they offer?" the unidentified voice queried as he sipped from a goblet.

"It concerns the son of Queen Elizabeth sire,"

"Which one?" the unidentified voice queried in an uninterested tone.

"Francis Bacon sire."

"Yes, what of him?" the unidentified voice continued as he let out a bored sigh.

"We have intercepted a letter confirming that Queen Marguerite of Navarre has taken Francis Bacon as a lover and has asked the Queen of England to sanction their wedding," the messenger replied as he read from the letter.

The startling news caught the unidentified man unawares and he jerked angrily as he drank from his goblet, forcing his drink to flood down his throat, giving him a coughing fit.

"What! Why was this not picked up before?" the unidentified voice spluttered, throwing his goblet to the ground in anger as he cleared his throat.

"This is the first news we have been able to intercept sire from Master Bacon," the messenger responded now feeling weary of his master.

"Has Queen Elizabeth responded?"

"Yes sire, she has stated that she will NOT sanction such an alliance," responded the messenger quickly, as he read the letter, his hands now shaking.

"How can they wed anyway? Is the woman not already married?" the unidentified voice mocked.

"It seems the King and Queen of Navarre live separate lives and they have been negotiating a divorce for some time sire," the messenger responded quickly as he read more of the letter.

"This union between Francis and the whore Marguerite will end immediately!" the unidentified voice ordered defiantly.

"Yes sire!" the messenger agreed quickly.

"Is there more?" the unidentified voice continued in a gruff voice.

The messenger scanned the rest of the letter.

"It seems Queen Elizabeth has outlawed any such match between England and France, and has instructed Francis to break off all liaisons with Queen Marguerite at once," added the messenger, his tone trying to be upbeat at this piece of news.

The heavy steps of the mysterious man could be heard as he rose from his chair and approached the messenger standing before him, his huge hand, laden with ring's, gripped the messenger tightly around the neck.

"Send word that this match must be stopped immediately! Do I make myself clear?" the unidentified voice threatened with the messenger nodding erratically, agreeing with his master's request as he gasped for air.

"Go!" the unidentified voice finishes, releasing his grip, allowing the messenger to collapse to the floor, gasping for air.

Catching his breath, the messenger scrambled to his feet and staggered out of the room as the unidentified man returned to his seat to ponder the news.

40. Exposed Secrets

Queen Marguerite entertains many dignitaries at yet another grand ball, and among the guests this time are Francis, Lord Beaumont and his nephew Damien.

At a particular point in the evening's festivities, Francis positions himself next to Lord Beaumont, who was distracted talking to a group of dignitaries, enabling Francis to slip a note into his pocket, but unbeknown to Francis, Damien had been keeping tabs on him and had seen what Francis had done.

Later that evening as Lord Beaumont found the note in his pocket, his face turned pale as he read its content.

Some days later at the grand home of Lord Beaumont, which he shared with his wife, daughter, and nephew Damien, he lay on a couch in his library with a book resting on his lap.

As he heard activity in the hallway outside his library, he grabbed the book up to his face as if he was engrossed with its contents.

In the hallway opposite the library, Damien exited a door leading up from the basement of the house, locking its door behind him before entering the library, to speak to his uncle.

Lord Beaumont pretended not to notice Damien entering, continuing the façade of reading his book.

"I am out for the evening," Damien informed his uncle, as he donned a coat and some gloves.

"Have a good time," his uncle returned happily as he pretended to be engrossed in his book.

"Yes, uncle," replied Damien, thinking his uncle had been acting strangely over the past few days. He made his way out of the house and into a waiting carriage.

As soon as Lord Beaumont heard the carriage leaving, he dropped the book and looked out of a window in the library that afforded a view of the path to the house.

Seeing the carriage making its way away from the house, he jumped up and out of the room into the hallway, making his way to the basement door.

He retrieved a set of master keys from his pocket and tried a number of them on the basement door lock, but was puzzled when none of the keys seemed to work.

He must have changed the lock! Lord Beaumont considered angrily.

As he dithered over whether to break the basement door down, he thought back to when Damien's mother, his sister, had died some 10 years before.

Seeing the fragile boy whose father, a soldier in the French army, had died when he was a baby, and had now lost his mother, Lord Beaumont felt obliged to take him in, being Damien's only living relatives left in the world.

Lord Beaumont remembered that he offered Damien the basement as a private place for him to use it as he wished, and Lord Beaumont was now faced with breaking the basement door down.

He knew there would be no way to cover up his actions.

As he made a run for the door, shoulder first, he smashed against the door causing an almighty *crack* as his body impacted hard against the strong wooden structure, causing him to bounce back onto the grand marble floor of his home.

As he wearily looked back up at the door still standing before him he realised the foolhardy thing he had just done, leaving one whole side of his body aching with pain. H was not at fit as he used to be.

As he stared at the lock, now hanging from a rotten hinge, he saw that his efforts had not been in vain, heaving a sigh of relief that he would not have to run at the door again.

"Whatever is the noise!" a woman's voice shouted down from an upper landing, a voice he recognised as his wife.

Realising his quiet investigation had now caught the attention of his wife and unsure of what he might find in the basement, Lord Beaumont decided it best to ensure that his wife did not get involved.

"Where is our daughter?" he shouted up to his wife.

"With me!" his wife replied, now looking down the large spiral staircase of their home and seeing her husband sitting a little out of view on his backside.

"Whatever is the matter?" she asked worriedly.

He got up and made his way to the spiral staircase and looked up to his wife with a serious face.

"I want both of you stay up there until I say otherwise!" he ordered.

"But why?" she asked, growing more concerned.

"Do not come downstairs! Do I make myself clear?" Lord Beaumont insisted, shouting back up at his wife.

"Yes, yes!" she replied, rushing worriedly back to their young daughter who was playing happily in a nearby room.

As Lord Beaumont eyed the open basement door, he reached into his pocket, taking out a folded note with some writing on it, pausing to consider its contents before placing it back in his pocket.

Lord Beaumont was following up on some disconcerting news he had received, from an anonymous note he found in his pocket after a palace ball some days before.

The note detailed distressing information about his nephew, stating that he had been dabbling in the occult. The note also stated that its anonymous author had actually seen Damien kill a woman in cold blood during a sacrifice.

Although the note was not signed with any name as such, it was signed at the bottom with the Egyptian symbol, the *Eye of Osiris*, signifying its author to be a member of the Order of the *Alumbrados*, an order where Lord Beaumont himself was a high ranking member. He had to take the note seriously.

He made his way down the wooden steps of his dark basement for the first time in many years, not knowing what to expect. As he got to the bottom of the stairs and entered the basement, he spent several minutes sifting through the junk that had collected there, letting out a sigh of relief as he found nothing out of the ordinary, thinking himself foolish for distrusting his nephew.

As he turned to leave, he contemplated how he was going to explain the broken lock on the basement door, but as he made his way back up the stairs, a small piece of white fabric with red blotches on it, hanging out of a chest caught his eye, and he stopped dead in his tracks.

Lord Beaumont made his way back down the stairs and headed towards the chest to get a closer look. Finding the chest locked, he forced it open and lifted out the fabric, holding it up in front of him.

As he reviewed the dress he tried to reconcile that the red blotches around the waist area of the dress must have been wine accidentally spilled on it, but seeing a small tear in the centre of the stain, he felt his theory was flawed.

Lord Beaumont deduced sadly that whoever had been wearing the dress had clearly been stabbed in the abdomen, and feeling physically sick, he threw up on the floor next to the chest.

As he wiped away the vomit from his face with a handkerchief from his pocket, he searched the rest of the chest and found jewellery, such as earrings, a wedding ring, and a necklace. As he sifted through more of the chest, his hand trembled as he picked up a dismembered finger, small and slim, with a feminine ring still attached to it.

Visibly shaking, he wrapped up the finger in another handkerchief, feeling queasy as he then put the wrapped item it in his pocket.

He closed the chest and made his way solemnly out of the basement back into his library, making his way to a drinks cabinet. He made himself a strong drink and gulped it down.

He sank into a chair, his face betraying the complete shock of what he had found in the basement.

The Past

41. EXPULSION

Some days later, Lord Beaumont stood at the doorway of his huge home as his nephew waited for the last of his belongings to be loaded onto a waiting carriage. Lord Beaumont felt saddened that he had somehow failed Damien.

"I thought I was doing a good deed when I took you in after your mother died, and this is how you repay me?" Lord Beaumont asked bitterly as Damien shuffled pass his uncle to the carriage.

"I was disgusted watching you and your pathetic friends in the secret order greeting our enemies with open arms! The English are our enemy, and you treat them as friends!" Damien started, seemingly disgusted with his uncles past actions.

"I lost all respect for you long ago!" Damien finished, shouting back defiantly as he boarded the waiting carriage.

"But you killed tha" Lord Beaumont started but stopped short, feeling sick about even discussing what Damien had done.

"Don't EVER come back!" Lord Beaumont continued shaking his head, feeling an utter contempt for his nephew.

"Oh, mark my words, I will be back, and YOU will be sorry!" Damien warned, his dark brown eyes blazing with anger.

The Past

42. The Revenge

𝔄 week later, Francis ambled aimlessly through a pretty village on the outskirts of the palace, oblivious of its splendour, having received a letter from his uncle, Lord Burghley.

The letter stated that his supposed real father, Robert Dudley, Earl of Leicester had recently wed Lettice Knollys, Lady Essex under a veil of secrecy, some years after her husband, Walter Devereux had died under mysterious circumstances. Lettice Knollys was a grandniece of Anne Boleyn and was a childhood friend of Queen Elizabeth.

As part of the marriage, Robert Dudley had become a father figure to the sole Devereux heir, Robert, who became the 2nd Earl of Essex.

Francis knew little of Robert beyond the knowledge that they both went to Trinity College and gossip that his grandmother, Catherine Carey, a close friend of Queen Elizabeth's, was a supposed illegitimate daughter of Henry VIII.

As the saddened Francis stopped to lean against a tree to read the letter again, feeling's of rejection from both of his real parents' tore at his very core, even more so as this news effectively meant that they had now gone their separate ways.

Lost in his thoughts, he paid little attention to his route back to the palace and walked aimlessly along a deserted cobbled pavement.

Unbeknown to Francis however, skulking in the shadows behind him was a burly man, the small scar on his chin and a nose broken in several places showed signs of his vicious nature. The man was following Francis.

As Francis attempted to cross the quiet street knowing he needed to take a left turn on the other side of the road to get back to the palace, the man following him took this opportunity to do some mischief and beckoned a coachman sitting on a horse-drawn carriage not too far behind him to draw down on Francis as he crossed the road.

On seeing the signal, the coachman whipped his horses into a frenzy, causing the carriage to bolt off towards Francis, who was now making his way across the street, but as Francis felt the rumbling of the earth beneath him, he realised something was wrong.

Turning to look for the cause of the disruption behind him, he momentarily froze as he faced two wild horses pulling a carriage bearing down on him.

"Move!" a soft, yet firm voice whispered within his thoughts, bringing Francis out of his shock, enabling him to jump out of harm's way in the nick of time.

As the wild carriage fired past him slowing to a halt not too far down the road, Francis angrily rose to his feet, gearing himself up make his way to the coachman to give him a piece of his mind. Taking a moment to check his surroundings, he heard someone approaching him from behind, and looking back, he saw a burly man closing in on him with violent intent in his eyes.

As the burly man locked eyes with Francis, he pulled out a dagger from inside his jacket causing Francis to jerk back away from him.

What the hell? Francis wondered, fearing for his life.

As he looked back to the coachman that nearly ran him over, he saw that the coachman jumped off his carriage and was making his way towards Francis, also with a violent intent in his eyes.

God's blood! This was no accident! Francis realised, unsure what these villainous characters were after.

Francis had no means of defence, just some recent publications he had hoped to read later than night. Instinctively, he wrapped up the papers he was carrying into a makeshift baton and held in front of him as he faced the burly man who was now upon him.

"Stay back! I am warning you!" Francis threatened the burly man, as he tried to defend himself with the makeshift baton.

Ignoring his plea, the burly man swiped his dagger at Francis, with Francis barely managing to deflect the dagger away.

Francis did his best to stave off the attack from the burly man and his dangerous knife, but it was not enough to cause his attacker to back off. What's more, Francis could see the coachman closing in on them.

I cannot fight both of them with the baton! Francis thought to himself, realising he was done for.

As Francis did his best to deflect the repeated knife attacks from the burly man, he began to realise that his only chance of survival was to try one of the incantations he had mastered from the Book of Raziel.

Francis was apprehensive about using the incantation as he was unsure of its impact, but time was running out and he had no other option.

As he whispered the incantation, he immediately felt a strange tingling sensation building up within his core, which then seemed to channel itself down his left arm, ending up in his clenched fist holding the makeshift baton.

The makeshift baton fell from his hand as his arm tingled with a strange sensation. As the sensation seemed to get progressively stronger within him, his fist started to glow, causing the burly man to stop his onslaught, covering his eyes as the glow turned into a brilliant white aura.

As the power continued to build within him, Francis could feel a dark foreboding taking hold of him, and although he had not realised it, the whites of his eyes had now turned black.

Suddenly, a lightning-styled charge shot out from the white aura, striking the chest of the burly man with such a force, the impact threw the villain some 30 feet in the air and away from Francis, landing him before the oncoming coachman.

The coachman stopped dead in his tracks and stared down at his partner in crime and then back at Francis. Frightened by what he had just witnessed, as well as Francis' blackened eyes. The coachman turned and made a run for it back onto his carriage, whipping his horses into action, disappearing off into the night.

With the mystical power now unleashed, Francis began to hear voices pulling away at his darkest thoughts pushing him to continue his onslaught on his attackers.

Kill them! Destroy them! Rip them apart!

As Francis tried to suppress the evil voices, it seemed like the newly awakened dark power within his consciousness reacted defensively by inflicting a sharp pain into the deep recesses of his mind, forcing him painfully to his knees. As he held his head in his hands fighting the pain, Francis could feel his very soul being consumed by evil.

The only thing he could think of to combat such evil was his faith, and already on his knees, he clasped both hands together and recited a biblical scripture close to his heart, over and over for many seconds until the dark whispers in his head began to subside, with his eyes finally returning back to normal.

As Francis came back to his senses he stared weirdly at his hands, fearing the power within them, not knowing exactly what he had unleashed from within himself, but before he could fully assess what had happened, he became aware of some of the villagers gathering around his attacker, and he felt a rush of guilt as he considered that he had possibly killed him.

As the lifeless body of his attacker began to move however, Francis let out a sigh of relief.

With more villagers forming around his attacker and a few making their way towards him, thoughts flashed through his mind about the witch burning he had to endure when he first arrived in Navarre. Not wanting to be recognised, or even worse imprisoned as a dabbler in magic, Francis jumped up and ran off into the night, making his way back to the palace.

As he made his way to his quarters, he began to have serious misgivings about opening the Book of Raziel, feeling angry and fearful about what he could achieve, and how, unleashing the powers had somehow unleashed dark inner desires within him that he was barely able to control.

In a fit of anger, he picked up a nearby vase and threw it across the room, flinching as it smashed into pieces against a wall, with some of the fragments clipping his portrait of Queen Marguerite, falling off its easel onto the floor.

Francis slumped to the floor, ending up next to the portrait, and stared fearfully at his hands again, still ashamed and angry at himself for what he had done, using magic to harm someone, even though it was in self defence.

His actions made him feel as if he had violated his own religious virtues.

As the Book of Raziel glowed from its hidden location in the drawer, almost beckoning him, Francis jumped up from the floor defiantly, and retrieved it, throwing it into one of his travelling suitcases, and then locking the suitcase with its key.

Staring intently at the key, Francis then opened one of his windows and threw the key out as far as his strength would allow, hearing a distant *splash* sound as it found its way into one of the many ponds that overlooked his apartment.

Finally, he staggered to the side of his bed, falling to his knees, and staring briefly at his hands in terror at the power within them, he clasped them tightly together in prayer, praying late into the night, asking God to forgive him for his evil doings.

Simultaneously, near the street where Francis had his earlier altercation with his attackers, Damien entered an alley with the coachman who had tried to run Francis over.

The coachman explained that he and his burly associate tried to attack Francis, but as he attempted to catch up to the fight between Francis and his associate, he saw a blinding light, and then his associate was laid out on the ground unconscious, but smelling alcohol on the coachman's breath Damien took little confidence in what the man was saying to him.

As the coachman led Damien down the alley, he explained how he had doubled back in his carriage after his altercation with Francis and collected his burly associate, stowing him in the alley.

When they finally reached the end of the alley, Damien finally saw the burly attacker in a bad way, slumped on the floor with a gag stuck in his mouth and a crazed look in his eyes.

As Damien surveyed the wide-eyed man, whose body seemed to involuntarily go into spasms, he realised something very bad must have happened to him, and removing the gag to question him, the man started screaming loudly, causing Damien to hastily replace the gag.

This man has lost his mind, Damien realised, wondering what Francis could have done to turn his man into a soft headed fool.

"I will deal with him," Damien told the coachman, paying him some money, and sending him on his way back out of the alley.

The coachman looked one last time at his associate slumped on the floor, took the money and then disappeared back out of the alley.

Could Francis really have done this? Damien wondered grimly, before covering the crazed burly man's mouth and nose firmly with his hand, struggling with him until finally, the man stopped breathing, Damien having suffocated him to death.

I will get you yet, Francis! Damien vowed to himself as he let the burly man's limp body slump back down on the floor.

43. PREMONITIONS

Queens Marguerite's bedchamber, Palace of Navarre

In the dead of night, Francis and Queen Marguerite lay asleep in a grand bed, but as she slept contentedly on her silk cushions, Francis tossed and turned, kicking off his side of the bed sheets.

As he continued twisting and turning in his sleep, his body suddenly tensed up before seemingly finding a release. A split-second later, a ghostly representation of himself separated from his physical body, floating up towards the high ceiling of the room.

As his ghostly body looked down, he briefly saw his physical form still lying beside his Marguerite before he floated uncontrollably upwards passing through the bedroom ceiling and a number of other ceilings for the floor above them, until he found himself hovering high above the palace itself.

Still feeling a strange pull as he floated above the palace to a certain direction, he followed this urge a great way over land then sea, returning to the familiar landscape of his own country, England, travelling a little more before finally slowing to a stop over a grand white building in the heart of London, the Strand.

After a few seconds spent gazing upon the grand building, its white bricks one by one turned black, before the whole building then crumbled to the ground, which in turn shrouded everything around him into complete darkness.

Back in Navarre, Francis immediately woke up from what must have been a nightmare. His whole body was drenched in sweat.

"No!" he wailed, as he jerked up, waking Queen Marguerite from her sleep.

"What is it Francis!" Queen Marguerite jumped up, asking Francis worriedly through her sleepy eyes, anxious to know why he was in such a state.

"You're as white as a sheet!" she continued, stroking his face as she tried to calm him.

Francis realised it was just an awful nightmare, and as he rubbed his forehead, he could feel the sweat dripping down his face.

"It felt so real," Francis responded trying to make sense of it all.

"What felt so real?" Queen Marguerite pressed.

"I dreamt of my boyhood London home, *York House*, plastered all over with black mortar," Francis sighed, confused by his dream.

York House, was a huge mansion on the Strand in London that boasted 40 fireplaces, and was located next door to York Place, the main residence of Queen Elizabeth, and as Francis thought about his London home, he mulled over the many times Queen Elizabeth would visit him as a child, now realising the visits and affections she laid upon him there were not as a Queen, but as a mother.

"What does it mean?" Queen Marguerite asked, pulling Francis back from his childhood thoughts.

"I do not know, but the country house is normally white. As a child I called it *the white temple*," Francis returned, shaking his head.

"I am sure everything is fine. It was just a dream," Queen Marguerite reassured him as she held him close.

"Yes," Francis responded nodding agreeably, not really knowing what to make of it all.

"Try and get some sleep," Queen Marguerite told him as she continued to caress his face, calming his senses.

Francis nodded in agreement.

"Yes, I will, but first I just want to go and wash off some of this sweat. Sorry I woke you!" he replied, gently kissing her as he got out of bed.

Francis made his way to an adjoining bathroom, where a bowl and a jug of water was laid out on a petite side table.

Francis poured some water into the bowl and then bent down over it, scooping up some of the cold refreshing water into his hands, splashing it over his sweaty face several times before picking up a nearby towel and drying his face and some of his hair that had inadvertently gotten wet.

As he straightened up to look into an overhanging gold encrusted mirror, he noticed in his reflection, that his hairline looked thinner and that some strands of his hair had also remained on the towel he had just used.

"Great, that's all I need!" he whispered to himself vainly as he considered his thick locks were thinning out.

After a quick scan of the rest of his hair and not finding any other noticeable hair loss, he lets out a deep sigh before returning to the bed where his love Marguerite was still waiting for him.

"Sorry, I thought you had fallen back to sleep!" Francis apologised as he jumped back into bed.

"My hair seems to be falling out!" Francis laughed, dipping his forehead down to show her.

As she examined a small thinning patch, she gave it a tender kiss.

"You are a man beyond your years Francis," she responded as Francis raised his head back to face her.

"I never cared that much for your boyish charms anyway!" she continued wryly, pulling herself closer to him and kissing him firmly on the lips.

As their kissing intensified, they began to make love for the third time that night.

44. Dreams Realised

Early March, 1579

As Francis and Queen Marguerite enjoyed breakfast together in her private quarters, their conversation was disturbed by a knock outside their room.

"Come." Queen Marguerite beckoned, and a male servant made his way into the room balancing a silver plate on one hand, which had a sealed envelope on it.

"An urgent message for Master Bacon, your Highness!" advised the servant to Queen Marguerite asking her permission to offer it to Francis, which she immediately gave.

Her eyebrows arched, wondering what the message contained.

Francis accepted the envelope, and noticing the Bacon family seal on it, immediately opened it.

As he read the letter it contained, tears fell from his eyes and his shoulders slumped in dismay as the dark cloud against the Bacon home he had seen in his recent nightmare had become a reality, for it would seem that a month earlier, Sir Nicholas Bacon had died in his sleep.

"My Father, Sir Nicholas Bacon is dead!" Francis offered up to his Queen, fighting the tears falling down his cheeks.

"Oh Francis, I am so sorry!" she replied, dropping her cutlery, saddened by the news.

Memories of his father's kindness, his laughter, his love, his friendship, their time together, and a thousand other brief glimpses tore through him in a flood of anguish.

During his three years in France, Francis toured many of its cities such as Fontainebleau, Blois, Tours, Poitiers and Chenonceaux, and Paris, Italy, Germany, and Spain, but now, it was time to go home.

The letter fell from his hand as Francis became lost in his grief for the only true father he had ever known.

45. RETURNING HOME

Some days later, Francis was dressed in English styled clothing in preparation for his journey back to England after the grave news concerning the death of Sir Nicholas Bacon.

As he prepared to leave his quarters in the palace, he caught sight of his receding hairline in a mirror. He had been trying to disguise his thinning hair in numerous ways, to no avail.

As he noticed one of the stylish French hats he had become accustomed to wearing whilst in France, he decided to put it on.

It will have to do! Francis thought, briefly looking at his hairline again in the mirror, ignoring the hat's French styling, thinking he would source an English variation when he returned home to English soil.

He sighed as he packed away the last of his things before leaving his quarters, making his way to the main entrance of the palace, where a number of carriages packed with his belongings waited for him to take him to the docks at Calais.

As he exited the palace he found Queen Marguerite waiting.

Although they had already said their goodbyes in private, Queen Marguerite had to see him one last time, and as they locked eyes, they both stared longingly at each other.

"I will miss you Francis," she revealed tearfully.

"And I will miss you my Queen," Francis responded sadly, thinking that he was also losing the woman he loved by his abrupt return to England.

"Parting is such sweet sorrow!" she whispered softly, fighting back the tears.

"I want you to know that you are my sun by day and my star by night. By my faith! I was in deepest darkness till you appeared and illuminated all that I knew and believed," she added.

Francis was touched by her words and smiled, admiring her eloquence.

"Do you remember when I first arrived, and you explained how you tried to model yourself on the Greek goddess Pallas Athena to inspire your programme of change?" Francis asked, trying to remain upbeat.

"Yes!" she responded happily thinking back to their early days together, wiping away a tear from her cheek.

"I see that goddess in you, my Queen, enriching the lives of your countrymen through literature, empowering their every French word, their every thought, and I have no doubt that in years to come the French language will be the envy of the world," he told her with great conviction in his tone.

Queen Marguerite gave a broad smile through her tears.

"In all my days I shall forever look to your strength for inspiration. You will be my example to follow," Francis added in a sincere tone.

He bowed, kissed her hand, and then got into the waiting carriage.

Francis gave a final wave to his Queen as the carriage led the entourage of coaches to the French coast where a galleon waited to ferry him back to England.

As he sat in the carriage all alone, he ached from the loss of the only woman he had ever loved and also the pain of losing the only father he had ever known, Sir Nicholas Bacon.

46. FINAL GOODBYE

A coachman entered the back of the church service where Sir Francis Bacon's funeral was being conducted and tapped the shoulder of the elderly man sitting in one of rear pews.

"Is it time already?" the elderly man whispered as he broke away from his fond thoughts about the life of the man whose funeral he was in attendance at.

He looked up at the coachman now standing behind him.

The coachman nodded.

The elderly man let out a sigh, and then rose from his seat at the back of the church, briefly eyeing the coffin one last time, before following his coachman out of the church.

As soon as the elderly man had managed to climb into the waiting carriage, the coachman jumped on top, and whipped the horses into action making their way out of St. Albans and on down to the London docks.

By late afternoon, the carriage arrived at a dockyard in Deptford, London, where a refitted galleon had just been loaded for a long trip.

The elderly man took his leave of the carriage and made his way onto the galleon, passing the galleon's name plate "The Golden Hinde".

As the Captain of the ship approached him, they exchanged smiles.

"Has everything been loaded?" asked the elderly man wearily.

"As per your instructions sire, we should be underway in an hour!" the Captain responded.

"Very good!" the elderly man replied, making his way down some steps that lead to his accommodation below deck.

As per the Captain's predictions, an hour later, the galleon pushed away from the dock, sailing down the Thames and eventually into open water with the elderly man watching from one of the top decks as the English coastline slowly disappeared from view.

47. POISONED

March 23rd 1579, England

A galleon finally docked in England, carrying a grief stricken 18 year old Francis Bacon as he returned home to England.

The French Court, although dissolute and its government corrupt, its culture was otherwise refined and glorious, whereas English culture at this time was uncouth with its English language, a sorry patchwork of almost incomprehensible dialects.

As he contemplated his future on his return journey, thinking back to his time in France, Francis had decided his purpose in life, which was to create, with the help of others suited to the task, a magnificent English language and culture just as the French poets and philosophers were striving to do.

It was a truly grand concept, and he knew it would be costly to fund, but he smiled at the idea of dedicating his life to the betterment of his kinsmen, and as he disembarked from the ship onto English soil for the first time in several years, he was happy to be home, but wishing it was under better circumstances.

Waiting for him on the dock was Anthony Bacon, dressed in black, and as Francis stepped off the ship, they embraced, mourning the loss of their father.

"How was the funeral?" Francis finally asked forcing a smile, realising it had been over a month since Sir Nicholas had died.

"It was a good send off!" Anthony replied, trying to sound upbeat.

"I am sorry we could not wait for your arrival," Anthony continued.

Francis nodded agreeably.

"I understand," Francis replied, letting out a deep sigh.

Anthony opened his mouth to say something but then changed his mind, turning away from Francis.

"What is it Anthony? Is there something you are not telling me?" Francis asked, sensing there was something troubling his brother.

"It's nothing!" Anthony replied, shaking his head.

"Tell me!" Francis pressed, not believing him.

"I cannot prove it Francis, but I fear our father was poisoned!" Anthony responded in frustration.

"Poisoned? But who would do such a thing?" Francis asked with a shocked look, trying to consider who could have hated Sir Nicholas badly enough to want to kill him.

"I do not know Francis. One of the maids found him dead in his sleep, and as she attended to him, she said she noticed a foul smell in his mouth," Anthony explained glumly.

"Where was mother?" Francis asked in astonishment.

"She was asleep beside him, and the maid had to shake her for some time to wake her, and when she finally did wake up, she said she felt as if she had been drugged!" Anthony continued angrily.

"I don't know what to believe," Anthony broke down.

Francis could not believe what he was hearing either.

"By the time our Doctor arrived, the smell had gone, and he couldn't find any trace of poison, so in any case, there was no proof that any crime had been committed!" Anthony added with an air of frustration.

Although Francis, Anthony, and the rest of the family did some investigations, they found no actual proof to suggest that their father had been poisoned.

It was to take Francis fifty years before he discovered the truth.

48. Gray's Inn

On his return from France, Francis was instantly embroiled in the trapping of making his way in the world due to uncovering the truth about his Tudor bloodline.

Sir Nicholas Bacon, in his will, left large sums of money to his children by his first wife, and a sufficient income for Lady Anne and her son Anthony, but nothing for Francis, expecting the Queen to provide for her son.

Francis spent the next few years petitioning the Queen and others in her circle that knew his royal secret, such as his uncle, Lord Burghley, with regards to obtaining a position worthy of his status as a secret prince.

On advice from his uncle Lord Burghley, Francis left the Gorhambury house he once called home and took up residence at Gray's Inn, a law court in Holborn, as he furthered his studies in the legal profession.

Queen Elizabeth herself, the Inn's Patron Lady, and, with his uncle, Lord Burghley, Sir Francis Walsingham, and his now deceased step-father, Sir Nicholas Bacon, among the members list of Gray's Inn, Francis was in good company.

Gray's Inn, one of four Inn's that would-be members of the legal profession were duty bound to join before they could qualify as a barrister, came into being as a result of the famed Knights Templar.

As the story goes, hundreds of years before, members of the Knights Templar bought a considerable amount of land on which they constructed their famed

Round Church and other buildings, which ultimately formed the grounds of the four Law courts, being Gray's Inn, Middle Temple Inn, Lower Temple Inn and Lincoln's Inn.

Although the Inn's were principally for the advancement of barristers wishing to practice Law, the rich culture of the Inn's, which included the training of good manners, courtly behaviour, singing and dancing (which occasionally spread to street processions and river pageants), aided the Inn's to become fashionable places for noblemen and country gentlemen to send their sons, even if their sons had no intention of ultimately becoming barristers.

It was December now, and as Francis ate in the *Great Hall,* an action compulsory for all would-be barristers, he looked on at some of the wasters around him who were only in attendance for the entertainment factor of the numerous revels and masque events that happened throughout the year.

As a December festive blanket of white snow covered the grounds of the courts, some of the active Inn students excitedly prepared the Great Hall for the annual Christmas revels, setting up a section of it to be used to stage some of the upcoming scheduled performances.

Although Francis looked forward to the boisterous affair he knew the celebrations would be, tonight he just wanted some peace and quiet to reflect on the year that had passed.

He finished his meal and headed back to his onsite lodgings, making his way up the spiral staircase of 1 Gray's Inn Square, passing the Inn library, situated across the landing from his lodgings.

Eyeing the darkness of the locked library, and still wide awake, Francis retrieved a bunch of keys from his pocket and stared at a long rusty old bronze key that stood out from the rest. He walked back to the library door and used the key to open the library door.

As the cost of his lodgings was paid directly by the crown, Francis had received many privileges by staying at Gray's Inn, and having his own personal key to its library was one of them. He smiled a little as he entered the empty library, trying to see in the dark as he squinted to read the titles on a nearby set of shelves.

Giving up, he turned back towards the library entrance and stopped at an unlit lantern resting on a small table.

He lit the lantern and turned up its strength before carrying it with him to make a clearer methodical scan of the walls of books, but as he made his way past a tall shelf of books, he heard a muffled noise behind him which caused him to turn abruptly.

"What the" he started, turning quickly, thinking someone was behind him, but losing his footing, he fell back against the wall of books, causing much of the books to rain down all over him.

He fell to his knees, purposefully arching over the lantern, protecting it so that he didn't start a fire.

As the avalanche of books eventually slowed to a stop, Francis saw the cause of the noise, a huge dusty rat, making its way through a space between two bookcases.

He moaned as he rubbed his now aching back from where the corners of thick volumes had dug into it.

Surveying the books that he now had to return to their shelves, he shook his head in dismay.

Still kneeling, he quickly grabbed armfuls of books from the floor around him and piled them back onto the shelves.

During his tidying up, he picked up a large thick book on some obscure subject which sparked his interest as the book felt much lighter than it should have been because of its supposed 1000 or so pages.

He opened the book and as he flicked through the pages, he was surprised to find that the book had been hollowed out in its centre, and that a smaller book had been hidden within it. He excitedly extracted the book.

As he smoothed his hand over the book's leather bound cover, Francis could see a subtle emblem of a cross, and looking a little closer, he realised that the emblem was not a typical Christian cross, but that of a shorter cross of four equal arms with widened ends, signifying the cross of the Knights Templar.

His interest was roused at once, and he immediately opened and flicked through the pages of the book, translating pages and pages of handwritten Latin text, each page of which was dated, referring to the early 1300s, dates around the time of the persecutions of the Knights Templar order.

The pages reminded Francis of the fateful journals he had read in his uncle's office that changed his life forever, and he froze on the spot fearful that his curiosity would cause him to get hurt again.

This journal precedes me by 300 or so years! It has nothing to do with me! Francis reasoned with himself until her was content enough that the book could in no way be related to him.

Francis put the leather bound book aside and then quickly returned the last of the stray books back to their place on the book shelf, before picking up the newly found book and the lantern, making his way out of the library.

As he got to the doorway, he doused the flame in the lantern, returning it to its rightful place near the entrance of the library and exited the library, locking the door behind him.

He paused to glance at the emblem of the Knights Templar cross on the newly found book before making the brief journey across the landing to his own lodgings. Unbeknown to Francis, a man stood, hidden in the shadows of the corridor out of view, watching him with interest.

In the confines of his room now, Francis browsed through the small book, reviewing the pages of handwritten text which he recognised as Latin, and discovered the annotations to be entries of the simple daily life of a monk in the Templar order.

The entries had been written over a two year period leading up to the dreaded persecutions of their order on Friday 13th October 1307, where the journal entries abruptly stopped.

The Templar order in their day were fierce warriors, devout monks, and international bankers, and the entries in the diary covered much of the typical daily chores of men in their order, detailing various conversations where the monk advised Kings, Queens, and Princes, brokered treaties, and built castles and preceptories on a massive scale. These advisory roles lasted over two centuries until their order was plunged into mass arrests, trials, and executions that shocked the Europeans of the day.

Francis was glued to the diary entries and flicked through the pages until the early hours.

His interest truly jumped when he read entries regarding old sagas, a supposed combination of genealogies, histories and legends written during the 1100s through to the 1300s, that related to the travels of a *Norse* explorer named *Leif Ericson* who colonized various islands from around the years 985 and 986.

Having read beyond the old sagas, the text became boring, but his interest was sparked as he noted down certain details the monk had written about the adventures of the explorer. Francis put down the diary and went to one of his suitcases, retrieving a long scroll, unrolling it onto his floor, which exposed an old map of the world.

As he referred to his notes taken from the diary, Francis began to pinpoint the supposed path that was taken based on the starting point of Norway, plotting a path with his faithful nautical instruments.

As Francis reviewed the supposed path of the Norse explorer, he realised that the sagas plotted a path from Norway to the land now described as the *New World* – some 500 years before Columbus was to have supposedly discovered it.

If this author of this diary knew of the Norse explorer, *could the Knights Templar have made a pre-Columbus voyage to the New World?* Francis thought critically.

Francis had doubts about Columbus being the first to discover the New World before when he took a recent trip to Scotland, visiting the Rosslyn Chapel, a famed church full of Templar influences.

In this church, as Francis admired the architecture, he noticed designs of ears of corn and aloe cactus sculpted into the stone structure that formed the archways and ceilings of the chapel, but seeing these artefacts caused a conundrum for him, because he knew that corn and aloe cactus plants were introduced to England in the early 1500s, supposedly brought back from the New World.

The conundrum for Francis was that the chapel was actually completed in 1486, some years before Columbus had even departed to the New World.

The only way the plants could have been incorporated into the chapel's design was if the architects had known people from the New World or indeed travelled there themselves, before Columbus! Francis resolved to himself.

As he rubbed the back of his head, he considered how the history he had always read and understood was now becoming more and more of an illusion.

49. DANGEROUS ENEMIES

𝔍n her palace at Richmond, Queen Elizabeth sat in front of a warm fire reading some state papers, when she was interrupted by a knock on her door.

"Enter!" she commanded, frowning at the interruption.

As the door opened, Robert Cecil, son of her close advisor Lord Burghley, entered. Robert was a slight, crooked, hump-backed young gentleman, of dwarfish stature.

As boys, he and Francis were friends, but once he learned of Francis' royal bloodline, he soon looked at Francis as competition in his quest for power and progression. At every opportunity, be it to the Privy Council or to Queen Elizabeth, Robert would report on any erroneous activities that Francis was engaged in.

Due to his disfigured back, Robert found it difficult to bow, and even when he did, he could not bow as low as other courtiers, but Queen Elizabeth had no sympathy for his deformity.

She would ridicule him often due to a long standing unnerving feeling of distrust she had for him, having only entertained Robert's services at the request of her dear trusted friend, Lord Burghley, his father.

"Your Majesty, the Privy Council has unearthed some damaging information relating to Francis Bacon," he informed her.

Queen Elizabeth huffed at the reasoning for interrupting her.

"What has he done now?" Queen Elizabeth asked impatiently.

"My father wishes me to inform you that Master Bacon has been petitioning his friends to further his hopes of becoming a Member of Parliament," he informed her, with a subtle wry smile.

Her eyes widened as she threw down her stately papers onto the desk in front of her.

"What?" she asked in an aggravated tone.

"He was told to desist in such activities!" she continued, shaking her head at Francis' disobedience.

Francis had a strong desire to enter politics just like his Bacon step-brothers, and their father before them, but this was against the wishes of his uncle, Lord Burghley.

Lord Burghley had convinced Queen Elizabeth that allowing Francis to elevate himself politically would give him power which could then allow him to possibly later usurp her own position, and felt Francis had to be pressured into complying with their wishes.

Queen Elizabeth gave Robert Cecil a stern look as she decided what action to take.

"Some days ago, your father spoke to me about an open position where we needed to nurture our international network of contacts?" she queried.

Robert Cecil nodded.

"Yes, your Majesty, his brother Anthony Bacon has recently returned from Europe on just a mission," he responded.

"Tell your father to pass the position onto Francis. He must be removed from these influences!" she ordered him shortly.

"Yes, your Majesty!" Robert Cecil responded agreeably finally making his leave.

"And ensure it does not involve a visit to France. I do not want him anywhere near the royal courts of Navarre!" she shouted as an afterthought as he reached the door.

Her advisor turned back to Queen Elizabeth, forcing a smile as he again bowed, the pain in his back now excruciating.

"Yes, your Majesty!" he confirmed once more, before turning to leave again.

As Robert Cecil left the room, he immediately straightened his back as much as possible to relieve the pain from bending for his Queen.

He hated how she mocks him, but knew one day that he would have his retribution.

50. Secret Rendezvous

June 1581, Spain

One late evening, a carriage stopped outside a village Inn and Francis exited the carriage, briefly reviewing a small placard outside stating that it offered accommodation.

He made his way into the busy Inn, and headed straight for the bar, which was manned by a big bellied bald man, who leaned on the bar twisting at his long curly black moustache.

"I need a room for the night." Francis explained.

The man, being the Inn keeper, looked Francis up and down, before taking out an attendance book and quill from under the bar.

"Your name?" the Inn keeper asked as he dipped the quill into a nearby inkpot, at the ready to allocate Francis a room.

"Spear-shaker," Francis whispered.

On hearing his name, the Inn keeper froze, looking up at Francis once again with a distrusting stare before putting the attendance book and quill back under the bar without writing anything in it.

Without another word, the Inn keeper turned to a key rack behind him and picked out a key, etched with the number 7 and dropped it on the bar.

"Up those stairs!" the Inn keeper told him, pointing to a nearby set of steps leading to the rooms for rent.

Francis took the key and made his way over to the stairs, feeling the Inn keeper's suspicious eyes on him. He climbed the steps to the first floor, walking past several doors until he arrived at the room numbered "7".

He used the key to unlock it and went inside.

The room itself was dimly lit with a lantern perched next to the doorway, and he could see it was a simple room, with a bed, desk, and another room which he assumed was the bathroom.

He closed the door behind him, and then adjusted the lantern to increase the light in the room, flinching as the increased light highlighted that he was not alone.

In a corner of the room, he eyed the silhouette of a petite figure looking out of the only window in the room.

As the hooded figure turned around and pulled back her hood, she revealed herself to be Queen Marguerite of Navarre.

Francis smiled broadly, bowing before her.

"Your Majesty!" he whispered with much happiness in his tone.

As he raised his head, they looked affectionately at each other for several seconds before Francis took the initiative and slowly approached her, putting his arms around her slim waist.

Although happiness filled her face from seeing him, Queen Marguerite did not respond, her hands remaining at her sides.

Realising she was not reciprocating his affection, Francis backed away, confused.

"It has been a long time Francis," Queen Marguerite finally responded.

"Yes, your Majesty. Maybe time and distance has changed us," Francis replied, trying to make sense of her dampened enthusiasm for seeing him.

Queen Marguerite turned her back to Francis as tears rolled down her cheeks, looking back out the window.

"I have a question to ask of you," she asked softly.

Francis knew that she was upset, but he also knew that he could not offer her comfort unless she allowed him to do so. She was a Queen after all.

"Anything, your Majesty!" he whispered desperately.

Queen Marguerite wiped away her tears, and turned around towards Francis, but finding it difficult to look into his eyes, stared down at the ground.

"It came upon me to defend your honour when my King said disparaging things about England, and more specifically, about you," she started, looking up briefly, seeing how well he had grown, before looking away again.

"My husband made a damning accusation that your only reason for being in Navarre was to spy on our Kingdom. To spy on our defences and my people," she continued, holding back the tears.

A look of guilt covered his face.

"Let me explain!" Francis begged her, as he quickly approached, but she slapped him as soon as he got within arms reach.

"So it is true?" she pressed, tears now streaming from her angry reddened eyes.

"Was it your duty to seduce me as well?" she continued, devastated that Francis had used her.

"It was not like that!" Francis replied defensively, shaking his head.

"But is it true?" she asked again, interrupting him.

Francis tried to think of an answer, but his indecision was enough, and Queen Marguerite felt she had confirmation that her husband was right, taking a few seconds to think before composing herself, willing the last of her tears to stop.

Francis tried to utter the right words to explain, but nothing came out.

As Queen of France, she knew that she had responsibilities far exceeding her own happiness, and had to now sever all future contact with Francis.

She had to be strong for France.

"It would please me, if you NEVER write to me again!" she screamed.

Francis could understand her anger, and believed she was just in her actions, knowing full well that if she was found out in a similar situation in England she would have surely been imprisoned and most probably beheaded.

It still hurt to have been spurned by her, and at this point, he understood for the first time, what it was to put a country *above all else*.

Queen Marguerite composed herself and drew her hood back over her head, and made her way past Francis to leave.

As she stopped at the doorway, she turned back towards him.

"You were the love of my life", she choked as she looked into his eyes one last time before rushing out of the room in tears.

"...and you were the love of mine," Francis whispered to himself with tears in his eyes as he stood alone in the empty room.

With sadness in his step, Francis left the tavern and continued his 12 month assigned tour for England, making reports on his observations regarding the *laws, religion, military strength and whatsoever concerning pleasure or profit* across Europe as he was instructed by Sir Walter Raleigh, the man in charge of the English Secret Service.

During his travels over this period, in addition to France and Spain, he also managed to visit Italy, Austria, Germany, Portugal, Poland, Denmark and Sweden, Florence, Venice, Mantua, Genoa and Savoy, liaising with many contacts in possession of useful information of benefit to the crown.

Upon his return to England in March 1582, he drafted a report detailing his travels and findings, presenting it as a State Paper to the Queen, entitled *Notes on the Present State of Christendom.*

51. THE GOOD PENS

Although Lord Burghley had urged Francis not to enter politics on several occasions and instead to continue a career in Law, Francis continued on regardless and started on a parliamentary service that was to span thirty-six years of his life, progressing his political ambitions to be raised Member of Parliament (MP) for Melcombe Regis (Portland) in 1584, aged just 23, a royal borough, and again as MP of Taunton two years later, in 1586.

Seeing the unfortunate state of religion in England, with authority from the Privy Council, he began writing down his ideas on the philosophical reformation of political parties in the church as well, eventually also becoming a bencher at Gray's Inn, which catapulted him to the prominent position of Reader there a year later.

Now with a viable income, Francis felt compelled to fulfil the promise he had made to himself when he first returned from France some years before, which was to set about the reformation of the English language.

With what little finances he had, he finally began to cultivate a "Pleiades" styled programme and met up with some of his friends from Cambridge, as well as other learned men who were authors in their own right, albeit writing mostly anonymously, he managed to bring together a formidable literary band of fellows.

At the meeting, Francis managed to assemble John Lyly, Thomas Lodge, George Peele, Robert Greene, Thomas Nashe, Christopher Marlowe, Henry

Neville, Thomas Middleton, Edward De Vere, and his step-brother Anthony Bacon.

Francis eyed his step-brother knowingly, having already discussesd his grand plans at length with him, and likewise, Anthony had aided Francis in understanding what was needed to accomplish his ideas but it was now time to convince the men that he had assembled.

Francis turned his focus to the assembled guests and addressed them.

"Every now and then in history there is one idea at work which is more powerful than any other, an idea which shapes the events of the time and determines their ultimate issues. As I watch the people who control the newspapers of our great country, I see the power they hold to sway public opinion to their own desires. These media moguls have not been voted into power, yet they have it nonetheless!" Francis explained to his friends.

Most of the seated audience nodded in agreement, whilst others looked at each other wondering what Francis was getting at.

"I ask you all to join me in the greatest collaboration of writer's that will form a renaissance of literature which in turn will make our people learned, informed, and independent!" Francis declared.

"What do you propose Francis?" asked his cousin, Edward De Vere.

"For far too long I have stood by and watched the English tongue fall by the wayside. I wish to clean up our current inflexible English language and give our kinsmen a usable vocabulary where we will be able to express ourselves with eloquence!" Francis explained in earnest.

"I see where you are coming from. You would like to stimulate our poor language as they did in France?" Edward De Vere queried as he began to understand what Francis was proposing.

Francis nodded eagerly.

Edward De Vere stroked his small beard as he contemplated whether they could achieve it without the backing of their government. He was uncertain.

"What type of writing do you have in mind?" Thomas Nashe asked eagerly.

"Everything and anything!" Francis responded excitedly, to the sniggers of a few of his guests.

"Seriously though, I want us to infuse the great work of the ancients, writing about our experiences, inspirations, taking some of the ancient Latin works and translating them to English and a lot more besides!" Francis added.

"If that is what you propose, we could also take some of the ancient works already translated by our friends in France, and simply convert them to English as well," Edward De Vere commented.

"I like it!" Francis replied, thinking that it would hasten things along as well.

"The only problem is that in France, they have their government backing them, I cannot see our government supporting us unless they have a hand in censoring what we publish," Edward De Vere continued, throwing a dampener on the discussions.

"I know, I know. I think we will have to do it alone for now and see where we get to," Francis responded grimly.

"But how are we going to get our countrymen to read our efforts if they are illiterate?" asked Henry Neville, not convinced.

"Controversy is always a good way to get a listening public. That is what they did in France," Edward De Vere clarified.

"Exactly, and that is how the media moguls that control the newspapers we read every day do it as well!" Francis reminded them, to the nodded agreement of many of them.

"Hmm," murmured Henry Neville, as he considered Edward De Vere's response.

"It could work, I suppose," he added thoughtfully.

"Whose name will be associated with the resulting works of such collaborations?" Edward De Vere queried, a secret author himself.

In his childhood, Francis had witnessed the consequence of attaching one's own name to controversial writings through his dearly departed father, Sir Nicholas. As Lord Keeper to Queen Elizabeth, a sound lawyer and a witty man, he also revelled in writing.

The greatest and almost the only regretful mistake that the very able man constantly complained about, was by assisting an author named *Hales* in a treatise he wrote on the title of the Scottish Queen. If Sir Nicholas had *concealed* his share in the book, and made Hales his instrument or mask, he would have saved himself, many years of worry and vexation.

Sir Nicholas Bacon's known connection with that book was the means of people excluding him from the Privy Council, and causing him to fall from the Queen Elizabeth's favour for many years.

Thereafter, Sir Nicholas wrote anonymously. He not only saw the joy of writing a book, but he learned the value of anonymity, and the use of a pen-name to hide his authorship of subsequent publications.

His mother also made several learned translations from Latin and Italian, but withheld her full name as well for fear of similar retribution.

"All literature built through this collaboration would be to the betterment of England, its language, culture, and more! One day, England will allow a writer free speech, but alas, that day is not here yet," Francis declared, looking to his cousin, Edward De Vere for support.

Edward De Vere winked at Francis, edging him on.

"Yes that is true. Maybe it would be best to keep the written works anonymous," Henry Neville agreed.

"I do not wish for any of us to be restricted in voicing our opinions, and due to the threat of imprisonment for doing so, I fear that is what we should do, for now," Francis added, trying to reassure the group.

The group had good reason to fear imprisonment, especially due to a series of proclamations restricting the free speech in playhouses. In 1559, which was the first year of Queen Elizabeth's reign where she instructed her officers not to permit any *interlude* to be *played wherein either matters of religion or the governance of the estate of the commonwealth shall be handled or treated*, in effect, censoring the portrayal of religion or government matters in any play.

Also, in 1570, another proclamation encouraged people to inform on authors of "seditious" (meaning a Catholic bias) books with the inducement that they *shall be so largely rewarded as during his or their lives they shall have just cause to think themselves well used*. In simple terms, this meant that their reward would be avoiding the imprisonment that would have resulted from failing to alert the authorities in the first place.

"Any works published by our group, will have a mark that will identify us, and we shall follow the ideas of Dante in his use of double-writing to aid us," Francis added.

This use of double writing in serious literature during Dante's time was the only method of free expression open to writers fearing retribution for airing their views on sensitive subjects such as politics and religion.

Dante's writing style was such that the authorities assumed his doctrine to be orthodox while the public, for whom it was designed, readily perceived its real focus. Except by resort to this old and time-honoured publication of independent thought, Dante's ideas would have perished altogether.

Over time, Francis' writing group would adopt all Dante's methods of secret writing (double entendres, word-play with words and phrases) and carried the methods to the farthest limits in a variety of ways such as by numbers, anagrams, printing errors, special type-setting, hieroglyphics, allegorical pictures, emblematic head/tail pieces, and watermarks.

"The road we are about to travel is a dangerous one, but one I think will be full of promise. If you believe my cause is just, then join me!" Francis added in an upbeat tone.

"I think we need a show of hands eh Francis?" Edward De Vere suggested.

"I suppose you are right," Francis replied, now thinking he may well find out if his peers considered him a fool for his crazy ideas, but one by one, each of the men raised their hand in agreement, to his amazement.

Francis smiled earnestly at the founding members of his new writing group.

✝

One evening, some weeks later, the group of men assembled once again for an initiation ceremony, where these same men were then initiated as founding members of a secret group called *The Knights of the Helmet*. The title was formed in honour of their newly recognised muse 'Pallas Athena' selected by Francis in conjunction with his cousin Edward De Vere, who was to be their guiding spirit to ensure they stayed their path of educating their fellow countrymen.

That night, Francis proudly led the initiation of each man through a ritual he devised based partly on some of the original initiations used by secret orders now long forgotten, which contained elaborate ceremonial exchanges of vows, and the reciting of age old proclamations of allegiance.

Each man was capped with a ceremonial helmet signifying their "Invisible" fight for human advancement, and then given a large Spear to hold, reminiscent of the spear Pallas Athena also held, when she would shake the spear of knowledge at those that stood in the way of the advancement of learning that they had now proclaimed to uphold.

As the writing group began their programme, it was not long before their publications, which included stories, poetry, and plays, rippled through the rich and poor alike, with plays being performed by the many play-houses that had sprouted up around London, with acting troupes travelling the land extending the reach of the plays.

This programme eventually drew in support from many prominent people who wanted to help and spread their efforts such as Robert Dudley, Earl of Leicester, still dear to the Queen, and biological father to Francis, who provided an enthusiastic patronage of the poets and artists, making his London home, Essex House, available to them as well as creating his own company of actors.

Out of these early years, Francis wrote several plays for as part of their programme, and they were *Venus & Adonis*, his initial offering to the writing group, *Love Labour's Lost*, and *Romeo & Juliet*.

Venus & Adonis, a narrative love poem, reflected his love affair with Queen Marguerite of Navarre.

Love Labour's Lost, a comedy play, which was initially performed at court in front of Queen Elizabeth, was first play, featuring many characters based on people he had met in Navarre. Four of the characters were specifically based on associates of his brother Anthony, being Lord's Biron, Dumaine, Longaville and Boyesse. The storyline itself was based on the King of Navarre who falls in love with a visiting princess, which was a reflection of Francis' own experiences in Navarre and his love for its Queen, Marguerite. At the end of the play, the princess's father dies forcing the princess to return home for the funeral, mirroring the reasons why Francis had to himself return to England.

Romeo & Juliet, a romantic play about a boy and a girl that fell in love, but due to their opposing families, they are destined never to be together also mirrored the Tudor and de Valois family objections to Francis marrying Queen Marguerite.

52. THE LIBRARY

As the writing group hungered for more resources to feed their literary expansion, Francis had accepted among others, Dr. Dee's offer of the use of his extensive library of reference books in Mortlake.

Although Dr. Dee had offered Francis access to his library many years before, the meeting had been delayed due to Dr. Dee spending some years abroad supposedly holidaying with his family, but secretly engaged in supernatural pursuits with an associate of his, Edward Kelly a supposed expert in communing with angelic beings via the use of a crystal-gazer.

Due to personal reasons, Dr. Dee had abruptly returned to England, and with a window of opportunity, Francis made the journey to visit him in his Mortlake home.

As Francis reviewed the great library, there was a noticeable change in the placement and ordering of the books within the library, and Francis was sure Dr. Dee's collection used to be larger than he had remembered, but dwelling on other matters, Francis was too distracted to care.

Seemingly oblivious to Francis' distracted thoughts, Dr. Dee sat patiently at a desk, focused on repairing the ruffled pages of an old book.

"How was your trip?" Francis asked, understanding that Dr. Dee had supposedly spent the last two years on a spiritual pilgrimage across Europe and was intrigued to know what he had been doing.

"I was recalled by the crown," Dr. Dee replied, seemingly vexed at his forced return.

Recalled? Francis thought ominously to himself.

"But why?" Francis queried.

"That I cannot discuss now Francis, but all will be revealed in due course!" Dr. Dee huffed before returning to the creases of the old book he was mending.

"Oh, OK," Francis commented, recognising his old mentor tone what he did not want to discuss the matter further.

What Francis was to learn later, was that Dr. Dee had been recalled by Sir Francis Walsingham, who was acting on information received from his European spy network, confirming that a Spanish armada was building to launch against England.

Sir Francis Walsingham had recalled Dr. Dee to use his knowledge of astrology to aid England in preparing to defend its shores.

"When I was last here Dr. Dee, I marvelled in the diversity of the fine books in your collection!" Francis queried, changing the subject.

Without looking up, his old mentor smiled a little, as he continued mending the ruffled book that had his attention.

As Francis looked back at the library, he was now certain that a large number of the books in the library had been removed as well as huge rows of books seemingly placed haphazardly back on the shelves, looking very much out of order.

"Master Dee, have you been rearranging some of these books?" Francis asked delicately.

Dr. Dee raised his eyes back up at Francis, now aggravated.

"While I was away, we had a break-in. The thieves stole some of my inventions, books and maps!" Dr. Dee confessed, finally revealing the reason for his anger at the violation of his home.

"What? Do you know who did it?" Francis asked, completely shocked.

Dr. Dee raised his hand to quell Francis' dismay.

"What's done is done!" his old mentor responded calmly.

"But did you find out who was responsible?" Francis continued, still angered at the violation.

"Let it go Francis, I have," Dr. Dee replied with a sigh, returning his attention to the old book in front of him.

Still shocked, Francis wandered past some of the bookshelves, passing an empty shelf he remembered that once housed several banned occult books, and he wondered whether these books had also been stolen.

Maybe Dr. Dee had seen the error of his ways Francis considered, thinking his old mentor had abandoned his occultist desires.

Francis desperately wanted to confess the occult experiences he had practiced through his limited understanding of the symbolism within the Book of Raziel to his mentor, but was now not so sure.

Looking beyond the many books, Francis began to eye the remaining strange objects in the library, noticing a small globe of the world on a rotating stand, seemingly not worthy of a thieves' treasure trove.

He made his way to the rotating stand, spinning its globe on its axis, and watching in earnest at the various land masses of the known world spun past, before turning back to Dr. Dee, taking in a wondrous view of the library.

"You still have a vast collection though, Dr. Dee," Francis commended his mentor, noting that there were maybe 400-500 fewer books in the library than before.

Dr. Dee stroked his beard for a few moments.

"Yes, the thieves seemed to be very specific about what they wanted, stealing certain maps, books on navigation, and a few of the inventions I was working on," Dr. Dee answered, as he surveyed the blank rows on some of the bookcases.

As Francis considered the value of some of the books he knew Dr. Dee held in his library, he began to think about the supposedly valuable book he now secretly possessed.

His blood ran cold as he considered just how far Damien would go to obtain the Book of Raziel from him, a book that Francis never wanted in the first place.

From the desk, Dr. Dee had been secretly watching Francis for some time and could tell that he was troubled and sat back in his chair, eyeing Francis squarely now.

"Francis, you know, you can tell me anything. There is not much that would shock me," he commented frankly, smiling warmly back at his former student.

Francis took comfort from his mentor's words as he considered the real reason for his visit.

"Is it that obvious?" Francis replied, embarrassed that his old mentor could still read him so easily.

Dr. Dee nodded as smiled back at Francis.

As he acknowledged Dr. Dee's astute observation, Francis took a deep breath as he considered how best to explain the real reason for his visits.

"Some years ago Dr. Dee, I heard whispers that you were looking for some sort of divine inspiration by talking to angels," Francis explained delicately, knowing that he was now talking about a very sensitive subject.

Dr. Dee's eyes flared angrily.

"Are you here to mock me Francis?" he returned in an angry tone, his eyes now wide with anger.

"No sire! I am here for mystical understanding!" Francis responded quickly raising his hands apologising, realising he had annoyed his old mentor.

"Mystical understanding?" Dr. Dee repeated, scrutinising Francis' face.

Thinking Francis to be sincere, Dr. Dee rose from his chair and began pacing his library, stretching his weary legs.

"Do you know why I amassed such a large collection of books?" Dr. Dee asked as he made his way pass Francis towards the globe.

"You once told me it was because you wished to have a centre of learning for England?" Francis responded sheepishly, remembering a conversation he had with Dr. Dee some years before.

"Yes, yes, but it was more than that Francis. It was about *knowledge*, *knowledge is power* Francis, and you would do well to remember that, no matter the cost!" Dr. Dee responded.

Francis was unsettled at hearing the phrase *knowledge is power*.

"What is it?" Dr. Dee queried, realising he had somehow hit a nerve.

"No, it's just that I have heard that phrase before," Francis answered, thinking back to his conversation with the ghostly aura years before in Navarre.

"And there I was thinking my advice unique!" Dr. Dee smiled before walking past him, making his way around the library reaching the world globe that Francis had been spinning earlier. He spun the globe gently, setting it rotating slowly on its axis.

"At one time, I believed that reading all that was available would give me immense knowledge of this world, perhaps even the meaning of life!" he started.

"Alas, I was mistaken," Dr. Dee sighed, stopping the globe from its spin abruptly.

"Although I did propose a national library to Queen Mary in her reign, it was only because I did not want to have to fund such an exercise of reading material at my own cost!" Dr. Dee confessed, laughing a little as he eyed Francis.

Francis himself began to chuckle a little at his mentor's honesty.

"When I exhausted all I could read and did not find what I was looking for, I took the unorthodox path of communing with angels in order to further my knowledge and understanding," Dr. Dee finally admitted.

Francis had heard whispers that Dr. Dee had been secretly trying to communicate with angels, but was nevertheless shocked at his mentor's confession that he did indeed dabble in what would have been deemed witchcraft.

"Did you have success?" asked Francis eager to know more, thinking about his own experiences with the apparition that visited him.

"Through my medium, yes," Dr. Dee responded looking into the expanse of his library.

"Alas, some people view me as a companion to hell hounds, a conjuror of wicked and damned spirits. As a result, I, and others like me that believe in this craft now choose secrecy to practice," Dr. Dee continued.

"There are others?" Francis asked.

Dr. Dee eyed him squarely again.

"You would be shocked to know how many, but enough of these questions Francis, why the sudden interest in the mystics?"

"It confuses me to believe one can speak to spirits. I once thought it a skill practiced by devil worshippers and witches" Francis confessed.

Dr. Dee's stern eyes on Francis softened a little.

"That's OK Francis. People fear what they do not know," Dr. Dee added with a knowing wisdom in his eyes.

Dr. Dee made his way back to Francis.

"Why would you want to understand such a thing anyway?" Dr. Dee pressed.

"It is a heavy burden to bestow on a man of religion such as you Francis," he continued in a concerned tone.

With all Dr. Dee's revelations, Francis decided he was now ready to confess his own deep secrets.

53. MYSTIC REVELATIONS

𝔍rancis inhaled deeply and then lifted his left hand out in front of him towards his mentor with his palm outstretched upwards.

Dr. Dee could see his hand was noticeably shaking but said nothing, waiting patiently for Francis to finish.

Francis closed his eyes and concentrated, whispering one of the incantations he had deciphered from the Book of Raziel before he had abruptly stopped deciphering its complex symbolism.

After a few seconds, above his opened palm, a small ball of swirling energy materialised.

Dr. Dee's eyes widened in amazement at what Francis had achieved.

"Well done my boy!" Dr. Dee responded in a jubilant tone.

As Francis smiled back to his mentor, this brief lapse in concentration set the once perfect circular small ball of energy to destabilise, changing its shape erratically.

"Oh no!" Francis shouted as he tried to stabilise his mystical feat, fearing something bad if he did not regain control.

Calmly, Dr. Dee waved a calm hand over the ball, whispering an incantation that immediately stabilised the ball, returning it back into a perfect circle.

Francis let out a sigh to relief as Dr. Dee came to his aid, and his face turned to amazement at how easily Dr. Dee controlled the situation.

Eyeing the amazement in his wide-eyed student, Dr. Dee decided to impress Francis some more, whispering another incantation which made the ball of energy grow in size, with the surface of the ball transforming into an accurate world map similar to the one in the corner of his library, showing the regions and countries of the world.

Francis was wide eyed in amazement as he stared at the large ball of energy that hovered in front of him.

"I knew it was right to come to you!" Francis exclaimed happily.

Francis came closer to the mystical globe and studied some of the coastal lines on the ball's surface.

"This globe is amazing! There are coastal lines on this globe that I have never even seen before!" Francis commented as he followed the coastlines.

Feeling he had impressed his student, Dr. Dee gestured with his hand to cause the globe to rotate, bringing the coastline of the *New World* into view.

Francis refocused on the coastline relating to the New World with renewed interest, reminding Francis of something that had been troubling him for some time. With his old mentor standing before him, Francis felt that if anyone would know the answer, it would be Dr. Dee.

"Dr. Dee, I happened to visit the Rosslyn Chapel as part of my travels to Scotland some time ago, and I had a question that no one could answer while I was there, relating to the New World," Francis asked as he continued analysing the various coastlines.

"What do you wish to know?" asked Dr. Dee apprehensively.

"As I surveyed its interior, I noticed clear depictions of ears of corn and aloe cactus on archways and ceilings," Francis added adamantly.

A slight frown formed on Dr. Dee's forehead, as if he could anticipate what was coming next.

"Go on," Dr. Dee beckoned him.

"I am sure from my learning's that corn and aloe cactus were brought to England early this century [1500] from the New World, but the chapel was built in 1486, some six years before Christopher Columbus even discovered this country," Francis finished, turning back to his old mentor with confusion in his face, hoping for Dr. Dee to give him a reasonable explanation.

"The designs must have been added afterwards," Dr. Dee responded defensively, avoiding eye contact with Francis.

"I do not think so sire. The carvings were an integral part of the chapel's initial design. I know that because I managed to view a copy of the original architectural diagrams for the chapel and the corn and aloe cactus designs were already detailed there too!" Francis replied, still pressing for an answer.

Francis could not help notice Dr. Dee's eyes widen in shock when he mentioned that he had reviewed the architectural designs of the chapel.

"I am sorry, I cannot help you Francis!" Dr. Dee responded sternly.

"The latest detail in this map has been updated with information passed on by the navigator Sir Francis Drake," he replied, attempting to change the subject.

"Drake? I have heard of him. Is he not a common pirate who ransacks Spanish galleons?" Francis responded in a disapproving tone for the man.

Becoming more agitated, Dr. Dee snapped his fingers causing the globe to disappear, startling Francis as he was still eyeing the coastlines it detailed.

"He is a 'privateer' Francis, remember that he shares his bounty with the crown, and on behalf of the crown, he has made numerous expeditions to the *New World* at great risk, and expense, to himself!" Dr. Dee responded defensively.

Francis, realising he had struck a nerve, went all quiet.

"I am sorry Francis, I got a bit carried away," Dr. Dee apologised, softening his tone as he realised he had overreacted to his once student, being unnecessarily rude.

Francis forced a smile back accepting his old mentor's apology.

"Now on to more important matters Francis!" Dr Dee continued, now eyeing Francis inquisitively.

"Tell me, how did you gain the mystical knowledge to summon the ball?" Dr. Dee queried with great interest.

"It all started in France sire," Francis admitted, thinking back to his discovery of the Book of Raziel.

"We came upon a woman who was accused of witchcraft. I went to her aid, but failed to save her life, and she was burned alive," Francis added with sadness in his tone.

Resting his hand on Francis' shoulder, Dr. Dee tried to console him.

"At least you tried Francis. I know you would have done everything in your power to save her," Dr. Dee responded softly.

"We?" Dr. Dee queried, seeking clarification.

"Yes, Master Paulet and I," Francis clarified.

"Ah, yes, the then French Ambassador," Dr. Dee nodded.

"Some days afterwards, she came to me in my dreams"

"She? Who do you mean?" Dr. Dee interrupted, now confused.

"The supposed witch sire. She came to me in my dreams!" Francis repeated, ominously.

"Oh?" Dr. Dee responded with great interest.

"Continue my boy!" Dr. Dee beckoned, yearning for more.

"Through a number of visions I had, I was able to recover a book, which I believe is called *The Book of Raziel!*" Francis then explained.

"The Book of Raziel?" Dr. Dee interrupted as his eyes widened in shock.

"I remember reading about this book! I didn't believe it actually really existed!" Dr. Dee continued as his face filled with amazement, having the sudden urge to sit down as he comprehended the books existence.

"Do you know of it?" Francis queried earnestly as his old mentor seemed to go into a fluster at the mention of the book.

"It is believed to be a very powerful mystical book." Dr. Dee explained, scratching the back of his head with earnest as he surveyed his vast book collection.

"I read something about it in one of these books, and I don't think it was stolen," Dr. Dee mumbled as he thought about which book he originally read about the book.

He immediately rose to his feet and went over to a book case in a far section of the library, grabbing a small mobile ladder with him on the way.

Dr. Dee latched the ladder against a particular bookcase and quickly made his way up to the top rung, selecting a book, and then sliding back down the stairs like an excited schoolboy and he returned to Francis, placing the book on the desk.

"Sit down my boy!" Dr. Dee invited Francis, pointing to a vacant seat, as he eagerly flipped through the pages of the book he had retrieved.

If there was anyone whom Francis could trust to understand what he had found and learned, it would be Dr. Dee, although Francis didn't believe it would have worked out quite this well.

As Francis looked over his mentor's shoulder, he noticed the text of the book was in aged Latin.

"If I remember the fable, the Book of Raziel was a book owned by the Angel Raziel, who was supposed to be a scribe for God, and sat near his throne, writing down everything that was said and discussed," Dr. Dee recited back to Francis from memory as he flipped through the pages of the book trying to find the correct section.

"Raziel was an angel?" Francis asked, intrigued by the revelation that the book was named after an angel.

"Yes, supposedly," replied Dr. Dee as he stopped abruptly on a particular page.

"Ah, here it is!" he exclaimed.

Dr. Dee scanned the text for a few seconds to get to the right paragraph.

"The Book of Raziel is said to contain all secret knowledge, and is considered to be a book of mystical knowledge. Raziel was said to have given the book to Adam and Eve after they ate from the forbidden tree of knowledge of Good and Evil, which resulted in their expulsion from the Garden of Eden, so the two could find their way back home and better understand their God," Dr. Dee recited out loud.

Adam and Eve? How old is this book supposed to be? Francis wondered in amazement.

"It seems his fellow angels were deeply disturbed by this, and as such and stole the book from Adam and Eve, throwing it into the ocean, but the book was eventually retrieved," Dr. Dee continued, supplying an abridged version of the Latin text into English.

"It then took on a new meaning as a book of knowledge, leaving a trail of references to it over the centuries, linking it to Enoch, the Archangel Raphael, and fables that Noah used its wisdom to help him build his Ark," Dr. Dee continued.

Francis just shook his head, bewildered at what Dr. Dee was telling him.

"It seems the trail went cold when the Book of Raziel was said to have come into the possession of King Solomon," Dr. Dee added as he read some more.

King Solomon? Francis repeated, now stunned, thinking the book must have been of great importance if the text was true that King Solomon himself held the book.

Francis took a deep breath and now feeling very guilty for even considering destroying the book because of its supposed importance, forgetting that the book itself was protected by a powerful force that meant it could not be destroyed.

"This woman who came to you in your dreams, did she have any strange markings?" Dr. Dee asked, drawing Francis out of his thoughts.

"Yes, she had a few, I remember a tattoo of a snake around her leg," Francis replied.

"Did you notice anything on her hand?" Dr. Dee asked, being more specific.

"Yes!" Francis agreed after pausing as he remembered back to his encounter with her. He remembered the strange Egyptian styled tattoo on the palm of her hand.

"Did it have the marking of an eye within a pyramid?" Dr. Dee asked apprehensively.

"Yes!" Francis responded agreeably.

Dr. Dee scanned through the book until he came to a reference on *Angels of Deliverance* and quickly read the Latin text, translating it into English.

"It says here that the book is supposedly guarded by one or more women wearing the sign of the Angel's of Deliverance," Dr. Dee told him.

"Angel's of Deliverance?" Francis repeated as his eyes widened with interest.

"The fable says that these angels wear the mark of the *all seeing eye*. Their one purpose is to protect and deliver the book through the generations to selected individuals, preordained to gain its secret teachings," Dr. Dee explained.

"It is said the book is delivered in advance of some forthcoming disaster," Dr. Dee informed Francis gloomily.

"A forthcoming disaster?" Francis repeated worriedly.

"Yes, if the fable is true," Dr. Dee replied, nodding ominously.

"It also says that the Angels of Deliverance are believed to have the ability to see into the future, which is partly why they wear the mark of the 'all seeing eye' in the first place, and last piece of text here states a fable that *only he that is preordained may read its mystical teachings,*" Dr Dee finished.

"Only he? What do you mean?" Francis queried.

"It means the secrets of the book are only visible to *he* that is preordained to read it. To everyone else, the book's secrets are supposedly invisible!" Dr. Dee answered.

"Invisible? I can assure you every page in the book sire is full of symbolism, I have seen it with my own eyes!" Francis explained.

Dr. Dee's face became serious.

"You sound like you still have the book?" Dr. Dee queried, his face hoping against everything that Francis would say YES.

"I do sire!" Francis replied, nodding.

Dr. Dee could not help but fell back into his chair overwhelmed at the revelation that Francis was still in possession of such a historic artefact. He swallowed hard.

"Where is the book now?" he asked anxiously.

"In my carriage outside, sire!" Francis replied quickly.

"You have it here? Bring it in, bring it in my boy!" Dr. Dee begged Francis hurriedly, amazed that he was so close to such an important book.

"Immediately sire!" Francis responded rising and quickly exiting the library back to his waiting carriage to retrieve the book.

Moments later, Francis returned to the library holding the mystical book at arms length, still afraid of its power, handing it carefully to Dr. Dee.

Dr. Dee gently placed the book on his desk before running his hand slowly over its brown leather cover, seemingly sensing its inner power.

After a little hesitation, he opened the book to find the first page blank, which left him perplexed, and ignoring this page, he very carefully turned the page finding a set of blank pages. He turned a few more pages, but again they were also blank.

Francis eyed the blank pages in confusion.

"But there were symbols, drawings, I swear to you sire!" Francis explained in defence.

Considering the text he had just read about the fabled book, Dr. Dee's initial confusion slowly disappeared and was replaced with a wry smile. He closed the book gently, stroking its cover once more, before moving out of the way to allow Francis access to the book.

"You open it Francis," Dr. Dee calmly advised him.

A confused Francis begrudgingly agreed and opened the book, but this time, the first page magically filled up with ancient symbolism right in front of their eyes and on turning the pages, each of the previously blank pages now magically filled up with the mystical symbolism as Francis had remembered as well

"That's unbelievable!" Francis exclaimed, relieved he was not going mad.

"Yes it is! But what this means is that the book is real, and that YOU are the rightful recipient of the book Francis. You thought you had found it, but in fact, the Angel of Deliverance had actually found you!" Dr. Dee explained.

For the rest of the day, Francis explained his mystical experiences, including his clash with Damien, explaining that Damien used a particular name *Allocen* when he communed with devils.

Dr. Dee immediately recognised that name "Allocen" through past conversations with his spirits through his *skryer* Edward Kelly, learning that Damien was known as a powerful sorcerer that dabbled in Dark magic and would stop at nothing to extend his already powerful mystical abilities.

From that day forward, Dr. Dee took Francis under his wing once again, offering a guiding hand in the training that Francis would need to fully exploit the mystical power hidden within the Book of Raziel.

54. THE NEW WORLD

Richmond Palace, January 1588

A pale looking young Francis, with a reddened nose and puffy teary eyes, navigated the many corridors of the palace, en route to an appointment with Queen Elizabeth. In his hand, he held a crumpled handkerchief.

His body ached as he recovered from a bout of flu.

As he arrived outside the designated stately office blocked by two royal guards, he tucked away his handkerchief into the sleeve of his doublet, and then took a deep breath before presenting himself to the guards.

"I have an appointment with her Majesty!" Francis explained through a blocked nose to the guards.

One of the guards nodded, knowing full well who he was, and knocked on the door of the office before entering to inform the Queen of his arrival, exiting a few seconds later to give Francis access to enter in.

As Francis made his way into the office, he performed the customary bow before his Queen who was sat at a gold encrusted marble desk, covered with piles of stately papers.

Queen Elizabeth looked up briefly from the state papers, purposefully making Francis wait until she was ready to receive him.

Feeling a sneeze coming on, Francis raised his hand in apology before quickly retrieving his trusty handkerchief from his sleeve and covering his nose just in time as the sneezing bout took hold of him, causing him to fight his bowed posture, as his Queen had not yet given him permission to rise.

Queen Elizabeth immediately covered her face to guard herself from the possible germs emanating from his violent sneezing fit.

"Rise, rise!" she ordered Francis, as she tried to contain a laugh watching him struggle to keep his bowed stature while simultaneously trying to contain his sneezing fit.

Acknowledging her, Francis straightened up, as he continued to control the tail end of his sneezing fit.

"Please accept my apologies, your Majesty!" Francis apologised as he regained his composure, completely embarrassed as he blew his nose one more time before quickly returning his handkerchief back to his sleeve.

Queen Elizabeth was at a loss for words and simply shook her head in dismay.

"You requested to see me your Majesty?" Francis sniffled as he peered through his reddened eyes.

Queen Elizabeth stared at Francis for some seconds as she decided whether to usher him away or not, finally deciding to be brief with her business.

"Yes, as my legal counsel, I require you to draw up a declaration of Independence for a piece of land discovered in the New World in my name," she responded in a quick tempo.

"This would be the land called 'Virginia' discovered by Sir Walter Raleigh?" Francis clarified, sniffling a little.

"That is correct," she replied, nodding.

Francis nodded in agreement.

"I will begin immediately! Is that all ma'am?"

"That is all, but you can start it tomorrow or whenever you get rid of that sickness you have," she replied, ushering him to leave the room immediately.

Francis nodded, forcing a smile before turning to leave.

Although, Francis and Queen Elizabeth, were indeed mother and son, their relationship would always be strained due to the deceit Francis felt at her hand in his upbringing by Lady Anne and Sir Nicholas Bacon.

Although she was an exceptionally proud woman and held her emotions close, sometimes it was difficult not being able to offer motherly love to her son.

"Wait!" she called out with a hint of anxiousness in her voice.

Francis let out a quiet sigh as he stopped just short of the door, turning back to face his Queen.

"Yes, your Majesty?" Francis replied, forcing another smile.

"I understand you have been feeling poorly of late?"

Francis nodded.

"It is just a cold, your Majesty. I am much better now!" Francis replied as he tried to put on a healthy smile.

"Well, just in case, make sure you book an appointment with my physician to ensure all is alright," she ordered him, immediately dipping her head back down to her state papers, not wanting Francis to see any possible hint of concern.

"I will your Majesty. Thank you!" Francis replied, taken aback by her concern for his wellbeing.

Awkwardly, he offered up a warm smile of gratitude.

Queen Elizabeth smiled a little herself as she pretended not to be interested, waving him out of the room in a quick motion as Francis again began reaching for his handkerchief, signalling the start of another bout of sneezing.

55. SPANISH ENEMIES

February 1588, Palacio de El Escorial, Spain

Kneeling before a large crucifix in the prayer room of his grand palace, King Philip II of Spain was in deep prayer.

He was deep in his devotions over the effect that his impending plans to attack England would have on his Spanish people, and a large cross hung from his neck, mirroring the heavy burden he had to bear due to his planned war with England.

As a zealous catholic, his deepest desire was to return England to a pure catholic faith, and to restore the damnable actions of Queen Elizabeth's father, Henry VIII, when he broke all ties with Rome and Catholicism.

In an ingenious plan, Henry VIII's powerful minion, Thomas Cromwell implemented a devious plot to dissolve all the monasteries, funnelling their wealth into that of the royal family, also confiscating their treasures and dismissing their sacred relics as frauds and turning out the monks themselves to become beggars, while their monasteries and lands were sold off.

Philip had the support of Pope Gregory XIII in his proposed invasion.

The Pope having excommunicated Queen Elizabeth, absolving her subjects from any duty they felt they had to her, also proclaiming that her assassination would not be deemed a mortal sin, a clear licence to kill her.

The pope went so far as to offer financial help and papal blessing to help Philip achieve a successful invasion, as long as he agreed to choose a new ruler for England, subject to the Pope's approval, who would be pledged to restore the Catholic faith.

As he prayed, he could feel someone had entered the room, and some seconds later one of his bishops quietly approached him in the middle of his prayers, leaning in and whispering into his ear.

"Damien Beaumont of France is here to see you, your Majesty!" his bishop whispered softly.

King Philip, with his eyes still closed, simply nodded, and then the bishop withdrew a few steps, waiting for further orders as King Philip cut short his prayers, slowly opening his eyes.

"Send him in!" he responded as he rose to his feet, taking a seat on a nearby throne.

The bishop nodded, and then left to fetch him.

Upon being presented to King Philip, Damien knelt before him.

King Philip quickly gestured for him to rise.

"I understand from your letter that you have information concerning the treasures stolen by the English pirate Drake?" King Philip queried, sneering as he uttered Drake's name in disgust.

"That is correct sire. It is well known now that Spain will soon be launching an attack on England for their treacherous execution of Mary Queen of Scots, the one true royal who could have taken England back to Catholicism!" Damien responded in a sincere tone.

King Philip nodded in agreement but stared inquisitively at Damien as he tried to make an assessment of his character.

"You have been well informed," King Philip eventually responded.

"I would like to help you return England back to the true church," Damien continued, still appealing to the King's strong religious virtues.

"Yes, yes, but how does this relate to the treasures stolen from Spain?" King Philip pressed impatiently.

Damien smiled, realising the King wished to get to the point.

"I have information that leads me to believe that much of the treasures plundered over the years by the pirate from your Spanish galleons are stored in secret locations across the *New World*," Damien explained.

The King's eyes widened with interest.

"The New World?" King Philip exclaimed, stunned at such a revelation.

"How did you come upon this information?" King Philip continued.

"My spies in England sire!" Damien responded lying, feeling that King Philip would not appreciate that he had really learned the information from conversations with demons he had summoned through dark magic.

"Do you know where in the New World?" King Philip asked.

"No, not yet sire. I have had success in securing some pertinent maps from those that share the secret, but I have not yet managed to pinpoint the precise whereabouts," Damien replied.

"Hmm," King Philip contemplated, wondering if there was truth in Damien's words.

"The locations are kept very secure by Drake and others, but if you allow my help in this war, I think I may be able to aid you in finding out where the treasures have been hidden," Damien continued.

Here, Damien was referring to the maps that he had stolen from Dr. Dee's Mortlake home some months before as he searched for clues as to the whereabouts of the treasures shipped to the New World.

"But why would they not keep the treasure safe in England?" the King queried, confused by Drake's actions.

"I do not know sire, I have heard that there is possibly a connection with the Knights Templar," Damien offered up.

"The bloody Templars?" King Philip exploded.

"Yes, but I personally thought they were all arrested and persecuted in the 1300s," Damien confessed.

"Most yes, but others fled abroad, whilst some simply changed their names," King Philip clarified, shaking his head as he considered his Templar knowledge.

"There were whispers that a large convoy escaped across the seas to the New World to safety, in any case, their treasure troves were never found," King Philip continued.

King Philip stroked his beard, considering the possibility of capturing the supposed bigger bounty of the Knights Templar treasure that was never recovered when the Templar monks were rounded up.

"Get me the details of these locations, and I will reward you greatly!" King Philip offered solemnly.

"It is not coin I seek sire. Like you, my strong catholic faith brings me here in this time of need. My desires are more historical. You have certain ancient artefacts among your stolen treasure trove, and I would like to pick and choose among a small selection of them if I may," Damien explained to King Philip in a humble tone.

King Philip stared at Damien, not fully trusting him.

"Hmm, so be it, as long as you bring that pirate to me and the location of the treasures, you will have your request!" King Philip finally agreed.

"But I warn you, do not cross me!" King Philip added, sternly.

Damien nodded uncomfortably, letting out a small smile at the chance to fight against the English armada, and get closer to the fabled ring that would ultimately pinpoint the location of the Book of Raziel.

56. THE NEW ORDER

On a late spring evening, a tired Francis leaves a printing company on Holborn high street, and began the short walk back to his Gray's Inn lodgings, lost in thought. As he made the journey, he was oblivious to two men that were following him from a distance.

As the men closed in on Francis, the first of the two retrieved a handkerchief from his pocket, while the second man revealed a small vial in his hand, which had a cork stuck in its slender neck, keeping its trapped liquid at bay.

The second man pulled the cork off the vial which let off an audible *pop* that did not register with Francis, who was deep in thought.

The second man promptly doused the handkerchief with the contents of the vial, turning his head away so as not to inhale its strong odour.

Almost immediately, both men pounced on Francis, one grabbing him and forcing his arms behind his back.

"What the" Francis started as his arms were painfully jerked behind him.

Before he could fight back or even whisper an incantation in defence, the second man forced Francis to inhale the strong sharp pungent odour of the handkerchief.

Almost immediately, his senses became clouded, and a few seconds later, everything went dark.

✝

As Francis opened his eyes, he found himself still in darkness, his eyes seemingly covered with a blindfold, tightly wrapped around his head.

He felt as though he was sitting on a hard wooden chair, and as he tried to lift his arms to remove the blindfold, he realised that both arms were tied to the arm rests of the chair.

Where am I? Francis wondered fearfully as he tried to stand before realising his legs were bound as well. He tried with all his might to loosen his restraints, but to no avail.

What the hell happened? He wondered angrily, thinking back to the last thing he could remember, which was his short walk down an almost empty path back to his lodgings at Gray's Inn.

As he considered using the power of the Book of Raziel to free himself, fear of the consequences made his skin crawl.

Wondering how long he had been unconscious, he thought he heard someone or something moving nearby and instinctively thought of shouting for help.

"Help!" Francis shouted frantically, but received no response.

"Someone! Anyone! Help!" Francis shouted again as he tried to loosen his restraints.

"There is no need to be fearful Francis," a calm voice with a hint of a French accent called out.

Francis jerked back in his chair as he deduced the voice came from someone that was some 15 or so feet away, causing Francis to tense up.

"Who's there?" Francis shouted, swinging his head around towards the sound of the voice.

"Where am I?" Francis continued angrily, pulling at his restraints some more.

"Be calm Francis, you are among friends!" another voice piped up, from behind him with an English nobleman tone in his voice.

"Friends?" Francis laughed incredulously.

"You kidnap me, blindfold me, tie me up, and then have the gall to tell me you are my friends?" he shouted in anger.

"I am a Member of Parliament, and have my own 'friends' in powerful places! Ones that would not kidnap me then tie me up!" Francis shouted angrily.

"The blindfold is there for your own safety, young Francis, because if you were to know who we were, we would have no option but to kill you to ensure our identities remained safe," an older Scottish voice added from a different location, causing Francis to turn again to the new location of this voice.

By now, Francis came to understand that there were a number of men encircled around him.

"We know full well who you are Francis, including knowledge of your Royal Tudor birth, and also of your secret writing group," the Scottish voice explained plainly in a seemingly unconcerned tone.

Although their knowledge of his secret writing group made him a little vulnerable, Francis was more interested in being freed from his restraints.

"What do you want from me?" Francis shouted, pulling at his restraints once again.

"Your help," replied a heartfelt plea from the man with the French accent that had first spoken.

"My help?" Francis repeated as a frown formed behind his blindfold.

"We represent the last of what was once called the High Council of the Templar Order," the man continued.

"The Knights Templar?" Francis repeated, surprised at the revelation.

"I had heard some of your kind survived," Francis returned sarcastically.

"Yes, some of our order in England escaped to Scotland before sailing further afield to safer havens," responded the man with the Scottish accent.

"We have been watching your activities young Francis, and have been impressed by how you have managed to extend your learning's across England and how your efforts have started to influence people's thinking," added the French accented man.

"You have been watching me?" Francis queried, feeling uneasy.

"We have read some of your earlier anonymous publications, and are impressed with your philosophical views of the world," commented another new voice.

"I personally like the way you have made use of Dante's double writing to get your ideas across on different levels. We would really like to use some of these ideas to communicate with our disparate members across the globe," another voice piped up.

"Your ideas are fresh, whereas we still cling too much to the old ways, which we know is preventing our growth!" added the man with the French accent.

All of a sudden, several different voices started to talk among themselves for some seconds, giving Francis an understanding that he was sitting in the middle of a circle of ten or so men.

"Order! Order!" the Scottish accented voice shouted, quelling the crossed conversations.

"Do not worry, young Francis, We know all your secrets, but that is not why you are here. You can keep your secrets as long as you help us with something," the man with the French accent continued.

With all the positive comments he had just received, the fear Francis had against his kidnappers had started to subside a little.

"What do you want of me?" Francis asked again, somewhat confused.

"Ever since our order disbanded, our order has been fragmented, and communication has been weak across the globe," the new voice of an English nobleman added.

"We would like you to help us form a new order based on the old Knights Templar doctrines, so that we may build an international network to more effectively connect with our members across the globe!" returned the Scottish accented voice.

"Do I have a choice?" Francis asked after some seconds of deliberation, knowing that he was in no position to negotiate.

"You always have a choice Francis. Just be sure you make the right one," responded the man with the French accent.

Francis sighed as he pondered their request, knowing he had no option but to accept.

"When do I start?" Francis replied coldly.

"Immediately!" advised the man with the Scottish accent, who now quietly waved to two men standing near to Francis, who were the same two men who had initially kidnapped him and brought him to the secret location.

"We will send you a contact to discuss how you can be of assistance," the voice continued.

Before Francis could say another word, a handkerchief was thrust over his mouth and nose by one of his original assailants, and he was forced to inhale the now familiar potent odour that rendered him unconscious yet again.

57. THE FREEMASONS

It was the familiar small crack on the ceiling that gave Francis the immediate confirmation that he was laying on his bed back in his Gray's Inn lodgings.

Sitting up in his bed, he realised he was still dressed.

As he wondered whether his kidnapping was just a bad dream, the red rope marks on his wrists and the familiar odour lingering on his face told him it was real, but he could not remember how he ended up in his room.

Just as he jumped out of bed, there was a knock on the door, and as he made his way to answer it, he remembered the last thing his captors had said to him.

We will send you a contact to discuss how you can be of assistance.

He froze on the spot, wondering what his captors wanted of him and who they would send to deliver their message, looking anxiously at the door as it shook again with another knock.

Apprehensively, he opened the door, but to his shock and delight, he found his old mentor, Dr. Dee waiting.

They both exchanged smiles, and as Francis was about to ask why his old mentor has turned up at his lodgings, looking in Dr. Dee's gleaming eyes, Francis knew he was facing the contact the High Council had spoken about.

Over a number of weeks, Francis was to help shape a new order based on the old doctrines of the original Knights Templar.

The remit of the founding nine knights of the Templar order was to guard pilgrims as they made a holy pilgrimage in Jerusalem, supported by the King of Jerusalem at the time, King Baldwin II. This King gave them their first headquarters in the sacred location Temple Mount, which was in the captured Al Aqsa Mosque, the Temple Mount having a mystique, because it was supposedly built above the ruins of the original Temple of Solomon.

As the order spread across Europe, they acquired much land and money, and became skilled masons as they built churches and headquarters for those in their order.

As Francis helped the secret order to refresh their ideals, it was explained that one of the new doctrines would be that the order would now be *free* of religious constraints, relinquishing its previous ties to Christianity, which led to the destruction of their original Templar movement.

This change and their original strength in stonemasonry influenced the naming of this new organisation to be *The Freemason Order*.

58. SEA OF SORCERY

Some months later, Spain declared war on England and dispatches a large Spanish armada of some 25,000 men and over 100 galleons, compared to England's paltry defence of 3,000 men and twenty or so galleons.

As England prepared for war, Queen Elizabeth appointed Robert Dudley, Earl of Leicester to Lord Lieutenant of England and Ireland, investing in him, more power than any sovereign had ever ventured to bestow upon one of their subjects.

As the war erupted, Queen Elizabeth and members of the Privy Council strategized how they hoped to defeat the Spanish armies in a makeshift war room within Richmond Palace.

England's defences were woefully inadequate.

Should Spain's army land in Sussex, Kent, or Essex, they would sweep past England's newly formed armies and descend into London leaving levels of bloodshed in the fields and towns the country had not seen for hundreds of years.

A selected few from the Privy Council huddled around an oversized map outstretched on a large table, covered with model boats in various groupings and locations, representing supposed English and Spanish strengths based on message dispatches from the battlefield.

The probability of losing to the *undefeatable* Spanish armada was high.

As courtiers came and went with message dispatches from the battlefield, the locations and quantities of the model boats on the map were continually updated and whenever a boat representing an English galleon was removed from the map, Queen Elizabeth's face dropped progressively further into despair.

A courtier arrived and Queen Elizabeth inhaled deeply as she wondered if it was another dire despatch from the battlefield, but had no dispatches and simply bowed to Queen Elizabeth.

"Dr. Dee has arrived as you requested, your Majesty," the courtier informed her.

Queen Elizabeth breathed out in relief, nodding and then ushering the courtier out of the war room.

"I will not be long!" Queen Elizabeth shouted to the busy Privy Councillors as they argued over their next move, following the courtier out of the room.

As she made her way out to the adjoining hallway, she found Dr. Dee waiting patiently.

"Your Majesty!" Dr. Dee greeted her, bowing immediately.

"Come with me Master Dee!" Queen Elizabeth ordered him as she darted into an adjoining room.

Dr. Dee quickly followed after his Queen, trying to keep up.

As they both entered the room, she closed the door behind her, locking it.

As Dr. Dee watched her lock the door, he realised their discussion would be of a serious nature, too secret even for the Privy Council.

"You called for me your Majesty?" asked Dr. Dee, as he eyed his Queen as she began pacing the room with a look of despair on her face.

"It is grave Master Dee! The attack from the Spaniards does not go well!" she explains to him worriedly.

"Yes, your Majesty. How can I be of service to my country?" Dr Dee asked knowing full well that England were in an undeniably losing position to the Spanish.

He was ready to take on any task she saw fit to give him if it would help England's cause.

"I have had dire messages from the field!" she responded gravely.

Dr. Dee's face dropped as he feared England's defences were already lost.

Queen Elizabeth shook he head and walked over to a desk in the room, opening a drawer and extracting an envelope.

"Is the war lost your Majesty?" Dr. Dee asked, afraid of the response, as he considered England's outnumbered army.

"Not yet," she replied, shaking her head as she handed him a water-stained envelope.

"This was sent to me by one of my best captains, now lost at sea!" she responded in a dejected tone.

Dr. Dee accepted the envelope, opening it to read its enclosed letter.

As he read the contents, his face quickly turned to shock.

The letter was written hastily by a Captain in charge of a now lost fleet of English galleons sent to do battle against the Spanish armies.

The letter detailed that the last of the galleons under his command had been destroyed by waves appearing from nowhere, but the comment that frightened Queen Elizabeth the most was when the Captain stated that many of the galleons had been overpowered by mysterious flying beasts.

Flying beasts? Dr. Dee considered in horror.

"Have my men gone mad Dr. Dee, or are the Spanish drawing on some dark magic? Tell me is all is not lost!" Queen Elizabeth begged him.

Dr. Dee shook his head as he wondered whether magic was indeed involved.

"I do not know your Majesty, but I am going to find out!" he promised her defiantly.

Queen Elizabeth nodded and made her way to the door and unlocked it.

"Make haste Master Dee, time is running out!" she begged with desperation in her tone, ushering him out of the room.

Dr. Dee nodded in agreement as he left the room, fearful by what he had just read.

59. CALL TO ARMS

𝔉rancis urgently arrived at Dr. Dee's home, and on being granted entry by a servant he was led into a darkened room, where Dr. Dee sat, deep in thought.

"I came as soon as I received your urgent message Dr. Dee! What is it?" Francis asked worriedly.

"Our war with the Spanish Armada is faltering, possibly due to dark sorcery Francis!" Dr. Dee informed explained in an ominous tone.

"Sorcery?" Francis replied, taken aback by the idea that sorcery was being used in the war between England and Spain.

"But how?" Francis asked, now flustered at the very idea.

"I don't know yet, but we are losing the war, and if England falls, you had best get used to speaking Spanish permanently!" Dr. Dee responded coldly.

Francis, weakened at the news, immediately took a seat, contemplating an England ruled by the Spanish.

"I have organised a meeting of druids I know that practice the secret teachings of the mystics tonight! We must fight fire with fire Francis!" Dr. Dee exclaimed angrily as he thought about their English soldier's possibly falling to dark forces.

A mystical fight? Francis thought grimly.

"What do you want of me in all this?" Francis asked, knowing Dr. Dee had a task for him.

"I have been mentoring you for some time now Francis in harnessing the power of the Book of Raziel," Dr. Dee began.

"I think you are ready!" Dr. Dee added with serious intent in his eyes.

"Ready? Ready for what?" Francis asked worriedly, remembering back to how hard his old mentor had pushed him in realising his true potential in the mastery of the mystics.

"Do you remember when I said the book of Raziel would choose a defender because of some impending disaster?"

Francis nodded uncomfortably.

"I think that disaster is our war with Spain Francis! I think the prophecy of the Book of Raziel is coming to pass!" Dr. Dee added.

Francis thought back some years when he saw a vision of England overrun with demons, with Damien leading them through the streets of England.

Can it be true? Is this war meant to be my destiny? Francis wondered, with a strange feeling that he knew it was.

"Dr. Dee, I was under the impression that your teachings were to help me attain a personal growth of realising my own true potential. That is what I believed!" Francis replied, weary of his mentor's request.

"To fight a mystical war using the pureness in the book is akin to defiling its very teachings! I do not think I can use my knowledge in that way!" Francis responded defiantly.

"I know how you feel Francis, but if you abandon your true potential now, the England you know may well disappear if we are overrun by the Spanish!" Dr. Dee argued.

"Ever since the incident in Navarre when I nearly killed a man, I lost faith in my powers and I still fear the book!" Francis confessed, a fact Dr. Dee knew too well.

"It was in self defence Francis, you must not blame yourself!" Dr. Dee told him, sensing Francis' anguish.

"Fear is a good thing Francis, it means you care, and you must use that fear now to bring caution to your powers," Dr. Dee explained.

Francis shook his head.

"I have never been a man of violence, and I'm not sure I can start now", Francis confessed.

"Francis, I do not know how many of your countrymen have been killed by our enemies practicing dark magic, but you have a duty to defend the men who you may one day rule," Dr. Dee reminded him, trying to appeal to his Tudor values, but Francis was still undecided.

Dr. Dee realised he would have to take a more serious stand, and eyed Francis squarely.

"This may be your only chance Francis before our country falls" Dr. Dee explained with a grave look in his face, which Francis finally took to heart.

After some seconds of serious thought, Francis finally agreed, knowing that Dr. Dee was right and that he had to put aside his own personal feelings, at least for now.

"Okay," Francis nodded apprehensively.

"You have made the right choice my boy!" Dr. Dee returned, resting his hand on Francis' shoulder.

Francis smiled, but deep down was uncomfortable with the whole situation.

"Meet me tonight!" Dr. Dee declared in an ominous tone, handing Francis a note detailing an address.

Francis nodded, while deep down also dreaded the prospect of using his powers in battle.

The Past
60. A MYSTICAL BATTLE

That evening, a horse-drawn carriage slowed to a halt in a small town called Wilton in Wiltshire, and Francis got out, paying the driver before continuing into the town on foot.

After walking a mile or two across the town, he arrived at an open area of land, eyeing the ancient structure of Stonehenge, glowing in the otherwise dark night, by what seemed an array of lit torches arranged within its interior.

As he got closer still, he could see the shadows of many men and women reflecting eerily against the age old stone boulders, created by the lit torches.

As he finally arrived within the stone structure enclosure itself, he found himself in a hive of activity with aged men and women rushing past, seemingly energised beyond the capability of their aged bodes.

Are all these men and women druids? Francis considered to himself as he gaped at their long white gowns.

As he made his way around the stone structure taking stock of what was going on, he paused as he watched the back of an aged man wearing a dark blue gown as he crawled around on all fours pouring out a white powder from a small bag as he meticulously etched out the last artistic symbols of a complex diagram onto the circular inner Stonehenge floor.

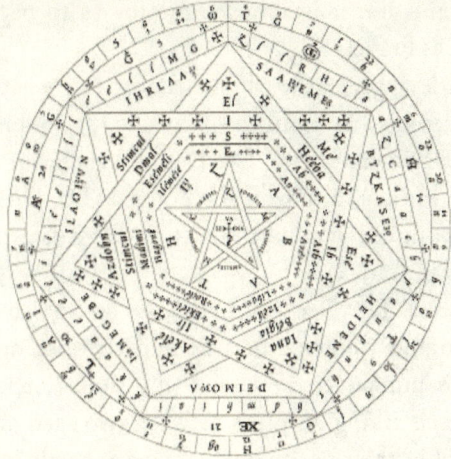

As Francis looked on in awe at the complex occult diagram, he noticed some familiar symbols within it that also appeared in the Book of Raziel.

Looking back at all the men and women around him, he realised they could all be tried for witchcraft and possibly burned alive for what they had convened to do.

His blood ran cold and he grew more and more fearful for his safety and the sanctity of his soul.

As he continued walking around the stone structure, he watched as the various druids prepared for the event ahead, some in deep meditation, whilst others resting up or talking among themselves.

As he watched the mannerisms of all the people around him, he got a strange feeling that they all seemed to know each other and knew what they were letting themselves in for. He also guessed that he was the youngest, based on the greying hair and aged bodies of the men and women around him.

As he stopped in front of a pile of white gowns, he felt a friendly hand on his shoulder.

"Francis!" a soft welsh toned voice whispered.

As Francis turned to the familiar voice behind him, he was relieved to see Dr. Dee smiling back at him, wearing the long dark blue gown he had seen earlier.

A sense of calm filled Francis now that he was no longer alone among complete strangers.

"Master Dee!" Francis responded smiling.

Master Dee picked up one of the white gowns from the pile and handed it to Francis.

"Welcome! Put this on, it is almost time for us to begin!" Dr. Dee added, smiling softly back at Francis.

Francis was a little apprehensive at the thought of what he was about to do, but Dr. Dee squeezed his arm gently as if sensing his doubts.

"Don't worry, just do your best," Dr. Dee added reassuringly.

Francis smiled a little, and put on the gown as Dr. Dee disappeared back to the centre of the complex symbolic structure for a last minute review before raising his hands in the air.

"Let us join forces!" Dr. Dee instructed the assembled druids with a raised voice, and the men and women stood up and crowded around in a circle and formed a complete human chain within the inner circle of the Stonehenge structure, with Francis taking his place between two aged men.

As they all settled in their positions, Dr. Dee seemed to take a deep breath as he readied himself.

"Everyone, please be seated!" Dr. Dee then instructed his followers as he began to mediate.

Simultaneously, all the druids sat down on the hard concrete ground, still holding hands, encircling the complex occult chalk markings etched on the stone floor.

"Let us begin!" instructed Dr. Dee ominously, as he clasped his hands together and bowed his head as he began to meditate. The druids all followed suit, bowing their own heads in meditation as well, including Francis.

As they each began to whisper, Francis could hear the words of ancient incantations recited in unison, over and over again. He himself began whispering the ancient words as Dr. Dee had taught him.

He shuddered, unsure if it was due to the cold evening winds or the fear of the dangers that lay ahead of him.

As the assembled druids continued their whispered chants, the previously calm and clear heavens above now seemed to cloud over in response to the power that was being called upon by the group's combined mystical chanting.

"What we desire is the amalgamation of power!" Dr. Dee shouted to the heavens, above the whispers of the druids, startling Francis.

"Who we ask is the giver of that power!" Dr. Dee shouted to the heavens again.

Slowly, the clear night above them began to crackle as if some mystical power was building.

"How we ask you to help us is to give us the power to leave our earthly guises and to deliver ourselves to our enemies!" He again shouted upwards.

"Where we stand is at one of the stations of your power!" Dr. Dee continued.

In among the clouds above, the skies grew even darker and then flashes of thunder and lightning caused the heavens to quake, jolting Francis momentarily from his concentration.

"We humbly desire this strength NOW!" Dr. Dee shouted, searching the sky for some divine inspiration.

As the flashes of lightning increased, a single bolt struck one of the Stonehenge stone boulders, illuminating it, with a strange luminous effect that seemed to spread from the first boulder to then somehow connect to both the boulders on either side of it, illuminating them as well. These newly illuminated boulders also connected to their adjoining boulders in a similar fashion until all the boulders that made up the stone structure of Stonehenge lit up like a shield around Francis and the druids.

As if the illuminated boulders were a sign, Dr. Dee began to whisper another incantation quietly to himself with his arms stretched down towards his occult symbol, seemingly willing unseen forces to do his bidding, and after some heavy incantation recitals, the occult etching below Dr. Dee's feet also began to illuminate with mystical energy.

One by one, each of the letters and symbols in the occult diagram began to light up, and when the final symbol was lit, a ball of energy materialised above Dr. Dee, hovering for a few seconds before slowly seeping into each of the people in the human chain, including Francis, and then finally into Dr. Dee, seemingly filling everyone with a powerful electric charge.

As Francis experienced the strange energy filling his entire being, he felt for the first time in his life, completely at peace with the world, seemingly feeling all wise and all knowing simultaneously.

All the intense meditation was for a specific purpose; they were attempting a mass *plane-walk*.

Francis had somehow managed to do it himself some years before, dreaming about his childhood London home, York Place, turning to rubble.

It seemed that being *the one,* through being chosen as the recipient of the Book of Raziel, he had somehow awakened this ability.

As Francis revelled in the euphoria of feeling like a higher power, he then had another strange sensation as if he had somehow split into two, now feeling as light as a feather, floating upwards into the heavens.

I am floating! Francis shuddered as he opened his eyes, finding himself actually floating in thin air.

Looking downwards, he could see that he was levitating some 30 or so feet above the Stonehenge structure, and looking further down to the ground level, he realised he could see his physical form sitting motionless below in the human chain between the two aged men.

From this height he also still managed to notice a thinning patch on his head in addition to the one he already knew about which aggravated him a little.

Looking up to the skies now, Francis realised he was not the only one having an out-of-body experience, as he saw the rest of the druids hovering with him as well, seemingly used to the experience but enjoying it nonetheless.

As he looked at their semi-transparent ghost-like forms, he lifted his hands in front of his face and realised his form was the same as the ghostly aura that once visited him.

Dr. Dee had achieved it; they were all now plane-walking, a transformation that allowed their spiritual selves to separate from their physical bodies, enabling them to float through different layers of existence.

As Dr. Dee's ghostly aura bobbed as he surveyed his small army, he hovered some more feet above them before speeding off into the night sky.

"Follow me! There is no time to lose!" he shouted to his makeshift army as he sped off into the night.

With Dr. Dee leading, the ghostly druids wasted no time in picking up speed following after him, followed by Francis, trying his best to keep up as they made their way a great distance across the English landscape, eventually passing an English coastline.

Eventually, Dr. Dee's aura hovered above a hive of vultures and crows making their way down towards some debris, he scanned the surrounding area, giving the druids and Francis time to catch up to his location.

As Francis and the druids wondered why they had stopped, the reasons became apparent as they focused on the debris floating in the sea below, seeing hundreds of fallen soldiers dressed in English regalia, their visible flesh being picked apart by scores of these hungry birds.

Francis felt sick to his stomach.

In the distance Dr. Dee spotted a faltering group of English galleons still fighting packs of flying demonic beasts.

"The game is afoot!" Dr. Dee shouted to his followers, pointing to the demonic forces laying siege to the galleons, and signalled his followers to bear down on the last of the English fleet to help defend them.

The last of the soldiers hanging on for dear life in their wrecked ships cringed in fear as they saw a ghostly army bearing down on them, but cheered as Dr. Dee's army began to fight the demonic beasts on their behalf.

The ghostly aura's split up, and battled the flying demonic beasts by using incantations that manifested fireballs and other spells. It didn't take them long to force the flying beasts back into the darkness from where they came.

As Francis did his best to defend himself against the few demonic beasts that came his way he was careful to use only the minimum power required to destroy them, still fearful of using some of the more powerful incantations that he knew.

Unbeknown to Dr. Dee and his followers, using similar powers of plane-walking, Damien was in their midst, floating through one of the remaining galleons still intact, the *Bonaventure*.

As members of the crew ran into his ghostly form they ran in the opposite direction, screaming like madmen.

Damien was on his own specific mission, and scanned the hands of each of the crew members that crossed his path as he searched for the magical ring that could locate the Book of Raziel for him.

Damien eventually eyed two men on the command deck, one of which he recognised as Sir Francis Drake due to the man's sharp cut golden beard and fiery-red curling hair.

As Damien eyed the lieutenant's fingers, he saw the elusive ring and grinned.

Sir Francis Drake stood with his lieutenant, Captain Stanley and they both turned to face Damien's ghostly form.

Sir Francis Drake, a stocky built man, stepped hesitantly forward and stood before Damien, trying to make sense of what he was looking at.

Without a word, as Sir Francis Drake made a move to unsheathe his sword, he and his lieutenant were both thrown back against a wall as a result of one of Damien's spells, knocking them out cold.

Damien then whispered another spell that magically extracted the ring from the lieutenant's finger, allowing it to hover in the air, while he whispered another spell that drew the ring towards him so he could review it more closely.

He smiled smugly as he surveyed his prize.

Looking out of a nearby open porthole, he scanned the debris until a crow caught his attention pecking at the carcass of an English soldier, and he whispered a spell that brought the crow under his command.

The crow stopped what it was doing, and flapped its wings towards Damien in the galleon, making its way through an open porthole.

The bird eventually landed on top of the unconscious Captain Stanley and locked its beady eyes on Damien, waiting for its orders.

Damien wasted no time and whispered his orders to the crow to collect the ring as it continued to hover in front of him and deliver to a secret location.

The crow immediately flapped its wings into action again and collected the ring in its claws before making its way back through the open porthole and up into the night sky to Damien's secret co-ordinates.

His work was now done, Damien quickly left the galleon.

As Francis destroyed the last of the demons in his vicinity, he eyed an aura fleeing a galleon away from the main fight, and as he managed to glimpse the face of the ghostly aura, he was shocked to recognise it as Damien.

I don't believe it! Francis thought as his heartbeat began to race.

He immediately chased after Damien.

As Damien floated up into the night sky, oblivious of Francis bearing down on him from behind, he could see Dr. Dee's ghostly army defeating his demonic manifestations.

No matter, I have the ring now! Damien thought as he made his escape, eyeing the crow flying off in the distance with the ring in its claws.

Damien was content.

As Francis watched Damien eyeing the crow in the distant, he noticed a glint in its claws, realising it must be of some importance to Damien and immediately whispered an incantation that caused a fireball to shoot out from his hand, hitting the crow dead on blowing it out of the sky right in front of Damien's eyes, leaving nothing more than its feathers and the ring to fall out of the sky.

The ring being too far away from Damien to recapture fell uncontrollably out of the night sky into the large expanse of the sea.

"No!" Damien shouted angrily, realising his prize was lost.

With his demonic forces diminished, he realised his efforts had been all for nothing. Knowing he should make his escape because he had drained his powers in manifesting his army of demons, his anger got the better of him as he searched the skies for the source of the attack.

As he turned in the direction of the bolt, he saw a ghostly aura whose face he also recognised closing in on him.

"Bacon?" Damien whispered to himself, shocked to see Francis had harnessed mystical powers.

He locked eyes with Francis, and they now hovered in the air facing each other.

"I should have known you were behind something like this!" Francis shouted angrily.

"It seems I have underestimated you Bacon!" Damien responded in a calm tone as he pondered his next step, knowing his powers had been severely weakened.

As Francis considered which incantation to use, Damien immediately whispered a spell that caused a rope to be manifested which wrapped itself around Francis' neck, strangling Francis physical self back at Stonehenge.

Damien gloated as he watched Francis suffocate.

From an initial confusion of not being able to grab the rope around his neck, Francis started to panic as he started to suffocate, grunting as he struggled to remove the rope around his neck, his ghostly aura began to weaken as his physical form back at Stonehenge started to die.

"How does it feel Francis?" Damien gloated.

Francis fought more frantically now, as the oxygen in his lungs began to deplete, still grunting and kicking to remove the rope, with no success.

"Now you will die for losing me my prize!" Damien shouted angrily at Francis.

Francis continued frantically to release himself from Damien's grip, but it was no use as everything around him began to fade into darkness.

Not too far away, as Dr. Dee assessed the efforts of his army's advances against the demons, he realised that Francis was missing.

As he desperately searched the carnage around him, he spotted Francis in the distance faltering to Damien's stranglehold.

"Francis!" he whispered gravely as he immediately charged off to his aid.

As Dr. Dee got closer, he could see the ghostly form of Francis nearly gone, and he immediately whispered an incantation causing Damien's own physical form, located in some secret location in Spain, to be inflicted with a searing pain through the chest.

In his secret location, Damien's physical form buckled to his knees as he tried to fight against the excruciating pain Dr. Dee had inflicted, while around him lay hundreds of dead men, with a handful still standing, all dressed in Spanish army attire.

All the men in the room had been enslaved under one of Damien's spells and each time one of Dr. Dee's army destroyed another demon, another soldier in the secret location would collapse, dead before they hit the ground.

Damien had used a *power of persuasion* spell to place the Spanish army under his control, and then used another more powerful ancient spell to draw out their smallest negative thoughts and desires to bend into that of an evil demonic beast which he then used for his own selfish needs.

Damien had taken a risk to push his powers to the limit in search of the ring, and it had all been for nothing as the ring was now lost at the bottom of the sea.

As Damien's ghostly aura whispered a spell to counteract Dr. Dee's attack, he realised he was not strong enough to fight Dr. Dee and his druid army that now also converged on him.

He quickly whispered a spell to command the last of the demons to attack Dr. Dee, at the cost of releasing Francis.

As the spell strangling Francis was removed, Francis coughed and spluttered as his physical form began to breathe again which in turn restored his ghostly aura back to a healthy look.

As Dr. Dee assessed the remaining beasts encircling him and his druid army, he realised he would have to let Damien escape for now, if they were to remain victorious.

Damien eyed Dr. Dee with loathing, before returning his gaze back to Francis.

"We will meet again Francis!" Damien shouted as he sped away in his escape.

By the time Dr. Dee and his army had destroyed the last of his demons, Damien was gone.

The battle was over and Dr. Dee led his tired army back to Stonehenge so they could reconnect with their physical selves. The war with Spain was over and England had won over the indefensible Spanish Armada.

It was at this point that Francis realised that Damien was too powerful for him, and that he would have to continue his mystical studies in harnessing the Book of Raziel if he was to ever have a chance of defeating Damien, if their paths ever crossed again.

61. THE BEAUMONT RETREAT

As Damien's ghostly aura reconnected with his physical self back at his secret location in Spain, the last of the Spanish soldiers King Phillip had assigned to him had fallen.

Some were vanquished by the lucky canon shots from English galleons, but the majority from the sorcery of Dr. Dee and his powerful druid army.

Damian's body was stiff.

He had pushed body and mind to their extremes because he thirsted for the chance to find the Book of Raziel, but it was not meant to be.

As he surveyed the bodies strewn around his secret location, he knew he would have to escape from Spain quickly before news of his failure reached the Spanish King.

He snatched a hooded cloak from one of the men that lay dead, and then began a fire to burn all traces of the soldiers who had died under his command.

As he sneaked out of what was an aged church 100s of years old, now smouldering in flames with the bodies of the innocent Spaniards forever hidden, he was in search of a carriage to take him back to France.

He walked on foot into a nearby Spanish village, and finding a lone coachman for hire, he quietly made his way over to him, grabbing him by the neck and whispered an incantation into his ear.

Damien used the last of his powers to take control of the coachman's weak mind, just as he did the dead soldiers who now lay burning behind him in the old church.

"Take me to the French border immediately!" Damien whispered with a weakened voice, before jumping into the carriage.

"Yes master!" the coachman responded in a dull emotionless tone, before climbing into his seat on top of the coach and whipping his horses into a gallop.

Unfortunately for Damien though, as King Phillip received news of his failed invasion, he was quick to send an army of guards to locate Damien and his missing soldiers.

Damien was captured just as he tried escape across the French border and was brought before the King.

Not being able to explain the whereabouts of the soldiers assigned to him, he was thrown into a Spanish prison and condemned to torture until he gave the whereabouts of the men put under his command.

The Past

62. BLOOD BROTHERS

November 1588. Parliament, London

With the Spanish war behind them, England moved to bring itself back to some level of normality, and being election time in Parliament, Francis revelled in his victory at the polls again, being returned MP [Member of Parliament] representing St. Albans, Ipswich and Cambridge simultaneously, having held previous positions as MP of Middlesex, Cornwall, Taunton, and Liverpool.

With an increasing knowledge of the legal system in England, Francis stood in the House of Commons, addressing other MPs as he talked about the corruption he saw in the current English legal system.

Francis opposed taxes for businesses and Government granted monopolies, and also moved that a tax bill to give monies to the Queen be extraordinary, such as if the country was at war. This amendment was passed thus finally establishing the base for the eventual ascendancy of Parliament over the Crown.

Francis also spoke out against feudal privileges and opposed the enclosure of common lands by land-owners and proposed to alter the language of the laws to make them accessible to the common man.

"As a lawyer, I have seen how the laws of the land are easily corrupted. Laws are made to guard the rights of the common folk, not to feed lawyers, and should be made so as to be read and understood by all!" Francis shouted fiercely to the loud cheers and agreement from his fellow MPs.

"Hang all of them, hang all the lawyers, but remember Bacon, you are a lawyer as well!" a backbencher shouted to the thunderous fresh applause and laughter of the rest of the house.

Francis merely smiled as he deep down knew his legal acumen was a means to an end to progress other matters that were closer to his heart.

In the public gallery, a young man stood up cheering in agreement with Francis and his name was Robert Devereux, 2nd Earl of Essex, dressed in the finest regimental regalia with a sword hanging from his waist.

In the aftermath of the death of his real father, Robert Dudley, Earl of Leicester, Francis uncovered another secret that he would have realised had he continued reading his uncle's day books, which was the revelation that Queen Elizabeth had TWO secret children. Robert Devereux was his younger brother.

Although Francis still had a stronger bond with his step-brother Anthony, Robert Devereux was his *true* blood brother and also a Tudor prince.

Like Francis, Robert was given to foster parents, and Walter & Lettice Devereux brought Robert up as their own child, and it now made sense to Francis why his real father, Robert Dudley secretly married Lady Essex when her husband died as he had read in a letter he received in France.

Robert Dudley did it because he wanted to be closer to his *son*.

With Robert Dudley taking a closer interest in Robert Devereux's upbringing, a unique bond formed between them, and they even joined forces on the battlefield in the recent victory against Spain.

Just as Francis and his newly revealed brother Robert had grown close since the recent death of their birth father, Robert Dudley, Robert [Devereux] had built up a bond with Queen Elizabeth, united in their grief for her childhood sweetheart.

As the brothers made their way down a walkway adjoining the Thames from Parliament, Francis, now sporting a flamboyant hat, complained about a recent reprimand he had received.

"I try to be a servant for the welfare of the people of England in parliament, only to be chastised and reprimanded for opposing the Queen's policies!" Francis complained.

"I think we have more machinery of government than is necessary. There are way too many parasites living off the labour of the industrious!" Francis moaned.

"I fear you are right Francis, but one day we will possess the power to make a difference!" Robert responded defiantly as a strong gust of wind forced the pungent smell of shit and rotten food into their faces from the Thames.

"God's bones!" Francis moaned again, shaking his head in disbelief.

Robert merely laughed.

"You get used to it!" Robert commented sniggering.

Francis continued shaking his head, wishing he had taken his carriage instead.

"Would you ever consider trying your hand at representing a borough at Parliament? I am sure you would be good at it." Francis queried, wanting to stop talking about himself.

"No, Francis," Robert responded.

"I would rather play the part of a great man on the stage, than the part of a fool in Parliament!" Robert continued, causing Francis to burst out laughing.

Robert Devereux, was a handsome young man, dignified and with great dash and spirit, but had a domineering egotism. His impulsive, ill disciplined and jealous nature, as well as an unreasonable ambition was as yet concealed.

From her disastrous confrontation with Francis when he discovered his true royal heritage, Robert Dudley ensured that Robert Devereux was informed of his royal birth at an earlier age, and being just 12, some years younger than Francis, helped him to more easily adjust to the news.

Although Francis served his Queen faithfully, he never really forgave her for deceiving him in his upbringing, and would forever distance himself from her emotionally, whereas Robert embraced her for all she was, and of course for what she could bestow upon him.

Those already in a position of power, such as Lord Burghley, saw that this could have dire consequences on his own position and also that of his son, having witnessed the influence Robert Dudley had on Queen Elizabeth.

One such scenario that highlighted such a risk to Lord Burghley's power was a period when Robert Dudley was still alive and Queen Elizabeth was very sick, and thinking she was going to die, she gave Robert Dudley the highest position in the land allowing him to have ruling power over England.

Fortunately for the Privy Council, she survived.

Due to this, Lord Burghley came to fear Robert Devereux, and this resulted in a policy of always trying to undermine Robert at every opportunity, and doing his utmost to block Robert's advancement and that of any of his friends and family, including Francis and his step-brother Anthony.

With regard to personality traits, Robert Devereux had unfortunately inherited a hot-headed temperament from his mother Queen Elizabeth, which placed them constantly at odds, arguing and disagreeing on many topics.

One such disagreement saw Robert stepping beyond reasonable levels of appropriate behaviour by unsheathing his sword in retaliation to Queen

Elizabeth slapping him across the face because he had mocked her aging looks in public.

Robert had to be dragged away from court by the guards, and reprimanded.

Although Queen Elizabeth was vexed by Robert's numerous outbursts and temper tantrums, she could not help but love her son.

63. WITCH HUNT

September 1589, North Sea

An armada of galleons flying the Danish flag progressed across a calm North Sea en route to Scotland with a royal cargo, Princess Anne, second daughter of the late King Frederick II of Denmark.

At barely sixteen years old, the Princess stood on the deck of her galleon, smiling as she inhaled the crisp sea air, contemplating her new life in Scotland, having recently married its Scottish King, James VI by proxy.

Suddenly, the Princess felt a dire change in the weather as the calm crisp breeze quickly whipped itself up into a whirlwind, and as she looked up to the sky to see what has caused the sudden change, the clear skies spooked her.

Looking down at the previously calm waters, she noticed that the undercurrents were also beginning to build up in an unearthly way.

Within a minute, the crews of each of the galleons in the Danish fleet began to scramble as they fought the fierce winds of an unearthly storm, frantically buckling down their cargo and loose items on deck.

Gripped with fear, the Princess held tightly onto a handrail in front of her for dear life as her crew frantically fought to control their ship through the storm.

"Princess! You must go down below!" shouted the voice of one of her guards from behind her, himself holding on to a strong rope to keep from being thrown overboard, but the Princess did not respond, focusing solely on maintaining her grip on the handrail in front of her for dear life.

At the same time, in a remote forest just outside of Copenhagen, Denmark, three powerful witches as ugly as each other, screamed and cackled around a cauldron bubbling over a fire.

They combined their powers to summon powerful dark magic to help them destroy the Princess and her Danish fleet.

The first old hag did her best to continue the onslaught of the strong winds as the second willed the undercurrents of the North Sea to build up causing high waves to crash against the ships, while the third witch held a small handmade doll whose face resembled the Danish Princess mischievously.

As the third witch forced a needle into the doll's stomach, the Danish Princess on board her wayward galleon felt an equivalent sharp stabbing pain in her stomach, causing her to let go of the railing as she collapsed to her knees in agony.

The guard, seeing the Princess fall to the deck and rolling around in pain, immediately let go of his own lifeline and fought through the billowing winds to go to her aid, edging progressively closer to her until he managed to reach her.

As the guard looked into her face, he could see was in a bad way and threw her over his shoulder and made the precarious short steps through the billowing winds to the safety of the lower decks of the galleon.

The first two witches back in the remote forest continued their mischief, now intent on forcing the air and sea to smash the Danish fleet into pieces, with the third witch still trying to kill the princess, forcing another needle into the handmade doll's stomach.

The Princess, back on the galleon, was now below deck, being helped by the guard who had saved her and her ladies-in-waiting immediately felt the sharp jab of the second needle and doubled over with pain again, crashing to the floor.

Amidst the fearful screams of her ladies-in-waiting, the princess was carried through the galleon's corridors as it rocked erratically from its battering by the strong winds.

As the storm got progressively worse, the positioning of the ships became more and more precarious as the strong winds pushed them dangerously close to each other, but suddenly out of nowhere, a mystical path emerged leading a calm exit out of the storm.

As the crews of each of the galleons spotted the pathway, they scrambled to steer their ships through it, one by one finding salvation out of the storm and back to calm seas.

Back in the remote forest, the witches were furious, and began fighting among themselves as they lay blame to each other's weakness in not maintaining their upper hand in destroying the Danish armada.

The Danish fleet, having sailed out of the storm via the mystical path now headed to safety in the nearby Scandinavian port of Norway.

Meanwhile, in the observation room of Dr. Dee's Mortlake home, a handful of druids together with Francis are in deep meditation around a small occult pentagram as Dr. Dee channelled their combined powers in maintaining the mystical path that had appeared as salvation to the Danish fleet aiding their escape from the unearthly storm.

Through his conversation with Angels via his *skryer* Edward Kelly many months before, Dr. Dee had received warnings that a group of witches were conspiring to block the union of King James with that of his Danish wife through the use of dark magic, so Dr. Dee had called an impromptu meeting of Francis and a handful of druids to set about negating the witches powerful magic.

Something was indeed rotten in the state of Denmark! Francis thought as he sat around the pentagram whispering ancient spells under his breath, which channelled his power into that of his mentor. Together they had succeeded in overcoming the power of the Danish witches.

It was the battle with Damien that made Francis realise the powerful threat of dark magic on the unsuspecting world, and now that he had proven to both himself and the druids that he had a formidable skill in the mystical arts, they invited him to join their secret order.

Francis accepted immediately, realising the good things he could achieve with the mystical powers he now possessed.

The secret order that Francis joined this time, was called *The Order of the Rosy Cross*, a secret society of mystics, whose English army was led by Dr. Dee himself.

The order was allegedly formed in late medieval Germany, and held a doctrine built on esoteric truths of the ancient past, which, concealed from the average man, provided insight into nature, the physical universe and the spiritual realm to those that could harness it. The order was symbolized by a red rose.

It was from this point onwards that Francis found out, that, just as there were *normal* wars going on all over the world, there were just as many mystical wars where those that wielded powerful dark magic such as Damien were a danger to everyone.

The battle against Damien was to be the first of many mystical battles Francis would participate in, and over the following years, Francis was to aid Dr. Dee and members of their order in their secret war defending all that was good, against the many powerful evil warlords that would rise up thirsting for world domination.

64. THE DUEL

It was early morning as Robert Devereux, who was in good spirits, manoeuvred the many corridors of Richmond palace, the newly favoured Thameside location of Queen Elizabeth, whom he was on his way to meet.

As he navigated the many corridors, he came upon one of her favoured courtiers, Sir Charles Bloutt, and as the early sunlight glinted through a nearby window it reflected off of a golden ornament on the courtier's arm, momentarily blinding Robert.

"Pray tell me how you came upon that grand ornament?" Robert asked pointing to the beautiful object with a hint of jealousy in his voice.

Sir Charles proudly shows off the ornament to Robert Devereux.

"This? It is a present from our fair Queen, given to me just yesterday for my exceptional skills at jousting!" he smiled.

"I see how it is going to be; every fool must have his trinket!" Robert added mocking Sir Charles as he continued past.

Sir Charles' smile immediately turned to an angry scowl.

"I resent that comment sire and demand you withdraw it!" Sir Charles ordered, blocking Robert's exit.

"I will not!" Robert objected childishly as he tried to continue past him.

"I will ask you again sire, otherwise I must challenge you to a duel!" Sir Charles continued, standing his ground.

"You are indeed more of a fool than I initially thought then!" Robert goaded him, his pride forcing him not to apologise.

Sir Charles took off a glove and threw it in Robert's face.

Angered by the glove hitting him, Robert raised his fist to punch Sir Charles, but Sir Charles immediately unsheathed his sword in defence, at which point Robert backed away from the sword that was now pressing against his chest.

"You prove to dishonour me, so I challenge you to a duel! Do you accept?" Sir Charles asked again as his sword pressed against Robert's exquisite doublet.

Robert paused for a moment as he realised the predicament he has just placed himself in, knowing that in addition to being an expert jouster, Sir Charles was also a formidable swordsman, much better than even he was.

"I accept!" Robert was forced to agree, his stubbornness not to apologise forcing him to accept the duel.

"I will meet you outside at the great oak tree in the grounds of the palace at noon!" Sir Charles informed him defiantly.

"Agreed!" Robert responded coldly, his mocking tone now gone.

With Robert agreeing, Sir Charles huffed as he stepped aside allowing Robert to continue past. As he made his way down the corridor, Robert contemplated how foolish he had been to get himself into such a situation.

Later that morning as news of the duel spread across the palace, a crowd gathered to observe the fencing dual between Robert and Sir Charles.

One female observer, her face disguised behind a dark hooded cloak, stood at the back of the crowd, watching the activities.

As the duel commenced, an adjudicator positioned himself between the two men, as they stood at the ready with unsheathed swords, finally flagging them both to begin.

As both men fought aggressively with their swords for a number of minutes, Sir Charles maintained the upper hand, eventually managing to disarm Robert, wounding him in the arm in the process.

The adjudicator ran to Robert, stopping the swordplay as he ascertained the extent of the wound before declaring Sir Charles the winner.

Robert's arm as well as his pride was wounded as he walked away a sore loser.

At the end of the duel, the hooded female spectator hurried away into the palace, and as she entered the court, she removed her hood to reveal that she was one of Queen Elizabeth's ladies-in-waiting.

She rushed down a number of corridors until she arrived at a particular room with guards posted outside, but on recognising her, they allowed her entry into the room.

In the room, Queen Elizabeth was pacing its full length like a caged and restless animal, worriedly turning a gold encrusted onyx ring around and around on one on her long slender fingers, knowing full well that Robert had foolishly involved himself in a duel.

"What news?" she shouted in a worried tone as her lady-in-waiting rushed into the room.

"He is wounded, but it is not deep - he lives!" the lady-in-waiting responded happily.

Queen Elizabeth let out a deep sigh of relief at the news, holding her hands against her breast, and saying a prayer of thanks to god before sitting down with her lady-in-waiting as she gave Queen Elizabeth an account of the duel and how it came about that Robert had lost.

"I am glad of it! Unless there is somebody to take down his pride, it will be impossible to get any good of him," Queen Elizabeth commented solemnly, angry that Robert had placed himself in such a dangerous position.

Queen Elizabeth ushered out her lady-in-waiting as she mulled over the event, shaking her head in dismay at her son's impetuous nature.

65. MENDING WOUNDS

A wounded Robert Devereux sat with Queen Elizabeth in a quiet room away from prying eyes, his arm bandaged in a sling, and was now having to endure a chastisement from his Queen for endangering his life.

"Today your impetuous nature almost got you killed!" Queen Elizabeth scolded him.

"Mother, I am not in the mood for" Robert replied angrily, before being stopped mid sentence by the Queen as she covered Robert's mouth with her own hand, touched at being addressed as his mother.

"Hush!" she ordered him.

As Queen Elizabeth stared at the many rings on her hand as it covered Robert's mouth, the moon shining in from a window behind her reflected off of one in particular that contained an image of a face.

"Do you see this ring?" she asked as she removed her hand from his mouth, clenching her fist tightly to highlight the many rings on her hand.

She pushed out one finger in particular where she wore a dark blue onyx ring with a small image of Queen Elizabeth on it.

"Yes?" Robert replied, nodding.

"Your father gave me this in celebration of your birth," she smiled, remembering her childhood sweetheart, Robert Dudley, Earl of Leicester, now dead.

As Robert eyed the ring, Queen Elizabeth removed it from her finger.

"Take this ring Robert, as a talisman of my protection. If you should ever become involved in troubles or difficulties of any kind and especially if you should lose my favour, either by your own misconduct or by the false accusations of your enemies, send me this ring," she told him as she put it on one of his fingers, finding it a perfect fit.

As Robert stared at the ring his eyes began to well up with tears.

"It will serve to remind me of my love for you, my son, and incline me to pardon and save you, whatever the troubles," she added in a soft motherly tone.

"Such a thing could never happen, my Queen!" Robert replied, feeling saddened, knowing deep down, that his impetuous nature may one day lead to him calling in such a favour.

"We are both of the same impetuous and excitable temperaments Robert, and this ring will always remind me of how dear you are to me," she confessed.

"OK," Robert whispered back, staring for a few seconds at the miniature cameo of Queen Elizabeth etched into its onyx face.

"I will wear it with pride," he added, kissing it.

Queen Elizabeth held his hand and they both continued to talk late into the night.

66. Making of a Hero

For Robert Devereux, the next few years were to shape his career and catapult him to the level of a hero among his countrymen. However, these years would also mark the beginning of his downfall.

1589

Due to Robert Devereux's thirst for battle, mixed with his stubborn nature, he disobeyed an order from Queen Elizabeth to join an English Armada sent to occupy Portugal and North Western Spain.

If the battle had ended well, there may have been little the Queen could have done to reprimand him, but it did not end well, and Robert made a hasty return to England after making an unsanctioned truce with the Spanish, which caused him a severe reprimand for his dishonourable actions.

1590

Robert Devereux marries the widow of Sir Philip Sydney, the daughter of Sir Francis Walsingham, and is chastised by Queen Elizabeth for taking a wife without her consent whom she felt was 'below his degree'.

1591

Robert Cecil, son of Lord Burghley, was knighted and made a member of the powerful Privy Council.

Robert Devereux was given command of a small English force sent to support Henry of Navarre against a Catholic uprising in France. During this campaign, his leadership proved inefficient and although he showed a certain reckless courage, the expedition, again, was unsuccessful.

Robert Devereux spends the next four years resolved to securing *domestical greatness*, becoming a Privy Councillor, and leader of a forward-thinking group at court, which were opposed to the entrenched Cecil family.

1593

The Queen awards Francis Bacon, Twickenham Park and a villa with nearly 90 acres of parkland, opposite her Palace in Richmond.

The play's *Faustus* and *The Jew of Malta* are performed by the Lord Admiral's Men at 'The Rose' playhouse.

1594

Francis becomes co-treasurer of Gray's Inn, a position previously held by Sir Nicholas Bacon.

At an annual Christmas revel, Francis directs a theatrical event for members of Gray's Inn, and on 28th December (Innocents Day), the play *The Comedy of Error's* has its first performance.

1595

On 3rd January, the Christmas/New Year revels at Gray's Inn finished with a performance entitled *The Order of the Knights of the Helmet*.

In August, a performance of *The Isle of Dogs* is performed at the Swan playhouse, written by Thomas Nashe and Ben Jonson, which was a satirical comedy based on the Queen and some other famous noblemen of the day.

Due to its popularity, it was not long before it incurred the wrath of the Privy Council which saw it as seditious, with news of the contents of the play reaching the Queen via the Privy Council, who immediately ordered the arrest of the people responsible.

Ben Jonson and two of the actors were immediately arrested and imprisoned, while Thomas Nashe, who was away at the time, avoided prison by claiming that he had only written the introduction and first act. As a consequence of these arrests, all London theatres were closed for two months and threatened with demolition. By the time Thomas Nashe returned, the Privy Council had censured all his works.

As Queen's Counsel Extraordinaire, and legal adviser at the time, Francis made use of all his skills of persuasion and contacts to ensure the three men spent minimal time in prison, but it was an important reminder to him and his writing group that England was anything but a society of free expression, and reminded Francis and his secret writing group that they had to be extra diligent in their publication to maintain their anonymity and safety.

1596

Robert continued to seek military honours, and as a result, when King Philip II of Spain planned an expedition to support Roman Catholics in Ireland, Queen Elizabeth was persuaded to counter this threat with an attack on Cadiz, with Robert joining as joint commander of the force.

This time, he proved himself as the hero of the hour, putting to land with a detachment of men and drove out all before him until he reached the market-place of Cadiz, which surrendered 'in great order'. He returned to England a hero, passing through the streets of London to the cheers of jubilation from his countrymen.

As the Earl of Essex reached the entrance of the Queens residence, York Place, there was an even bigger crowd waiting for him and his men. As a sign of success and his achievements, he raised his sword high in the air again, to the thunderous applause of the crowd.

From one of the windows, Queen Elizabeth looked on at the popularity of the Earl of Essex. Her face turned from happiness to jealousy as they cheered for him. As one of her advisors, Robert Cecil, entered the room, she turned to face him.

"Ma'am, I must warn you that the Earl is becoming dangerously popular to the people of England and to his army. For a soldier to rise above his station as he does, his popularity could exceed your own," he explained in no uncertain terms.

Queen Elizabeth frowned but did not respond, and turned back to the window to watch her son enjoy the applause of his kinsmen.

Further notable plays generated by Francis and his *good pens* in the following years were *The Merchant of Venice, A Midsummer Night's Dream*, and *The Two Gentlemen of Veron.* Each of these drew on many personal and professional experiences of Francis' life such as his knowledge of Law in *The Merchant of Venice*, also including historical facts concerning a wreck that occurred earlier in the year into its storyline.

1597

Robert continued his expeditions, this time to intercept the Spanish treasure fleet in the Azores, but the attempt failed, largely due to his own mismanagement of his army.

Francis publishes the Essays *with Colours of Good and Evil* and *Meditationes Sacrae.*

Francis writes *Maxims of the Law.*

Francis courts and then proposes marriage to the wealthy Lady Hatton, who refuses, instead marrying his rival and enemy, Sir Edward Coke, now Attorney-General and extremely rich.

King James writes a short piece of literature entitled *Daemonologie* to persuade sceptics on the importance of knowledge about witchcraft.

Late one night in the back room of *The Hartshorn*, an alehouse that bordered his Gorhambury estate in St Albans, Francis and other men were dressed in ceremonial gowns adorned with ancient symbols, enrolled new members into a secret order.

Beyond a stone altar at one end of the room adorned with ceremonial objects, three of the room's walls were decorated with the death scene from the play *Venus and Adonis,* also containing references to the Bacon family home Gorhambury as well as the animal kingdom.

1598

The play *All's Well That Ends Well,* written by Francis' writing group, is first performed and is based on the difficult marriage between Edward De Vere and Anne Cecil, Lord Burghley's daughter.

The Past

67. EXPOSED

The play *Richard II* written by Francis' writing group is first performed, which focused once again on royal succession, playing on the question of the deposing, and voluntary abdication of a king.

Unfortunately, the storyline incensed and horrified Queen Elizabeth immensely, causing her to order the writer to be found and imprisoned for the treasonable aspects of the play.

With the stakes increased that their cover was now seriously at risk, Francis needed a scapegoat, as although many of the play's by his writing group had the name 'Speare-shaker' on their title, there was no actual author that it referred to.

Remembering a conversation with a printer's apprentice by the name of Richard Field, who worked for a George Bishop, one of his principal printers, the apprentice once spoke of a boyhood friend of his that had travelled to London from Stratford-upon-Avon to make his fortune. This friend had a surname that stuck in Francis' mind, 'William Shakespere'.

Francis, now 36, in his advisory role to Queen Elizabeth managed to avoid the association with the writing group by devising an ingenious plan of displaced identity, using the man from Stratford-upon-Avon's name as a scapegoat, paying him handsomely for the use of his name.

Subsequent performances of the play were performed with the offending portions removed, in particular, a deposition scene, and although some plays had previously been published with the name 'Shake-speare' in its title, all further plays by the writing group were now to be published with the full name 'William Shake-speare' appearing on their title pages for the first time.

Although forced to use the name "William" as the forename for the many plays being written by his writing group, as Francis considered the Germanic version of the forename, which was *Wilhelm*, he soon dawned on him that he was meant to associate with the Stratfordian.

Breaking down the Germanic version, the first part "Will" meant *will or desire*, and "helm" meant *helmet, protection*, meant that the name "William" actually meant to *Will of the Helmet* in German.

To Francis, it seemed that fate had already decreed the pseudonym 'William Shake-speare' was always meant to adorn the title pages of the many plays penned by his writing group.

The Past

68. MYSTICAL CAMPAIGN

Under the cover of night, a handful of small boats filled with what seemed to be a band of missionaries due to their matching dark hooded cloaks, slowly rowed their way from the Northumberland coast out to Lindisfarne Castle on Holy Island.

As the castle came into view, dramatically perched on a rocky crag, one of the passengers stood up and removed his hood to reveal it was none other than Dr. Dee, with the face of Francis Bacon peering out from the hood of another cloak.

As the moonlight shone on the other men in the small boats, their faces of the other hooded passengers were members of 'The Order of the Rosy Cross'.

Dr. Dee looked uneasily at the fortified castle built atop a volcanic mound in the distance.

As the boats moored quietly at the bottom of the mound, some of the men gasped at the rocky mountain they knew they would have to climb.

As Francis looked up at the overwhelming sight of the castle, he could not help but compare it to the mythical Greek palace *Mount Olympus*, home of Zeus and other gods and goddesses, which also supposedly stood on a similar styled elevated mound.

As Francis scanned the faces of the other members of the order, seeing only men instead of the usual male and female mix, it highlighted the severity of the mission.

Some, including Francis even wielded swords as a secondary means of defence in case their mystical powers proved insufficient on this dangerous mission.

Dr. Dee, having received reports from scores of villages on and around the Northumberland coast, that a there had been an increasing occurrence of women disappearing without a trace, that is until one young girl who managed to escape from her captors in Lindisfarne Castle on Holy Island.

This young girl risked her life by jumping into the sea, barely avoiding the rocky shore below, describing her ordeal at being told she was to be a sacrifice by a crazed supposed sorcerer. That was all the information Dr. Dee needed to mobilise his men.

"Onward and upwards!" Dr. Dee whispered loud enough for his band to hear as he led the way up the side of the steep mountain, aided by a long staff.

A few of the men did a double-take, but were not going to abandon their leader and made haste after him up the rocky mountain to the unknown dangers of the castle above.

After a hard climb up the side of the mountain, they all successfully reached the top, arriving at the closed drawbridge of the castle which also afforded a deep moat leading down to a perilous drop, but before any of them could decide the next move, Dr. Dee had already whispered an incantation that mustered up a sorcerer's fire blast, which he aimed at the ropes holding the drawbridge in place, forcing the drawbridge to come crashing down.

The ground shook as the drawbridge collapsed in front of them removing their element of surprise. With their element of surprise now gone, Dr. Dee dispensed with his whispering.

"For the crown!" he shouted defiantly as he charged across the drawbridge with his small army now invigorated for battle. As they kept close, some unsheathed their swords and held them up in an attacking position as they ran, ready for anything.

As they all crossed the drawbridge, they found themselves in an open courtyard and regrouped in a defensive circle, but they were confused to find no enemies to fight, just the eerie emptiness of the courtyard.

As Francis and the other men scanned the rooftops and dark recesses of the courtyard, they were perplexed.

"Are you sure this is the right place?" Francis asked Dr. Dee as they all scanned the empty courtyard, barely noticing a line of ten or so black crows that had perched on the top of the inner wall of the castle, sitting motionless watching their every move.

"There was supposed to be a full regiment that guarded this castle!" Francis commented as he stood by Dr. Dee, with a broadsword raised high in the air.

Dr. Dee nodded as his inquisitive eyes seemed to penetrate the closed doors leading into the castle. He could feel the unspeakable devilish activities that had been going on within the castle walls.

"Do not be mistaken men. There is a dark evil here!" Dr. Dee responded defiantly, staring up at the crows that were still looking down on them.

Dr. Dee could feel that he and his men were being watched through the eyes of the crows and immediately whispered an incantation that brought forth another fireball, sending it in the direction of the crows.

The crows reacted quickly by taking flight to dodge the fireball, and magically transformed themselves into a pack of hungry fire breathing dragons.

The battle was afoot and the men all scrambled to action fighting off the onslaught of dragons while dodging their fiery breath that could incinerate any one of them if they were not careful.

Dr. Dee, sensing a powerful evil from deep within the castle, followed his instinct and forced his way through a set of unwelcoming doors leading to the inner depths the castle.

Francis and the other men battled the dragons using a mixture of magical power and swords when they did not have enough time to muster an incantation.

Having seen Dr. Dee break away from the fight and enter the castle, Francis also felt the pull of some powerful evil, and decided to follow his old mentor through the same doors, but as he did, a number of dragons swooped down in front of him, seemingly blocking his entry.

Francis had no option but to continue the fight in the courtyard with the other men.

✝

Inside, Dr. Dee made his way down a myriad of darkened empty corridors with an uneasy feeling about him that he was being watched and held on tightly to his long staff as he continued down a corridor, feeling as if he was being drawn towards some dark evil presence.

The long corridor finally led him into a large dining room, which housed the longest dining table he had ever seen. The room was dark and miserable.

As he moved around the room he closed in on the table and eyed a set of manacles that had been nailed into the thick oak of the table, set in such a manner as to shackle a set of arms and legs of some unfortunate prisoner.

In the middle of the set of manacles was a large red mark that had stained the table surface.

Dr. Dee deduced that table had been used to either torture someone, or more likely as a sacrificial table where the women that had disappeared may have met their unfortunate deaths.

Dr. Dee could feel the scores of sacrifices that had been performed in this very room of innocent young girls.

"Hell's spawn! Where are you? Show yourself!" Dr. Dee shouted in anger, his voice echoing across the huge expanse of the room, but there was no answer.

As he tried to focus on pinpointing the source of the dark evil that he could sense, he was drawn to look at the furthest end of the table where there seemed to be a single place setting with a half eaten mound of flesh on the plate.

Dr. Dee was adamant that the dark evil he sensed was hidden somewhere in the room.

"I said show yourself!" Dr. Dee challenged again before whispering an incantation that seemed to reverberate around the whole room, forcing an invisible form to forcibly solidify into the lone chair at the end of the table.

The bearded man with greying hair dressed in a blood red cloak, seemed to be of a similar age to Dr. Dee.

"Bravo Master Dee!" the unknown man commended him, seemingly knowing Dr. Dee.

As Dr. Dee eyed his prey, he recognised him as a one-time friend, and old member of 'The Order of the Rosy Cross', having both learned the art of the mystics from the same teacher many decades before.

Dr. Dee was taken aback.

"Lord Strange? I thought you had given up your foolhardy attempts at world domination a long time ago!" Dr. Dee scowled.

"It is true. I have abandoned that particular quest!" Lord Strange confessed in a mocking tone.

"I now merely seek the power to control the fools who run our fair country. They bleed us, so I thought why not bleed a few of my own eh?" he mocked.

"Please, I beg you! Stop these evil ways before it is too late!" Dr. Dee replied, trying to appeal to Lord Strange's sensibilities.

"It is already too late for me Dee, for indeed my soul is truly damned due to my many past deeds. Satan's creatures will take me one day that I am sure," Lord Strange replied, seemingly talking to himself.

"Give up your sinister ways! My men will soon defeat your dragons and come and help me to defeat you!" Dr. Dee told him, his words recognising Lord Strange as being a stronger master of the mystics than he ever was.

Lord Strange gave Dr. Dee a condescending sneer.

"Do not be so sure Master Dee!" Lord Strange laughed.

"Why? Have you set some sort of trap for them?" Dr. Dee shouted worriedly, looking back in the direction of the men he left to fight in the courtyard.

"I knew you and your merry band would come after that silly girl escaped, so I have taken certain precautions to ensure you interference will be short lived!" Lord Strange confessed mischievously causing Dr. Dee to fear for the life of his men.

"They were your friends once! Think about what you are doing Lord Strange! Stop this!" Dr. Dee begged.

Just as Dr. Dee decided to return to help his men, Lord Strange whispered his own incantation, which lifted Dr. Dee in the air and slammed him forcefully against a far wall, disorientating him.

Back at the courtyard where Francis and his friends seemed to be making good progress against the dragons, a set of double doors blew open, revealing the missing soldiers that had previously manned the castle, all brandishing bows and arrows.

Just as Francis and the men were about to cheer at their support, they noticed a cold look in their faces and that their eyes were black and devoid of any life.

These men were now the walking dead army of whoever controlled them.

"Stop! Snap out of it!" Francis shouted to the soldiers, but their souls, like the lives they once lived, were lost forever.

The soldiers stepped forward and lined up together in unison like puppets and simultaneously raised their bows, jerking back their bowstrings and loading in an arrow, taking aim at Francis and his friends.

The soldier's then let their arrow's take flight.

"Everyone watch out!" Francis shouted as he and many of his order ran for cover as they tried to dodge a hail of arrows.

Most, like Francis managed to get to safety in time, but some were not so lucky and fell under the heavy onslaught of arrows to their death.

Francis and the remaining members of the order realised they were no match for the soldiers and the last of the dragons, but nonetheless rose defiantly to avenge their fallen comrades.

As they fought for their lives, Francis saw that the soldiers were mere puppets and knew the only way to stop the bloodshed and to ensure victory was to stop the puppet master.

With a heavy heart, Francis fought his way through the heavily defended path into the castle, leaving the other members of the order to fight on without him.

As the doors closed behind him separating him from his friends in the courtyard, he knew he had to be quick.

69. UNLEASHED POWER

As Francis rushed down lit corridors that reminded him of the royal palaces of Hampton Court, his senses pulled him towards the same dark evil he had felt earlier.

As thoughts raced through his mind about whether Dr. Dee was safe, Francis heard an almighty crash coming from a room up ahead.

He quickly gathered speed as he headed towards a set of closed doors where the crashing sounds seemed to be coming from, and as he rushed at the doors, he whispered an incantation that blew the doors off its hinges.

With his sword raised high, he slid into the room, finding himself in a large dining room where Dr. Dee was being strangled by a man he did not recognise.

"Master Dee!" Francis shouted as he saw the battered face of his old mentor.

Lord Strange merely glanced at Francis as his stranglehold continued to drain the last of Dr. Dee's life, whispering an incantation that fired off a powerful fireball that should have decimated Francis.

Francis was ready, having whispered an incantation of his own into his sword, raising it just in time to deflect the fireball away.

"Who the hell are you?" Lord Strange barked as Francis managed to deflect his onslaught.

"My name is of no importance, but I think you are the one that will know hell!" Francis shouted defiantly fearing the life of his old mentor and leader.

As the thoughts within Francis finally clouded over with anger at how his old mentor had been battered, the full power of the white and black magic became twisted into one and was drawn into his fist clenched around his broadsword.

Feeling the power within him fighting for a release, Francis had no time to think about what to do next and just relinquished control, allowing the fullness of the power within him to manifest.

He aimed his broadsword at Lord Strange and then stopped fighting the black and white powers within him, and with a calm release, his inner power used the sword as a conduit, and shot out an almighty blast that penetrated deep into Dr. Dee's attacker, causing his whole body to burst into flames.

As Lord Strange cried out in pain, his scream echoed across the large room, sending a shiver down Francis' spine.

Seconds later, the body that was Lord Strange disintegrated into ashes, leaving a mound of smouldering dust where he once stood.

Francis fell immediately to his knees, not sure whether the sudden weakness was from the strain of his mystical outburst or the anguish at having killed a man.

Eyeing Dr. Dee's unmoving body nearby, Francis mustered up the last of his strength to crawl to him, and as his trembling hand checked for signs of life, he was relieved as his old master let out a groan.

"Master Dee!" Francis shrieked with joy.

Dr. Dee groaned again, but gave Francis a pained smile through some broken teeth and a bloodied face.

"How are you feeling?" Francis asked.

"I'll live my boy. Help me up?" Dr Dee responded as he slowly regained consciousness.

With that, Francis helped his old mentor back to the remaining members of 'The Order of the Rosy Cross' where they paid tribute to their fallen comrades.

The Past

70. INVISIBLE COLLEGE

In the aftermath of the grief of those that had fallen at the battle on Holy Island, the severely depleted membership of 'The Order of the Rosy Cross' had become a concern as it had left Europe vulnerable to attack from other's like Lord Strange.

Due to the hardened persecution of those that were accused of practicing the mystical arts many druids went underground and out of sight, so new druids joining the order were few and far between.

Because of this, there was a consensus to take the drastic steps of publicly canvassing for new members.

Dr. Dee colluded with Francis on an idea to create an *invisible college* where those that understood the ancient teachings of mysticism could gather and collaborate in secrecy for the greater good of mankind, and as Francis made use of his international contacts across Europe, it did not take long before news of this college spread across the globe.

With a high demand in interest to join their secret order, it quickly regained its numbers and also managing to create a truly global network of members to continue the fight.

71. LOSS OF FAVOUR

Greenwich Palace, 1599

Robert Devereux in typical fashion continued to press the Queen for advancement, and was eventually appointed Earl Marshal of England, a remarkable sign of Royal favour, even though Robert and the Queen continued to have many disagreements.

Finally given the opportunity to remove a rebellion in Ireland, the expedition proved disastrous despite having a well-equipped army.

In late September, upon Robert's unsanctioned return from Ireland before the battle had been finished, he immediately went to see Queen Elizabeth at Nonesuch Palace in Surrey.

Without waiting for his arrival to be announced to the Queen, he barged straight into her bedchambers finding her not yet fully dressed or wigged and as a penalty for his disrespect, she immediately confined him to his private rooms.

The next day, the Privy Council met with him, and after a five hour interrogation of his actions during his charge of putting down the rebellion in Ireland, they found his flight from Ireland tantamount to a desertion of duty and put him under house arrest at York House.

With Queen Elizabeth's most trusted ally, Lord Burghley, dying the year before, his only surviving son, the slightly deformed hunched back Robert Cecil, whom Lord Burghley had groomed to continue in his footsteps, followed in his father's efforts to keep Robert Devereux from growing in power and stature.

The following year, on June 5th, many months after his confinement, Robert was finally tried for his crimes, which resulted in him being deprived of public office, and sent into virtual confinement, committing him to Essex House.

Enraged at his sentence, Robert believed this reprimand was purposefully brought on by his enemies in the Privy Council, namely Robert Cecil and Sir Walter Raleigh in their attempts to keep him on a short leash.

Having lost much of his power and creditability due to him being deprived of public office and stripped of much of his privileges, Robert now sat forlorn at his desk in Essex House.

With fire in his eyes, he placed a newly written letter into an envelope and sealed it, before having it secretly delivered to Scotland where a final messenger accepts it and makes his way down a darkened hallway into a grand room decorated with gold and expensive tapestries.

As the messenger enters the room, the door fails to close and is left ajar as he enters.

"Sire, I have a letter from Robert Devereux, 2nd Earl of Essex," the messenger explains to a mysterious man in the room.

"Read it!" a Scottish voice orders impatiently.

"He asks for your renewed support in his attempts to perform a coup against his enemies," the messenger reads with surprise.

"Does the boy still desire to usurp his mother, and take the throne?" the mysterious voice asks.

"It seems so sire," responds the messenger, now feeling a little unsettled that the letter contained details of a planned coup against England's Queen.

"He also states that he has the support of his army still fighting in Ireland, and believes the people of England will follow him," the messenger continued, now feeling even more unsettled at the news.

The mysterious voice began to laugh out loud. His chair creaks as he rises from it and paces the grand room as he considers what to do.

"He is a fool! Reply to his letter and confirm our support!" the mysterious voice finally barks back at the messenger.

"You are going to support his coup sire?" the messenger asks with a confused stare, unsure that he had understood his master's response correctly.

The mysterious voice made his way out of the room, revealing his face to be King James VI of Scotland, with the messenger immediately behind him.

"Of course not you fool! I will ensure that he does not obstruct my succession by helping him to his own downfall!" he laughed.

"Send a message also to our spies in London and advise them of the Earl's activities and ensure my cousin Elizabeth is notified of his plans on the eve of his supposed attack!" King James finished as he walked down the hall laughing even more loudly.

"Yes sire!" the messenger nodded, now understanding that his master was planning to expose the Earl of Essex a traitor to his cousin.

King James bellowed with joy as he disappeared down the hall.

72. THOUGHTS OF TREASON

Essex House, London

Essex House occupied a location where the Outer Temple, part of the original headquarters of the Knights Templar had previously stood, and was immediately adjacent to the Middle Temple, one of the four principal Inns of Court, one of which was Gray's Inn.

Having just finished a hearty meal, Francis and his brother Robert Devereux retire to a cosy room where two chairs were placed beside a small fire as spiced wine warmed in a cauldron above it.

The house was substantial, boasting 42 bedrooms, plus a picture gallery, kitchens, outhouses, a banqueting suite, a study as well as a chapel, originally built for their father, Robert Dudley, Earl of Leicester.

Robert had inherited the house on his father's death.

"I fear you have eaten me out of house and home Francis!" Robert jibed, staring at Francis' rounded stomach.

Francis could not contain his laughter, as his rounded stomach shuddered from a hearty meal they had just finished.

"It was indeed a dish fit for a King!" Francis smiled as he rubbed his bloated stomach.

Robert nodded and chuckled at Francis' response.

Robert had been drinking heavily that night which always brought out his darker side and had spent much of the dinner complaining about his many demotions over the years, and as he ladled some of the wine into his half filled goblet, Francis could tell he had no intention of slowing down.

Now finished complaining about his loss of public office and many privileges, he began to complain about the fact that their aging Queen had still not handed the Royal crown down to Francis or himself.

"Francis, we both know that you, as the secret Prince of Wales, are next in line to the crown, if our mother so commands it," Robert started.

Francis nodded.

"You also know of the information retrieved by your brother Anthony from our spies in Spain that key Privy Council members to our Queen are in receipt of a Spanish pension to ensure neither of us succeeding the throne!" Robert added, angrily.

"That may be true Robert, but we have no proof. It would be extremely difficult to be a louder voice than the Privy Councillors without it!" Francis explained.

"Yes, I know Francis, but we must do something!"

"I know Robert, but all we can do right now is be patient," Francis told him, resting his hand on Robert's shoulder, to calm him.

"The tides will turn again in our favour," Francis advised him.

"I am fed up waiting while those pompous fools in the Privy Council destroy what is left of our England Francis!" Robert moaned.

"That hunched back Cecil pours poison in our Queens ears! We will never get a chance to govern what is ours!" Robert shouted angrily.

"Robert," Francis responded softly, resting a calming hand on his shoulder again.

Robert smiled and then nodded, agreeing he needed to calm down.

"Francis, I fear we may have to use force to oust them," Robert explained in a grave tone.

Francis was shocked by what his brother was suggesting.

"You know I am against that course of action Robert, and you would do well to be careful of even discussing such a thing. If you are contemplating such an idea, then I would say you are playing a dangerous game!" Francis advised him in the strongest terms.

"In any case, our Queen has the right to choose whomever she wishes as her successor when she decides to give up the crown, and I am against the use of force to bring that about!" Francis added defiantly.

"Francis, the Queen is getting older, and refuses to name an heir! She abdicates her powers in favour of her advisors Robert Cecil and Walter Raleigh!"

Robert shouted, spilling some of the wine from his goblet as he jerked around angrily.

"Sorry," Robert apologised as he spilled a little red wine on Francis.

"It is fine Robert," Francis returned making light of the small red stain on his new breeches, taking a handkerchief to wipe it dry.

"Anyway, she may one day transfer the crown to one of us Francis, but I fear the enemies that surround her will have us dead before that happens!" Robert complained in a dejected tone.

Francis pondered his brother's statement as he looked into his own half empty goblet of red wine.

"To be or not to be king is something I have pondered at great length Robert," Francis started, again resting his hand on Robert's shoulder.

"I will not stand in your way if you feel the Queen will relinquish control to you," Francis continued.

Robert's eyes widened.

"You would denounce your rights to the throne of England? You are the first, Francis, it is your right!" Robert told him.

Francis looked briefly at the reddened stain on his breeches, and turned back up to face his brother.

"What costs blood is surely not worth blood Robert, and if I am to be honest, I do not believe I am destined to rule England, whether it is my birthright or not!" Francis admitted.

Robert was confused.

"Why do you say that, Francis?" Robert queried, taken aback by his brother's frank confession.

"I do not believe our Queen holds me in such high esteem that she would relinquish control of our fair country to me," Francis confessed.

"My country does not even recognise me as the Prince of Wales!" Francis laughed a little as he took a sip from his goblet.

"But it does not matter. England holds *you* in high esteem, and if you believe the country will support you, I will step aside," Francis added, wondering if the strong wine had finally gone to his head.

"Are you sure, Francis?" Robert asked, eyeing his brother with an increased sense of seriousness.

"I am certain Robert," Francis confirmed, nodding sadly.

"I thank you for you honesty brother, and if you are giving me this opportunity, I will not wait a second more, I must strike now!"

Robert took his brother's hand.

"I have a meeting planned which includes many prominent people who will aid in removing the enemies of state, but I also need more support from the people," Robert explained.

As Francis listened to Robert, he realised his brother's patience had grown thin, and it seemed he was already conspiring against the Privy Council.

"I know you are persuasive Robert, but if you are considering what I think you are, and I would strongly advise against it!" Francis warned him.

"I have waited too long Francis, and time is running out. I know the dangers, but I have a just cause!" Robert argued.

Robert's impatience and hot temper had landed him in much trouble over the years, and Francis worried that this plot may be the death of him.

"Robert, please think seriously about what you are doing!" Francis begged.

"My mind is made up Francis, there is only one way ahead!" Robert told him grimly.

Francis sighed as he realised he would not be able to change his brother's hot tempered mind.

"I would ask one thing," Robert queried.

"What?" Francis replied, fearing he would now be somehow implicated in his brother's bad decisions.

"I wonder if you could organise a performance at 'The Globe' playhouse?" Robert queried.

The Globe? Francis thought, a little confused.

"What did you have in mind?" Francis asked back in confusion.

"Richard II? How it plays with the royal succession, in terms of raising the question of the deposing and "voluntary" abdication of a King would set the tone for what I plan to do!" Robert explained.

"Oh," Francis responded under his breath, now understanding Robert's intentions.

"Will you do it?" Robert pressed.

Francis nodded reluctantly, eyeing his half empty goblet of wine, wondering if he had made a terrible decision in passing up on his chance to become King of England.

73. THE GLOBE THEATRE

February 7 1601, London

𝕿he Globe, a playhouse on the bank of the London Thames, was a 20-sided open-air amphitheatre, giving it a cylindrical shape, three stories tall and 100-foot wide, able to house some 3300 spectators, drawing in the rich and poor alike to its numerous performances.

Tonight was to be an unusually busy night for an old performance of the play *Richard II*.

As the final patrons took their seats, the play orator walked into the centre of the circular stage to introduce the play.

"Welcome to the Globe Theatre! The play Richard II by William Shakespeare is proudly sponsored by Robert Devereux, 2nd Earl of Essex!" the orator shouted to the rapturous applause of the audience, as he bowed in the direction of Robert Devereux sitting in one of the higher balcony seats, causing many of the attendee's to stand up clapping and cheering in appreciation of the heroic soldier in their midst.

Robert stood up and bowed to his fellow kinsmen waving thanks for their welcoming cheers.

"For those of you who are not familiar with this play, let me summarise it for you!" the orator continued as the cheering started to die down, reading from a parchment detailing a summary of the play.

"Richard II, who ascended to the throne as a young man, is a regal and stately figure, but he is wasteful in his spending habits, unwise in his choice of counsellors and detached from his country and its common people!" the orator finished to a thunderous applause from hundreds of the assembled patrons, seemingly in agreement to the current state of their England.

As Robert listened to the thunderous applause, he took it as a sign that his kinsmen agreed that the current government was indeed detached from the needs of the common people, believing it was his duty to lead the charge for a necessary change. As the applause died down, Robert took his seat and the play commenced.

The Past

74. THE COUPE

The next day, a group of some twenty people met in Essex House, home of Robert Devereux, to discuss their planned coup against the English government, believing that the England they knew had changed for the worse, not just politically, but also economically, and they were not wrong.

During Queen Elizabeth's reign, the population of England rose from 3 million to 4 million, putting unprecedented pressure on the country's resources.

It was hardly surprising that, with so many people flocking to the towns, London was by now the biggest city in Europe with between 130,000 and 150,000 inhabitants, a colourful metropolis containing the best and worst of city life.

London's streets filled up with alehouses, gambling dens and brothels, as public entertainment was provided by street performers, playhouses, and spectacles such as bear baiting. London was filthy but intriguing, lively but dangerous, becoming a magnet for beggars, thieves and tricksters from across the country.

As the standard of living dropped, the problem of vagrancy worsened and this was to have repercussions for the country as a whole.

In addition to this, the country had also been hit by a number of poor harvests, which put increasing pressure on a limited supply of food. The resulting rise in food prices led, in some cases, to starvation among those who could not afford to pay.

The personal character of the Earl of Essex had given him a very wide-spread popularity and influence among those that realised the government and its monarchy was not working, and Robert wanted to gain the sympathetic vote of many influential people to believe in his rebellion against the crown.

The plot and the membership of the coupe were gradually expanding, and with time, the plan was to extend support in the course of the next few months, not only throughout England, but also into France and Spain.

"My plan to oust the enemy party and establish a true voice about the Queen is almost upon us!" Robert shouted to the group assembled in his home to a rapturous cheer, but his speech was short-lived as a servant rushed into the room.

"Master, you have a visitor!" The maid informed him worriedly.

"I said NO visitors right now!" Robert barked back at the servant.

"I know sire, but the gent says it is urgent!" the servant responded.

"Who is it?" Robert asked impatiently.

"The Earl of Southampton sire!" the servant responded in a strained tone.

"What is he doing here?" Robert whispered to himself with a worried look.

"Send him in, send him!" Robert ordered impatiently.

The servant nodded and then rushed out of the room, and while Robert and his rebellious group waited, Robert started wringing his hands in worry, fearing something has happened.

The servant quickly led in the Earl of Southampton, before disappearing back out of the room, wanting to have nothing to do with the secret discussions.

"Robert, we must talk!" the Earl of Southampton whispered in a low tone as he entered the room, uncomfortably eyeing some of his friends.

"What is it?" Robert asked worriedly as he took the Earl of Southampton aside.

"It is grave, I'm afraid. News of the plot has reached the Queen and also the Privy Council!" the Earl of Southampton replied, his voice strained.

"What? How is that possible?" Robert asked, as the group behind them began to realise that their planned coup had been uncovered and started talking among themselves about the prospect that they could be arrested at any moment.

"There are whispers at court that King James of Scotland knew of our efforts and warned Queen Elizabeth!" the Earl of Southampton continued.

Robert Devereux went quiet as he realised that King James had gone back on their deal.

"Then time is of the essence! We march on to Whitehall today!" Robert shouted, realising there was no other option, as they would all be arrested for treason sooner or later anyway.

This will not have been all for naught! Robert thought defiantly.

By now many of Robert's rebellious group had started to think about the stark reality that they could be imprisoned or worse hung and quartered for their treasonable thoughts and actions.

"We are done for Robert! We have lost the element of surprise! We should abandon this plot!" begged the Earl of Southampton, now downbeat.

"Yes, I think we must go into hiding, or even flee England for a period until it all blows over!" another person in the group piped up in fear, to the nodding agreement of others in the group.

"No! I would rather be shot in the head than spend the rest of my days abroad, wandering as a vagabond or fugitive. We cannot leave England to rot! We must rally on to Whitehall today!" Robert shouted defiantly as he tried rally his small group.

The crowd that had cheered Robert only a short while ago where now like lost sheep, not knowing where to go or what to do.

Robert realised he would have to appeal to their sensibilities.

"Listen! If you believe in the poison being spread by the Queen's advisors, fight with me! If you believe we can bring back to England what has been lost, follow me now - to London!" he cried out to the group.

Many of the group cheered while others were still unsure, but as Robert led them out of his house, most of them followed him, not knowing what else to they could do.

As they all poured out of Essex House, Robert and a handful of others mounted horses, while other followed on foot, making their way into central London.

Robert pretended not to notice as some of his group that walked with him on foot, slipped away, trying to distance themselves from him and his rebellion.

As Robert lead the way into central London passing through many poor towns, he tried in vain to spur on his fellow countrymen to arm themselves and follow him.

"For the Queen, for the Queen!" he shouted as he rode through the roads as he tried to drum up support for his cause.

Robert's design was to convey the impression that his actions are not against the Queen herself, but against his own enemies in her counsels, and he pretended that the Queen herself was on his side.

The people of London, however, were not so easily fooled.

Thinking in advance, the Mayor of London had already received prior warning from the Privy Council, to be ready to suppress an imminent uprising, if one should be made.

Additionally, one of the Queen's principal ministers of state, at the head of a small troop of horsemen, rode through the streets, proclaiming Robert a traitor, and calling upon all the citizens to aid in arresting him, with the people seemingly disposed to listen to him, and to comply with his demand.

After riding through some of the principal streets to get a feel for the state of the supposed uprising, the minister returned to the Queen, and reported to her that all was well in the city and there was no danger that Robert would succeed in raising a rebellion there.

In the meantime, the farther Robert advanced, the more he found himself environed with difficulties and dangers. The people began to assemble here and there with evident intent to impede his movements. They blocked the streets with carts and coaches to prevent his escape.

His followers, one after another, finding all hope of success gone, abandoned their despairing leader and fled.

Robert himself, with a handful of supporters, wandered about trying unsuccessfully to increase their numbers until the early hours of the morning, finding every way of retreat hemmed up against them.

He finally fled to the river side to take a boat with the few followers he had left, ordering the watermen to row as quickly as possible up the river landing at Westminster and then retreating to Essex house, entering with the utmost trepidation, before barricading the doors.

Robert himself was excited in the highest degree, fully determined to die there, rather than surrender himself as a prisoner.

As an army of the Queen's men hammered away outside his home, it soon became clear that he would have to surrender, as he could not possibly withstand a siege in his own home against the whole force of the English realm.

He finally surrendered at about six in the evening and was solemnly taken to the Tower of London.

75. The Trial

Robert's trial, along with that of his co-conspirators proved to be a very ominous affair.

Although the public were not in support of bringing charges against their war hero, they understood that laws had been broken and those responsible had to be held to account.

Edward Coke, a revered lawyer was appointed by the state to defend the crown, with Francis chosen as his junior counsel.

Francis viewed his selection as a cruel joke, firstly, because he and Edward Coke were long time rivals, and secondly as the trial continued, he knew he would ultimately have to prosecute his own brother, Robert Devereux, the ring leader of the attempted coupe itself, as well as friends and family, such as Sir Henry Neville, his nephew, and the Earl of Southampton.

Due to an ultimatum offered to him by Queen Elizabeth, Francis was given the choice to either aid the crown and prosecute Robert and his co-conspirators or watch as his brother, Anthony Bacon, also faced charges of treason as an accomplice, the Queen arguing that Anthony must have had prior knowledge of the coupe, due to his position as private secretary to Robert at the time.

As Anthony was at that time seriously ill, Francis knew that imprisonment could have meant certain death for Anthony.

"*Nolens volens*" [Latin for 'whether willing or unwilling'] Francis thought to himself as he sat in court next to his grinning rival, Edward Coke, while they prepared themselves for their first prosecutions in the Essex rebellion.

Francis had no option but to defend the crown.

As the trials commenced, courtiers, commoners, churchmen, students, scholars, and interested foreigners all crowded into the court, rubbing shoulders as they jockeyed to get a seat or at least stand, seeking a first hand view of the prosecutions.

As Edward Coke laid into the accused prisoners, he took great joy in proving their guilt and destroying their characters, which would sometimes carry him off the rails into unseemly wrangles time and time again, with Francis as his junior, having to interrupt the procedures to bring him back to the points at issue.

As part of the prosecutions, Sir Henry Neville and the Earl of Southampton were sentenced to the Tower of London for their part in the uprising.

Edward Coke revelled in having Francis to do his bidding, and was one of the few noblemen that knew of his secret Tudor lineage, once ridiculing Francis about it in public calling him *The Queen's Bastard*.

As part of the prosecution, many people were examined in the dock as the trial progressed, and specifically, one of the principal actors of the staged play *Richard II*, was called in to give an account of the circumstances that led to the play being performed the day before the failed coupe.

As the actor gave an account that he and his fellow actors were paid extra to perform the old play, even though there were newer and more popular plays that could have easily sufficed, it again put emphasis on the efforts of Francis' writing group.

Luckily for Francis, Edward Coke was merely looking for ammunition to infer that the performance of the play was intended to stir up support for Robert Devereux, the play's sponsor that night.

At one point, Francis exchanged an uncomfortable stare with the actor in the dock, whom he knew well, and Edward Coke thinking he had seen a friendly exchange with the witness and Francis, seized the opportunity to explore the possibility that the actor was holding something back.

"Sir, please tell me, has any effort been made to induce you to tell a different story?" Edward Coke asked the actor in a serious tone.

"A different story from what I have already told you sir?" the witness queried in an innocent tone.

"That is what I mean!" Edward Coke continued, still very serious.

"Yes sir! Several people have tried to get me to tell a different story, from what I have told, but they didn't succeed!" the witness continued.

Edward Coke's eyes widened.

"Now, sir, upon your oath, I wish to know who those persons are!" he pressed to the gasps of some of the crowd, as well as Francis.

"Well, I guess you've tried 'bout as hard as any of them!" the actor replied, laughing merrily.

Unimpressed, Edward Coke dismissed the actor, but the judge, jury, and spectators, all indulged in a hearty laugh at his expense.

Francis let out a cool exhale as he leaned back in his chair relieved that his writing group remained secret.

When it was Robert's time to be prosecuted, he protested a heartfelt innocence for trying to dethrone the Queen, consistently declaring that he was simply trying to rid her of the damaging advisors in her Privy Council, declaring that he believed they were secretly bankrolled by Queen Elizabeth's enemies in Spain.

Unfortunately for Robert, he had no proof to support his claims, and after a number of days deliberating over Robert's fate, the judge finally declared his verdict.

"Guilty of treason, punishable by death!" the Judge declared.

Edward Coke was ecstatic by the result.

Although it was inevitable that such a conclusion would be reached against Robert, as he was indeed guilty, it was still a shock for Francis to hear the outcome that he had forcibly played a part in bringing about.

Francis was ashamed and distraught with the result, and many shouts of uproar echoed in and around the court against the decision to the anger of the judge who tried for many minutes to bring about order in his court, banging his hammer on the desk several times.

Queen Elizabeth had punished Robert many times in the past, but this was now deadly serious, and out of her control.

Justice had to be served, and although his brother had been found guilty of treason, Francis felt certain that Queen Elizabeth would never sign an order for the execution of her own son.

"Take him away!" the judge shouted to more disapproving boos and hisses of the crowds in the courtroom at the decision.

Guards escort Robert Devereux out of the court and back to his cell in the Tower of London.

76. DEVEREUX'S FATE

Tower of London, London

𝕽obert Devereux, 2nd Earl of Essex, sits on the floor of his cell awaiting his fate in the Beauchamp Tower.

As the day edged towards noon, Robert closed his fist around a small black bag that hung from his neck, he prayed in silence, wishing he was back in the luxury of his magnificent 42 bedroom London home, Essex House.

His thoughts were interrupted as he heard footsteps making their way towards his cell, and as a set of keys clinked against the other side of the door he jumped up.

As the broad oak door to his cells opened, his gaoler, a brutish looking unattractive man, entered.

"You have a visitor Master Devereux!" the gaoler grinned, revealing his brown teeth, some of which were missing.

As the gaoler moved out of the way, Robert locked eyes with the diminutive hunched figure of one of the Queen's advisors, Robert Cecil.

The Queen's advisor gave the prisoner a sly grin, and grimaced as he inhaled the putrid stench of the dirty cells.

"I must admit, I never realised you had so much support by the amount of your supporters we have arrested!" the advisor started, focusing on Robert now.

"No matter, it is just a matter of time before we have them all," he continued in a mocking tone, raising his chin a little to eyeball Robert.

"What do you want?" asked Robert bitterly.

"To gloat a little I suppose. Of course I will be even happier to see you executed though!" the advisor responded with a grin.

"It will never happen. My countrymen won't allow it!" Robert replied defiantly.

"Don't be so sure. You are a traitor, and *your* countrymen know what we do to traitors!" the advisor replied with an eerie confidence in his tone.

Robert Cecil turned to the gaoler.

"The Queen has given explicit orders that he is not allowed any visitors. Is that understood?" he explained to the gaoler in a stern tone.

The gaoler nodded in agreement.

"No doubt I will see you at your execution!" the advisor sniggered back to Robert as he left the cell.

Now alone and dejected, Robert turned and walked over to the only luxury his cell afforded, which was a small arched window that looked out over a courtyard below.

As he looked out and stared down at the courtyard, he eyed a yard boy battling against strong winds as he worked on his task of clearing away the last of fallen leaves from the many trees surrounding the tower.

As Robert peered out the window upwards, he saw birds flying without a care in the world, and considered how wonderful it would be to be free again like them.

He lifted up his hand to gaze at a dark blue onyx ring on one of his fingers given to him by Queen Elizabeth in case he should ever need her help, twisting the ring around on his finger anxiously, contemplating what to do.

This ring will save me, but I must have it delivered to my mother safely Robert considered, staring back out the window at the yard boy still diligently sweeping up the loose leaves.

As the boy swept away a mound of leaves, his actions uncovered a bird laying motionless, and as the boy closed in to remove it thinking it dead, the bird flapped its wings madly trying to protect itself, but did not seem to be able to lift itself off the ground.

Robert watched the event with interest, mainly because he did not have anything else to do.

As the boy looked closer he realised the bird had somehow trapped one of its legs, but as he got closer to release bird, it flapped its wings madly again.

Considering his options, the boy took out a small bundle wrapped in paper from his pocket, opening it to expose some bread he had made for his lunch and broke away a piece of it, using it to calm and distract the bird, allowing him to get close enough to release its caught leg.

With its leg now free, the bird flapped it wings and flew straight up into the sky, perching briefly on the window ledge of Robert's cell, chirping at him for a few seconds before it flapped its wings again, continuing on its journey upwards from the Tower of London, until it was out of sight.

Robert laughed a little as he wondered what the bird thought as it eyed him locked in his own cage.

Returning his attention back downwards to the courtyard, he saw the boy looking back up at him.

"You did a good deed boy!" Robert shouted down at the boy, jovially.

"His wing was caught sire. He just needed a little help!" the boy responded proudly.

Robert nodded agreeably.

As Robert pondered the boy's response, he looked back at the lone guard snoring loudly on the other side of his cell in the tower.

He turned back to the boy in the yard below.

"Do you know who I am?" Robert asked, shouting back down to the boy.

The boy began to smile.

"Yes sire, everyone knows how you smashed the Irish rebellion!" the boy replied, smiling back up at his hero, giving Robert cause to smile broadly for the time in many days.

"Some of my earlier triumphs!" he shouted back.

"Will you do one more good deed boy, but for me this time?" Robert asked as he began to remove the onyx ring.

"Name it sire!" the boy responded eagerly.

As Robert squeezed the ring into his hand, he explained his dilemma about the urgent delivery of the ring to the boy.

77. THE PLOY

$\mathfrak{S}$ome days later, Queen Elizabeth sat quietly in a room, reading a bible to help give her solace, having heavy thoughts on her mind about the treason inflicted upon her by her own son, Robert Devereux.

She had been deliberating on what she should do about his plight for days with no resolution that would be legal in the eyes of the people of England.

A knock on the door brought her wearily out of her thoughts.

"Come in!" she shouted tiredly.

Her advisor Robert Cecil made his way into the room, bowing as low as his humped back affliction would allow, and Queen Elizabeth waved her hand unenthusiastically giving him authority to stand upright.

"Your Majesty!" he greeted her.

"What is it?" she asked impatiently.

"The Earl of Essex has been in the tower for a number of days now, awaiting execution. I have taken the action of drafting his execution order," he explained, dropping a prepared execution order on her desk.

"All that it requires is your signature," he informed her.

"Shall I fetch you a quill, your Majesty?" he continued casually.

The Queen looked up at her advisor, her eyes now wide with rage.

"The impertinence!" she shouted incredulously.

 Get out!" she barked as she stood up.

"My apologies, your Majesty!" her advisor responded quickly, backing out of the room in haste closing the door behind him, leaving Queen Elizabeth again alone in the room.

In the unnerving quietness of the room, Queen Elizabeth eyed the execution order with contempt, before bursting into tears at the prospect of her son being executed for his crimes.

The Past
78. No Reprieve

$\mathcal{L}$ater that day, a dishevelled and anxious looking Robert Devereux peered out onto the courtyard for some time, staring at the courtyard below strewn with stray leaves, leaving it unusually unkempt.

He finally turned to the guard outside of his cell that sat in a small chair eating his lunch.

"What happened to the boy that was maintaining the yard the other day?" Robert queried.

The guard shrugged his shoulders, as he scooped a spoonful of a brownish sludge in his bowl, putting it into his mouth.

"Very peculiar!" the gaoler commented as he chewed then swallowed hard.

"Apparently he was caught stealing, although he didn't seem the type to me, but in any case, he won't be back," the gaoler continued, before scooping up another spoonful of the brownish sludge into his mouth again, spitting out a piece he didn't like.

Stealing? Robert thought worriedly.

"Why do you think he won't be back?" Robert asked, waiting for what seemed like an eternity for the gaoler to finish yet another mouthful of his soup.

"Well, apparently he was sent up North somewhere to a boy's home I think," the gaoler responded as he devoured another spoonful.

If he had delivered the ring, I would have already had my reprieve! All is lost! Robert considered as he slumped to the floor depressed.

79. HASTY DECISIONS

Hampton Court Palace, England

The next day as Queen Elizabeth sat on her golden throne in a great hall attending to her daily matters of state, having just finished her morning's schedule of affairs, her thoughts were distracted as she looked longingly over the single finger of her right hand devoid of a ring.

As someone neared her, she looked up annoyed, eyeing a courtier with an urgent look about him.

"An urgent message for you, your Majesty!" the courtier offered as he handed her a message given to him by Robert Cecil, her hunched backed advisor.

"Who is it from?" Queen Elizabeth queried wearily.

"It is a report received from the guards at the Tower of London, your Majesty!" the courtier informed her, causing Queen Elizabeth to jerk upright as she worried that something had happened to her Robert.

"Read it!?" she asked anxiously, now alert.

They say the Earl of Essex has gone quite mad, throwing away all his possessions to the common people," stated the courtier as he read the report.

"What? What does that mean?" she snapped with a confused stare.

The courtier continued to read the message, his hands now visibly shaking.

"The guards report that the Earl of Essex has thrown all of his rings out the window of his cell as he awaits his execution." The courtier continued in a strained tone.

Queen Elizabeth shook her head in disbelief, eyeing her bare finger again before raging orders back at the courtier.

"If he awaits his execution then he shall have it!" she shouted in anger at Robert's supposed last act of defiance against her.

"Come with me!" she ordered the courtier, getting up from her throne and storming out of the hall to a private adjoining room, with the courtier almost having to run to keep up with her.

"Wait here!" she shouted to the courtier as he abruptly stopped at the door to one of her private stately offices, nearly bumping into her.

Queen Elizabeth stormed into the room, making her way to dainty mother-of-pearl and ebony inlaid writing table, pulling on an almost invisible drawer to retrieve the execution order that her advisor, Robert Cecil, had previously left for her to sign.

Dropping the execution order on the table, she picked up a quill and dipped it briefly into some ink before signing the warrant. She folded the execution order up and inserted it into an envelope.

Her nostrils still flaring with anger, she left the room with the envelope in her hand, coming upon the same courtier in the hallway who waited feverishly for her.

"Here!" she shouted to the courtier, frightening him with her hot tempered demeanour, shoving the envelope in his hand.

"Deliver this immediately to the Tower of London!" she shouted.

The courtier trembled as he accepted the envelope and gave a quick nod before rushing away down the hallway towards the palace exit.

As the courtier reached the main gate of the palace, he came upon the hunched back Robert Cecil.

The courtier sheepishly approached him, and Robert Cecil took him aside.

"Did you deliver the message?" Robert Cecil quizzed the courtier.

"Yes sire!" the courtier responded worriedly, fearing the situation the advisor had involved him in.

"What did she say?" Robert Cecil pressed.

The courtier handed over the envelope.

As Robert Cecil opened the envelope and saw which document it contained, he smiled mischievously as he re-inserted the document and handed the envelope back to the courtier.

"Come with me!" Robert Cecil advised and the courtier followed him out of the palace to a carriage rank.

Robert Cecil waved one of the carriages over.

"What are you waiting for? Get this order to the Tower immediately!" Robert Cecil shouted at the courtier.

"Yes, sire!" the courtier jumped, eyeing the carriage stopping now in front of them.

"Take this courtier to the Tower of London immediately!" Robert Cecil ordered the coachman on top of the carriage handing the coachman some coins.

The coachman nodded agreeably, as the courtier jumped on board.

As the carriage made its way from the palace, Robert Cecil rubbed his palms together as he considered how his mischievous plan was working.

He made his way back inside the palace.

The Past

80. EXECUTION ORDER

To pass the monotonous hours in the tower, Robert carved an inscription on the stonework above his cell, using the handle of a spoon as a lasting testament of his time in the Tower, etching the words "ROBART TIDIR" a Welsh versioned spelling of his name.

As he looked out of his cell window to inhale some cleaner air than the stench in his cell, he saw the governor of the Tower of London making his way inside.

This cannot be good! Robert thought gravely, shaking his head.

He sat down on his bed, waiting for the governor, squeezing the small black bag that hung around his neck in his fist and whispered another prayer, hoping that it would be good news.

Moments later as the governor arrived at his cell, Robert stood up, bracing himself for the news, be it good or bad, but from the governor's a saddened face, Robert realised the news was bad.

"It saddens me to inform you that a warrant for your execution has arrived Robert. It has been signed by Queen Elizabeth herself," the Governor explained.

Robert's shoulders slumped as tears rolled down his cheeks.

"So it has come to this! My Queen has finally forsaken me!" Robert lamented, slumping back down onto his bed.

The governor bowed his head apologetically.

"I am sorry. Is there anything I can do for you before I call the executioner?" the Governor queried.

"I don't suppose I have time for a hearty meal?" Robert asked, trying to stay upbeat.

"The warrant states an immediate execution, I am afraid," the governor replied.

Robert sighed and squeezed the small black bag that hung around his neck again, nodding.

"Maybe you could do one favour for me when the deed is done?" Robert asked.

"What is it?" the governor queried.

Robert pulled the black bag from around his neck and handed it to the governor.

"Will you promise that the Queen will receive this bag directly after the" Robert's eyes began to fill up with tears, as his voice dried.

"After the execution?" he continued, rubbing his neck shuddering at the thought of the executioner's axe.

The governor nodded solemnly, accepting the small bag, putting it in his pocket.

81. RETRACTIONS

Some minutes after Queen Elizabeth had handed off the signed execution order to the courtier in a moment of hot headedness, she again rushed into her private room.

As she entered the room, she hurried again to her dainty writing table, pulling out a single blank parchment from its drawer and anxiously wrote a retraction to the execution order she had signed just minutes before, her hand visibly shaking as she wrote.

Finishing the short letter, she quickly inserted in an envelope and added her royal wax seal before rushing back out of the room.

Almost immediately, she came upon a passing courtier wearing a bright white smart doublet, nearly knocking him over.

"You!" she shouted, causing the courtier to jump.

The courtier realising it was Queen Elizabeth, immediately bowed.

"Your Majesty!" the courtier exclaimed.

"Take this letter to the Governor of the Tower of London immediately, and make haste, there is no time to delay!" she ordered, thrusting the envelope into his hand.

"As you wish, your Majesty!" the courtier stuttered, accepting the envelope and immediately rushing down the hallway towards the Hampton Court exit, coming upon Robert Cecil.

Behind the hunched back Robert, a couple of courtiers stared at him.

"My mother was touched by a hunched back beggar once, and she came up in a bad rash," whispered one of the courtiers.

"Hmm," the other courtier murmured, nodding.

"He's a bad one alright and only got to where he is because of his father, Lord Burghley" the second courtier continued to the agreeable nod of the first courtier.

As Robert scrutinized the two courtiers whispering with his beady eyes, the two men ceased their chatter and quickly went about their business.

As the Privy Councillor continued into the palace, he passed the courtier with the urgent retraction in his hand, and noticing the Royal seal on the envelope, Robert quietly followed him out of the palace.

As the courtier exited the gates at Hampton court looking for a carriage to take him to the Tower of London, Robert Cecil approached him.

"You there!" he shouted to the courtier, not knowing his name.

"Yes sir!" the courtier nodded, seeing that Robert Cecil was wearing the distinguished colours identifying him as a senior member of the Privy Council.

"Where are you going with such haste?" he quizzed the courtier.

"The Queen has given me an urgent letter to deliver to the Governor at the Tower of London sire!" the courtier quickly informed him, urgently scanning the carriage rank for a free carriage.

"Let me see that!" Robert Cecil demanded, pointing at the envelope.

The courtier hesitated.

"Give it to me!" Robert Cecil now shouted, snatching the envelope out of the courtier's hand.

The courtier was lost for words.

As Robert Cecil reviewed the letter, he could see that it did indeed possess the Royal seal, and as the seal had not yet hardened, he opened the envelope carefully and read its contents, much to the embarrassment of the courtier.

Upon seeing that it was the Queen's instruction to stop the previous execution order against Robert Devereux, Robert Cecil decided that the letter must be delayed, if his plan of ensuring Robert Devereux's execution was to succeed.

He looked out to the carriage rank and eyed his own carriage and coachman parked up, before returning his gaze back to the courtier, who looked back at him flustered.

Robert re-inserted the letter in the envelope, and closed the envelope carefully, pressing down hard on the wax seal.

"Here," Robert told the courtier, handing the envelope back to him, and then waved his own carriage over.

"My carriage will take you to the tower," Robert Cecil continued, pointing at his carriage as it came to a stop before them.

"Thank you sire!" responded a thankful courtier, not realising his luck.

Robert Cecil opened his carriage door and the courtier gratefully jumped inside.

Robert Cecil beckoned his coachman down from his seat, to which the coachman willingly obliged, and being a huge man, he then bent over to bring his ear within earshot of his diminutive master.

Robert Cecil whispered into his ear.

"The courtier's destination is the Tower of London, but I want you to take the longest route possible. Do you understand me?" Robert Cecil explained in no uncertain terms.

His coachman nodded and then Robert ordered his coachman on his way with the courtier.

Soon it will all be over for him! Robert Cecil thought playfully as he again made his way back into the palace, rubbing his spine which now pained him from the excessive walking he had been doing that day.

The Past

82. THE EXECUTION

An hour later, Robert was led out from his cell to Tower Green, a private courtyard in the Tower grounds, generally reserved for royalty.

To his surprise, Robert was greeted by a small crowd of his friends and family that had heard of his immediate execution. Their mood was sombre.

The lieutenant of the Tower presided, dressed in a black velvet gown, over a suit of black satin standing at the *scaffold*, a platform about twelve feet square and four feet high, with a railing around it, with steps by which to ascend. The chopping block was positioned in the centre of the scaffold, covered, as well as the platform itself, with black cloth.

As Robert ascended the platform with a firm step, he surveyed the solemn scene around him with calmness and dignity, and called out to God for forgiveness and then to his Queen, acknowledging his guilt and the justice in his condemnation.

His mind was deeply subdued with a sense of his accountability to God, and he expressed a strong desire to be forgiven for all his sins, which he admitted had been many over the years.

He asked the spectators present to join him in his devotions, and he then proceeded to offer a short prayer, in which he implored further pardon for his sins, and a long life and happy reign for the Queen.

The prayer ended, and all was ready.

The executioner, according to custom on such occasions, then asked his pardon for the violence he was about to commit, which Robert readily granted, then requesting Robert to lay his head upon the block, exposing his neck.

Robert knelt down, and after the briefest of hesitations, he laid his head on the block.

The executioner prepared himself, making a judgement on the swinging pattern of the huge axe he wielded, he heaved it up with his muscular arms, but as it hovered high in the air on the tail end of a swing, the courtier on his way from the royal court with the stay of execution letter from Queen Elizabeth entered the Tower Green momentarily distracting the executioner's concentration.

As the executioner's heavy axe then fell, slicing through the air down towards Robert's neck, it missed and crashed into the back of Robert's skull.

The sharp sound of steel cracking bone sent a shiver down the courtier's spine as Robert's blood splattered onto the courtier's face and fine white doublet.

The courtier, seeing the full gory details immediately threw up where he stood.

As the executioner looked down at the mess, he was aggravated to see he had missed Robert's neck due to the courtier's inopportune entry into the grounds.

He was fuming.

"Now look what you made me do!" the executioner shouted back at the courtier spilling his guts.

"It's not a complete cut; I will have to swing again!" the executioner moaned, shaking his head in dismay.

As the courtier picked out pieces of bone which must have come from the Robert's crushed skull, he became sick again, oblivious of the executioner's further corrective swings.

As the executioner swung his axe repeatedly, making corrective hacks until finally severing Robert's semi-shattered head from his body, the females in the small crowd that had come to support Robert were all sobbing at the cruel gruesome end of one of England's champion's.

Finally having severed the head, the executioner picked up the bleeding head, and shouted solemnly, "God save the Queen!" before dropping it in a nearby basket.

The courtier could only look on in disgust.

After cleaning the sick from his mouth, the weak courtier made his way to a senior looking gent standing near the scaffolds.

"I have a letter for the Governor of the Tower of London!" the courtier explained, taking in deep breaths as he tried to control his nausea.

"I am that man," the man revealed.

Relieved, the courtier quickly handed him the letter he was to deliver as he breathed in deeply as he tried to calm his now sensitive stomach.

The Governor eyed and confirmed the Royal seal on the envelope before opening and reading the letter within it.

"The Queen asks me to revoke the warrant for the execution of Robert Devereux, 2nd Earl of Essex?" he read back quietly to the courtier so no one else could hear their conversation.

The courtier nodded.

"Do you have a response for her?" the courtier asked.

"Yes, tell her the retraction came too late and that Robert Devereux, 2nd Earl of Essex has been executed," the governor informed him, looking down at the bloody severed head in the nearby basket.

As the Courtier also stared into the basket and saw the bloodied head, he threw up again on the grass, nearly messing the governor's shoes.

The Governor gave the courtier a stern look.

The courtier apologised profusely and quickly retrieved a handkerchief from inside his doublet, and as he cleaned away more fresh vomit from his mouth, the courtier wondered why Robert Devereux had been executed in the Tower Green, a private area of the Tower normally reserved for Royal prisoners, when, as a traitor, he ought to have been hung and quartered at Tyburn.

As the governor turned to leave, he remembered the small bag that Robert had given him, and his own promise to ensure Queen Elizabeth received it.

He turned back to the courtier.

"Are you going directly back to the Queen?" The Governor asked.

"Yes!" the courtier nodded.

The governor reached into his pocket and pulled out the small black bag that had been entrusted to him by Robert.

"The prisoner requested that the Queen alone should receive this. Can you please ensure his last wish?" the governor asked, thrusting the bag into his hand.

The courtier gave the small black bag a brief glance before nodding in agreement.

"Good!" the governor responded finally as he left, making his way back to his office within the Tower.

The courtier looked at the simple black bag again before putting it in his own pocket, and with that, he left the Tower Green, jumping into the first carriage-for-hire he saw to shuttle him back to the palace.

As he sat in the carriage, he dwelled on the ominous task of being the bearer of bad news when he presented himself back to Queen Elizabeth.

83. TOO LATE

The courtier arrived back at Hampton court much more quickly than it took for Robert Cecil's carriage to get him to the Tower, but he had more pressing things on his mind, being nervous over the possible reaction of his Queen when he informs her that the retraction arrived too late to save England's hero, Robert Devereux.

As he made his way into the great hall, where she sat distraught on her throne, all the attended patrons around her stopped their individual conversations, staring at his blood stained doublet and face.

As Queen Elizabeth noticed the blood on the courtier's garment, her eyes bulged with tears.

"I apologise for my attire, your Majesty!" the courtier apologised with a touch of fear in his voice.

Queen Elizabeth was speechless as she stared at the courtier's blood stained clothing.

"Did you deliver my letter?" she asked nervously.

As the courtier began to speak, he noticed the Queen seemed very strained as she waited for his response.

"Yes, I did your Majesty!" responded the courtier in a saddened tone.

Queen Elizabeth held her chest as if her heart was about to burst, breathing erratically, fearful of the response to her next question.

"And?" she asked, not able to finish her own sentence.

As the courtier stared up at his Queen, he could see she had stopped breathing, waiting for his response.

"The governor wishes to inform you that the Robert Devereux, 2nd Earl of Essex was executed earlier today, your majesty," the courtier solemnly declared, finally breathing a sigh of relief for telling her.

At that confirmation, the Queen cried out so loudly that her piercing scream seemed to echo through the whole palace, finally collapsing in a heap as her ladies-in-waiting rushed to attend her.

As the court patrons stood in shock at their Queen for her execution order against their favourite hero, many left the hall in disgust.

Just as the courtier turned to leave, he remembered the pouch in his pocket, and turned back, mounting the steps up to his Queen as she was being attended to by her ladies-in-waiting, and asked for one more moment with the tearful Monarch.

"Your Majesty, I was told to deliver this item to you directly. I believe the prisoner wanted you to have it," the courtier whispered, as he stretched out his hand, revealing the small pouch.

As Queen Elizabeth paused from her crying and looked down at the courtier and the item in his hand, she recognised the pouch, remembering how it always hung around Robert's neck.

She accepted the pouch from the courtier, opening it immediately, finding a small parchment scroll with some writing on it that she felt looked familiar.

As she wiped away tears from her eyes to read the small writing on the scroll, some twenty seconds of silence passed before she broke down into another uncontrollable fit of hysteria.

Queen Elizabeth immediately recognised the writing to be by her one love, Robert Dudley, and was a declaration by him, stating that Robert Devereux was an English prince, having the royal blood of the Queen of England and himself, and should be treated as a Prince of England if he was ever captured.

The declaration was signed by Robert Dudley and bore the seal of the Leicester Earldom.

The parchment scroll was to be a lifeline for Robert by his father, so that he could identify himself if he was ever captured during one of his campaigns.

Queen Elizabeth had never known about the parchment scroll, and its revelation on Robert's death was to serve as a final reminder that she had 'killed' her own son.

Robert Devereux had been a hero, renowned for his powerful intelligence, his uncanny ability to read his enemies mind and act immediately upon his intuition to his Majesty's advantage. He willingly took risks where other men would have wavered and backed away. He had been bold, dauntless, and had died fighting for something he believed it.

England would miss him sorely.

Over the many months following Robert's execution, Queen Elizabeth began to lose favour with her countrymen as they blamed her for his death, and when she made appearances in public, she was no longer greeted with cheers as before, but silence, while her Ministers were insulted and jeered at.

Francis was completely devastated at the loss.

84. LOSS OF A BROTHER

The following year, Francis looking thin and pale, walked with his brother Anthony, who also had a sickly look about him as well but more so.

They both walked slowly, in a sombre mood around the town of St. Albans, not too far from their Gorhambury home.

"It worries me to see you so sad Francis. You must stop blaming yourself for Robert's death," Anthony commented.

Francis had no enthusiasm about him and dragged his feet as they walked, but managed to stretch out his arm and wrap it around Anthony's neck.

Although he was still grieving for Robert, he was also worried about Anthony's ill health.

"It was I that sent him to his death Anthony, I am to blame!" Francis returned as his head hung low, staring at the cobbled pavement.

Anthony put her arm around Francis' waist and they both carried on a while looking like two best friends.

"You did what you had to do Francis, but remember, Robert was the instigator of his own demise," Anthony assured him.

"I knew what he was planning! I should have done more to deter him, stopped him, something!" replied Francis angrily as he thought about Robert's reckless actions.

Just as Anthony was about to respond, he had a small coughing fit, causing Francis to remove his arm, allowing Anthony to retrieve a handkerchief, covering it over his mouth as he coughed and spluttered with his sickness.

"Are you alright brother? Maybe going out was too much for you? Come let us turn back!" Francis insisted.

"No, no, I will be fine Francis. The air will do me well," Anthony told him, pushing away from Francis and continuing down the street.

We are both in such a state! Francis thought shaking his head in dismay as he watched his brother amble ahead.

He quickened his step to catch up to Anthony.

It was bad enough that Francis blamed himself for Robert's death, putting his own health in a downward spiral, but he also had to contend with worrying about Anthony, who had been seriously ill for some time.

"These are not good days at all. The air seems to be filled with gloom and darkness since Robert's death," Francis commented as he eyed the poor people lining the streets where they walked.

Anthony nodded, covering his mouth with the handkerchief as he coughed some more.

"Yes, I agree. When Robert died, it seemed a little of England died with him, even our Queen seems lost," Anthony responded as he lifted his mouth from his handkerchief.

As Anthony checked his handkerchief, he was stunned to see a small splatter of blood that had stained his handkerchief from his recent coughing bout.

His shoulders dropped in despair knowing that his time was running out, but closed the handkerchief up in his fist and hiding the despair in his face as he turned back to his brother.

As Francis looked around him at his countrymen on the street, it saddened him to see so much poverty and hunger permeating their every action.

"You are right Anthony. Everything does seem lost," Francis responded.

"You need to focus back on your writing Francis!" Anthony told him adamantly.

"Your countrymen need you now, more than ever," Robert added, wheezing a little.

"Yes, I know, but all my recent writing seems to be dark and tragic," Francis responded in a dejected tone.

"You need to remind our kinsmen that there is still love and hope left in this world. Promise me Francis!" Anthony begged.

Francis eyed his brother thoughtfully, wondering why Anthony had a sudden need for him to continue writing, unsure whether he actually had anything left to give, but he duly agreed.

"OK brother, I will do it for you," Francis told him, to a thankful smile back from Anthony.

They hugged and continued down the street, coming upon a drunken beggar.

"Spare any change geezer?" the beggar asked, bringing a strong pungent odour into their midst.

Anthony's nose crinkled as he could smell the rotten odour coming from the beggar.

"Get a job you filthy animal!" Anthony replied, coughing a little at the beggar's pungent smell.

The beggar shrugged his shoulders, and staggered off, not even responding.

Francis laughed at Anthony's actions in total contradiction to what he had just asked Francis to promise, and hurried after the beggar, giving him some coins from his pocket.

"And that is why you are always broke Francis!" Anthony scolded Francis, shaking his head.

"Riches are for spending!" Francis told him, smiling.

"Yes, but you need to be rich to do the spending!" Anthony laughed back heartily.

Francis nodded, smiling in agreement.

"You know one of the main endeavours in my writing was to explore human nature, and like the ancients, to teach wisdom through entertainment. To hold a mirror up to human nature, so that both good and bad might be seen for what they are and what they do," Francis commented, thinking positively about the future.

"You achieved it Francis, many, many times," Anthony informed him proudly.

"Yes, but I think all of that has been forgotten," Francis responded looking around him at his poor kinsmen.

As Anthony was about to respond, he began coughing again, but this time his coughs became more violent, causing him to collapse to his knees.

As Francis reached for his brother, the handkerchief Anthony had been holding in his clenched fist, dropped to the ground, opening to reveal its blood stains.

To his horror, Francis realised Anthony was much sicker than he had let on.

"Anthony!" Francis shouted as his brother fell unconscious.

"Please, someone get a doctor!" Francis shouted frantically as a crowd gathered around him.

Anthony never recovered from that day, and for Francis, it was not long after that his tower of strength, friend, co-writer and partner in his grand scheme, passed away.

The Past

85. CONFESSIONS

January 1603

As the Queen felt a need for more privacy in her ensuing grief over the death of her son Robert Devereux two years before, she decided to be removed from Westminster to her Richmond palace across the Thames from the Twickenham lodge which Francis once owned.

She made the journey to Richmond on a cold and stormy day, refusing to be deterred by the weather, but as a consequence, she caught a fever and became even more frail and weaker than before.

On her good days, Queen Elizabeth would sit in the chamber closets connected to the chapel, where she could listen to the divine service, the closets themselves in the form of small galleries, allowing her to be accompanied by her immediate attendants.

It was the middle of February when she received a message from her dear friend, Catherine Howard, Countess of Nottingham, begging an audience with her Queen.

On further investigation, Queen Elizabeth found out that the Countess of Nottingham was on her deathbed, and therefore felt she should make an effort to fulfil her dear friend's request before it was too late.

✝

Catherine Howard, Countess of Nottingham, in her 56th year, lay in her bedchamber, trying to tame her unkempt long greying hair with an ivory comb.

The dark rings around her eyes and the empty look in her expression showed her failing health.

She knew she was dying, but wanted to look her best for an impending royal visitor.

After a brief knock on the bedroom door, a withered looking Queen Elizabeth, now in her 70th year, a dear friend of the Countess, made her way in, and as the Countess tried to get out of bed to greet her, Queen Elizabeth rushed to her side, stopping her.

"No need to rise old friend, you are very weak, just rest," Queen Elizabeth told her as she performed the unusual step of personally propping up the Countess by doubling up her pillows.

They had been friends for a long time, but today the Countess felt uncomfortable with the kindness she was receiving from her Queen, feeling unworthy.

"Thank you for coming, your Majesty," the Countess whispered in a croaky embarrassed response.

"I came as soon as I could. I am sorry for not visiting you sooner, but I have not been well myself," Queen Elizabeth explained, thinking of her own grief at the loss of her son, Robert Devereux.

As she eyed the Countess' wild hair and the comb she held in her right hand, Queen Elizabeth gently took the comb from the Countess and began working it through the Countess' mass of tangles.

With that, the Countess could no longer contain herself and burst into tears.

"Please, stop!" the Countess whispered weakly, her eyes betraying a look of shame for the warm affections of her Queen.

"Hush now, you have lived a good long life, let us not be sad. Your fair husband will be waiting for you when it is your time to go," Queen Elizabeth explained to the Countess, trying to console her, but the Countess continued to cry.

Queen Elizabeth, thinking that the Countess was afraid of dying, wrapped her arms around her old friend.

"It's ok, there is nothing to fear," Queen Elizabeth whispered, but the Countess could not take her kindness any more and broke away from her.

"I have done such a wicked thing!" the Countess confessed abruptly, shaking her head.

"What is it? Whatever is the matter?" Queen Elizabeth asked in a concerned tone.

"Your Majesty, I know I do not have long to live, but I cannot leave this world without confessing a great injustice I have done to you!" the Countess explained.

"Me? You have done *me* an injustice?" Queen Elizabeth asked, now taken aback.

Visibly trembling, the Countess held out her left fist, which had been clenched the whole time of the Queen's visit, slowly opening it to reveal a gold encrusted onyx ring.

As Queen Elizabeth studied the onyx ring, she immediately recognised it, grabbing it and looking at it more closely, not believing what her aging eyes had confirmed, recognising the unique ring to be the same one she had given to her son, Robert Devereux, some years before.

"Where did you get this?" the Queen demanded angrily.

The Countess began to shake, unable to speak.

"I gave this ring to the Earl of Essex! Tell me how it came to be in your possession!" Queen Elizabeth pressed, trying to control the urge to accost her friend.

The Countess inhaled deeply as she mustered up the strength to explain.

86. A Queen's Anger

The Countess explained how two years earlier, when Robert Devereux awaited his fate in the Tower of London, a certain yard boy approached her at the home of Lady Scroope, her sister.

The Countess continued to explain that as the boy approached the house, she happened to greet him just as she was about to leave, having dropped off a book she had loaned from her sister.

The boy told her that he worked in the Tower, and had an urgent message for Lady Scroope, directly from Robert Devereux, 2nd Earl of Essex, as he sat imprisoned on charges of treason in the Tower.

The Countess admitted to the Queen that she was intrigued to know what the message was, and convinced the yard boy that she could be trusted with the message, making an excuse that her sister was away for some days.

Hesitantly, the boy, unsure of what to do next, relayed the important message told to him by Robert Devereux.

The boy told her that Robert had instructed him to ask Lady Scroope to present a special ring to Queen Elizabeth immediately, begging for her Majesty's mercy, stressing that it was a matter of life or death if the message was not delivered, handing the ring to the Countess of Nottingham before taking his leave.

The Countess then explained, that upon receipt of the ring, she returned home to discuss the matter with her husband, who was still alive at the time.

In view of Robert Devereux's treasonable activities, her husband discouraged the Countess from delivering the ring to her sister or Queen Elizabeth, and made arrangements that the yard boy would not be able to tell anyone he had spoken to her.

The Countess cried some more as she found out some days later that the yard boy had mysteriously disappeared, fearing he may have been killed through her misdeeds.

"I know now that the ring could have been his salvation, and I pray that you and God will forgive me," the Countess begged, her confession complete.

With that, Queen Elizabeth became furious and reproached her in the bitterest terms before grabbing her by the neck and shaking her violently for some seconds before her withered body was too weak to continue.

The Queen rose wearily to her feet in disgust.

"God may forgive you, but I never will!" she screamed at the Countess who now gasped for air in her worsened state of ill health as Queen Elizabeth stormed out of her house.

The Countess, full of grief and sorrow for her actions, wept for many days at her deception, and was found dead in her bed not long after.

87. DEATH OF A QUEEN

As Queen Elizabeth realised the implication of the Countess' confession, her exasperation against the Countess was soon replaced by inconsolable grief.

Feelings of the hopeless and irretrievable loss of her son, Robert Devereux, whose image the ring recalled so forcibly to her, felt as sharp as a dagger pushed deep within her heart.

Her imagination wandered in wretchedness and despair to the gloomy dungeon in the Tower where Robert had been confined, and she imagined him pining there, day after day, in dreadful suspense and anxiety, waiting for her to redeem the solemn pledge by which she had bound herself to him by giving him the ring.

All the sorrow she had felt at his untimely and cruel fate was awakened afresh, and had now become more poignant than ever.

No longer wishing to sleep in her bed, the Queen ordered her ladies-in-waiting to place cushions for her upon the floor in the most inner and secluded area of the private apartments. Her hair dishevelled, her dress neglected, her food refused, and her mind a prey to almost uninterrupted anguish and grief.

One day, feeling considerable pain in her hand, she asked her attendants to remove the wedding ring with which she had commemorated her espousal to her kingdom and her people on the day of her coronation.

Unfortunately, due to the flesh around the ring becoming swollen, natural removal was prevented, and the attendants had to procure an instrument to cut the ring in two, in order to relieve the pressure on her finger.

The task was carried out in silence as the Queen and her attendants, regarding the event as a symbol that the union, of which the ring had been the pledge, was being sundered forever.

The Queen's health continued to diminish with each passing day, and it became clear to all that she would soon cease to live.

Still feeling heartbroken for her actions in the demise of her son, Robert, she continually refused Francis his audience with her, feeling sorry for herself, and wishing to die.

One by one, the nobles and statesmen who had been her attendants at court for so many years began to withdraw from the palace, leaving London secretly, with eager dispatch to Scotland in order to be the first to hail King James, the moment they should learn that Elizabeth had ceased to breathe.

Though her strength of body was almost gone, her mind remained sharp and active within its failing tenement, watching everything, noticing every movement, and growing more and more irritable as her situation grew more helpless and forlorn. Everything seemed to conspire to deepen the despondency and gloom which darkened her dying hours.

With his patience now gone, Francis made a pact with one of the Queens ladies-in-waiting one evening to gain access to her Richmond residence to visit her, and as he travelled down one of the darkened hallways towards her apartments, he heard a wailing noise ahead of him.

In the distance, he saw a frail old woman in her night dress, swinging a sword to and fro, high in the air, as if she fought some invisible demons.

As he got closer, he realised the frail old woman was his fact his Queen, his mother, in the midst of madness, her thinning grey unkempt hair devoid of one of her stately wigs.

The danger of the sword she was wielding faded away as Francis remembered how this now frail woman once ruled the nation and extended colonies of England.

Tears fell from his eyes as his whole body shook with sadness at how she had become.

As he grew closer however, he realised he could be maimed by the Queen's erratic swinging of the sword and worried about how best to approach her.

"Who is it? Who is there? Is that you Satan come to take me?" she babbled as she tried to identify Francis in the darkened hallway, swinging her sword vigorously in front of her as she neared him, seemingly protecting herself.

"Please, stop this!" Francis begged her in despair.

Queen Elizabeth stopped dead in her tracks.

Her eyes widened as she focused on Francis standing before her.

In her madness, and her worn eyes from extreme sleep deprivation, she thought the voice to be her childhood sweetheart, Robert Dudley, Earl of Leicester, now long dead.

"Sweet Robin, is that you? Have you come for me at last? I have missed you so much!" she responded in a weak, longing voice.

As she dragged her feet slowly to Francis she dropped the sword to the ground, and Francis flinched as it hit the marble floor with an almighty *clang*.

As tears fell from her cheeks for her lost love, she stretched out her arms as her legs began to fail her, weak in her grief, with Francis just able to catch her as she sank to her knees on the cold marble floor, taking Francis down with her.

"Our son is dead Robin, our son is dead," she sobbed sorrowfully.

"I know, I know. It is going to be alright," Francis whispered soothingly back.

"It is my entire fault!" she cried through her tears, shaking her head.

Francis held her close and helped her back to her private quarters, consoling her throughout the night.

Over a few days, Francis tried to nurse her back to health, but it was no use, she had no will to live.

Speaking to the Queen's physician, Francis finally understood that there was no hope for her – she was dying, and had but a few days left to live.

As a few more days passed, her voice grew more and more faint, until, on March 23rd, she could no longer speak, and in the afternoon of this day, she roused herself a little, and contrived to made signs to have her Privy Council called to her bedside.

Those members of her Privy Council who had not yet departed for Scotland reported to her bedside pressing her for an answer to the all important question. Who did she wish to succeed her on the throne?

On her death bed, some of her councillors sat in vigil, pressing the Queen to name a successor, knowing full well that the statute she previously passed through parliament some 32 years before allowed her to name a *natural issue* as successor to the throne, if she so wished.

Unable to answer, when the assembled Privy Council suggested King James VI of Scotland, she raised her finger, making a sign of assent, and with them all in agreement, the counsellors left her.

At six o'clock in the evening she made a sign for the archbishop and her chaplains to come to her, and when they arrived, they approached her bedside and knelt before her.

The Queen lay on her back speechless, but with her eyes still moving watchfully and observing everything, she made those around her understand that the faculties of her mind were unimpaired.

As one of the clergymen asked her questions regarding her faith, she responded via hand and eye movements, still unable to speak as bystanders looked on with breathless attention.

The aged bishop, who had asked the questions earlier, began to pray for her, continuing for a considerable time, pronouncing a benediction upon her, and as he was about to conclude, Queen Elizabeth made a sign.

Not understanding her wishes, one of her ladies-in-waiting explained to the bishop that the Queen wished him to continue his devotions and although weary from kneeling, the bishop continued his prayers for a further half hour, and as he closed his bible the Queen again repeated the sign.

The bishop, realising that his prayers were providing some comfort, resumed with greater fervency than before, and continued his supplications for some time. This went on for so long, many of those that had been present eventually had to make their excuses to enable them to leave for their homes or other duties.

When at last the bishop retired, the Queen was left alone with her physician and ladies-in-waiting, and they remained at their dying sovereign's bedside for a few hours longer, observing her failing pulse, shallow breathing, and all the other indications of approaching dissolution.

As the hours passed slowly, they began to long for an end to their weary task and rest for both themselves and their patient. Their vigil finally ended at midnight, when it was communicated throughout the palace that Elizabeth was no more.

A messenger was despatched to Scotland to inform King James VI that he was to become the King of England, with subsequent messages then despatched to inform key persons in the realm that their Queen was dead, one of these messages being sent to the Bacon Gorhambury home in the dead of night.

Francis, his wife, Lady Anne Bacon, and much of the maids and servants was awakened by the load urgent knocking of the messenger with bad tidings.

On receiving the news that England's Queen was dead, Francis collapsed in grief, while Lady Anne broke down into a fit of tears, and the maids and servants who listed from the door let out muffled cries of sadness.

Francis staggered emotionally to the Chapel within their Gorhambury home, dropping down to his knees, wondering just how much more he could take.

With hands clasped tightly in desperate prayer for his Queen, he lifted his tear stained face up to the crucifix and benevolent, sad-eyed statue of the virgin, and bawled for the mother he never really knew.

In the meantime, all routes to Scotland were covered with eager aspirants for the favour of the distinguished personage there, who, from the instant Elizabeth ceased to breathe, became King of England and Wales in addition to the Scottish title he already held.

Eager patrons of the new King arrived in Scotland by sea and by land, urging their way as rapidly as possible, each wanting to be foremost in paying homage to the rising sun.

As Elizabeth lay neglected and forgotten, the Privy Counsel assembled and proclaimed King James, the rightful King of England. The interest she had once inspired had been awakened only by her power, and with that gone, few seemed to mourn her loss.

The attention of the kingdom was soon universally absorbed in the plans for receiving and proclaiming the new monarch from the North, and in anticipation of the splendid pageantry, which was to signal King James taking his seat upon the English Throne.

The Present

88. THE ISLAND

Heavy rain poured down on a deserted stretch of beach as the elderly man stepped from a boat and onto a foreign island, still wearing his wide brimmed hat, which kept the hard cold rain from hitting his face. He was immediately greeted by a darkly tanned looking English man.

"Hello sir, I am the foreman in command of the dig!" the man introduced himself, speaking in fluent English.

A small smile appeared from under the hat which still obstructed much of the old man's face as he faced away from the rain, and they immediately shook hands, and in the ensuing wrist action, there was a subtle give and take, as if they had just acknowledged each other in some secret way.

"Is everything going to plan?" the elderly man queried in a serious tone as they released hands.

"Yes. As per your instructions sir!" the man replied back agreeably.

"Good, good!" the elderly man nodded, as he looked up at the rain bearing down on the island.

"If you will follow me sir, I will get you in out of the rain and tomorrow if the weather is kind we can visit the dig?" the man explained.

"Yes, yes! That sound like a very good idea!" the elderly man responded eagerly as he shivered under his coat, hurriedly following the man into the island via a man made path.

89. A New Era

July 23rd 1603, Whitehall, London

Heavy rainfall poured down on some 300 or so well dressed noblemen standing impatiently in a line outside Whitehall, waiting to be formally presented to their new King, James I of England.

Many of their faces showed their frustration as they stood drenched in their best clothes as they waited to be presented to their new King.

As Francis stood next in line, his thoughts had blocked out the sound of a multitude of musicians playing jovial tunes for the large crowd that had travelled from across England to catch a glimpse of their new King.

King James stood magnificently under a waterproof tarpaulin wearing a velvet coat which reached down to his knees, obscuring most of his finely laced doublet, which was adorned with a frenzy of jewels and detailed embroidery.

As Francis looked at his own clothes, which looked damp and lifeless, he wondered what the future now held for him.

He was painfully aware that the naming of James VI of Scotland as the successor to the departed Queen Elizabeth ended the Tudor line, but due to his philanthropic literary work in the reign of Elizabeth, and the largely unpaid legal work for his sovereign, it had left him in dire straights financially.

Anthony's recent death had also left him with debts that had to be paid, in addition to his own debts covering his mortgaged Twickenham Park home.

Therefore, even though he had inherited the manors and estates of Gorhambury from Anthony, which had been bringing in a modicum of financial security, Francis still needed to earn a reasonable income, even if it meant practising law more fully and to possibly also try to obtain an official position in the King's service.

Being next in the queue, King James ushered him forward.

Francis bowed and then knelt before the newly pronounced King of England, who stood above him, clasping a sword in his hand.

After a brief pause, King James tapped the sword on each of his shoulders to knight him.

"Arise, *Sir* Francis Bacon!" King James proclaimed.

Francis glanced up to the new King of England, who looked solemnly back at him and sighed.

Hearing the impatient moans of the noblemen still waiting behind him, Francis realised there was no time to dither, and stood, briefly bowing to his King before leaving.

As he made his way pass a long crowd of other noblemen who were still waiting to be received, he passed his half-brother Edward Bacon also in the queue, and they exchanged a brief smile as they crossed each other.

With Queen Elizabeth now dead, Francis felt he was finally free to publish works under his own name with a lesser level of prejudice, publishing *Valerius Terminus of the Interpretation of Nature*, *Temporis Partus Masculus* (The Masculine Birth of Time) and *De Interpretatione Naturae Proaemium* (Preface to 'Of the Interpretation of Nature'), some of his philosophical efforts concerning nature.

He also began work on a series of manuscripts about the new union of England and Scotland which he hoped would capture the King's attention.

90. THE BIBLE

$\mathfrak{I}$n 1455, a man named Johann Gutenberg invented the first printing press in Mainz, Germany and the first ever book to be printed was a bible, in Latin, and this historical fact plagued King James.

Being a very devout man, born during the period between the Geneva and the Bishop's Bible, King James believed there was a need for a new Bible version, as the current offerings were, in his view, not true to the original Hebrew version.

Due to the Bible editions being available mostly in Latin, the tongue of scholars, lawyers, and priests, King James felt it was time to make a change and print an accurate version that was accessible to all.

"I have yet to see a Bible well translated into English, but I think that, of all, Geneva is the worst. I wish special pains to be taken for a uniform translation, which should be done by the best learned men in both Universities, then reviewed by the Bishops, presented to the Privy Council, lastly ratified by the Royal authority, to be read in the whole Church, and none other!" King James was heard to say in one of his earliest public speeches.

One of the first official actions of the new King in January of the following year was the calling of a Hampton Court Conference.

Here King James gave the go-ahead for the creation of a new bible, and five months later, 54 men deemed to be the best biblical scholars and linguists of their day were nominated to start work on it.

The first draft of the Bible was to be completed by organising six groups, who would meet regularly at three key locations; Westminster, Cambridge, and Oxford.

Ten at Westminster were assigned Genesis through to Kings; seven had Romans through Jude. At Cambridge, eight worked on Chronicles through Ecclesiastes, while seven others handled the Apocrypha. Oxford employed seven to translate Isaiah through Malachi and eight occupied themselves with the Gospels, Acts, and Revelations.

By January 1609, drafts of the three parts that made up the new bible had neared completion.

Each of the three companies created a draft copy of their efforts, one made at Oxford, one at Cambridge, and one at Westminster, which were then sent to London, with two members selected from each company forming a committee to review and polish the completed manuscripts.

The members met daily at Stationers' Hall in London over a nine-month period at which time, these newly drafted versions were entrusted to Dr. Thomas Bilson and Dr. Miles Smith, who then formally presented the hand written draft manuscripts over to King James.

A year later, King James returned a final *revised* hand written version of the Bible back to Dr. Thomas Bilson and Dr. Miles Smith, which was promptly sent off for publication.

91. LATER LIFE

Under the rule of the new King, the next few years would be busy ones for Francis as his writing groups worked feverishly under a more relaxed royal rule.

1604

Francis publishes *Apology in certain imputations concerning the late Earl of Essex*.

Francis is appointed to the King's Counsel.

Measure for Measure is first performed, a play dealing with the issues of mercy, justice, and truth, and their relationship to pride and humility.

One night as Francis watched a bright new evening star in the night sky, he thought back to his scriptures and wondered if 1600 years before, men also looked up and likewise considered a similar star to be the star of Bethlehem.

Francis, like many astronomers of his time, wondered whether the appearance of this wondrous sight, confirmed the significance of a period of great change based around an 800-year cycle, such as the rise of Charles the Great (800 years earlier) and the birth of Christ (1600 years earlier).

1605

The history of Don Quixote is published in Madrid. Over and over again in the book, thirty-three times in fact, we are told that the real author is an Arab historian named *Cid Hamet Benengeli*.

Francis publishes *The Advancement of Learning*.

King James sends Ben Jonson to prison for his play *Eastward Ho*, due to its derogatory reference to his Scottish kinsmen.

1606

Francis designs a garden within the grounds of the Gray's Inn law court where he was held in high regard, filling it with cherry, birch and groves of elms, which were recently delivered from a galleon returning from the island of *Acadia*.

One night in the secrecy of darkness, he buries certain original manuscripts close to his heart under a newly planted birch tree as a lasting tribute to the many plays he had written during his time spent at Gray's Inn.

Francis, wearing a purple robe of Genoese velvet, with shoes to match, adorned with rosettes and a cap of the same material, married Alice Barnham, the daughter of a rich London alderman. She was a young woman, 30 years his junior, bearing a striking resemblance to his old love, Queen Marguerite of Navarre.

The Virginia Company creates a charter together with help from Francis, finances and promotes the inhabitation of a colony in the America's.

In December, the Virginia Company's funds three ships to sail to the America's.

1607

Francis Writes *Cogita et Visa* (Thoughts and Conclusions).

Francis is appointed *Solicitor General*, one of the highest positions in England.

1608

Francis attends the funeral of his old mentor and friend, Dr John Dee and is bequeathed Dr. Dee's most important books, and promising on Dr. Dee's deathbed, to lead and expand the membership of 'The Order of the Rosy Cross'.

1609

The first settlers sent by the Virginia Company land in Jamestown and build a three-sided fort.

The Virginia Company issues a second charter signed by King James, which assigns Francis and 51 other names, the positions for governing the colony from London, and then sends an expedition of nine more ships, carrying some 600 passengers from Plymouth to reinforce the colony.

During the expedition, one of the vessels becomes shipwrecked off the island of Bermuda, but eventually makes it to Jamestown, whilst the remaining eight ships that did reach Virginia were subjected to infectious diseases, starvation, and the inhospitable natives.

92. THE CURSE OF AGING

Eyeing a sombre reflection of his self in a full length mirror as he stood in a dressing room at his Gorhambury home, Francis lets out a deep sigh.

Now aged 46 and dressed in black for a funeral, he reflected on the new lines on his aged face in the mirror as the sun's rays beamed through a nearby window, reflecting off his shiny balding head.

His eyes are full of sorrow.

After many years of caring for his step-mother, Lady Anne Bacon, as she battled dementia, she finally dies at the tender age of 82.

Francis solemnly puts on a wide rimmed black hat and then leaves the room, meeting his wife in the hallway, and they both make their way down the stairs of their home to a waiting procession for her funeral.

93. REVENGE

Spain, 1609

In the Spanish town of Logroño, Northern Spain, not far from the town of Navarre, the Spanish inquisition had begun the Basque witch trials, Spain's most ambitious attempt to root out witchcraft.

In the local city prison, a plump grey haired woman awaiting trial for practicing witchcraft is thrown into the adjoining cell of a wild haired man snoring loudly as he lay fast asleep on a dirty cell floor.

Unable to see the man's face, hidden amidst a mop of long wild hair, wearing nothing more than a pair of shorts, the old women sadly eyed scarred streaks on the man's bony back revealing years of whipping's the prisoner had to endure as part of his confinement.

After many hours agitated by the man's incessant snoring, the woman finally becomes angry for some peace.

"You there on the ground!" the woman barked, trying to rouse the sleeping man from his slumber

"You there!" she shouted at him again.

"What do you want witch!" mumbled the man as he stirred a little, moving his head a little.

"Who said I was a witch? It's a damned lie I say!" the woman shouted defensively, deciding not to say another word.

Through his long wild black hair, the man's dark grey eyes twitched a little as he considered the woman's curious response.

"Only a witch would antagonise a man while he slept!" the man groaned a little, faking his agitation as he waited to hear her response.

"Oh, I see!" the woman replied, understanding the logic of the man's outburst to her.

The man digested her response for a few seconds before slowly rising to his feet, and as he did, his long wild hair dropped around his gaunt and dirtied face, which now sported an overgrown beard as well.

He brushed off the stray dirt that had stuck to his sweaty chest and face, leaning against a wall for support as he slowly opened his weary eyes.

"How long have you been here?" the woman asked after a few tense seconds, eyeing the man's long locks and beard.

"What year is it?" the man groaned, not really knowing the answer.

Her eyes widened.

"You don't know what year it is?" the old woman asked, feeling a hint of sadness for the man.

"What year is it woman!" the man pressed impatiently with a raised voice.

"1609! It's 1609" she stuttered back quickly.

As the man heard the old woman's response, his eyes dropped to the floor in a seemingly lost stare and then sighed before sliding back down onto the dirty floor using the wall as support for his slow decline.

He paused for some seconds as he took in the information.

"Twenty years," he groaned.

The woman gasped and dropped her head, fearful of what the witch trials had in store for her.

The man parted the long locks that covered his face, tucking them behind his ears, revealing a battered and bruised looking Damien.

His broken nose and gaunt face left permanent traces of the 20 years of torture he had endured at the hands of the prison guards that used him as their plaything.

Staring into the darkness of his cell, his dark grey eyes seemed devoid of any real emotion, and he stared blankly at one of the walls for several seconds before remembering that he was not alone.

"Why are you here?" Damien asked, turning to the old women, eyeing her intensely with his dark grey eyes as if seeing her for the first time.

The woman felt a cold chill as he stared at her.

"I am here for the inquisition," she told him, looking away.

"The inquisition?" Damien asked with a grave stare.

"The damned Spanish inquisition is putting people on trial for practicing magic," the woman explained, realising he obviously didn't know what happened beyond his prison cell.

A trial? Damien thought worriedly as he wondered whether they would come for him as well.

"They are scouring the surrounding areas of Navarre, Alava, Guipuscoa, Biscay, La Rioja and even in the North of Burgos and Soria, making their arrests!" she moaned.

At the mention of Navarre, Damien thought back to the life he had been living before he was locked up in this stinking prison some twenty years ago.

He then remembered how his uncle, Lord Beaumont, had rejected using his influence that could have released him when he was first arrested.

Damien now hated his uncle with a passion, but somehow though, he knew that today, everything was going to change.

"So, are you a witch?" Damien asked her coldly.

"No, I am not!" the old woman immediately responded defensively, crossing her arms and pouting her lips.

Damien was not convinced, but he said no more and simply curled back up on the floor to sleep, but for the first time in many years, he let out a wry smile.

As Damien feigned a quieter sleeping pattern than before, it was not long before the old woman closed her eyes and fell into a sombre sleep, snoring quite loudly herself.

As Damien gently rolled over onto his back and eyed the old woman asleep, he quietly rose to his feet and made his way to the adjoining cell bars which separated them.

I can feel your magic, witch! Damien thought to himself as he reached one of his arms between the bars, and closed his eyes in concentration, opening them a few seconds later with a mischievous grin, the first time in many years.

Weakened from his bad diet and the many beatings during his imprisonment, Damien had no way to rebuild his depleted mystical powers, until now.

Damien closed his eyes again and mustered up an ancient incantation that drew on the little mystical power he could draw from within the old witch into himself.

As the incantation did its job, Damien's whole body felt euphoric, and he revelled in the small but powerful fill.

The following day when a young guard entered the prison to relieve one of the older officers on night duty, he found his fellow guards murdered in the most gruesome of deaths.

Damien had claimed his retribution against the guards that had inflicted many years of torture against him. Lucky for them, their torture was short due to Damien's minimal mystical powers.

As he searched the cells nervously and discovered that Damien had escaped, he also discovered the old woman, who was now nothing more than a dead withered corpse.

✝

Some days later back in Navarre, in the early hours of the morning, Damien looking in better health, stood partially disguised in a stolen oversized long dark coat, waiting patiently in front of a bridge, blocking its entrance.

As he glanced over the bridge edge, he smiled at the sheer drop beneath him of some hundred feet with a streaming river bank some fifty feet wide at its bottom.

Feeling the ground rumbling beneath him, he turned back towards the path.

Looking in the distance, he confirmed that a carriage was heading towards the bridge he was blocking.

Within the carriage, was Damien's uncle, Lord Beaumont, his wife, and their daughter, making their weekly trip to church.

It had been over 20 years since Damien had last seen the only family he had left in the world, and the years had been kind to them, no doubt helped by his uncle's wealth.

As the coachman spotted Damien standing purposefully between the carriage and the bridge, he pulled on the reins, bringing his two mares skidding to an abrupt halt, causing his passengers to fall about inside the carriage.

"What the hell is going on?" Lord Beaumont shouted up angrily to the coachman, as he managed to get back into his seat with his wife and daughter following suite.

"I am sorry sire, but there is a gentleman blocking the bridge!" the coachman shouted down from his elevated seat to the side of one of the carriage windows.

"What?" Lord Beaumont replied angrily, peering out of the carriage window to see for himself.

With his long unkempt wild hair blowing in the wind covering his face, Damien tucked one side of his locks behind an ear, exposing his face to his uncle who was now looking directly at him from the carriage.

As his uncle recognised Damien, his brows collided ferociously above the fear in his eyes.

He popped his head back into the carriage and slumped back into his seat, contemplating his predicament.

Lord Beaumont had a flashback of some twenty years before when Damien was first imprisoned, receiving a letter from Damien begging for help to get him released, which he had refused.

"Whatever is the matter?" his wife asked, seeing he husband's now sombre face.

"It's Damien. I think he intends to do us harm!" Lord Beaumont responded with fear in his voice.

His wife gasped, while his daughter could not really understand why they were so fearful of her cousin.

As his wife and daughter looked out the other carriage window, they became frightened themselves as they witnessed Damien's crazed demeanour.

Lord Beaumont feared the worst in that Damien had come back for retribution against him and his family. Lord Beaumont knew there was only one option.

He popped his head back out of the carriage.

"Continue onwards!" he shouted to his coachman.

"But the gentleman sire?" the coachman continued in a strained voice, apprehensive about going any further.

"He'll get out of the way if he knows what's good for him!" Lord Beaumont shouted back up impatiently.

"Get this carriage moving!" Lord Beaumont pressed, banging impatiently on the roof, unsettling the coachman topside.

Uncomfortably, the coachman whipped his horses back into action, forcing the carriage to bolt towards the bridge and Damien.

The coachmen's heart raced as he approached Damien, and he swung his arm madly warning him to get out of the way, but the emotionless Damien stood his ground defiantly.

Just as the carriage was within a few feet of running him over, Damien whispered an incantation that caused the horses to jerk wildly and then change their direction, veering away from Damien and towards an unprotected edge next to the bridge that led perilously downwards into the deep rocky gorge below.

In the blink of an eye, as the coachman tried in vain to stop the horses, he, Lord Beaumont, his screaming wife and daughter, flew off the edge of the sheer drop.

Almost majestically, for a brief moment, the wild mares pulling the carriage seemed to have achieved the impossible as they left the road and hovered in mid air before they and the heavy carriage they were strapped to, dropped like a lead weight down into the deep rocky gorge beneath them.

"Goodbye uncle, and oh yes, give my regards to my parents," Damien commented coldly as the screams of the last of his family in the world, grew more and more feint until it abruptly stopped, replaced by the even more feint cracking noise of wood and bone against the river and stone of the gorge.

Damien solemnly made his way towards a horse that had been secured nearby, climbing atop it and directing it off into the town of Navarre.

With Damien being the sole surviving relative of Lord Beaumont, he now hoped to inherit his uncle's wealth, but he was soon to realise that his uncle had put a clause in his will bequeathing his wealth, upon the death of himself, his wife and daughter, wholly to the secret order *Alumbrados*.

Angry that his uncle's wealth had been taken from him, Damien spent the following year regaining his strength, and then used his power of persuasion to infiltrate the *Alumbrados* secret order, enabling him to eventually take control of all the high ranking members of the order and pollute the order's doctrines with dark magic, ultimately turning each of its members into his slaves and in turn giving him immense power.

94. THE TEMPEST

𝔉rancis begins work on a new play entitled *The Tempest*.

As he wrote well into the night, he referred to a worn bound document that bore the title *True Reportory*; a 2000-word report written by William Strachey, the returning secretary to the intended Deputy Governor of a colony in the America's funded by the Virginia Company.

In this restricted document, William Strachey gave a detailed account of important events that he had witnessed, which included rapes, murders and insurrections of the natives.

In this new manuscript, Francis had decided to recognise his old mentor Dr. Dee as the character of *Prospero* within it, portraying Dr. Dee's tireless efforts of ridding the world of those that wielded the power of Black magic and wished to use it for the destruction of all that was good.

In addition to adding mysticism to the play, Francis had decided to encode some of the spiritual doctrines that had been created for new initiates of the Freemasonry secret society that he was helping to build.

In encoding some of the *degree's* of Freemasonry, Francis explained the character 'Prospero' as being a man of goodwill and beloved by his people, highlighting to the secret initiate the 1st Degree of the Freemasonry, its lowest level, and as having earnestly studied the Liberal Arts and Sciences, then showed that the Prospero earned himself the 2nd Degree.

Having his hero then face death by drowning and starvation, being then brought up by his daughter with charitable care on the island on which he was cast, the character then earned himself the 3rd level degree of Freemasonry.

Giving Prospero a hat and rapier, which he donned when he wished to reveal his true self to others, Francis could indicate some of the Freemasonry symbolism that initiates would recognise and also encode a subtle link to the helmet and spear that was associated to his muse, Pallas Athena.

Here then, Prospero was described as a Freemason Master, who had started at the lowest degree in the beginning of the play and his elevations up further degrees during the course of the play.

This manuscript being the last play that he wished written under the Shakespeare pseudonym, would also contain his signature 33, derived from the final word of the play:

As you from crimes would pardon'd be,
*Let your Indulgence set me **free**.*

The meaning of the final word was as personal as it could be, as the Latin meaning of 'Francis' meant "Frenchman: *Free* Man", and coincidentally, the simple cipher count of *Free* also equated to 33, the same cipher for the name "Bacon" as well.

95. THE FIRE

29th June 1613, Globe playhouse, London

Francis and some of his closest friends made their way to some seats in an elevated private balcony of the playhouse that looked down over the stage.

He was attending a performance of the 'William Shake-speare' play *All is True*, a history of Henry VIII by the playing troupe *The Lord Chamberlain's Men*.

As the play commenced, Francis was as usual enthralled to see a production of his writing group's efforts again, but not being able to settle in his seat, he knew something was wrong.

He had an unshakable feeling that he was being watched, and as he scanned the audience in the lower aisles, he received confirmation, recognising a face he thought was a ghost.

Damien's face looked back up at him.

The years had not been kind to Damien, but it was definitely him, looking up at Francis with a deadly stare.

As Francis considered Damien's disregard for human life, he began to fear for the lives of the patrons in the playhouse and his own friends.

He knew he had to draw Damien away from the playhouse.

He rose, making an excuse to get some air, and made his way down some steps to ground level to face his old enemy, and similarly, Damien left his seat, gesturing with a tilt of his head for Francis to follow him through a side door near to him, which led down to the basement level of the playhouse.

Francis nodded in agreement and followed Damien through the side door and down the stairs into the darkened room of the playhouse basement, finally facing each other amidst old props and boxes full of costumes from past plays.

As loose sawdust fell down around them, escaping through the cracks in the ceiling from the antics of the ongoing performance above them, they eyed each other for many seconds, seemingly testing each other's nerves.

"What are you doing here Damien?" Francis asked finally, fearing for the safety of the people watching the performance above them.

"Francis, I thought you would be glad to see me!" Damien responded mockingly.

"I am. I have old scores to settle with you!" Francis responded as he braced himself for a fight, summoning mystical energy within him that immediately powered into both of his fists, allowing him to draw on them in an instant if he needed to defend himself quickly.

"The last I heard of you, was that you were imprisoned in a Spanish jail!" Francis started with a glint of disappointment in his eyes.

"I rather hoped you had died there," Francis continued.

Damien, desperately wanting to strike out at Francis, held back and instead forced a smile at his enemy.

"Be careful, now Francis. Remember, Dr. Dee is not around to save you this time,"

"Don't you dare talk about Dr. Dee!" Francis growled as his anger began to strengthening the power within his clenched fists.

"What are you doing here Damien?" Francis pressed again, wishing to fight him and get it over with.

"I am here for revenge Francis. You lost me an important prize, and for that you must pay!" Damien shouted back.

As the play continued above, a sliver of sawdust fell down between them seemingly creating a makeshift dividing line between them.

"An important prize?" Francis queried with a heavy frown.

"Are you talking about the Book of Raziel?" Francis queried in an almost mocking tone.

Damien was speechless for some seconds, amazed that Francis even knew of the book's existence.

"What do you know of the Book of Raziel? Tell me dammit!" Damien demanded.

Francis laughed a little as he realised that Damien had no idea that he possessed the book all these years.

Damien became even more impatient.

"Tell me!" Damien pressed, now losing his cool.

"I have the book and I alone wield its power!" Francis responded calmly, raising his hands, as its mystical power pulsated in his fists.

Damien staggered back, fearful of Francis for the first time.

"You have had the book all along?" Damien replied, stunned at the revelation.

Is the Book of Raziel really that powerful? Francis considered as he saw the fear in Damien's face.

"Yes!" Francis responded darkly.

"Where is it?" Damien shouted angrily.

"You have no appreciation of its power! Give it to me!" Damien barked.

"You will never have it Damien!" Francis told him frankly.

"Then you will have to die Francis, because I <u>will</u> have that book!" Damien replied defiantly, and immediately began an onslaught of powerful magic against Francis, shooting a series of fire blasts at him, which Francis managed to block with his own onslaught.

As they fought for several minutes in the confines of the basement, Damien quickly realised that their powers were on an equal footing, realising Francis must have been either holding his power back or had not fully harnessed the book's true potential as yet.

To be sure, he decided he would have to retreat and find another way to defeat Francis if he hoped to have a chance of finally possessing it.

"When you least expect it Francis, I will be your downfall, and then I will be back for the book!" Damien warned him as he stopped his attack.

"You are not going anywhere Damien. There is no way I am going to let you leave!" Francis declared, as he thought about the scores of men that had died at Damien's hand when they last fought in the war with Spain.

"You think you can stop me Francis?" Damien mocked, surveying his surroundings, eyeing the wooden beam foundations that made up the playhouse around them.

"You know, this playhouse is constructed entirely out of wood and is a sure risk to the people above us if a fire was to break out!" Damien threatened.

"I could just imagine how high the causalities would be if it were to catch fire during a packed performance, like the one tonight!" Damien added smiling devilishly.

"You would be wise to leave this playhouse peacefully Damien!" warned Francis as he realised that Damien's threat was very real, knowing full well that the wooden frame foundation of the playhouse around them was like a tinderbox.

As they stood face to face Damien whispered a short incantation which created a small smouldering fireball in his hand, which he playfully jerked in many different directions, taunting Francis who was at the ready to dispel it.

"All it would take is a well placed fireball to hit one of these supporting beams and I could literally bring the house down!" Damien teased.

"Don't do it Damien, or I promise you, you will regret it!" Francis warned him.

Damien made a thoughtful facial expression, seemingly considering the idea, before quickly shooting the fireball towards one of the supporting wooden beams.

"No!" Francis shouted, immediately whispering his own incantation to dispel the fireball, but it was too late. As the fireball hit its target, a main wooden structural beam, it immediately burst into flames.

As Francis tried to contain the inflamed wooden beam by calling on an incantation to manifest a jet of water onto the flames, Damian fired off another one at the ceiling of the basement which smashed through the stage floor, careering into a curtain hanging on one of the walls, causing it to catch fire.

As the curtain burst into flames, panic set in for the playhouse patrons and actors above them, and Francis began to hear screams and the urgent footsteps of people above them escaping the building for the safety of the outdoors.

"We will meet again Francis!" Damian shouted above the noise, making his escape back up the side door to the ground floor.

As Damien turned back to Francis however, he could see Francis had almost put out the fire on the wooden beam, and thinking that Francis would nothing to delay him chasing after him, he realised he would need to cause more damage to ensure his escape.

Looking at the other supporting beams around him, he launched a number of further fireball's at two of the supporting wooden beams, which immediately began to destabilise the basement structure, bringing the playhouse down around them.

"No!" shouted Francis, looking at the other beams now on fire.

Francis knew he would not be able to stop the now irreversible damage Damien had caused.

As Damien stood at the small steps that led back up the ground level, he gave a final laugh at Francis before making his escape, just managing to escape out of the playhouse as it collapsed around Francis.

As Francis eyed the side entrance that was to be his escape collapse, he realised his only exit was now blocked because of falling debris.

Francis desperately searched for another way out, now terrified that he would become buried alive under the collapsing structure.

In an act of desperation, he decided to shoot a powerful a fireball at a nearby weakened wall, which successfully smashed a way out of the basement to the exterior of the playhouse, and just managing to escape the basement as the whole building collapsed.

Now out of the burning building, he searched desperately for Damien, but he was gone.

Full of soot like the rest of the playhouse patrons, Francis returned to the playhouse as it burned to the ground, shaking his head in disbelief at Damien's escape.

Francis could not believe he had let Damian get away *again*.

96. REVELATIONS

Some months after the first version of the King James Bible had been published and distributed to all the churches across England, batches of it were also sent out across Europe, with a copy reaching Damien, now back in France.

Sitting in a darkened room sparsely lit by numerous candles, he studied the text of the huge book on an equally large imposing desk.

Next to this great book was a small parchment containing notes he had made referring to certain passages that had intrigued him during previous readings, and the notes listed Deuteronomy 18:10, Revelations 13:18, and Job 38:31 among others.

Damien had become interested in this new version of the bible ever since he had been informed by a demon he had previously communed with stating that the Bible had been encoded with certain secrets relating to Francis Bacon and a recently emerging order called *The Freemasons*.

Damien was on a mission to seek out anything scandalous about Francis in the hopes of blackmailing him into giving up the Book of Raziel, and reviewing his notes, he opened the great bible to particular scripture, **Deuteronomy 18:10**, reading the passage quietly to himself.

There shall not be found among you any one that maketh his son or his daughter to pass through the fire, or that useth divination, or an observer of the times, or an enchanter, or a witch, or a charmer, or a consulter with familiar spirits, or a wizard, or a necromancer.

He scoffed at the text before referring back to his notes to find the next entry to review, turning the pages of the bible to stop at **Revelations 13:18** and again read the passage silently to himself.

Here is wisdom.

Let him that hath understanding count the number of the beast: for it is the number of a man; and his number is six hundred threescore and six.

"Six hundred and sixty six," he whispered under his breath as he wondered if there was a hidden meaning to the number.

Closing his eyes, he concentrated on the text, and as he reopened his eyes, he could sense that there was something more to the passage, something hidden.

...count the number of the beast: for it is the <u>number of a man</u>; and his number is six hundred threescore and six

Feeling this fragment stood out in particular, he immediately jumped up and scanned some books on a nearby shelf, selecting one entitled *Proficience and Advancement of Learning Divine and Humane*, written by Francis Bacon.

He lifted the book from the shelf and opened it to a bookmark he had set earlier, and read an underlined passage 'for Cyphars; they were commonly in letters or alphabets, but may be in words.'

It must be a cypher of some kind Damien considered defiantly, closing the small book and replacing it back on the shelf before returning to the biblical text of Revelations that seemed to call out to him.

...count the number of the beast Damien thought logically, thinking the book was a beast of a volume.

Having a strong analytical mind, he opened the Bible back to its contents page, and reviewed the index of chapters, and then from the first page, he began to *count* the number of pages, ignoring the title page and the following blank page. As he counted, he paused briefly when he came to a blank page after the first 33 pages of content, but then continued, excluding a count of the blank page.

He continued counting the pages, and turning the page to reveal the 666th page, he arrived at the end of Psalm 45 and the beginning of Psalm 46, and excitedly, he reads the last line of Psalm 45 at the top of the page.

<u>I will make thy name</u> to be remembered in all generations: therefore shall the people praise thee for ever and ever.

"I will make thy name?" he repeated to himself quizzingly, concluding that the text was alluding to a name of some kind.

There must be a name hidden in these pages! Damian considered as he tried to decipher what was actually hidden in the text.

Reading Psalm 46 and not find anything out of the ordinary, he reluctantly returned to the contents page to try alternative counting methodologies, with 666 as the numerical *key*, and began to count the chapters, realising there were indeed over 666 chapters in the edition, searching for the 666 link.

He tried it two different ways, firstly he counted from the *first* chapter of the bible, and then from the *last* chapter of the bible and on checking the 666th chapter from the end of the bible, he found it again pointed to Psalm 46.

His face lit up.

There has to be something of note in this Psalm! Damien thought excitedly.

OD is our refuge and strength: a very present helpe in trouble.
2 Therefore will not we feare, though the earth be remoued: and though the mountaines be caried into the midst of the sea.
3 Though the waters thereof roare and be troubled, though the mountaines shake with the swelling thereof.
4 There is a riuer, the streames wherof shall make glad the citie of God: the holy place of the Tabernacles of the most high.
5 God is in the midst of her: she shall not be moued: God shall helpe her, and that right early.
6 The heathen raged, the kingdomes were mooued: he vttered his voyce, the earth melted.
7 The LORD of hosts is with vs, the God of Jacob is our refuge.
8 Come, behold the workes of the LORD, what desolations hee hath made in the earth.
9 He maketh warres to cease vnto the end of the earth: hee breaketh the bow, and cutteth the speare in sunder, he burneth the chariot in the fire.
10 Be still, and know that I am God: I will be exalted among the heathen, I will be exalted in the earth.
11 The LORD of hosts is with vs, the God of Jacob is our refuge.

He jumped up and looked back at his bookshelf, retrieving a 1602 version of the *Bishop's* Bible, which was an earlier translation of the Hebrew text, placing it next to the King James edition, opening it also at Psalms 46.

Comparing the text of Psalm 46 in both bibles, he noticed that the Bishops Bible omitted the words *Selah*, which he knew to be Hebrew punctuation text.

Damien was more intrigued to find a matching pattern of words at the top and bottom of the King James Version of the text which did not exist in the Bishops Bible version.

Focusing his attention back on the King James text, he now recognised three of the four key alchemical elements, *Earth*, *Water*, and *Fire*, which he had not picked up on before.

As Damien retrieved a quill, he noted down the numerical patterns of the elements he had identified in the psalm, counting the word location for these initial words.

For the word location of 'Earth', he marked it as the 20th word and 'Water' being the 37th, partially validating a similar pattern by counting backwards from the bottom of the text, finding the word for the element 'Fire' at the 37th word.

Curiously, Damien found the text 'will' at the 20th word, where he thought the last element 'air' should have been located.

Thinking the elements texts as coincidence, he tried alternative number pattern sequences, and eventually decided to use the Psalm '46' number as the key. He counted 46 words from the first word of the psalm, which he identified as "shake" and then counted 46 words from the end of the psalm, identifying the word "spear" there.

As he leaned back in his chair thinking about the power of the Book of Raziel, remembering Francis had revealed to him that he possessed it at their last encounter when they fought at 'The Globe', it struck him that the play being performed that night was written by a *William Shake-speare*.

Now filled with a knowing look of astonishment, he jerked his head back down at the text for Psalm 46 and smiled at finding a *shake-speare* signature connection encoded in the King James Bible, revealed initially in *Revelations 13:18*.

It was no coincidence, it was encoded in Revelations! Damien thought as he leaned back in his chair, his eyes wide in amazement at his find.

Now I need to understand what connection there is between this man William Shake-speare and Francis! Damien thought defiantly as a frown rose on his forehead.

Over a number of days, searching the pages of the King James Bible for more clues, he uncovered many numerical associations relating to the number 33, one in particular, found when he reviewed the exact middle pages of the bible, being *Psalm 117*.

This biblical text, being the shortest chapter in the whole bible, contained exactly 33 words, which by no coincidence was the number of years in the life of Jesus Christ, the number of generations from Adam to David.

Unbeknown to Damien, 33 was also the number of degrees Francis had defined for the secret Freemasonry order and of course was also the cipher number for 'Bacon'.

97. Accolades

Over the next few years, all the hard work Francis had put in to progress his political career started to bear fruit and he began to receive many elevations of power.

1613

English Colonists in Virginia destroy the French settlements at Port Royal, Nova Scotia.

Francis arranges a house purchase from a Henry Walker to William Shakspere to ensure the Stratfordian's silence was maintained. The house in question was originally owned by his step-mother, Lady Anne Bacon.

1614

Sir Walter Raleigh writes "The History of the World".

In a dimly lit cellar of his Gorhambury home, Francis worked feverishly in a makeshift laboratory on a number of experiments amidst an array of strange instruments such as aged manuscripts, skulls, and animal specimens.

1616

Francis is appointed *Privy Councillor*.

Francis takes on a forty year lease of Canonbury Manor, a fine mansion which afforded panoramic views over London, which quickly became the venue of choice to enrol new initiates into the secret Freemasonry order.

William Shakspere dies on April 22

Miguel de Cervantes, author of 'Don Quixote' dies on April 23

Francis reviews a written manuscript entitled *Macbeth* in the study of his Gorhambury home with its author John Middleton.

Francis helps the Privy Council to dismiss Edward Coke, his long time rival, from the post of *Lord Chief Justice*.

1617

Francis is appointed *Lord Keeper*.

While King James toured his old Kingdom in Scotland, he names Francis, *Regent of England*, which gives Francis ruling power over England for many months in the King's absence.

1618

Francis publishes a book to commemorate the King's tour of Scotland.

Francis leads many battles against the forces of evil with his druid army, in the name of *The Rosy Cross*.

Francis is appointed *Lord Chancellor*.

Francis secures a lease of his childhood home, York House, giving him a London residence for himself and his wife, Alice Bacon.

Francis uses a magnifying glass as he makes use of his artistic skills in calligraphy, carving curious strokes around a prominent letter "B" on the side of a wooden printing block.

Francis is given the title *Baron Verulam*.

1620

Francis Publishes *Novum Organum* (The New Organon).

Francis continues to influence the Freemasonry secret order across Europe.

1621

Francis is given the title *Viscount St. Albans*.

98. THE ACTOR'S GRAVEYARD

$\mathfrak{M}$aking their way out of a carriage in the east end of London, a balding Francis Bacon in his 60th year and a similarly aged Ben Jonson, makes a visit to Saint Leonard's Churchyard in Shoreditch, more commonly known as *The Actor's Graveyard.*

Although Francis continued to grow in stature under the rule of King James, the accolades he received felt hollow as he mourned the loss of key people in his life such as his step-parents Sir Nicholas and Lady Anne Bacon, his blood brother Robert Devereux, his step-brother Anthony, and his real mother and father, Queen Elizabeth and Robert Dudley, Earl of Leicester.

As Francis led the way into the cemetery, they passed the many gravestones for actors famous in their day. One particular gravestone catches Ben Jonson's eye, which was the grave of an actor called *Gabriel Spenser,* who died 22nd September 1598.

Ben Jonson's s face filled with guilt and in a panic he quickly distanced himself from the grave, wanting to forget he was the man who had killed him in bar brawl.

As he caught up to Francis, he found him standing over the grave of James Burbage, founder of England's first playhouse, *The Theatre.* Ben Jonson was amazed and saddened at the same time as he noticed headstones for James' two sons, Richard & Cuthbert, who inherited two theatres upon their father's death, "The Blackfriars Theatre" & "The Theatre".

As Francis thought back to how the Babbage brothers created 'The Globe' playhouse, he could not help but laugh a little at their ingenuity.

The story of the 'The Globe' was a strange one and came about because of a legal dispute against rent due on the land of "The Theatre" was built.

The Babbage brothers owning the building, but not the land, had disagreed to an unfair increase in the rent by their landlord, and promptly decided to relocate it, timber by timber, across the Thames, renaming it to *The Globe*.

Sadness covered Francis' face as he felt the guilt in being the cause for the playhouse to be burned to the ground during a mystical fight he had with Damien.

"The Bacon family has been connected to the Burbage family for over 40 years," Francis commented in a sad tone back to Ben Jonson.

Ben Jonson's eyes widened.

"You knew the family that long?" Ben Jonson asked in amazement.

Francis nodded solemnly.

"It was James Burbage that introduced me to the stage, and I will forever be grateful to him and his family for that. He and his wife, as well as Richard, Cuthbert, and his three daughters, are all gone now," Francis added sadly.

As Ben Jonson surveyed the surrounding graves and realised the extended graves, he was now even more saddened for the Burbage family.

"I will just say a prayer before we go?" Francis asked.

"Of course!" Ben Jonson replied, nodding profusely, bowing his own head.

As they both bowed their heads, Francis whispered a prayer for the Burbage family, calling out each of the many family members names one by one that had been buried in the cemetery.

As Francis finished, they turned and left the cemetery, with Ben Jonson taking a slightly longer route out of the cemetery, not wanting to pass by the headstone of the man he had killed, for fear of being haunted for the rest of his days by the dead man's ghost.

99. THE NEW ATLANTIS

𝕿wisting and turning in his bed, Francis had another troubled sleep as his wife lay beside him snoring loudly. The dreams eventually became more vivid.

In one dream, Francis saw himself making his way across the seas to an unknown land, the *New World*, and further visions, seemed to cycle through this new land, seemingly accelerating timelines and showing the barren land, being built upon as years, then decades passed.

Images flashed of many wars, the signing of the Declaration of Independence, more wars, and notable figures including Hitler, Martin Luther King, the KKK, free love of the 1960s, Presidents, Rosa Parks, Stalin, nuclear missiles, Beatrice Hicks, and the collapse of the twin towers on 9/11.

Francis woke up in a sweat.

This dream was not the first he had experienced, where he envisioned a new utopia defined by an ideal commonwealth that would ultimately be a global controlling force, but with each dream he could see how that new utopia would operate and evolve, be it good or bad.

This last vivid dream was all that he needed to complete the picture of how that new utopia would be realised, and as he looked over to his perfect wife still asleep beside him, he quietly got out of bed and made his way downstairs to his study.

With a bust of Athena staring down at him from the mantel of his study, he took his seat, pulling out some blank parchment and a new quill from his desk drawer.

As he dipped the quill briefly into a nearby inkpot, he paused to take in the euphoria of what he was about to write.

Thinking of the title he had already selected, he wrote the words *The New Atlantis* at the top of the first blank piece of parchment, a legendary island he was introduced to in his studies of the Greek philosopher Plato in his dialogues, *Timaeus* and *Critias*.

As he lingered on the title, Francis thought back to the secret Knights Templar diary that he had discovered in the library at Gray's Inn, he remembered the entries of the Norse saga's which alluded to the location of a legendary island that was now recognised to be the New World.

In this, his *Magnum Opus* [Latin for 'Great Work'], Francis would detail his aspirations and ideals in the form of an idealised utopia and a vision of the future of human discovery and knowledge.

In this new manuscript, he would describe a land where there would be greater rights for women, the abolition of slavery, the elimination of debtor's prisons, the separation of church and state, and freedom of religious and political expression.

100. THE MONOPOLY

House of Parliament, 1621

Due to his recent elevation to Lord Chancellor and Keeper of the Great Seal of England, Francis had become the *single* authority of approval for all official documents of England.

Of all his previous political appointments, it was this one that he was most proud of, as it was a position also held by his deceased step-father, Sir Nicholas Bacon.

As the British parliament grew in power, King James was finding it more and more difficult to control and prosper from *his* England, with much of his historical regal powers being continually scrutinised by parliament.

Of the few historical powers King James still controlled, was the rights and letting of monopolies and patents for commodities such as for gold, silver and thread, which meant that no one could deal in such commodities or goods, unless a patent was approved by him.

It was the talk of parliament that King James was known to only approve patents on the proviso that the recipient would give him a share in any profits they received. One of the prominent recipients of the most lucrative monopolies manufacturing gold and silver lace was to the Duke of Buckingham and two other lucky men being a Sir Giles Mompesson and Sir Francis Michell.

As these fortunate men prospered greatly through these monopolies it was not long before jealousies arose from other nobles and questions started to be asked as to whether the King actually owned the powers to grant such patents in the first place, but until the question was settled, these dealings were legal, and Francis, in his role as Lord Chancellor, had no option but to approve them.

As Francis could see the backlash that this was causing around the realm he wrote to the Duke of Buckingham, who had the ear of the King, stating:

Care must be taken that monopolies, which are the canker of all trades, be by no means admitted under the pretence of the specious colour of the Public Good,

When it came time to settle the question as to whether King James owned the right to approve such patents, a King's Counsel was created and named *The Referees* based on advice from Francis himself.

King James very grudgingly gave his consent, which was necessary as any matter concerning the legality of the monopolies could not be authorised without it. Francis also commented on this at the time, stating:

…the King did wisely put it upon a consult whether the patents were at this time to be removed by Act of Counsel before Parliament,

This comment gave some credence that King James was being responsible in the ensuing investigations.

"The patents and monopolies were right in law but wrong in convenience and action, and that any that was being exploited for private gain and not for the national interest should be declared illegal!" Francis declared at a meeting of 'The Referees', which caused ripples throughout parliament as no one previously dared to give a public opinion on the matter.

The King and the Duke of Buckingham naturally objected to this as they were both sharing in the profits, and as the majority of 'The Referees' knew this, when it came to a vote to declare their opinions on the matter, they dared not vote against the King's wishes.

On a count being taken, it was found that the majority had decided that the King did indeed possess the necessary legal rights, with Francis, voting with a minority of people against the continuation of such patents.

However, some Members of Parliament were still determined to obtain redress of the grievances caused by the monopoly patents, and decided to mount a stronger case intended to attack the offensive patents, and pushed through another request in Parliament to question their legality once more.

Although Francis had voted at the meeting of 'The Referees' against the continuation of the monopoly patents, it was still his responsibility to authorise them, which gave Sir Edward Coke, his longstanding adversary, the opportunity that he had been waiting for, to come back and ruin him.

Speaking in Parliament, Sir Edward Coke moved that there should be a committee to enquire into 'The Grievances of Monopolies'.

Another committee was appointed, which eventually decided that the monopoly patents were indeed invalid and reported accordingly to the Commons, who as a first step proceeded against Sir Giles Mompesson and Sir Francis Michell, the former fleeing the country while the other was publicly *degraded* and sentenced to a prison term of 162 years.

Sir Francis Michell's degradation essentially meant he was stripped of his knighthood, and this was done at Westminster Hall, taking the form of his spurs being broken and thrown away, his belt cut and his sword broken over his head, then finally, he was pronounced to be 'no longer a Knight but Knave'.

"I am not guilty of these grievances which have been discovered. I based my judgement upon others who have misled me!" stated King James as he tried to clear his name in the ensuing investigations as he appeared before the House of Lords defending himself.

King James laid blame entirely on 'The Referees'.

Speaking again in Parliament, Sir Edward Coke and two associates, Cranfield and Phillips, then openly attacked 'The Referees' by name.

"Enough has been done to condemn Mompesson, now let us now dig deeper!" stated Sir Edward Coke in parliament as he gave Francis Bacon, who was sitting in a nearby pew, a cold stare.

Phillips and Cranfield then added that Francis Bacon, as Lord Chancellor, was one of 'The Referees', and should therefore share the guilt.

A conference was called by the Lords, in which 'The Referees' were named, with the Lord Chancellor at its head who then made it clear that, under a pretext of a general attack on 'The Referees', Francis was the one man whom the House of Parliament were disposed to making the scapegoat, although he had voted against the monopolies when the question first arose.

101. THE PLOT

𝔍ollowing on from the monopolies' scandal, Sir Edward Coke set up another committee to enquire into *the abuses of the Courts of Justice and to receive complaints from litigants with particular reference to the Court of Chancery*. Little did Francis realise that a new plot was being hatched against him.

In his first four terms as Lord Chancellor, Francis had made no less than 8800 orders and decrees and not a single one of which had ever been questioned.

Francis welcomed the enquiry and gave the Commons committee free reign to make any searches in his court that they deemed necessary as Francis knew of no miscarriages of justice.

The remuneration of the land at the time was that very few officials actually received government salaries, and instead had to depend on fees and gifts from clients, and this was so from the Lord Chancellor position downwards.

All the functionaries of law and justice took fees and even litigants were allowed to give gifts and presents, which would also have been termed as fees.

In the Courts of Justice the amount of the fee was left open, but a fee was due and paid for every act that was fulfilled. A judge was not considered to be a public servant, but his income also depended on the fees that he received.

No fixed salary was paid to the Lord Chancellor, but the position was worth between ten and fifteen thousand pounds a year, derived from fees.

The Attorney General's position was worth six thousand pounds a year and his fixed salary was £81 a year, while the Solicitor General's position was worth three thousand a year with a fixed salary of £70 a year.

All these men lived in great style and could accumulate goods and land with their payment fees paid by those who resorted to justice in their courts.

Francis held a view that this system ought to have been abolished by law, and he was no doubt referring to this when he said that he welcomed the inquiry suggested by Edward Coke into the abuses of the Courts of Justice.

On being appointed to the post of Lord Chancellor, his office had the power to make new rules, but not enough to change this system of rewarding Court officials, which was immoral, but so long as it was in existence, he had to abide by it.

Additionally, Francis had no authority to appoint any new staff, and instead had to manage with the existing government assigned employees. He also had no power to dismiss his staff, even for gross misconduct, his only power was to suspend them from active duty.

Among his Chancery staff was a man called John Churchil, who had complaints made against him for pocketing fees and cheating clients, and being informed of this, Francis suspended him from his duties and thus made an enemy of him for life.

As Francis had no power to dismiss him, he could only forbid Churchil from appearing in court, hinted at a prosecution in the King's Bench if he did.

Unbeknown to Francis however, his enemies contacted John Churchil and instructed him to dig into all past cases to find persons that may bear a grudge against Francis in his role as Lord Chancellor.

John Churchil was successful, and on the 14th March, the Commons heard a rumour that a charge was to be made against Francis for bribery and corruption.

The next day, Sir Robert Philips reported to the House that two witnesses, Kit Aubrey and Edward Egerton, were prepared to make complaints against Francis in his role as Lord Chancellor.

Kit Aubrey detailed to a House of Commons Committee that on having a suit in Chancery, he was advised by his counsel to send a present of £100 to the court, a sum he then paid to Sir George Hastings.

Edward Egerton also detailed to the same Commons Committee that he had presented the Lord Chancellor with a basin and ewer worth fifty guineas, and then on the persuasion of Sir George Hastings and Sir Richard Young, had given them a purse of £500.

Each complained that, although they had paid monies, they received nothing for their gifts.

Francis on hearing of these accusations was fuming and immediately called a private hearing in the House of Commons before a senior official, Lord Cavendish, requesting Sir George Hastings and Sir Richard Young to attend.

As the two men sheepishly arrived at the hearing, Francis laid into them.

"What is this story about the £100?" Francis queried Sir George Hastings.

"It is true. I did accept the £500 from Kit Aubrey," Sir George Hastings immediately confessed, embarrassed at his actions.

"Until this moment, I had never even heard of Kit Aubrey's fee or bribe and must deny it upon my honour!" Francis complained to Lord Cavendish as he turned back to now face Sir Richard Young.

"And what is this story of the purse?" Francis pressed Sir Richard Young.

"I did indeed receive the sum of £500 from Edward Egerton," Sir Richard Young also confessed under pressure as Lord Cavendish looked on.

"Take note, my Lord. If they say I took this money, it is a falsehood, and I shall deny it upon my honour!" Francis declared to Lord Cavendish angry at the lies made against him.

Lord Cavendish having made notes of the discussion ended the private hearing, so he could confer with members of the House of Commons, but the next day Sir George Hastings also confessed that he had taken Aubrey's money and kept it for himself.

By their own admission, Sir George Hastings and Sir Richard Young were rogues, and in the House of Commons, Sir Thomas Wentworth denounced them as guilty men, although neither man confirmed nor denied it.

The Commons moved that these two accusations should be laid before the peers *without prejudice or opinion* and on the 20th March the two cases were accordingly sent to the House of Lords.

Francis at once wrote a letter to the Lords saying, *I would be glad to preserve my honour and fame, so far as I was worthy, hearing that some complaints of bribery were coming before their Lordships and requesting that they would maintain me in their good opinion until my case be heard.*

102. A Weak Case

With the aid of Churchil, enemies of Francis continued their character assassination by compiling a list of criminal abuses, extracted from the 8800 cases Francis had presided over, selecting a total of twenty two cases in which bribery was supposedly alleged.

Churchil now appeared before the Commons.

"I would like it noted that I protest that a forger, rogue and cheat by his own admission should not be heard, nor any credence paid to his stories in these proceedings!" Sir Thomas Meautys declared, to a muted response as the case proceeded. In not one of the twenty-two cases could it be shown that any fee traced to the Chancellor could, by any fair construction, be called a bribe.

None of the cases appeared to have been given on any promise made, none appeared to have been given in secret, and none appeared to have corrupted justice, but at the preliminary inquiry, Sir Edward Coke construed every fee paid into a bribe.

"No fee could be called a bribe, unless it could be shown to have been taken as part of a contract to pervert justice, and asked how could a judge retain in his recollection the name of every suitor in his court?" Heneage Finch declared interrupting Edward Coke's weak arguments concerning fees paid.

By the end of Edward Coke's clever defamation of Francis' ethics, the House of Commons consented to let the case go to the Lords, but as an inquiry only and not as an impeachment. The Commons also concluded that they wished the system of fees amended, and also that there should not be a personal charge against the Lord Chancellor.

Reconfirming his innocence of all charges, Francis, wrote a letter addressed to the House of Lords:

There are three degrees or cases, as I conceive, of gifts or rewards given to a judge. The First is of bargain, contract, or promise of reward, pendente lite and this is properly called Venalis sententiae, or baratua, or corruptelae numerum, and of this my heart tells me I am innocent; that I had no bribe or reward in my eye or thought when I pronounced my sentence or order.

The second is a neglect of a judge to inform himself whether the cause be fully at an end or not, what time he receives the gift, but takes it upon the credit of the party that all is done, or otherwise omits to enquire and the third is when it is received, sine fraud, after the cause is ended; which it seems, by the opinion of civilians is, no offence.

Only the first of these cases, a contract to defeat justice for a personal gain implies moral guilt or invites legal censure.

For the first, I take myself to be as innocent as any babe born on St. Innocent's day in my heart.

For the second, I doubt in some particulars I may be at fault, and for the last, I conceive it to be no fault

On the 19th March, the case went to the House of Lords, who appointed a committee to investigate the matter.

When Francis heard that the case had gone to the Peers, he had at last realised that he was being singled out and that his enemies were closing in on him.

He immediately made a declaration to the House that he would defend his innocence.

The King and the Duke of Buckingham were aghast at the thought of Francis defending himself in court.

A defence was the very last thing they wanted.

The King and the Duke of Buckingham knew full well that if Francis made a good case for himself and was acquitted, the wrath of the people would fall on them, and that the vexed questions of the monopolies would arise once more, bringing light to the gross immorality of the court, the squandering of public monies by King James, and the conspiracy against Francis.

The Duke of Buckingham immediately wrote to Francis to ascertain whether he really meant to defend himself, and in an indignant letter back, Francis responded stating:

I praise God for it, I never took a penny for any benefice or ecclesiastical living, I never took a penny for releasing anything I stopped at the Seal, I never took a penny for commission on things of that nature, I never shared with any servant for any second or ulterior profit.

It was then that the King and the Duke of Buckingham had confirmation that he would indeed defend himself.

A few days later, on 26th March, Parliament adjourned and Francis retired to his country seat at Gorhambury, riding there accompanied by a large retinue of his friends who shared their belief in his innocence.

On arriving at his Gorhambury home, Francis started preparing his defence, being resolved to battle for his honour in spite of the hostile attitude of the King and the Duke of Buckingham.

If the Lords had already made up their minds to brand him as a criminal, he had made up his mind that it should only be after a public trial, so that there should be a full record made to enable future generations to judge whether he was guilty or innocent.

103. FALSE GUILT

16th April, Whitehall

Becoming fearful of being implicated in Francis' defence, King James requested Francis to appear before him at Whitehall.

As soon as he arrived, he was brought before King James, and knelt in his presence.

"You requested to see me your Majesty?" Francis asked, forcing a smile,

"Yes, Lord Chancellor!" King James returned in an irritated tone.

I understand that you intend to make a defence for yourself against the charges being laid out against you?" King James quizzed, frowning as he waited for his response.

"That is true, your Majesty!" Francis confirmed.

King James turned in his chair feeling uncomfortable at Francis answer.

"Are you aware, that this course of action would be detrimental to my credibility, and also again focus on the issue of the monopolies affair?" King James barked, asking Francis to understand that his actions were putting the King's credibility in question.

"I was not aware, Majesty. I mean only to prove my innocence in the eyes of my peers," Francis returned innocently, sidestepping the issue of the monopolies' affair and redirecting the issues back to him wanting to prove his innocence.

"But at what cost to your King?" King James pleaded.

"I implore you, do not resist your charges and abandon your defence. Trust in your position, and your honour, as well as your faith that the crown will do you justice!" King James begged.

Francis realised he was being placed in a difficult position as his King begged him to desist from his proposed defence.

What could he do? He had never before allowed his own interests to interfere or conflict with the interests of the State, and he passionately remonstrated with the King for asking him to abandon his defence and to plead guilty, but his protests proved fruitless.

With a heavy heart, Francis agreed he would abandon his defence for his King and country, and as he left, he felt that his honour was being sacrificed, hoping his trust in King James would not be betrayed.

Francis had never opposed the wishes of a reigning sovereign unless he thought that such wishes were unreasonable, in which case he was not afraid to speak out boldly and without regard for the consequences.

He worried that his sovereign would not come to his aid if everything went badly wrong.

The next day Francis deserted his defence and prepared to plead guilty to all the charges, sending a letter to King James, reminding him that he had sacrificed his good name to safeguard the position of the Monarch and implored him to support him in his time of need.

On 27th April, the Prince of Wales signified onto the Lords that the Lord Chancellor had sent a letter to them, which had previously been approved by King James.

In an extract of the letter, Francis wrote:

I do ingeniously confess and acknowledge that, having understood the particulars of the charge, not formally from the House but enough to inform my conscience and memory; I find matter sufficient and full to move me to desert the defence and to move your Lordships to condemn and censure me.

He then also professed:

Gladness in some things: "The first is that hereafter the greatness of a judge or magistrate shall be no sanctuary or protection of guiltiness; which, in few words, is the beginning of a golden world.

The next, that after this example, it is like that judges will fly from anything that is in the likeness of corruption (though it were at a great distance), as from a serpent; which tendeth to the purging of the courts of justice, and the reducing them to their true honour and splendour. And in these two points, God is my witness that, though it be my fortune to be the anvil whereupon these good effects are beaten and wrought, I take no small comfort.

Unfortunately, when his letter was received, the committee agreed that his submission was not enough, as it contained no plea of guilt.

"There is no confession of any corruption in the Lord Chancellor's submission!" commented Lord Southampton uncomfortably as he read the letter in a private chamber with members of the committee investigating the supposed corruption attending.

"It is necessary to have the party hear the charge and we to hear the party's answers!" he added solemnly.

With this, the Lords demand that Francis should plead guilty to each particular offence in turn.

Without a plea of guilt, the House of Lords were powerless, because no part of the case against Francis had been proved, no court to try him had been constituted, no evidence against him had been taken under cross examination, no particulars of the charges against him had been supplied to him, and no counsel in his defence had been heard.

The Lords could not vote on rumour alone, what they must have was a plea of guilty, so particulars on the charges of corruption were at last sent to Francis.

This was the first time he had ever seen the details of the charges of corruption against him. The list contained particulars of the twenty-two counts that Churchil had unearthed by raking through the 8800+ suits overseen by Francis.

Of the twenty-two cases where there was a suspicion of any bribery, only 12 persons were found who were willing to come forward and give evidence. Eight of the counts fell through as they were not suits in law but debt cases or arbitrations. Ten of the cases related to fees had been paid long after the cases had been decided, which finally left four cases.

Therefore under scrutiny, except for four possible cases, not a single fee traced to Francis himself could be called a bribe, not one appeared to have been given on any promise, not one appeared to have been given in secret, and not one appeared to have corrupted justice.

Yet Francis had promised King James to plead guilty, so on 30th April, he sent to the House of Lords, a confession in which he pleaded guilty, answering the various counts fully.

Francis admitted the receipt of several gifts, fines, fees and presents, some by his officers, some by himself, re-stating that, if the receipt of such fees and gifts held by the Peers to be proof of corruption, he confessed to the offence, but nowhere did he admit or allow his judges to infer, that he had ever accepted a fee or reward to pervert justice.

On 3rd May, the Peers met and the charges and submissions were read, after which, they adjourned to consider what sentence should be passed.

Upon resuming, the Lords, having agreed upon their sentence, sent a message to the House of Commons to say that they were indeed ready to pass judgement.

The Commons convened, headed by the Speaker, who in their name, demanded and prayed judgement against the Lord Chancellor as the nature of his offence and demerits demanded.

The Lord Chief Justice then passed judgement declaring that Sir Francis Bacon, Lord Chancellor of England would be required to pay a fine of £40,000 and also be imprisoned in the Tower of London at the King's pleasure.

His once spotless reputation was shattered forever.

The Lord Chief Justice then further stated an even greater blow that Francis would never be allowed to hold office, place, or employment, in the State or Commonwealth, and never again be allowed to sit in Parliament or come within the verge of the Court.

After Francis had been sentenced, the reformation of the Court of Chancery was dropped by the reformers, as was the enquiry into the practices of the King's Bench.

The plot to discredit Francis had succeeded, ensuring that officials would continue to receive presents and fees, and that the vaunted desires of the government for reform, was killed off.

104. LETTER OF DISCHARGE

31ˢᵗ May 1621, Tower of London

Two days passed as Francis paced the cramped confines of his cell reflecting on how his political life now lay in ruins, the loss of his job, and even worse, being imprisoned. The thought had crossed his mind to use his mystical power to break free of his confinement, but he knew that would only exacerbate his situation.

Hearing someone making their way up the stairs of the tower to his cell, his hopes rose as he thought it would be a welcome release from his degrading ordeal.

He crossed his cell, making his way towards the entrance to greet the visitors but recoiled in shock as Damien, his most hated enemy, strode in.

"You? What are you doing here?" Francis barked.

"Hello Francis!" Damien smiled as he calmly made his way to Francis' cell, taunting him. "Oh, how the mighty have fallen!" Damien sneered.

As Francis eyed the confines of his cell, he realised he may have to smash his way free if he was to fight Damien, and braced himself for a fight.

"Don't worry Francis, I am not here to fight," Damien told him as he watched Francis assuming an attacking posture.

"What do you want Damien!" Francis asked again, still readying himself for battle.

Damien eyed Francis with a mocking smile.

"I took great satisfaction in aiding in your downfall Francis" Damien started.

"You?" Francis quizzed angrily as he tried to understand what Damien could gain from his downfall.

"In part, yes, but there were many that wanted to see your fall from grace," Damien smiled.

As Francis became more angered, he scanned his cell as he considered smashing a way through the cell to attack Damien.

"Give me the Book of Raziel Francis, or your time in these cells may end as badly as your brother Robert's did," Damien informed him, eyeing the inscription "ROBART TIDIR" above one of the cells.

As Francis followed Damien's eyes to stare at the lasting inscription his brother Robert had made when he himself had been locked up in the Tower, a chill ran down his spine.

"Give me the book Francis, NOW!" Damien demanded in a raised tone.

"Not on my life!" Francis shouted back, causing the gaoler to rush up the stairs and into the cells.

The gaoler was a huge man, with a heavy woollen smock and wide leather key-belt strapped around his belly.

"Is everything alright here Master Bacon?" The concerned gaoler asked, wondering what all the raised voices were about.

"This gentleman said he was a friend of yours, so I let him up," the gaoler explained, scrutinizing Damien.

"He is no friend of mine!" Francis returned shortly, eyeing Damien with contempt.

The gaoler looked back angrily at Damien.

"I think you better leave then sir, eh?" the guard asked, clapping his shovel-sized hand on Damien's back, not knowing that Damien was a dangerous villain and could kill him in an instant.

"I will be seeing you again Francis!" Damien told Francis calmly as he turned to leave, stopping briefly at the stairs, turning back to Francis.

"Next time I see you though, you would be wise to surrender the book," Damien continued in a defiant tone before making his way down the stairs and out of the Tower.

"Sorry about that Master Bacon!" the guard apologised as he followed after Damien down the stairs, escorting him out.

Now alone in his cell again, Francis slumped down to the floor, staring fearfully at Robert's inscription above the cell doors opposite him.

As the hours passed, Francis started to panic, fearing the same fate that had befallen his brother Robert and jumped up.

"Guard!" he shouted frantically, causing his guard to come racing up the stairs to his cells.

"Yes sir? What is it?" the guard asked, flustered, thinking something bad had happened to his important prisoner.

"Could you please provide me with a quill, ink and some paper?" Francis asked impatiently.

The guard dropped his shoulders in disbelief.

"Is that it? You called me up here like someone was murdering you, only to tell me you want to write summit?" the guard complained incredulously.

"It's a matter of life and death!" Francis returned in desperation.

"I don't have any here, and will have to request it!" the guard huffed.

"Please, it is urgent!" Francis pressed.

"It's always urgent!" the guard moaned as he walked back out the cells and down the stairs to the lower levels.

A few minutes later as Francis overheard some muffled noises from the guards, his guard returned with some cheap paper, a worn quill and some ink, begrudgingly handing them to Francis before again leaving his cells and making his way back down the stairs.

Francis immediately sat up on the cold floor of his cell and wrote an appeal of leniency to his King, reminding him of the sacrifices he had made for the crown, stating:

Good my Lord, procure the warrant for my discharge this day, when I am dead, he is gone that was always a true and perfect servant to his master, and one that was never author of any immoderate, no, nor unsafe, nor unfortunate counsel, and one that no temptation could ever make other than a trusty and honest and thrice loving friend to your Lordship; and howsoever I acknowledge the sentence just, and for reformation sake fit, the justest Chancellor that hath been in the five changes since Sir Nicholas Bacon's time.

Your Lordship's true friend, living and dying, Fr. St. Alban. Tower, 31st May, 1621.

He folded the letter and then clambered to his feet.

"Guard!" Francis shouted in a lowered tone, having to do this a number of times before the guards downstairs finally heard him.

"What now?" the same guard asked impatiently, as he made his way to Francis' cell.

"Could you please ensure that the King receives this letter urgently?" Francis asked.

The guard frowned as he heard the *urgently* word again, shaking his head in dismay as he took the letter, giving Francis a final disgruntled stare as he left his cell.

As the guard got to the bottom of the stairs from his cell, Francis heard the conversations of the guard ordering one of the other guards to deliver a letter to the Royal palace of King James.

Francis gave a sigh of relief that his request had been honoured, and a few days later, Francis was indeed released from the Tower, and the great fine of £40,000 was quashed.

Some months later, King James also signed a warrant absolving Francis of the majority of the charges against him, except for the charge that barred him from ever holding office or sitting in parliament.

During his political career, Francis was the first man in history to become a member of the House of Lords and the House of Commons at the same time, and while in Parliament, he had served on no less than 29 committees, and was regarded as one of the most eloquent orators ever to have stood before the House of Commons.

105. ADULTERY

Due to his many elevations early in his career under King James, Francis became very wealthy, and literally poured jewels in his wife's lap, also spending huge sums decorating their many homes.

Power was also available, as four years earlier, when Francis was made temporary Regent of England which gave him ruling power over England, if only for six months. In this period his wife, Lady Alice Bacon, revelled in being elevated as *first lady in the land*, taking precedence over all other baronesses.

Lady Alice Bacon had extravagant tastes and revelled in the wealth and power afforded to her husband, but it all disappeared with the charges that were laid against him.

In an attempt to return to the life she was accustomed to, she personally pleaded with the Marquis of Buckingham for the restoration of her husband's salary and pensions, to no avail, and it was not long before Francis was also forced to relinquish their prized London home, York House.

Due to the tightening of financial resources, Francis and Alice fought more and more as she wanted to know where Francis was spending their diminishing funds.

Money was an issue, but Francis was resolved to continue the funding of his writing programme, which also included his own personal publications, but the strain on their marriage ultimately caused them to drift apart.

One night, as Francis was walking through the grounds of his Gorhambury home to take in the warm night air, he was drawn to strange muffled moaning sounds deep within the wooded area of his grounds and decided to investigate its source.

As he closed in on the source of the noise, he was shocked and saddened to come upon his wife engaged in a sexual act with a gentleman-in-waiting known to Francis, a Mr John Underhill.

Greatly angered and saddened at such an act of unfaithfulness by his wife, he and John Underhill scuffled but being the now aged man he was, Francis resigned himself to a life without her and returned to the manor, turning his wife out of Gorhambury manor a short time later.

Although John Underhill was originally listed as a gentleman-in-waiting at York House, his initial acquaintance with Francis was to harbour an agreement for the purchase of a property in New Place, Stratford-upon-Avon for a certain William Shakspere, and Francis kept John Underhill employed as a favour.

Due to Francis uncovering his wife's adulterous affair, Francis subsequently amended his will, which had once been quite favourable to her, leaving her lands, goods and income, to revoking it all, writing:

What so ever I have given, granted, conferred, or appointed to my wife in the former part of my will, I do now for just and great cause, utterly revoke, and make void, and leave her to her right only.

The Past

106. THE FIRST FOLIO

April 1623, London, England

A few years later, Francis sits in a carriage, deep in thought, as it made its way to the studio of the famous artist, Martin Droeshout.

For over thirty years, the Knights of the Helmet's writing efforts had permeated England and Europe, aided by the expansion of playhouses, quarto publications, and word of mouth, enriching English literature.

In recent years however, as the progress of disease, and the rapidly increasing infirmities of old age ravaged the founding members, the rate of new releases and publications by the group had slowed literally to a stop.

As Francis travelled the rocky London roads to meet with the artist, he thought back to a meeting he had with the remaining members of his writing group some weeks before.

In this meeting, Francis and the remaining members had agreed to draw a line under their efforts, effectively bringing their writing programme to an end.

When the question came up about what to do with their stockpile of some seventeen plays that had never even been performed, let alone registered in the Stationer's Register, it was agreed to revise the existing list of authored plays, with the aim of publishing a complete final collection, in one bound folio.

In addition, the remaining members unanimously agreed that a portrait of the author should appear along with the introductory pages of the folio, and that it should be a picture of Francis as a final tribute to the plays *true* author.

Although Francis was flattered by their desires, he still had not wanted to bring undue attention to himself, especially since their scapegoat author, the Stratfordian William Shakspere, had been dead some nine years already.

Knowing the group would most probably be making some necessary revisions to the current plays in advance of the final folio, Francis was worried that people would start to ask questions, but his writing group were adamant, feeling that, at their old age, they were now beyond the persecution of the crown.

With this, Francis agreed to honour his writing group's request, but to also recognise their contributions as well, and had made an agreement with the artist he was en-route to meet, that he wished the portrait not to bear a direct resemblance to himself, and to somehow also indicate that the plays being published in the folio were a collaborative effort.

As Francis arrived at the studio, he was greeted by Martin Droeshout himself, who looked the part of an artist, being covered from head-to-toe in paints and oils.

"Master Bacon! Welcome" the artist exclaimed as they shook hands.

As the artist stood before Francis, Francis could tell the artist seemed worried.

"Would you like something to drink before we" the artist started.

"No, no. Let's get down to business shall we?" Francis interrupted, having other appointments that day. Francis was also eager to see the portrait.

"Yes, yes of course!" The artist returned, wringing his hands as he worried whether the portrait would be well received or not.

The artist immediately escorted Francis to a small room at the back of the studio which was practically empty apart from a single canvas upon an easel, hidden purposefully behind a cloth, no doubt to protect it from the dusty elements of the studio and prying eyes.

"Behold, Mr Francis *Shake-speare* Bacon!" Martin Droeshout declared as he removed the cloth to reveal the portrait he had painted, staring intently at Francis' expression to get an idea if Francis liked the portrait or not.

As Francis reviewed the portrait, he immediately recognised it as a mesh of two of his own personal paintings that he had loaned to the artist, the first, a painting of himself some five years earlier when he was dressed in formal wear celebrating a recent promotion at the time, and the second, when Francis was just 16 years old, wearing a smart blue doublet.

Francis grimaced as he eyed the balding head of the portrait, and rubbed the back of his own head in embarrassment.

"I have removed your signature hat sir, as the resemblance was much too familiar!" the artist commented as he saw Francis focused on the head of the portrait.

Francis smiled a little uncomfortably before pulling his gaze away from the balding head, reviewing the rest of the portrait, assessing its every stroke and shadow, as if he was valuing it for some great gallery.

As Francis continued his assessment, he noticed the subtle irregularities of the portrait's neckline, tracing a strange series of line running from the ear down to the chin,

"What does this line signify?" Francis queried as he followed his finger down the line from the right ear to the chin.

"Ah!" the artist exclaimed excitedly, hoping Francis would spot the irregularity.

"This line subtly signifies that the face itself a mask," the artist clarified, as he explained the multiple lines on the neck.

"If you also notice," The artist started.

"The head is not truly connected with the body, but rests on the collar? This is to signify that the head does not truly belong to the body, and that there is more to the portrait than the eye can see," the artist explained, still looking for some complimentary comments from Francis.

Francis made a subtle nod in acceptance of the explanation and then continued his evaluation of the portrait and stopped at the doublet, remembering its design came from one of his childhood portraits.

As he remembered back to the day the portrait was made, he realised that this was the very same fateful day when he discovered the truth about his hidden Tudor heritage in his uncle's office, which changed his life forever.

So much has happened since then Francis thought sadly, remembering back to the many funerals of friends and family, Sir Nicholas, Robert Dudley, Robert Devereux, Lord Burghley, Queen Elizabeth, Anthony Bacon, Dr. Dee, Lady Anne, his fall from grace, his adulterous wife. He sighed quietly as he turned away from the painter's eyes.

"If you look carefully at the coat as well sire, you will see one-half of it is on backwards. This is to signify that the effort of the plays rests on more than one shoulder," the artist added, bringing Francis back from his thoughts.

Francis smiled back at the artist as he refocused on the portrait, reviewing the jacket, eyeing how the artist had indeed painted it with the left arm drawn the correct way, and the right arm painted with the back of the shoulder facing to the front.

"You do not like it?" asked the artist finally, his hopes waning for a positive response about the painting.

Disappointed, the artist dropped his head into his paint stained hands, fearing Francis was not impressed with the portrait, and began mumbling to himself that he had failed in his task.

As Francis turned back to the frustrated artist, he smiled, putting a friendly hand on Martin Droeshout's shoulder.

The artist removed his face from his hands and locked eyes with Francis, letting out a heavy sigh.

"I wished a portrait to contradict and confute, and to force people to weigh and consider," Francis explained to him, returning his eyes back to the portrait briefly.

"It is a masterpiece, Master Droeshout!" Francis assured him, smiling broadly, finally giving the artist reason to be happy.

"You like it? Wonderful!" the artist shouted with joy raising his hands in the air in success.

Francis was content with the portrait aside from it revealing his balding hairline, but agreed with the artist that adding his now signature hat into the painting would have brought too much of a resemblance back to him.

"Will you have the engraved version ready as agreed?"

"Yes!" the artist assured him, jubilantly.

"Good. I will send for my original portraits to be collected later today," Francis added, shaking hands with the artist before leaving the studio and making his way back to his waiting carriage.

"To the printers!" Francis shouted up to his coachman as he boarded his carriage.

"As you wish master!" the coachman shouted back, whipping the horses into action, causing the carriage to jerk off on the short journey to the printers assigned the task of publishing the folio.

The printing of the folio was to be carried out by Isaac Jaggard and Ed Blount, gentlemen with whom Francis had had a long prior relationship.

With Ed Blount, Francis had worked with him on an earlier publication entitled *Don-Quixote of the Mancha*, while Isaac Jaggard had printed many of Francis' own early essays.

Many of the old plays had already been published in previous years in their own dedicated Quarto's but there were many that required revision changes.

As such, edits to some of the plays were as minor as a few line additions, growing to 300+ new lines against the plays of Othello and *Richard III*, to even more extensive changes such as the 1200+ line additions to *The Merry Wives of Windsor*, while *Henry V* received so many edits, its size doubled that of its previous publication.

True to Dante's philosophy of double-writing as implemented in previous Shake-speare publications, after all the revisions to the plays were completed for the folio, it was garnished with symbolic headpiece designs and cryptic wordings such as the strange, long word, 'honorificabilitudinitatibus' in the text of Venus & Adonis.

This strange word was an anagram for the Latin phrase, *hi ludi F. Baconis nati tuiti orbi*, which meant **These plays F. Bacon's offspring preserved for the world.**

Isaac Jaggard was already accustomed to the arduous work of inserting these cryptic wordings through the use of *accidental* typeface errors for Francis and members of his writing group in the past, and this folio was to be no exception,

As Isaac Jaggard was an initiate in the Freemasonry order, he was sworn to secrecy and could be trusted completely.

The end folio was entitled "Mr. William Shake-speare's Comedies, Histories & Tragedies", and although not all the stockpiled plays made it into this version, there was hope for a later revision of the folio to accommodate them.

The front cover of the first folio displayed a copper engraved version of the portrait by Martin Droeshout with an additional cryptic statement about the portrait on its facing page by Francis' friend Ben Jonson.

The folio was dedicated to William, Earl of Pembroke and Philip, Earl of Montgomery, close associates of Francis that supported him when he fell from power, and were also fellow founding members of the Virginia Company.

As Francis held the first printed copy of the folio and reviewed its 900 or so pages, he was shocked by how much of his life had permeated the pages of many of the plays.

He was amazed at how many times his brother's name, 'Anthony' was used across the plays, how little some of the plays portrayed a motherly figure, mirroring his estranged relationship with his real mother, and also, how many of the plays toyed with the idea of royal ascension.

He had had never fully realised how much of his thoughts had lingered on the possibility about one day leading his countrymen as King of his England, but all that was now behind him.

The end version of the First Folio contained some 36 plays and was registered on 8th November with a print run of 500 copies, each of which were to be sold for £1.

107. THE FINAL BATTLE

April 9, 1626, Highgate, London

Three years later, a bleary eyed Francis steps out from the offices of a printing company one late evening into a blanket of white snow.

As he stood at the doorway looking out at the bitter cold weather, he shook his head in dismay, wishing he had told his driver to wait for him.

He turned back to the main door of the printers, balancing a stylish walking stick on his arm as he searched through a big bunch of keys on a ring, selecting a long bronzed one, using it to lock the office up.

As he turned back to survey the snowy downfall, he pulled his wide brimmed hat down over his forehead and then stuck his stylish walking stick into the blanket of snow to judge how deep the downfall had been.

He inhaled deeply, raised his chin, and then began on the precarious journey to a nearby carriage rank on foot to pick up a carriage for hire to transport him back to his Gorhambury estate.

Unbeknown to Francis however, a mysterious figure was lurking in the shadows waiting for him, and as Francis made his way down the road, the mysterious figure followed behind from a distance.

As Francis made his way down the road and turned a corner, a group of children having a snow fight playfully turned their attention to him, and he suddenly comes under attack from a barrage of snowballs.

"What the" Francis exclaimed as a hail of snowballs hammered him, before realising the group of children hiding behind a nearby fence ahead of him, and shaking his head initially in anger, he began to laugh out loud, remembering back to his childhood when he and his brother Anthony used to have such fun together.

As a snowball hit him in the face, Francis faced the start reality that he would be battered if he did not either run or find shelter from their attack, and deciding it would be risky running in the snow, he knew he needed to find shelter against their onslaught instead.

Thinking quickly, he crossed the road and took refuge behind a nearby row of thick bushes.

As he hid behind his newfound shield, he found he was next to a mound of snow, and decided he would get his own back on the children and quickly made up a few snowballs of his own to defend himself with.

As he sneaked a peek at the activities of the children, Francis caught a glimpse of a mysterious man skulking in the shadows on the other side of the road, watching in his general direction.

Remaining calm, Francis picked up his pile of snowballs and sneaked to where the children were hiding behind the shield of the fence and jumped up, laying into them, pelting them with the snowballs. Realising they had been rumbled, the children all ran out from behind the fence pass Francis, making their escape down the high street away from Francis.

Francis was jubilant at his success but kept track of the mysterious man as he continued on his journey towards to the nearby carriage rank, but as he turned another corner and noticed an empty alley, he instinctively decided to dart into it and surprise his stalker, raising his walking cane in the air to defend himself.

After a few seconds, the mysterious figure passed the alley after him, and Francis jumped out to confront him from behind.

"Watch yourself sire, I can defend myself!" Francis warned, waving his walking cane in the air above him, ready to strike.

The mysterious figure was initially surprised at being found out, but immediately backing away a few steps from Francis, removing his hat to reveal it was Damien, his old enemy.

Francis was stone-faced.

"Damien!" Francis shouted with fury in his voice.

"Hello Francis!" Damien responded in a tone seemingly colder than the snow that surrounded them.

Francis immediately whispered a spell that fuelled powerful mystical energies to build up in his clenched fists and took a defensive stance.

"You should not have come back to England Damien!" Francis shouted angrily.

Damien stood his ground and just smiled mischievously.

"Before we get down to a fight, I want you to hear me out," Damien explained calmly.

"We have nothing to talk about!" Francis shouted back.

"Oh, I think we do Francis. I have built a dossier on you that will make the bribery charges that destroyed your political career seem like a slap on the wrist!" Damien joked.

"I think you would be wise to hear me out before you try and best me with your mystic powers!" Damien continued.

"I will not be fooled by you again Damien and this time, there is no one here for you to use against me!" Francis responded angrily as he scanned their surrounding vicinity.

Damien looked in the direction of the printing building that Francis had just left.

"You know, ever since our last encounter at 'The Globe', I have become an avid reader of the works of this 'Shake-speare' fellow, especially since his first folio was printed!" Damien started, stroking his greying beard.

"Correct me if I am wrong, but that printing company you just left tonight actually printed the Shakespeare folio, did it not?" Damien queried in a teasing tone.

"Those printers have many clients," Francis replied, puzzled at Damien's line of conversation.

Damien eyed the shape of a bunch of keys in one of Francis' coat pockets, knowing that Francis had locked up the printer's when he left the premises.

"Oh, Yes, but I am sure not all of their clients have their own keys to the premises, eh?" Damien smirked.

"You know, as I reviewed the folio, I happened to stop to admire the scroll work around the first letter of the first word of the first play, *The Tempest* I believe?" Damien commented.

"You wouldn't happen to know what that first letter was, would you Francis?" Damien continued with a quizzing look, not really expecting an answer.

Although Francis was a little rattled by Damien's conversation topic, he didn't show it, and merely gave Damien a cold stare.

"The first letter was the letter 'B' for *Bote-swaine*," Damien continued smoothly, answering his own question.

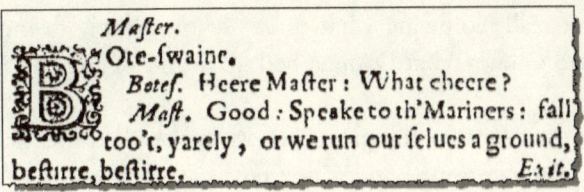

> Mafter.
> Ote-fwaine.
> Botef. Heere Mafter: What cheere?
> Maft. Good: Speake to th'Mariners: fall
> too't, yarely, or we run our felues a ground,
> beftirre, beftirre.   Exit.

"I initially thought 'Bote-swaine' to be quite a strange word to start such a major folio, but to those that had a deep understanding of astronomy would immediately know that the words 'Botes' and 'Wain' referred to the *Boötes* and *Ursa Major* star constellations," Damien explained.

"If I remember correctly, you have a keen interest in astronomy, don't you Francis?" Damien queried, again not really expecting an answer.

With that, Francis became a little unsettled at Damien's astute observations, and seeing a small reaction, Damien was spurred to continue.

"Of course, one of the stars within the 'Ursa Major' constellation refers to one of the seven stars of the *Pleiades*' star cluster, a name that we both know Ronsard and other's have taken to distinguish themselves by," Damien added with a knowing grin.

Francis looked away as he appreciated Damien's knowledge of astrology had unearthed him paying homage indirectly to the work of the *Pleiades* writing group back in Navarre.

"As I paused on this first page, I then began to admire the scrollwork design of the first letter 'B', something curious caught my eye, so curious in fact, I had to retrieve my magnifying glass so I could get a closer view!" Damien laughed.

Francis did not want to give anything away and maintained his cold stare, but deep down, Damien was touching upon matter's that he had rather hoped would remain hidden.

"To my amazement I noticed a peculiar arrangement of letters around this prominent letter!" Damien added, feigning a look of shock by what he had discovered.

"On closer inspection, I found that these random letters were not random at all, but actually spelled out a name, *f-r-a-n-c-i-s-b-a-c-o-n* in fact!" Damien continued, now eyeing Francis critically.

Francis, not really knowing what to say or do, simply feigned a laugh, but now felt he had to know that Damien had up his sleeve and had to hear Damien out.

"After that discovery, I took great interest in the plays themselves as you can imagine!" Damien continued, mocking Francis some more.

"On reading the play *Love's Labour's Lost*, I thought how strange that it was set in Navarre, where we met, and what was even stranger was that some of the characters of the play seemed to have been named after real people we both knew!"

Damien eyed Francis squarely.

"I wonder if these friends are aware that their names have been taken in vain so?" Damien asked as he raised a brow.

Francis raises his hands, still glowing from the hidden power within them, and clapped them together, mocking an attempt at commending Damien for his deductive skills.

"Well done Damien!" Francis replied as he clapped his hands together some more.

"If you have a point to all this, I suggest you get to it as my patience is wearing thin!" Francis responded back angrily.

"Oh, allow me a little indulgence Francis, after all I have been waiting quite some time for this conversation!" Damien goaded him.

"Another quite interesting play was *Romeo & Juliet*, and again I found many parallels there, to your romantic liaison with our fair Queen Marguerite, although not quite the romance in reality really, more like an *affair* doomed to failure!" Damien mocked.

With the reference to Queen Marguerite, Francis almost lost his cool as his anger increased, causing more power to be channelled to his fists, causing them to flare momentarily, but calmed himself, feeling Damien was purposefully trying to rattle him.

"Also, as I read *King Henry the IV*, I noted that the word *Francis* appears 33 times on a single page. Thirty three times Francis! Were you trying to make a statement Francis? You certainly did to me!" Damien scowled.

"I think this conversation has gone far enough Damien, get to your point or prepare yourself to fight!" Francis barked impatiently, taking up an attack posture.

Damien seeing Francis now powering up, believed it was indeed time to get to the point.

"I believe YOU are Shakespeare Francis, a name no doubt derived from the Speare-Shaker herself 'Pallas Athena'," Damien huffed.

"What if I am the author? What is it you plan to do?" asked Francis, finally having had enough of Damien's accusations.

"Blackmail me?" Francis continued, laughing incredulously.

"I have already been removed from office, I no longer have any political influence, and I have no money to pay you, not that I would ever give you coin anyway!" Francis barked.

As Francis fought his inner rage, trying to resist using his mystical powers in anger, he tried to focus on his muse, Pallas Athena, remembering that she was a warrior and a peacemaker, and looked at warring as a final resort, but Damien had already done enough that warranted a fight.

"You may have heard that I have taken over the Alumbrados order," Damien declared, changing the subject.

Confusion covered Francis face as he considered fearfully what Damien had done to take control of the Alumbrados order.

"Lord Beaumont would never allow it!" Francis shouted defiantly, remembering that Damien's uncle knew what sort of monster Damien was.

"My poor uncle died of an unfortunate accident," Damien explained with a sly grin, that Francis immediately took to mean Damien had some part to play in his uncles death.

"I understand you have are now affiliated with a new order emerging across Europe called the 'The Freemasons' as well?" Damien queried, looking for a reaction from Francis.

Francis did not flinch.

"Listen to me Francis. After pouring through the plays in the folio, I finally understood the deepest desires of its author and realised that they were also my desires," Damien continued.

Francis was perplexed.

"What are you talking about?" Francis shouted with a confused look.

"Join me Francis!" Damien declared defiantly.

"What?" Francis queried with a wild confused stare.

"Join me! As I read the many plays in the Shakespeare folio, I finally understood what it is *you* as the author have been lamenting about all these years, and I am here to make your dreams become a reality!" Damien clarified.

Francis was dumbfounded and just looked on at Damien with confusion.

Damien merely smiled a knowing smile.

"It struck me how one of the themes that kept on appearing in the plays was concerned with royal ascension and the quest for power," Damien started as he gave Francis a sincere look.

"Because of the Alumbrados order, I knew about your royal blood before you even arrived in France, and reading the folio plays, 'Hamlet', 'King Lear', 'Richard III', 'Macbeth', and many others, all relating to the high-born, the royals and nobles, it struck me that they reflected your life, your struggles," Damien continued, causing some deep emotions to stir within Francis.

As Francis maintained a statue-like angry stare at Damien, he pushed the sad thoughts of his unrecognised royal Tudor lineage to the back of his mind, but Damien could still see his arguments were having an effect as he had hoped.

"As I read about the fierce irresolution in prince Hamlet, and how he could not succeed to his father's throne any more than you could succeed to your English Queen's. I could only imagine what it was like living on the sword-edge of a balance, not knowing what to do for the best," Damien explained in the same sincere tone, although an evil glint in his eyes told a wholly different story.

"Join forces with me Francis, and together we can remove the Scottish King who has stolen your crown! With the power of the Book of Raziel and our respective secret societies, we would be undefeatable!" Damien declared, extending his hand to Francis.

As Francis stared at Damien's extended hand his thoughts drifted on the seed Damien had sown and dwelled on the subliminal desires that had manifested themselves in his writing.

However, As Francis thought about the Book of Raziel and Damien unrelenting search for it, his senses came back to him, remembering that Damien was only interested in the power of the book and what it could do for him.

Francis inhaled deeply as he considered the fullness of the life he had lived, and looked back up into Damien's eyes with a renewed confidence.

"My crown, Damien, is in my heart, not on my head, not decked with diamonds and Indian stones, not to be seen. My crown is called content!" Francis responded confidently as he resolved the mental demon's that Damien had inserted in his thoughts concerning his birthright being taken away from him.

"If you also noticed, another theme in my writing was the corruption of power in the hands of people like you!" Francis continued defiantly.

"There is to be no deal, Damien!" Francis finished, shaking his head adamantly.

Damien's coolness now disappeared as he finally realised that Francis would never join with him.

"You will submit to me Francis, and if you will not join me, I will have no choice but to take the book by force!" Damien warned as his arrogance returned.

"Do your worst Damien. I am ready to die, are you?" Francis returned, now goading Damien to fight.

"We will see Francis!" Damien barked, frustrated by his failed attempt to convert Francis to his way of thinking.

With that, both men immediately engaged in an almighty fight, unleashing their powers to the limits, with Damien using his dark magic to summon many demonic apparitions to aid his fight, while Francis used his white magic, harnessing the earth's natural elements.

As Damien's flying demons attacked him through the snowy streets of Highgate, Francis darted into a nearby park to find refuge in its thick forest.

Although Francis make good use of the strong winds he controlled to aid the destruction of some of Damien's host of flying demons, it was not enough for him to gain a victory as he still held back the darkest of his own power's, fearing them more than Damien.

The flying beasts eventually overpowered Francis and forced him to the snowy cold ground, causing Damien to immediately make his way over to Francis, and kneeling over him he grabs Francis by the neck, and whispers an incantation that vanquished the remaining demons he had summoned.

"You should have known Mother Nature would fail you Francis, just as your own mother failed you!" Damien goaded smugly as he gripped Francis by the neck.

My dear God, please help me! Francis thought in a weakened, as he fought hard not to pass out. He wearily stared up at Damien, fighting to free himself but realised he was too weak.

"Tell me where you have stored the book and I promise that you will receive the same painless death that I inflicted upon your father!" Damien boasted.

As Francis could feel his life ebbing away, he managed to regain enough strength to utter a response.

"You?" Francis whispered as he gasped for air.

"Yes Francis, it was me that had your father poisoned!" Damien confessed smugly as he stood over him.

"You lie!" Francis exclaimed, shaking his head in disbelief.

But how could he have known about the poison otherwise? Francis thought as he lay on his back fighting to stay conscious.

"It was bad enough you had relations with my Queen, but to consider marriage? There were far greater powers above me that would not let such a union occur," Damien explained in a mocking tone as he tightened his grip on his neck, causing Francis to gurgle as his body was deprived of oxygen.

As the inner turmoil mounted within Francis at the thought that he was the cause of his step-father's death, he finally decided that there was no reason to hold back the dark foreboding within him that fought to be freed.

Whenever he used the power of the Book of Raziel he felt the dark foreboding, but always preferred to keep it at bay, but now, all he wanted to do was to unleash its full force against Damien.

As he relaxed his mind and let go of the deep mental blocks he had put up to help him forget the knowledge of all the dark incantations that he had memorised, he could feel the darkness take hold of him.

"I was glad to have arranged your father's death if it meant we were rid of your English influences!" Damien continued as he continued his grip.

As Francis let his body go limp, Damien became enraged as he still did not know where his treasure was.

"Don't you die on me yet Francis! Tell me the location of the Book of Raziel!" Damien shouted in frustration.

All colours will agree in the dark Francis thought as everything around him began to fade to darkness, believing his time was up, not realising his eyes had actually turned black as his inner darkness took hold of him.

As Damien began to shake Francis to revive him, he was aghast as he saw the transformation in Francis' eyes and recoiled back in terror.

"What the" Damien started, but was dumbstruck as Francis levitated off from the ground and hovered up a few feet in front of him.

As Damien realised that Francis had now become consumed by the innate power of the Book of Raziel, he fumbled back as he tried to consider what to do next.

Realising Francis had now become consumed by the innate power of the Book of Raziel, Damien became fearful, and his instincts of self preservation forced him fire to off a fireball at Francis in order to destroy him.

As the fireball was about to make impact though, Francis raised his hand smoothly as if he was controlling the very fabric of the gravity that surrounded the fireball, and turned it into a blob of water, which immediately dissipated into the snow covered ground below him.

Feeling that he was now in trouble, Damien laid into Francis, unleashing everything he had, but Francis smoothly protected himself from being harmed.

As Damien was about to summon some more demons to battle on his behalf, Francis again raised his hand smoothly and fired an almighty ball of energy straight into Damien's chest.

In the split second after Damien's body consumed the ball of energy, he exhaled briefly and then smiled uncomfortably as he felt his body become unstable.

"What have you done Francis?" Damien shouted as he shuddered fearfully at his body destabilising.

A split second later, Damien's whole being exploded, leaving pieces of his body strewn across the blanket of snow that covered the park.

As Damien disappeared, the dark forces that had possessed Francis finally receded, causing Francis to fall out of the sky and down to the cold snow laden grass beneath him, ending up on his back.

As the snowflakes continued their own onslaught, Francis laid there as his body healed itself to a level where briefly regained consciousness, slowly opening his eyes, revealing his dark brown mixed with hazel eye colouring had returned.

As he lay on his back looking up at the full moon obscured by another wave of snow carried on their way by the continual cold winds, he was almost certain that the snow flakes were falling from the moon itself.

Not having any strength left within him, he let his eyelids fall shut again, letting out a sigh of relief.

The Present

108. The Pit

As intense rays of sunlight did its best to weaken the progress of a large group of men working hard on various aspects of a major dig, the mysterious elderly man sat on a small boulder, dwarfed by a huge aged tree that afforded a good shade from the suns heat.

Although he felt cool under the tree and the wide brimmed hat he also had on, his patience was starting to become irritated at the heat that burned down on his men, slowing down their work.

The efforts of the men were to excavate a pit that extended some 200+ feet underground.

Apart from the first *thirty-three* feet, the majority of the hole lay below sea level.

Finally, a tired tanned foreman made his way over to the elderly man, wiping some sweat away from his forehead with the back of his hand.

"We are ready sir. The excavations are now complete!" the foreman informed him as he exhaled a sigh of relief.

"Thank god!" the elderly man responded as he licked his dry lips.

He got up and made his way over to the pit, fishing a coin from his pocket and dropping it into its mouth.

As he listened, it took the coin a few seconds to hit the makeshift pit's wooden bottom, which caused the elderly man to smile broadly. He now had his own confirmation that the pit contained no water.

"Fill it!" the elderly man shouted gleefully, throwing his fist in the air as a sign of achievement.

The foreman immediately waved over to some men who sweltered in the sun next to a cache of 20 or so crates brought by the elderly man from England.

On the foreman's instructions, two workmen were lowered into the pit by a manual hoist, and when they had both reached the bottom, the rest of the workmen began lowering each of the crates down to them via the same hoist.

All was going well until one of the crates that had been damaged during transport, split open as it was being tied to the hoist before it was lowered into the pit, causing a number of thickly bound manuscripts to fall out onto the muddy ground.

The elderly man immediately rushed over, followed closely by the foreman.

"Be careful with those manuscripts!" the elderly man shouted as he made his way to the broken crate.

"I am sorry sire! We will get these items into another crate immediately!" the foreman assured him as he caught up.

As the elderly man shook his head in despair at the manuscripts now exposed from the split crate, he picked up a couple of them that have fallen out onto the muddy ground around the pit, and cleaning them up.

Exposed within the crate were titles such as Don Quixote, Romeo & Juliet, Macbeth, and a manuscript of the King James authored Holy Bible.

"Bring over an empty crate!" the foreman shouted to one of the workmen, who immediately jumped into action, nodding briefly and disappeared, before reappearing, dragging an empty crate across the muddy sand, dropping it next to the broken crate.

Two workmen immediately got to work transferring the manuscripts into the new empty crate, but as they threw the books into the new crate as if they were throwing rocks, their reckless actions inflamed the wrath of the elderly man.

"Careful with those books!" the elderly man shouted in anger again, shaking his head in dismay at their non-caring actions.

The two workmen froze eyeing each other, wondering why there was such a fuss about the books, but nevertheless, they continued more slowly, transferring the books across carefully.

The new crate was quickly hoisted back up with the others and lowered into the man-made pit, along with other items, such as stone boulders, clay, sand, and oak trees to a meticulous plan.

The two workmen who had transferred the books to the new crate took a much needed break, and as they ate, they discussed the dig.

"All this for a bunch of books?" the younger workman sneered as he retrieved an apple from his pocket.

"You got that right!" responded the older workman, shaking his head in disbelief.

"Apparently, where the pit is situated, it should be full of sea water!" the younger workman added, as he took a bite from his apple.

"It is true. There is some ingenious science at play here. The flow of sea water to the pit seems to be blocked. When all the crates have been lowered, I hear that they intend to let the sea water flow back into the pit, filling it up!" the older workman responded with a confused look.

"What? That is madness! How will they be able to retrieve the crates?"

"I think that is their intention. I heard that the crates will never be retrievable, unless you know the secrets of the islands!" responded the old workman.

Both men looked on in bewilderment as to what they were witnessing.

A few days later, after the elderly man had confirmed that everything had been completed to his satisfaction, the foreman gave the final order to his men to clear up their tools and equipment in preparation to finally leave the island.

The men worked well into the night packing their tools equipment away into many crates that were then transferred back to their ships anchored nearby, before they themselves boarded canoes taking them back as well.

As the last of the men boarded the ships and pulled up their anchors, they finally sailed away from the island.

On the deck of one of the ships that made its way from the island, the elderly man, his face still hidden by the night sky and his trusty wide brimmed hat, stared out at the island's coastline as the ship glided beyond the island's western section. As the ship passed a bay entitled *Bay Francoise*, named after Francis Bacon, the elderly man's face creased into a smile.

As the islands finally disappeared into the distance, the moon reflected off the sea to illuminate the side of the ship, revealing its name 'The Golden Hinde'.

109. VIRGINIA

$\mathcal{S}$ome days later, the 'The Golden Hinde' docked in Virginia, a colony of the New World, so named after Queen Elizabeth, the *Virgin* Queen.

As the elderly man wearily exited the ship, he was immediately escorted into a waiting carriage, and after a few of his items had been secured, the carriage left the dock, and after a seemingly never-ending journey, the carriage entered a town and slowed to a stop outside a grand building.

As the elderly man exited the carriage without his hat finally revealing him to be none other than a balding Francis Bacon, now 66 years old.

Francis and his '*good pens*' had accomplished a great deal in assisting the revitalisation of knowledge, literature, education, philosophy and science in England, but Francis looked even further ahead to an inspired vision of a democratic society supported by such an educated citizenry, believing he would have made his vision a reality had he become King of England.

Francis had convinced High Council members of the Freemason order of his inspired vision of a democratic society as detailed in one of his last literary achievements, the *New Atlantis*, and their belief in his idea gave them reason to help him realise it by mobilising some of their order to *The New World*.

Over a number of months, Francis and members of the Freemasonry order systematically relocated collections of historical documents, original literary works, artefacts, jewels and gold to this land of opportunity to help Francis build his *utopia*.

The fight with Damien had finally highlighted to Francis that there were people watching him and the actions of his secret order, forcing him to accelerate his plans at the extreme cost of feigning his own demise, having barely survived his battle with Damien.

Francis made his way to the building and knocked on the door, and a few seconds later, a doorman opened the door, staring at Francis.

"Yes?" the doorman asked inquisitively.

"My name is Francis Bacon!" Francis whispered.

Without a word, the doorman swung the door open and bid Francis to enter.

The doorman led Francis into a large room where a number of men were already in mid debate over matters relating to the direction of the New World, discussing economics, agriculture, and land, but their heated conversations stopped as soon as Francis entered the room.

As Francis surveyed the men, recognising some to be high ranking council members of the Freemason order that he had eventually come to meet, including some members of the secret order *Alumbrados* that Damien had previously taken over.

With Damien's magical powers of persuasion over the members of the *Alumbrados* order broken on his death, their key leaders were indebted to Francis and formed an alliance with his Freemasonry secret order, changing their name to *The Illuminati* as they tried to disassociate themselves from the stain of the dark practices Damien had introduced into their initiation process.

Although Francis had dedicated his life to the betterment of England, he felt he had gone as far as he could there, and with most of his family and close friends now dead, and his wife estranged, Francis knew it was time to move on.

In time, his life would not be regarded solely as a man, but rather as the focal point between an invisible institution and a world which was never able to distinguish between the messenger and the message which he promulgated.

Bene visit qui bene latuit
(Latin: *One lives best by the hidden life*)

The Future

EPILOGUE

A tourist speed boat bounced along strong waves as it made its way across the sea towards a familiar island, where extensive excavations were carried out on a man-made pit nearly 400 years before.

A disinterested tour guide on the speed boat recites the history of the island loudly over the deafening noise of the boat's engine.

"You should now be able to see the famous *Oak Island* in the distance, where for the last 200 years people have been trying to uncover the fabled treasure supposedly buried within a mysterious man-made pit! Some even losing their lives," she shouted as the engine noise grinded loudly.

As the group of tourists looked out at as the island came into view, many of them scrambled for their cameras and began taking pictures.

When the boat finally docked against a small pier on the island, the tour guide jumped off first and then took out a bright pink umbrella, raising it high into the air as the rest of the tourists followed her off the boat.

"Okay! Please stay close, and follow me!" she shouted with a sense of authority.

"If you cannot see my umbrella, you are already lost!" she warned jokingly, to the smiles of some of the tourists.

The tour guide then proceeded to make her way through a path into the centre of the island as she has done countless times before, followed closely by her tour group, eventually arriving at a man made clearing where a handful of other tour groups had already congregated around the main focus, a man-made pit.

The tour guide led her group to the edge of a barrier put up around the man-made pit to ensure the pit itself was not disturbed, and waited for the last of her group to catch up and gather around her before she continued her history of the island.

"It has been the focus of the world's longest and most expensive treasure hunt and one of the world's deepest and most costly archaeological digs, as well as being Canada's best-known mystery. Indeed, it is one of the great mysteries of the world!" she shouted with little enthusiasm above the noise of similar speeches by a number of other tour guides placed around the pit.

"Some say it may even represent an ancient artefact created by a past civilization of advanced capability!" she added with a little disbelief.

"For some two centuries, greed, folly, and even death have followed the supposed 'Money Pit' enigma" she continued.

"So what is actually down there?" asked one of the men in her group.

"No one really knows for sure, different things have been found, jewellery, iron scissors dating back some 300 years, and bits of paper with writing on it," the tour guide responded plainly.

"Over the years different groups of people have spent millions of dollars trying to uncover what is down there and it has bankrupt a number of companies in the process," she added, still with a feigned interest in the history of the pit.

"Millions?" asked another tourist.

"Yes! Makes you wonder if it's even worth it!" another tourist piped up.

"You mean, with all the technology at our disposal, no one has been able to retrieve what is down there?" asked a Chinese tourist holidaying with his wife and young child.

The tourist was draped with an array of technology, such as a video camera in one hand aimed at the pit, his phone in another, and what looked like a laptop bag straining on his frail shoulder.

"That's right! The depth of the pit is supposedly about 200 feet, containing traps to the complexity of the ancient Egyptians," the tour guide explained.

"It is said, whoever designed it had a brilliant mind!" she finished.

"So have they given up?" asked another man in her tour group.

"No, they are still working on a way to uncover the hidden treasures," the tour guide responded as she turned briefly to watch the Chinese man in her group focusing his camcorder on the pit.

"Supposedly, in the pit lay a number of oak trees that may unlock the puzzle one day," the tour guide continued turning back to her group.

"How so?" asked another tourist.

"It seems that over the years, a number of oak trees have obstructed the hidden treasures in it from being able to float to the top. The majority of the oak trees have slowly rotted and broken away. There is only one left," she finished with a smile.

As the Chinese tourist next to her finally corrected the focus on his camcorder as it pointed at the pit some feet away and peered through his viewfinder, he noticed a series of bubbles of air breaking the pit's surface.

He pulled away from his camcorder and turned to his tour guide.

"Excuse me, but is that supposed to happen?" he asked, pointing back towards the air bubbles in the pit.

As the tour guide and most of her group strained to look into the pit from the edge of the barrier, they also saw the bubbles appearing, now in increasing quantities.

"Well, no, not really," responded the tour guide, now frowning as she wondered why the bubbles were appearing.

As she swung her head considering who she could inform, she began to feel a small rumbling beneath her feet.

"I think I can feel something rumbling!" shouted one of tourists in another tour group, also standing at the edge of the barrier.

"It's an earthquake!" a small male Malaysian tourist shouted worriedly, causing mass hysteria to everyone that heard his cry.

As everyone on the man-made clearing scrambled to find a refuge from what felt like an imminent earthquake, a large oak tree shot out of the pit high into the air.

In its trail, a stream of the muddy murky water followed it, with the tree eventually conceding to gravity and landing some twenty feet on the outskirts of the clearing into some trees.

Amidst some bushes, the rotted soaked oak tree gleamed in the sunlight exposing a piece of bark with a familiar faint emblem etched into it - 'F. B.', 'Anthony', and an image of a pig.

Some seconds later back at the pit edge, the tour guide and some of the people from her tour group cautiously rose from the edge of the barrier where they had taken refuge, and stared fearfully at the pit.

The tour guide, critically gazing into the opening of the pit let out a sigh of relief as she eyed its now calm watery surface.

"It's OK, I think the worst of it is over!" she shouted to some of the people around her, causing cautious heads to slowly appear from various places as people came out of their hiding places.

From a shelter on the far edge of the pit, the Chinese male member of her tour group excitedly made his way back to the pit edge, followed unenthusiastically by his wife and child.

He excitedly made his way back to the barrier surrounding the pit, smiling to his tour guide as he reached her.

"What a show!" the Chinese tourist exclaimed to his tour guide as he again setup his camcorder, aiming it at the pit surface.

"I am going to upload this stuff to YouTube as soon as I get back to our hotel!" he exclaimed excitedly.

The tour guide shook her head in disbelief that the tourist had a seemingly adrenalin rush from the series of events, and became fixated with wanting to know what shot out of the pit.

As the tourist fixed the zoom of his camcorder back on the pit and pressed his eye against the viewfinder, his face dropped when he saw the bubbles beginning to appear on the pit surface again.

"Oh no, it's not over!" the Chinese tourist moaned.

"What?" the tour guide exclaimed as she turned back to the pit edge, getting her own confirmation that the bubbles had started appearing again.

"Go back, go back!" the Chinese tourist shouted as he rushed back towards his wife and child as they were making their way back to the pit.

"Everyone get down, there's another one coming out!" the tour guide screamed as she ducked for cover again.

With the tour guide's warning, everyone around her started in a mad panic again, scrambling to their various safe havens as they braced themselves for another eruption.

After a few pensive seconds however, instead of an eruption, a familiar crate, as deposited hundreds of years before, bubbled to the surface of the pit.

After a few more seconds, another crate popped up, then another, then another, filling the mouth of the pit.

The End

Acknowledgements

I would first and foremost like to thank my wife for her encouragement and support over the past 3 years it has taken me to write this novel and her painstaking efforts in proofreading the manuscript way too many times to mention.

I would also like to thank all of my close friends and work colleagues for tolerating me whilst I rambled on about new discoveries for the book.

Without all of your constant nagging for a release date, we might never have made it to print!

I thoroughly enjoyed writing this book about one of the most incredibly gifted men of our time, whom I have greatly admired for many years. I hope I have managed to do justice to his memory and portrayed his countless achievements with the utmost respect.

I can confidently say I gave this my best shot and this novel is all I wished it to be and a lot more.

Thanks again to all.

Kenric McKenzie
Author of **Spearshaker: Francis Bacon's Legacy**